Praise for the
Maximum Security series

D0376985

Also available from Kat Martin

Maximum Security

The Ultimate Betrayal
The Deception
The Conspiracy

Maximum Security novellas

Come Midnight
Before Nightfall
Shadows at Dawn
Wait Until Dark

The Raines of Wind Canyon

Against the Mark
Against the Edge
Against the Odds
Against the Sun
Against the Night
Against the Storm
Against the Law
Against the Fire
Against the Wind

Season of Strangers
Scent of Roses
The Summit

For a complete list of books by Kat Martin,
visit her website, www.katmartin.com.

KAT MARTIN

THE

PERFECT
MURDER

HQN

ISBN-13: 978-1-335-45345-7

The Perfect Murder
First published in 2021. This edition published in 2022.
Copyright © 2021 by Kat Martin

Come Midnight
First published in 2021. This edition published in 2022.
Copyright © 2021 by Kat Martin

Recycling programs
for this product may
not exist in your area.

This edition published by arrangement with Harlequin Books S.A.

For questions and comments about the quality of this book,
please contact us at CustomerService@Harlequin.com.

HQN
22 Adelaide St. West, 41st Floor
Toronto, Ontario M5H 4E3, Canada
www.Harlequin.com

Printed and bound in Barcelona, Spain by CPI Black Print

CONTENTS

To my husband, Larry, for his years of love and friendship. Here's to sharing many more.

THE PERFECT MURDER

CHAPTER ONE

Galveston, Texas
The last day of July

SECONDS AFTER THE chopper lifted off the pad, Reese felt the odd vibration. Along with the pilot and copilot and five members of the crew, the Eurocopter EC135 was headed for the Poseidon offshore drilling platform.

For a moment, the ride leveled out and Reese relaxed against his seat. As CEO of Garrett Resources, the billion-dollar oil and gas company he owned with his brothers, he was always searching for the right investment to expand company holdings, the reason he was flying out to the platform.

For months he'd been working with Sea Titan Drilling, the owner of the offshore rig, to complete the five-hundred-million-dollar purchase—an extremely good value when the average price of a similar rig was around six-fifty.

The vibration returned and with it came a grinding noise that put Reese on alert. The men in the cabin began to glance back and forth and shift nervously in their seats. A sharp jolt, then the chopper seemed to fall out of the sky. It climbed again, began to dip and sway, dropped then climbed as the pilot fought for control.

The pilot's deep voice rumbled through the headset. "We've got a problem. I don't want you to panic, but we need to find a place to set down."

There was definitely a problem, Reese realized, as the vibration continued to worsen. The chopper was out of control and the whole cabin was shaking as if it would break apart at any minute. His pulse was hammering, his adrenaline pumping.

Along with the men in the crew who rode to and from the rig every few weeks, he stared out the window toward the ground. They were no longer above the heliport. Clearly the pilot was looking for an open space big enough to handle the thirty-six-foot blade span. All Reese could see were the rooftops of nearby warehouses and metal commercial buildings.

The chopper kept shaking. The crew was grim-faced but resigned. The pilot did something to take the pitch out of the rotors, and the chopper started falling.

"No need to worry," the pilot reassured them. "We'll autorotate down. I've done it a dozen times."

Autorotate down. Reese knew the concept, the technique helicopter pilots used to land when the engine failed. The trick was to find a safe place to hit the ground.

Both engines went silent. The blades were flat now, the wind whistling through them, tying his stomach into a knot.

"Brace for impact," the pilot said. Below them, Reese spotted an open flat slab of asphalt in the yard of a small trucking firm—the only possible landing site anywhere around. Trouble was it didn't look wide enough to handle the blades.

At the last second, the pilot flared the helicopter's engine in an effort to slow the descent, then the ground rushed up and the chopper hit with a jolt that racked Reese's whole body.

For an instant, he thought they were going to make it. Then one of the spinning rotor blades clipped the corner of a building and tore free. The Plexiglas bubble of the cockpit shattered as the long metal blades exploded into a hundred deadly pieces, careening like knives through the air, slicing into buildings and the cabin of the helicopter.

Reese didn't feel the impact. One moment he was conscious, then the world suddenly went black.

Seconds later, he awoke to urgent cries in the cabin, which was filled with smoke and the orange-and-red flicker of flames. The guy seated across from him had a piece of iron sticking out of the middle of his forehead, lines of blood running down his face. Blank eyes stared at nothing.

Cursing, his head throbbing, Reese popped his seat belt and tried to get up, but his body refused to cooperate. His vison blurred, his mind went blank, and again darkness descended.

SOMETHING STIRRED IN his consciousness.

When Reese opened his eyes, monitors beeped next to his bedside and he realized he was lying in a hospital room. He had no idea how much time had passed since the crash, but by the end of the day, he knew the pilot and one of the Poseidon crewmen had died. He remembered the man's blank stare and thought how it could have been him.

What had happened? No one seemed to know. Reese wanted answers. The National Transportation Safety Board would be in charge of the investigation. He would leave it to them, he thought. *For now.*

Reese closed his eyes and let the pain meds suck him under.

CHAPTER TWO

Four weeks later
Dallas, Texas

FOR MCKENZIE HAINES, her day as executive assistant to
Reese Garrett started as usual. After a few minutes spent
with her own assistant, Louise Dennison, an older woman
with short, iron gray hair, Kenzie began her early-morning
briefing with Reese to go over his daily schedule and discuss what he needed from her.

Seated across the desk from the CEO of Garrett Resources in his spacious office, she waited as he finished an
unexpected phone call. With his wavy jet-black hair and
amazing blue eyes, Reese was one of the best-looking men
Kenzie had ever seen. Keenly intelligent and highly successful, he was a combination of virile masculinity and brooding
reserve that attracted women of every age, shape, and size.

She could still see the faint scar on the side of his head
near his temple from the helicopter crash that had killed
two men and put Reese in the hospital.

At the time of the accident, Kenzie had worked for the
company only five months, but in that time, she had come
to admire and respect her employer. She could still recall
the sharp stab of fear when his brother Chase had phoned
to inform her of the accident.

Three days later, Reese was back at his desk, running the

company with the iron control he was known for. Unfortunately, even now, four weeks after the incident, NTSB investigators remained unable to pinpoint the cause of the crash.

Reese's phone call ended and his dark head came up, his intense blue eyes locking on her face. No matter how she worked to ignore it, Kenzie always felt the impact.

"Where were we?" he asked.

"You wanted me to reschedule your visit to the offshore platform."

"Yes. I've put it off too long already."

"I probably shouldn't say this, but after what happened, I don't blame you."

The corner of his mouth kicked up. "Maybe not, but I want this deal done. We've been working on it for months. We need to finish our due diligence and make it end."

"Yes, sir. Would you like me to go with you?" Traveling with Reese when he needed her assistance was part of her job, though he hadn't asked her to go with him the day of the crash, thank God.

One of his rare smiles appeared. "You want to hold my hand in case I get scared in the chopper?"

Kenzie laughed, a little embarrassed he had hit so close to the truth. She liked him, admired him. He could have died that day. "I just thought you might need me."

Reese shook his head. "Not this time. I won't be discussing business while I'm out there. I just want to get a feel for the way things operate out on the rig."

She nodded, not surprised since he had said something similar before. "I'll make the arrangements."

As she looked down at his calendar on her iPad, thinking of what she would need to rearrange, a soft knock sounded at the door. The knob turned and Louise stood in the opening.

"I'm sorry to interrupt, sir, but the police are on the

phone. They're looking for Kenzie. Apparently it's some kind of an emergency."

Kenzie shot up from the chair in front of Reese's polished dark walnut desk.

"Put the call through on my line, Louise," Reese said before she had taken a step. "She can talk to them in here."

"Yes, sir." As the older woman backed out of the room, Kenzie's pulse began to pound. The police were calling. What could have happened? She prayed it wasn't Griff, her nine-year-old son. Or, dear God, maybe it was Gran.

Her long dark hair swung forward as she leaned over to pick up the phone. "Hello...this is McKenzie Haines?"

"Ms. Haines, this is Sergeant Bothwell, Dallas Police Department. I'm afraid there's been an accident involving your son."

Kenzie's fingers tightened around the receiver. "Is he... Is Griff all right?"

"He's been taken to Baylor Medical at Uptown, ma'am. That's all I know."

Kenzie swallowed. "Baylor. Thank...thank you for calling." Desperate to get to the hospital, she started to hang up, but Reese grabbed the phone out of her hand.

"This is Reese Garrett. I work with Ms. Haines. Can you tell us what happened to the boy?"

She couldn't hear what Sergeant Bothwell said but Reese's expression looked grim. She was trembling by the time he set the phone back down in the cradle.

"What did he say?"

"Griff was riding his bicycle in front of the house. He swerved to dodge a car, fell off, and hit his head. The babysitter called an ambulance."

Suddenly light-headed, she swayed on her feet, gripping the edge of the desk to steady herself. "What was he doing in the street? He's not supposed to be riding out front by himself. Tammy Stevens was watching him while my grandmother went to her doctor's appointment. Oh, God."

"Take it easy. You'll know more when you get to the hospital. Come on, I'll drive you." Before she could object, he called down to the garage to have his car brought up.

"You don't have to do that," she said. "I can drive myself."

"You're in no shape to drive. Get your purse and let's go."

Since he was right, she didn't argue, though she was surprised he had offered. Reese was her employer, CEO of the company. They didn't really know each other on a personal level.

Somehow she managed to walk out of his office on legs that felt weak and unsteady. Louise's desk sat in the open area out front, Kenzie's desk and credenza in a spacious, more private location closer to Reese's impressive executive office.

He paused at Louise's desk. "Kenzie's son was in an accident. He's been taken to the emergency room at Baylor. I'm driving her to the hospital. If you need me, call my cell."

"Yes, sir." She turned to Kenzie. "Let me know what you find out about Griff, okay? I'll worry till I know he's all right."

Kenzie nodded, her stomach clenched tight with nerves. "I will, Louise, I promise." Hurrying over to her desk, she grabbed her handbag then continued with Reese to the private wood-paneled elevator that serviced the executive offices on the fourteenth floor of the building in the nineteen-hundred block of North Akard.

The elevator descended, then the doors opened in the underground parking garage behind the valet stand. A shiny black Jaguar idled in front, the air conditioner running, the September temperatures still uncomfortably high.

Reese walked her around to the passenger side of the car and opened the door, waited while she settled herself in the sporty, red-trimmed, black leather seats. Tugging down the navy blue pencil skirt she was wearing with a matching jacket and heels, she pushed her dark hair out of her face.

"Put your belt on," Reese commanded as he slid behind the wheel and put the car in gear. He was the kind of man who was always in charge, always in control, yet somehow he seemed more efficient than overbearing. Working with him had been exhilarating, challenging, and exhausting. It was a job she truly loved.

Her heart was still racing as he drove the Jag out of the parking garage. The brakes slammed the instant they pulled into the street, and Reese softly cursed.

Dozens of people carrying signs and banners rushed up to surround the car. *SOS, Save Our Shores. Stop Deep Sea Oil. No Drill No Spill.*

"Son of a bitch." Reese eased the car out into the street, nudging protesters aside, the vehicle crawling along when it was clear he would rather have hit the gas and charged forward. There weren't more than a couple of dozen, most of them young, in their twenties or early thirties, wearing everything from purple hair and nose rings to Bozo the Clown masks.

"I'm sorry, Kenzie," Reese said. "I knew there'd been some trouble at the Houston office, but this is the first time we've had protests here."

She'd known about the recent protests to halt more drilling in the Gulf. She hadn't realized they had expanded as far as Dallas. The odd thing was, the deal to buy the platform had been in progress for months and the rig had been producing oil for years.

She looked at the jeering crowd blocking their way and

fear for her son intensified. Griff needed her. She had to reach him.

"Don't worry, they aren't going to stop us from getting there," Reese said, reading her mind.

He increased his speed, the Jag's powerful engine purring, the vehicle forcing the crowd to separate and really pissing them off. Though the windows were up and the air conditioner was running, she could hear the foul things they were saying about Garrett Resources, some specifically aimed at Reese as head of the company.

Reese ignored them and increased his speed, breaking free of the unruly mob and leaving them ranting and raving in the middle of the street behind them.

As he continued along North Akard toward Baylor Medical, Kenzie's mind remained on her son. She checked her phone messages, found call after call from Tammy Stevens, her next door neighbor's teenage daughter who'd been babysitting Griff. But when she tried to return the call, Tammy's phone went directly to voice mail. Kenzie's worry continued to build. *Dear God, let him be okay.*

As soon as Reese pulled the Jag into a space in the emergency parking lot, Kenzie opened the car door, jumped out, and ran for the entrance, praying all the way that Griff would be all right. He was only nine years old, his life just beginning. The thought that something terrible might have happened to him clogged her chest with fear.

Reese's long strides caught up with her before she reached the glass doors. He was tall, his expensive suits custom tailored to his broad shoulders and narrow hips. She knew he enjoyed sports, played tennis, and worked out with a martial arts trainer three times week. As his personal assistant, Kenzie knew a lot about Reese Garrett.

He held the door as she hurried into a scene of organized

chaos: nurses and doctors in scrubs, carts rattling by pushed by lab technicians, worried family members huddled together. The hospital smells of antiseptic and ammonia made her stomach roll. Vaguely, she wondered if Reese's recent hospital stay had left him feeling equally unsettled.

He steered her directly to the nurses' station, identified himself, and introduced Kenzie as Griffin Haines's mother.

"We'd like to see the boy and speak to the doctor," Reese said. "As soon as possible."

Kenzie was still trying to wrap her head around the fact that Reese Garrett had driven her to the hospital and instead of leaving was staying to lend his support. Reese had never met her son, yet she could sense his concern. It steadied her, kept her from sliding into total panic.

A petite, redheaded nurse behind the counter took one look at Reese and couldn't move fast enough to help him. "I'll find the doctor for you." She took off at a run, and as they waited, Kenzie's heart continued to pound.

Where was Griff? How badly was he injured?

"He's just a boy," she said, unconsciously speaking her thoughts. "He's got to be okay."

Reese caught her shoulders, turning her to face him. It was the first time he had ever touched her, she realized. In today's business climate, there could be no hint of impropriety. As her boss, Reese had been scrupulous in his treatment of her. Never once had he stepped out of line.

"He's going to be okay," he said firmly. "You need to believe that unless you learn something different. If that happens, you can deal with it then. I learned that lesson a long time ago."

She swallowed. "You're right. I need to be strong for Griff." But it wasn't that easy to do.

CHAPTER THREE

KENZIE PACED THE HALLWAY, willing her son to be okay. She glanced up to see a small, white-coated doctor striding toward her, a stethoscope and a pair of wire-rimmed glasses on a short silver chain around his neck.

"Mrs. Haines?"

She hated to be called that. She would have gone back to her maiden name after her divorce if it hadn't been for Griff.

"I'm McKenzie Haines."

"Dr. Marshall. Your son suffered a concussion when he fell off his bicycle and struck his head on the pavement. He was unconscious for a few seconds, so we're doing a CT scan to be sure there are no complications."

Her stomach quivered. "Is he…is he going to be all right?"

"He's scraped and bruised and he's got a nasty headache. We'll want to keep him a couple of hours for observation, but if the test results are clear, you can take him home. By tomorrow he should be feeling better."

Kenzie's legs went weak and she felt Reese's hand at her waist to help keep her upright.

"I think you'd better sit down." After guiding her the few feet to a row of hard plastic chairs, he settled her in the seat.

"I'll let you know the test results as soon as they're available," the doctor said. Turning, he headed back the way he had come.

Kenzie looked up at Reese. She hadn't realized how terrified she had been until now. "He's going to be okay."

Reese smiled. He didn't do it often and it made him even more handsome. "Like I said, best not to worry until it becomes necessary. Something I learned on the job."

Kenzie felt that smile all the way to her toes. Just four years older than she was, Reese posed a dangerous attraction she had carefully avoided since her first day as his executive assistant, a job that paid a handsome six-figure salary, money she needed to take care of her family.

As her worry receded, she heard a commotion and looked up to see a tall, lean, sandy-haired man marching toward the nurses' station. Lee Haines, her ex-husband. A shiver of dread moved down her spine.

"I want to see my son!" Lee demanded, overbearing and condescending in a way Reese never was. When she'd first met him, she'd been attracted to his good looks, Harvard education, and upper-crust social status. Coming from working-class parents who constantly worried about bills and occasionally where the next meal was coming from, she had craved the kind of security Lee's family represented.

Still, she wondered how she ever could have fallen for the man's phony charm.

She rose as he approached.

"The police called," he said. "What the hell is going on?"

"Griff's going to be all right. They're doing a CT scan to be sure, but it looks like he'll be okay."

"Where was Florence? I thought your grandmother was supposed to be taking care of him."

"Gran had a doctor's appointment. She was only supposed to be gone a little over an hour." Kenzie and her grandmother, seventy-year-old Florence Spencer, were Griff's primary caregivers. Kenzie's job demanded long hours and an occasional business trip with Reese. Her grandmother took care of Griff during the workday and whenever Kenzie was gone. Gran loved him and he loved her.

"This is your fault," Lee said. "You should be home taking care of him yourself. If Griffin lived with me, this never would have happened."

Anger slipped through her. "He was riding his bike. He isn't supposed to go into the street unless one of us is out there with him. He's a kid. He doesn't always follow the rules. He fell off his bike and hit his head. Things like that happen."

"Why wasn't he wearing his helmet? That's the reason I bought it. It's your job to make sure he's safe."

She didn't bother to answer. Instead, feeling Reese's presence beside her and accepting the inevitable, she turned to introduce him. "Reese, this is my ex-husband, Lee Haines. Lee, this is Reese Garrett, my employer. He was kind enough to drive me to the hospital."

Lee looked Reese up and down, his gaze moving between the two of them as if he knew some dirty secret.

"Garrett. I've seen you and your brothers at charity events over the years." Lee didn't offer to shake hands and neither did Reese, who seemed to understand exactly the kind of man Lee was.

"Is that right?" Reese said coolly. "I don't remember seeing you."

Lee's mouth thinned.

The doctor walked up just then. "You're Griffin's father?" he asked.

"That's right."

"Then you'll be happy to hear nothing unexpected showed up in the tests. As I told your wife—"

"Ex-wife," Lee corrected.

"As I told Ms. Haines earlier, we'd like to keep the boy a couple more hours, then he can go home. The nurse will provide a dos and don'ts list, but he should be feeling better by tomorrow. I'd advise keeping him out of school at least for a couple of days."

"Of course," Kenzie said.

"The nurse will let you know when you can see him." Turning, the doctor hurried off to take care of another patient.

Lee stared down at her. With her five-foot-four-inch stature compared to his six-three, about the same as Reese, Lee used his height to intimidate her. Not that it worked anymore.

"This is just one more example of your incompetence," he said. "Griff's accident will be duly noted in the custody suit I'm filing against you."

Her chest constricted. "Custody suit? What are you talking about?"

Lee smirked. "You heard me. I'm tired of all this shuffling back and forth. Griff should be living with his father. I plan to make that happen. You can contact your attorney, but it won't do you any good. You don't have the money to fight me, and we both know it."

He turned to Reese. "If you haven't already found out, she isn't even good in bed." Turning, he walked away.

Reese's jaw looked iron hard, and she had never seen that particular shade of ice blue in his eyes.

"You all right?" he asked.

Kenzie managed to hold back tears. For the first time, she wished Reese hadn't come with her, hadn't met Lee and witnessed her humiliation.

"He didn't even wait to see his son." She released a shaky

breath. "I'm sorry that happened. Lee has never forgiven me for divorcing him."

Reese's gaze flicked toward Lee's retreating figure. "Clearly a good decision."

Under different circumstances, she would have smiled. "No doubt about that." She took a shaky breath. "I appreciate the ride, but I need to stay, and I know how much work you have to do at the office. You should get back. I'll call my grandmother, have her pick me up. It won't be a problem."

Reese's eyes shifted toward the exit as Lee walked out the door, and the glacial blue returned. "I take it you didn't see the custody battle coming."

She shook her head. "The divorce was my idea and it was brutal." Worse for her, since she'd given up alimony and taken a very low amount of child support in order to get it done. She wanted as little to do with her ex as possible.

"Lee never wanted custody of Griff," she said. "In his own way, he loves his son, but he's never wanted the inconvenience of having a child around. Not until now. Arthur Haines, Lee's father, always wanted him to go into politics and I heard Lee's considering it. Raising a son would appeal to a certain segment of voters."

"Fighting the suit could get expensive. If you need some help…"

Appalled, she stared up at him. "Thank you for offering, but this isn't your problem, Reese. I can handle it on my own."

A flush rose beneath the olive skin over his cheekbones. "I'm sorry. I didn't mean to offend you."

She relaxed, felt the faintest hint of a smile. "I didn't mean to take offense." She glanced anxiously toward the nurses' station, eager to see her son. Her cell phone vibrated and she pulled it out and read the name.

"It's my grandmother. She's probably frantic." She pressed the phone to her ear. "Everything's okay, Gran. I'm at the hospital with Griff. He's going to be okay, so you don't need to worry." Gran explained that Tammy had misplaced her phone during all the commotion and they wouldn't let her go in the ambulance.

"Tell her Griff's okay. I'll call you back as soon as I can and explain what's going on."

She ended the call and turned to Reese. "Thank you for bringing me. If it's all right, I'll take Griff home and stay with him for the rest of the day. I'll see you at the office in the morning."

"You've been working a lot of overtime. Why don't you take tomorrow off to be with your boy?"

Warm gratitude slipped through her. "That would be wonderful."

The red-haired nurse came up just then, cast a quick glance at Reese, but spoke to Kenzie. "I'll take you to see your son now."

Kenzie smiled at Reese. "Thank you again." He just nodded. As she turned to follow the nurse, she could feel his eyes on her until she disappeared into Griff's curtained cubicle.

CHAPTER FOUR

ASIDE FROM ARRIVING at the office the next morning in the back of a limo to avoid dealing with the protesters milling around out front, Reese's day started like any other.

Except that Kenzie wasn't there. Since she had never taken a sick day in the months since he'd hired her, she had been at her desk every morning before he arrived. Been there for their morning briefing and the list of what he needed her to do.

What he needed from Kenzie was a thought that led in a direction he couldn't allow. In six short months, she had become a necessity, as essential to his job as his laptop or his cell phone.

Which meant he had to ignore the kick he felt every time he looked at her. Kenzie Haines was by far the best executive assistant he had ever worked with. And with the heavy mahogany hair curling softly around her shoulders, perfect curves, and a peaches-and-cream complexion, she was also by far the most beautiful.

Kenzie was the kind of woman who drew a man's attention without even trying, and there was a kindness about her that shined through her careful reserve. Unfortunately, any physical attraction he felt for her had to be ruthlessly suppressed. Except for riding next to her in the back of a limo, he had never made any sort of physical contact.

As CEO of a billion-dollar corporation, Reese was in an

extremely vulnerable position. He had to be careful of every word he spoke, every untethered glance, every thought.

He amended that. So far no one had been able to police the thoughts running through a person's head, but who knew when that could change.

Until today, he had managed to quash any notion of Kenzie as anything but a highly valued employee, and though her fear for her son had touched him in a way he hadn't expected, he intended to keep his distance, just as he had before.

Reese sighed as he leaned back in the black leather chair behind his desk. The office was done in a modern motif with dark wood paneling and chairs upholstered in rich pearl gray.

There was a separate conversation area, a fully stocked wet bar behind the paneling of one wall, and the most advanced high-tech equipment available. Everything from a top-of-the-line iMac Pro to a seventy-inch flat screen with a wireless HDMI transmitter and receiver kit.

Reese checked his schedule for what seemed the fiftieth time. He was used to Kenzie keeping track for him. Without her there, he had run poor Louise ragged. He almost smiled. Kenzie's assistant would be even more grateful to have her back than he would.

He thought about her ex-husband. Since Kenzie rarely spoke about herself, Reese had never made the connection to the wealthy Haines family until he had seen Lee Haines, who looked a great deal like his father.

Reese had never met Lee before, but he knew Arthur. Old Dallas oil money, an empire built by Arthur's father. Along with Troy Graves, his late partner's son, Arthur owned half of Black Sand Oil and Gas, one of Garrett Resources' fiercest competitors.

He wondered how much Kenzie had collected in the divorce settlement. Surely enough to fight Haines's suit and maintain custody of her son.

Or maybe not. He remembered hearing something about the senior Haines's divorce. Rumor had it that Arthur had managed to leave his wife next to penniless. Her depression had eventually led to suicide. He wondered if Lee had managed to leave Kenzie with little or nothing, just as Arthur had done.

Thinking of his assistant and her ex-husband's foul attitude toward her, Reese felt an unexpected surge of protectiveness. If Kenzie needed help, he would find a way to help her—whether or not she was too proud to accept it.

Rising from his desk, he wandered over to the window and looked down on the street. About the same number of sign-carrying protesters today as yesterday. He'd been surprised this morning to find them still there.

In Texas, drilling was a way of life. At least for now, fossil fuels were a necessity, though the company was heavily invested in sustainable energy, including geothermal, solar, and tidal. Reese sincerely hoped there would be enough alternate energy to run the world someday, but in the meantime, there was very little choice.

The intercom buzzed. The unfamiliar sound of Louise's voice still surprised him.

"You have a call from Mr. Stiles, sir. He says it's urgent."

Derek Stiles was his VP in charge of mergers and acquisitions, working out of the Houston office. He was a good-looking guy, thirty-four, same age as Reese, and one of his top executives. "Go ahead and put him through, Louise." Reese picked up the phone and leaned back in his chair. "I wasn't expecting to hear from you until tomorrow."

"I know, but unfortunately, another problem came up— more trouble with the rig."

The deal to purchase the rig was being dragged down by unforeseen problems. For months, they'd been trying to close the deal with Sea Titan without success. The platform was only ninety miles off the coast, but the purchase couldn't be finalized until a series of tests and safety drills had been performed and successfully completed.

"What's going on?" Reese asked. He rarely involved himself in the day-to-day business of actual oil production, but this deal was important.

"There's a situation with the lifeboats. They keep getting hung up once the men are aboard. The rig can't pass inspection until the boats launch properly, and the problem needs to be fixed before drilling can resume. That definitely has to happen before we close the deal."

"So get it fixed," Reese said.

"The installation manager has been doing his best, but there's some kind of equipment malfunction that's going to require replacement parts. Getting them is going to take time, which will delay the drilling restart. I wouldn't bother you except…well, as you know, this isn't the first delay we've experienced lately."

"Problems always arise in purchasing a project this big."

"I know, but…"

Reese's hold tightened on the phone. "What are you not telling me, Derek?"

His sigh came through the phone. "I really hate to put this out there without any proof, but I'm worried these delays aren't accidental."

Reese sat forward in his chair. "You think someone is sabotaging the rig?"

"I think it's possible. That's the reason I called. Maybe someone doesn't want the deal to go through, or a competitor wants to buy the platform out from under us. It's a helluva good price."

"Which we've got completely tied down. No way can Sea Titan back out."

"Maybe they're having second thoughts, sabotaging the deal themselves."

It was possible, he supposed. Or one of the whack jobs marching around out front in a clown mask could be involved, which raised the question, how far would the protesters be willing to go to make their point?

"Or it could just be a run of bad luck," Derek said.

"Let's hope that's it. The Poseidon's an important part of our latest market-share strategy. It represents months of hard work by a lot of good people—to say nothing of the money we've invested in the option. I'm glad you took the initiative on this. Keep me in the loop and let me know if any other problems come up."

"Will do. Thanks, Reese."

Reese could hear the relief in his VP's voice. It was never easy to call the CEO with problems, or even potential problems.

He thought of the people waving signs in front of the office. They wanted to stop the purchase. They were using the deal to bring attention to their cause. He understood that, in many ways agreed with their concerns.

A notion that brought another thought squarely to mind. So far the NTSB—National Transportation Safety Board—hadn't been able to pinpoint the cause of the helicopter crash. It was some kind of equipment malfunction, of course, but there had been no indication of a problem before the day of the crash.

He wouldn't discount Derek's phone call.

But he hoped like hell his VP was wrong.

KENZIE SPENT A leisurely day at home with Griff. She could tell he was feeling better because he was starting to get restless, pressing her to let him go outdoors.

"Mo-om." He dragged it out like a two-syllable word, making her smile. "My head doesn't hurt anymore and it's boring just sitting around doing nothing. Can't I at least go out and ride my skateboard in the driveway?"

Unlike some kids who spent every hour on their digital devices, Griff was an outdoor kid. He loved sports and any kind of outside activity, like hiking and baseball and especially swimming. Kenzie was usually grateful. Not today.

"The reason you're staying home from school is to give yourself a chance to heal. You hit your head hard enough to knock yourself unconscious. The doctor wants you to take it easy."

"He said I was only out a few seconds."

"I know, but still…"

Griff grumbled something she was glad she couldn't hear.

"If you want some fresh air, why don't you take your iPad out on the patio? You can sit in the sun and play a game or do a puzzle or something. It's not too hot today."

They had a small fenced yard behind their town house. Someday she wanted to buy a house with a big backyard. It was one of the reasons she was grateful for her high-paying job.

Griff shrugged his shoulders. "I guess." He ambled away, resigned to taking it easy at least for the next few hours. Kenzie watched him go, the fear she'd experienced yesterday still haunting her.

At every opportunity, she had walked up and simply hugged him, or ran her fingers through his thick dark brown hair. It carried the same touch of red as her own, his eyes the same golden amber. He was finally losing his baby fat, growing taller and leaner, more like his father.

Though that was the end of the resemblance. Griff was sweet and loving, always helpful and optimistic. Not demanding, mean-tempered, and completely self-centered, as Lee was. She liked to think Griff got his good qualities from her side of the family.

Which turned her thoughts to Gran. Kenzie found her seated at the kitchen table, a romance novel open in front of her. A ray of sunlight illuminated the heavy silver hair she wore in a sleek, chin-length bob. At seventy, Flo Spencer was still attractive, the few extra pounds she carried minimizing the lines in her face.

Gran looked up from her book. "You've been edgy all morning. I know you're used to being at work, but an extra day off once in a while is good for you. Why don't you go for a swim? Do something to relax."

Kenzie was used to working long hours and when she was home, sometimes it was hard to shift gears and unwind. Swimming definitely helped. She'd been captain of the high school swim team, still did laps after work as often as possible in the condo association pool to stay in shape.

"Maybe I will." But if she did, Griff, who seemed to have the same love of swimming she had, would want to go with her. Usually she was thrilled to have him along, but today she wanted him to stay quiet.

"On second thought, I think I'll go up and check my email. Louise isn't used to working directly with Reese. She might need help with something."

Gran took her reading glasses off, folded them, and neatly set them on the table. "It was nice of your boss to take you to the hospital yesterday."

"Yes, it was."

Gran had seen photos of Reese Garrett in the online digital version of the Dallas *Morning News*. Pictures of him were constantly in the society pages, attending one charitable event or another, always with an extremely beautiful woman. Rarely the same one more than a couple of times.

Since Kenzie kept track of his calendar, she knew most of their names. Gran knew Reese was an amazing-looking man and extremely successful. Divorced with plenty of family money, Reese Garrett was one of the most eligible bachelors in Dallas.

Gran closed the novel she had been reading and gave Kenzie an assessing glance. She'd always been amazingly perceptive. "In my day, it was all right for a boss to go out with one of his employees. I guess that's all changed now."

Kenzie poured herself a cup of coffee from the fresh pot on the counter. "It's completely changed, Gran. Even if Reese were interested in me as more than just an employee, which I'm sure he isn't, there's no way he could risk getting involved. And if I want to keep my job, there is no way I could risk getting involved with him."

Gran sighed. "I suppose. But it's kind of a shame, since the two of you have so much in common."

Kenzie cocked a skeptical eyebrow. "Really? Like what?"

"Like you're both very intelligent, both career-minded, both very attractive people. Probably a lot of other things, too."

"Reese is a lot more than above-average in looks, and he has never shown the least interest in me, so you can just stop your matchmaking efforts right now."

Gran's faint smile was unrepentant. She held up her paperback, the cover showing a gorgeous half-naked medieval warrior. "It could be risky, but the right man might be worth it."

Kenzie rolled her eyes, but she couldn't help smiling. Gran was the ultimate romantic. She had loved Kenzie's grandfather every day of their fifty-year marriage, loved him until the day he'd died of a heart attack five years ago. Kenzie wasn't sure that kind of love even existed in today's modern world.

On that sad note, she took her cup of coffee and headed upstairs to her computer.

CHAPTER FIVE

THE FOLLOWING MORNING, Reese arrived a few minutes later than usual. Reese had been out late last night, attending a political fundraiser for the mayor.

Mark Rydell was doing a good job, had lent his support to a number of projects Garrett Resources had undertaken, and in return, Reese was supporting the mayor's bid for reelection.

What hadn't worked out so well was his date for the event. Reese had been seeing Fiona Cantor off and on for the past few months. She was a beautiful, statuesque blonde, an attorney at one of the big Dallas law firms. She was pleasant company and a satisfactory bed partner who didn't expect more than being friends with benefits.

Unfortunately, last night when he'd driven her home after the gala, things had taken an unexpected turn.

"I've got a nice bottle of champagne chilling in the fridge," Fiona had said with an inviting smile. "Or if you'd prefer, a glass of that Oban single malt I bought just for you." She leaned over and kissed him, wet and open-mouthed, ran a red polished nail down his cheek. "Or we can just go straight to bed."

He'd looked into her big blue eyes and tried to muster some enthusiasm. When none surfaced, he shook his head. "I've got a lot on my mind, Fi, and a long day tomorrow. I think I'll head on home."

Fiona frowned. "I'm tired of excuses, Reese. We haven't

had sex the last three times we've been together. What's going on?"

He thought about brushing her off, telling her it was just problems at work, which was certainly true. Instead, he told her the truth. "I think it's time we moved on. It's been fun, but I've just got too much on my mind right now. I need a little space. I hope you understand."

Her spine stiffened. "Oh, I understand, Reese. Who is she?"

He blocked the image before it had time to surface. "It's no one, Fi. That isn't what's going on." Well, not exactly.

Fiona released a slow, resigned breath. "It's all right. We never were exclusive." She was right. They had dated a lot of different people, always kept things casual and open. She was undemanding and he had enjoyed her company. But it wasn't serious and both of them knew it.

"Call me if you change your mind," Fi said, but he knew he wouldn't. He had lost interest in Fiona sometime back. The next time he needed a date, he'd go through his contacts, find someone else to accompany him. He'd never had trouble attracting women. He was more than decent looking, and he had lots of money. That was all it really took.

Which wasn't saying much.

Lately, it wasn't enough.

The memory of the evening slipped away as he strode across the office, then paused next to Kenzie's desk. "How's Griff?"

When she rose from her chair, he tried not to notice how her skirt and simple white cotton sweater showed off her curves. She always wore business clothes but somehow still managed to look sexier than he would have liked.

"Griff's okay. He was going crazy cooped up in the house and he seemed completely fine, so I let him go back to school today." She smiled and he worked to ignore the heat that washed through him. "I really appreciate what you did. I'm not usually one to panic, but it's different when it's your child."

He nodded. "I'm sure it is." Having kids was one of the reasons he'd gotten married. He and Sandra were already on the brink of divorce when they'd discovered she couldn't have children. Instead of being upset, Sandra had been relieved.

"I've got a few things I need to add to my schedule," he said. "Derek Stiles called yesterday. Looks like we're having more problems with the rig."

"You'll get them sorted." She flashed him a smile. "You always do."

But there was one thing he was having more and more trouble handling and she was standing right in front of him.

Reese clenched his jaw and went to work.

He was sitting at his desk later that day when his intercom buzzed.

"It's Frank Milburn," Kenzie said. "He has news about the crash."

Milburn was in charge of the NTSB investigation. "Put him through." Reese pressed the speaker button and settled back in his chair.

"I know you've been anxious to hear from us," Frank said, a small man with close-cropped brown hair. "I wish we could have completed the investigation sooner, but these things take time."

"I'm aware. So what have you found out?"

"The last of the reports came in. We'd been waiting for some metal structural tests. Combined with the rest of the information we've assembled, the reports revealed what we had recently begun to suspect but until today weren't able to confirm."

"Go on."

"Sometime before the flight took off the morning of

the crash, someone tampered with the engine. A piece of metal in one of the gears was filed just enough to cause it to grind itself to pieces. The flight control mechanism disconnected, rendering the helo uncontrollable. To put it in layman's terms, the helicopter was sabotaged."

Tension tightened Reese's shoulders. He didn't ask Milburn if he was sure. The NTSB team had been investigating the crash for weeks. Two men were dead. The authorities had to be extremely thorough. The question now was who had done it? And why?

"Have you found out who's responsible?" Reese asked.

"Unfortunately, not yet. As we've known from the start and you were informed, pilot error contributed heavily to the event. There should have been room for the chopper to safely autorotate down, but the pilot misjudged his position. He came in too close to the building, one of the blades clipped the corner, and the helicopter was torn apart."

"So what, exactly, *do* you know?"

"We know a criminal act was committed that ended up causing the deaths of two men. As of this morning, the FBI will be taking over the investigation. They'll be actively pursuing whoever is responsible for the crime, now a double murder."

Murder. The news sent a chill down Reese's spine. He leaned over his desk, shut off the speaker, and picked up the phone. "Whatever you find out, I'll expect you to keep me in the loop."

"I'll do my best," Milburn said. "It'll be more difficult once the gears of the FBI begin to turn."

He understood how a federal agency worked. Lots of interlocking pieces and parts that inevitably slowed things down. The call ended, but Reese had no intention of leaving the matter in the hands of some governmental bureaucracy, not even the FBI. The feds would have to start over, look at the crash from an entirely different angle. It could take weeks, even months.

Two men were dead and he could have been the third. He thought of the accidents that had been plaguing the Poseidon. The helo crash hadn't been accidental. The chopper was meant to go down.

Was it possible he had been the target?

He couldn't wait weeks or months, not when his life could be in danger. He needed answers. Finding them sent his mind immediately to his brothers.

Chase owned Maximum Security, the best private security firm in Dallas. There wasn't a better investigator in the city than Chase. But once his brother heard the NTSB's findings, he'd demand Reese have round-the-clock personal protection. Brandon, their younger brother, a highly sought-after bodyguard, would be the logical choice. But Reese had too much going on to be dogged 24/7.

Not when there was no proof Reese had been anything but an unlucky passenger. Especially not when he was more than capable of taking care of himself.

In high school, he'd fallen in with a dangerous crowd, older kids who were in and out of trouble. He'd found himself on the police radar, a troublemaker, minor car thief, fringe member of a local teenage gang, and street brawler. Activities that, combined with being picked up for using an illegal firearm, had led to a yearlong stint in juvenile detention.

His mom, divorced from his far-too-lenient dad and already raising his brothers, had taken custody and moved Reese in with her and her family. His grandfather, a former Texas sheriff, along with half a dozen relatives in the military or law enforcement, had stepped in and helped him turn his life around.

One of his uncles had convinced him to use his fighting skills in the boxing ring instead of on the street. By the time he was in college, he'd added kickboxing, then tae-kwondo, leading to a brief interest in mixed martial arts. Though he'd left those days behind, he still trained weekly to keep in shape.

No, he didn't need Chase or Brandon, or his half brother, Michael, a computer nerd who lived in Houston, a recent addition to the family.

What Reese needed was information. He phoned Tabitha Love. Tabby worked for The Max as a computer special-ist. She was one of the smartest people he had ever known, smarter even than the experts who worked for Garrett Re-sources. And she would be discreet.

She answered on the second ring. "Is that Reese Gar-rett's name I see on my screen?" He could hear the smile in her voice. He rarely called her, though she was always happy to help.

"No way to deny it, I'm afraid. I'm hoping you can carve out some time for me. It's a personal matter, one I need you to handle quietly and fairly quickly."

She must have heard something in his tone. "For you, chief, I have all the time in the world." She said it as if he were the editor of a newspaper or the leader of a tribe, not the chief executive officer of the company. It always made him smile.

Tabby was in her late twenties, tall, with very short black hair shaved on the sides and moussed on top. Her face glit-tered with enough studs to drive up the price of silver on the stock market: ears, tongue, eyebrow, plus a nose ring, and who knew what else beneath her clothes.

Fortunately, not him. Tabby's boyfriend, Lester, took up most of her free time.

"So what is it you need?" Tabby asked, suddenly all business.

"You may have heard about the drilling platform the company is purchasing. The Poseidon?"

"It's been all over the news. Apparently not everyone's happy about the deal."

"Exactly. We've got protesters marching on the street outside our door. They're using the sale to bring attention to the problems caused by offshore drilling."

"I'm thinking Deepwater Horizon and the BP oil spill, right?"

"That's the argument and there are problems, for sure, but not as many as people believe. Unfortunately, until we find a reliable energy alternative, fossil fuels are necessary to our survival."

"I get it. So what do you need me to do?"

"I need to find out who sabotaged the helicopter I was riding in four weeks ago."

"Wow, your accident wasn't an accident? That's not good news."

"No, it isn't. It's not public info, but there's no way they can keep it quiet for long. I'm planning to do some legwork. I'll come up with a list of names—passengers and crew, anyone with access to the chopper. I'll need background info and I'll need you to go deep. I want to know if I was the target."

Tabby's voice tightened. "Get me the names. I'll get everything you need."

"Thanks, Tab, I'll be in touch." The line went dead and Reese leaned back in his chair. He'd have to find time to go to Houston to start his search. His schedule was packed, so it wouldn't be easy.

A light knock sounded, then Kenzie opened the door. Her pale scoop-necked sweater hinted at the fullness of her breasts, something he shouldn't have noticed, but did.

"What did Milburn have to say? Have they found the cause of the crash?"

He didn't want to worry her, but sooner or later the information was bound to hit the news. He was going to need help with this. He needed Kenzie in the loop.

"Someone tampered with the chopper. The crash was intentional."

"Oh, my God. Reese, you could have been killed."

He forced the tight muscles across his shoulders to relax. "The investigation's ongoing. The FBI is taking over. Eventually, they'll find whoever's responsible and arrest them."

"Eventually? What about in the meantime? What if whoever did it does something like that again?" She began to realize the implications, as he had known she would. "You don't...you don't think you were the target?"

"A lot's been happening. According to Derek Stiles, there have been an inordinate amount of accidents that involve the rig."

She stiffened. "You need someone to protect you. You have to call your brother."

"Which one?" he joked. "And the answer is no. I'm not calling either of my brothers. I won't be cosseted twenty-four hours a day. I am, however, going to find the bastard who crashed the chopper and killed two good men. I'm going to make sure he doesn't hurt anyone else."

Kenzie just stood there. She handled his schedule, knew about the hours each week he set aside for his martial arts instructor. She had to know he was proficient—more than proficient—in self-defense. She didn't know about his dark past or his skill with a weapon.

But she should know him well enough to realize he wasn't going to change his mind.

"All right, then," she said resignedly. "What can I do to help?"

A faint smile touched his lips. "I'll fill you in as soon as I figure it out."

"Fair enough." She took a deep breath, focused back on work. "I assume that means you'll be carrying on with your schedule for today and this evening."

"Unless something changes, yes. Remind me…what's on my calendar for tonight?"

"You have a charity event, the annual Dallas Youth Homes fundraiser. You bought a table for eight that includes your brothers and their wives, Kade Logan, Chase's friend from Denver, and his date, Marla Steiner."

"Who am I taking?"

"Andrea Wellington. You mentioned something about meeting her at an event at the governor's mansion when you asked me to arrange for a limo."

He remembered now. When he'd called her, he'd already been trying to distance himself from Fiona.

"Follow up. Give her the time the limo will arrive and tell her I look forward to seeing her again." And he hoped like hell it was true. Hoped an evening with Andrea Wellington would be more appealing than the ones he'd spent with the last few women he'd dated.

"I'll take care of it." Kenzie turned and walked out the door and Reese's gaze followed. Her spine-erect posture should have kept his mind on business, but the sexy sway of her hips sent a rush of heat straight to his groin.

Cursing softly, Reese jerked his thoughts back from where they'd gone and began to formulate a plan that would help him find a killer.

CHAPTER SIX

KENZIE MADE THE phone call, dreading the sound of the woman's voice. Reese dated the most beautiful women in the world: movie stars, TV personalities, and fashion models, though he seemed to prefer women less interested in the spotlight. Businesswomen, a high school principal, and attorneys like Fiona Cantor had all spent time in his company.

And undoubtedly in his bed.

Though he never dated a woman very long, they usually remained friends and rarely refused to see him again. Perhaps he kept things superficial as a result of his divorce, a bitter, expensive dissolution from what Kenzie had read in the gossip columns. She figured Reese wasn't ready to go down that particular road again—if ever.

In a way it made her sad. Reese was a great guy. She knew he had coached Little League baseball and was a Big Brother to kids from broken homes. He also donated heavily to underprivileged teen charities, including Dallas Youth Homes, the benefit he was attending tonight.

The woman answered and Kenzie took a deep breath. "Hello, Andrea, this is Reese Garrett's personal assistant, McKenzie Haines. I'm calling to let you know the limo will be arriving at seven o'clock to pick you up for tonight's event. Reese said to tell you he's looking forward to seeing you again."

"Oh, dear. I was just getting ready to call him. A family emergency came up and I have to cancel. My mom's in the hospital. Shall I call Reese or can you give him the message?"

"I can let him know. Don't worry, I'm sure Reese would want you to be with your mother."

"Thank you."

The call ended and Kenzie felt a shocking sense of relief. It was ridiculous. Reese would just call someone else to take Andrea's place. She glanced at the clock. It was Friday night, the office closed. Except for the few people on the executive floor who were still working, everyone had gone home. Reese was going to be late if he didn't leave soon, and he still needed to find a date.

She knocked lightly on his door and pulled it open. Reese stood in the middle of the room talking on the phone as he unfastened the row of buttons down the front of his white dress shirt.

She knew he kept several suits and miscellaneous extra garments in his office. There was a private bath with a shower so he could change if he was running late.

But tonight was a black-tie affair. He motioned toward the closet, shrugged out of the shirt and tossed it onto the sofa. She tried not to stare. She had imagined his lean, tanned, broad-shouldered torso more times than she cared to admit, but not the powerful chest with the crisp black hair arrowing down over six-pack abs, across a flat stomach, disappearing into the waistband of his slacks.

Her heart drummed. Her palms felt damp. Trying to block the image, she walked briskly to the closet to retrieve the tuxedo she found inside, but the sight of his naked torso was burned into her brain.

She took down a black designer tux and the pleated white shirt next to it. Still on the phone, Reese had turned and was looking out the window, giving her a view of his broad shoulders and muscular back.

She told herself to move, but her legs felt frozen and she couldn't seem to take the first step. The tux and shirt hit the floor and her mouth dried up. Stretched across all that smooth, tanned skin was the most amazing tattoo she had ever seen.

The wings of a beautifully drawn bird, its head in profile, spread from one feathered tip to another across that broad back. Not an eagle, she realized. Something darker, more compelling, something she couldn't have imagined in her most erotic dreams.

Reese turned away from the window and the beautiful bird disappeared. Face flushed with embarrassment, she reached down and picked up the hangers, carefully draped the tux over the arm of the sofa.

Reese ended the call and tossed his cell on the matching chair. "I'm running late," he explained. "I had my housekeeper go by my apartment and pick up my tux. I figured I could save time if I dressed right here."

She managed to nod. Clearly, she must not have looked as astonished as she felt.

Reese crossed to the sofa, took the dress shirt off the hanger, and slipped it on, covering those wide shoulders and most of his powerful chest.

"So I guess this is the first time you've seen my tattoo," he said mildly. "I suppose I should have prepared you."

But he had been clear from the beginning. If she wanted to be his personal assistant, it was her job to do whatever he needed done. Not including sexual favors, of course.

If she was offended by bringing him a cup of coffee or helping him arrange a date, he would hire a man for the position. Because of the social climate where male-female business relations had become so strained, he had preferred to do just that. Kenzie had convinced him she could handle the job.

"It's not a problem," she said. "It's not like I'm in danger of being assaulted. You're standing ten feet away."

His mouth edged up in that sexy way of his.

"Your tattoo," she couldn't resist adding. "It's incredible. What kind of bird is it?"

He buttoned the shirt, but made no move to take off any more of his clothes. Reese never pushed the boundaries between employer and employee. She didn't believe he ever would.

"It's a falcon," he said. "I had it done when I was in high school. Kind of a *fuck you* to my family, I guess. I should probably have it removed, but I see it as a reminder of the rotten kid I was back then. In some odd way, it keeps me centered."

Surprise filtered through her. Though she'd read some of his background in the papers, she couldn't imagine Reese Garrett ever really stepping out of line. "The tattoo is beautiful. It's part of you now. I don't think it's something you should destroy."

His features softened. She could feel his intense blue eyes on her. "Maybe not. I like it, if you want the truth." He flicked a glance at the tux, Armani or something equally expensive. "You came in here for a reason. What is it?"

She felt like a fool. At the sight of his amazing body, she had completely forgotten the reason she was there. "Your date for the evening, Andrea Wellington? She had a family emergency and had to cancel."

He frowned. "I can't go to this thing alone." He checked his gold Bulgari wristwatch, adjusted the black alligator band, and looked back at her. "I don't have time to find someone else. How long would it take you to get ready?"

"What?"

"I need a dinner date. If you have something formal to wear, I'd appreciate it if you'd fill in."

She had traveled with him. Joined him for business lunches and dinners with associates whenever he needed her. This was no different.

"I attended all sorts of formal functions when I was married to Lee. I have the right clothes. Once I get home, I can be ready in twenty minutes."

He looked back down at his watch. "We'll save time if I just go with you. Reggie has the limo waiting downstairs. As soon as I'm dressed, we can go."

KENZIE RODE IN silence all the way to her town house. She was going to be Reese's date for the evening. She'd had a dream like that one night, a dream that had ended with Reese kissing her, doing a lot more than that. She'd awakened with a start, her skin hot and her body damp. Fortunately, the erotic part of the dream had slipped away, for which she was especially grateful now.

She thought of the beautiful tattoo on his back, a falcon, wings spread the width of his shoulders. The sight had hit her with a shot of lust unlike anything she had ever felt before.

She and Lee had had an adequate sex life. At least in the beginning. Until he'd started cheating and she had found out. She had threatened to leave him. For Griffin's sake had stayed, but her desire for him had faded along with her trust.

Their limo pulled up in front of the town house, a two-story redbrick building on Colby Street in Uptown.

"I can wait out here," Reese offered.

Kenzie shook her head. "Absolutely not. Besides, it's time you met my grandmother and my son, Griff."

He nodded, a little surprised, she thought, and maybe pleased. "All right." The front door wasn't bolted. She opened it and both of them walked into the foyer. She noticed Reese frowning.

"Be smarter to keep your door locked. Criminals are always looking for an easy mark."

He was right. She tried to keep the house secure but it was difficult with three people going in and out.

"I'll try harder."

Reese just nodded.

As they walked into the living room, Gran rose from the overstuffed chair next to the beige tweed sofa. Except for Griff's skateboard propped against one wall and a stack of paperback romances on the end table next to a brass lamp, Gran always kept the place neat and clean.

"Gran, this is my boss, Reese Garrett. Reese, this is Florence Spencer, my grandmother."

"Nice to meet you, Mrs. Spencer," Reese said.

Gran smiled. "I'd rather you just call me Flo." Her pale blue eyes ran over him boldly, from the top of his gleaming black hair, along the shiny lapels of his tuxedo, down his long legs, to the glossy black shoes on his feet. "Pleasure to meet you." She turned to Kenzie. "Griff's over at the neighbor's. He should be home any minute."

"Reese's date canceled at the last minute. I'm filling in for her, so I need to get upstairs and change." Kenzie turned back to Reese. "I won't be long."

He just nodded. She wondered what he thought of the town house. With its inexpensive, durable furniture, knick-knacks on the shelves, and framed family photos on the walls, the place was at best comfortable and homey. She wasn't much of a decorator. Or rather, she was too busy earning a living to worry much about it.

In time, she planned to make improvements, but for now it was enough.

She headed upstairs, quickly went to her closet, and started searching through the clothes left over from her former life. She'd been the wife of Lee Haines, a wealthy businessman, daughter-in-law of Arthur Haines, both members of the Dallas elite. The clothes weren't new, but the designer labels were exclusive and the garments beautifully made in timeless styles that rarely changed.

Quickly sorting through her options, she chose a modest dark blue crepe gown with a beaded bodice and narrow spaghetti straps. It fit snugly at the waist and hips, then flared gently to the floor.

She tossed the dress on the bed and hurried into the bathroom to freshen her makeup, adding a little extra for the occasion. Brushing her heavy dark hair, she plaited it into a loose braid and pinned it in a knot at the nape of her neck, careful to leave a few loose strands beside each ear.

Satisfied with her appearance, she added a pair of rhinestone earrings and slipped into matching dark blue satin heels. Blue beaded clutch in hand, she headed out of the bedroom and started down the stairs, pausing halfway when she heard her son's laughter mingled with Reese's deep chuckle.

Her stomach fluttered and it wasn't from nerves. Pressing her hand there, she took a deep breath and continued down to the living room.

CHAPTER SEVEN

WHATEVER REESE WAS about to say froze in the back of his throat. The blue beaded gown worked perfectly with Kenzie's coloring, her mahogany hair, golden brown eyes, and fair complexion. It was modest for the most part, displaying her curves but only a hint of cleavage. The fabric rustled when she moved, an erotic sound that stirred the blood already pounding through his veins.

The dress was simple and in perfect taste. On Kenzie, it was the sexiest gown Reese had ever seen. He wanted to tell her how beautiful she looked, but it was exactly the wrong thing to do.

"So what do you think about the coaching job, Mr. Garrett?" Griff asked, giving Reese the moment he needed to compose himself. Griffin Haines was a handsome kid with his mother's good looks and similar coloring, the golden brown eyes and thick, dark, reddish-brown hair.

He was smart, too, same as Kenzie. Fortunately, Lee Haines's weak chin and pale eyes had been overpowered by Kenzie's stronger genes.

Reese's gaze went back to her and he restarted the conversation. "Griff mentioned he played Little League baseball and I told him I'd coached a team a couple of summers ago. Griff says his coach recently quit and asked if I'd be interested." He looked back at Griff. "Tell you what, let me give it some thought."

Kenzie just nodded, clearly not excited at the prospect. He wondered if she could be thinking along the same lines he was. The last thing they needed was more time together.

"If you don't want to be late, we'd better get going," she said with a glance at the door.

Gran walked them to the entry. "You both look gorgeous. You make a beautiful couple."

Reese managed to smile. "Thank you, Mrs. Spencer."

"It's just Flo, like I said."

He nodded. "We won't be late, Flo." He turned to Griff. "I'll have your mom home as early as possible."

"That's okay, Mom doesn't have a curfew like I do."

Reese managed to hold back a smile and just nodded.

They left the town house, Kenzie walking beside him. She missed a step in her sky-high heels but quickly righted herself without his help. Reese felt a trickle of irritation at the forced propriety. It felt strange to be escorting a woman he wasn't allowed to touch.

Kenzie flicked him a sideways glance. "Maybe we could set aside some of the politically correct protocol, just for tonight."

Reese smiled broadly, relieved she felt the same. "That sounds great. Just remember it was your idea."

Kenzie smiled back. He felt the kick but managed to ignore it. As he guided her down the slightly uneven path to the long white stretch limo, the warmth of her body beneath his hand, seeping through her gown, sent his mind once more where it didn't belong.

He focused on the limo driver, who opened the rear passenger door. A big, beefy African American, Reggie Porter owned the limo company. He was former military, tough as nails, and a longtime, trusted friend of the Garrett family.

Reese helped Kenzie settle inside then slid onto the deep

red leather seat beside her. He couldn't help thinking how good she felt next to him, which made him wonder if setting aside the rules for the evening had been the best plan.

One thing he knew, dating his executive assistant was completely out of the question. If he wanted to see her, he'd either have to fire her or find her another, less desirable position in the company, which, for both their sakes and especially his, Reese refused to do.

With the investigation he was beginning, he needed Kenzie now more than ever.

THE BENEFIT FOR the Dallas Youth Homes charity was being held at The Adolphus, an elegant older hotel on Commerce Street in the financial district.

The hotel, built in 1912, had once played host to presidents and even the Queen of England. The ballroom, with its elegant molded ceilings and parquet floors, held a sea of linen-draped tables, each with a blue-and-silver floral arrangement.

Most of the guests were seated by the time Kenzie and Reese walked to their table near the stage at the front of the room where his brothers were waiting, along with a friend from Colorado and his date.

Her nerves were on edge. Being with Reese tonight felt different than previous business events. Part of her loved being with him this way. Another part worried it might intensify the forbidden feelings she carried for him.

To protect herself, Kenzie concentrated on the evening ahead. She knew from Reese's schedule who would be sitting at the table. She had met Chase and Brandon during Reese's hospital stay, but none of the others.

"Sorry I missed the cocktail hour," Reese said. "My

date had a family emergency. This is my assistant, Kenzie Haines. She was kind enough to fill in for her."

He turned to Kenzie. "You've met my brother Chase."

She nodded. "It's nice to see you again."

"You, too, Kenzie," Chase said. "And under far more pleasant circumstances. I appreciate the way you helped us take care of my brother after the accident."

She felt the heat creeping into her face. After the crash, she had gone to see Reese at the hospital every day, explaining her presence as necessary to keep the office running smoothly. Reese never knew how worried she had been and she wanted to keep it that way.

"Looking out for Reese is my job," she said mildly.

Chase's smile widened. "Yes, I suppose it is." He was maybe an inch shorter than Reese, the edge of his jaw defined by a short-cropped dark blond beard.

"The lady next to him is his wife, Harper," Reese continued.

"Nice to meet you, Kenzie." Harper Garrett was a tall, willowy young woman with gorgeous silver-blond hair.

"You, too."

"You know my younger brother, Brandon."

Brandon touched his forehead in a faint salute. "Nice seeing you." He grinned. "Anyone who can put up with my prickly brother all day is okay by me." He had dark brown hair and the lean, hard-muscled build that ran in the Garrett family.

He was also gorgeous, with a movie-star face and beautiful blue eyes a less intense shade than Reese's. She couldn't help noticing the affection in Brandon's eyes whenever he looked at his wife.

Jessie Garrett smiled and greeted Kenzie warmly, and Reese moved on to Kade Logan, a rancher from Colorado, a handsome, well-built man with dark hair and golden brown eyes. His companion, talk-show personality Marla Steiner, was a date Chase had arranged for his friend.

Once Kenzie and Reese were seated, there was a brief welcome from the president of the charity, then the dinner service began—chicken swimming in lemon cream sauce and green beans with slivered almonds. She'd eaten similar meals with Lee on dozens of different occasions.

Kenzie shifted in her chair. With eight people at the round linen-covered table, she was sitting close enough to Reese to feel the occasional brush of his thigh against hers. She remembered his magnificent tattooed back, and her body flushed with heat. It was frightening. She couldn't wait for the evening to end.

It seemed hours before it was over. At one point, Reese got up and gave a brief address, followed by several others describing the work done by the charity, thanking people for coming, and imploring them to be generous.

She made a trip to the ladies' room with Harper and Jessie, found both of them easy to talk to and totally accepting of her as nothing more than Reese's substitute date. She'd been worried something in her expression would give away her attraction.

All evening, Kenzie worked to keep up a businesslike facade, which Reese seemed to do without the slightest effort. A thought that was oddly depressing.

Deep down, she couldn't help wishing she were there with him for real, something she had never remotely considered. It wasn't going to happen, could not possibly happen, not when her job meant so much to her and she needed the income so badly. More so if Lee actually filled a custody suit for Griff.

The hours slipped past. Finally, the benefit was over

and they were back in the limo. The vehicle was driving toward her town house when Reese mentioned the investigation he was pursuing.

"I'm flying into Houston," he said. "Driving on to Galveston. I'll be asking questions, tracking people down, digging up basic information."

"I've scheduled your trip to the platform," Kenzie said, "but I really think, under the circumstances, you should postpone it."

Surprisingly, Reese agreed. "Until we know what's going on, that's probably a good idea."

"I'll take care of it."

"I could really use your help while I'm down there," he said. "If leaving town for a couple of days isn't too inconvenient."

"Gran's there to take care of Griff and they're both used to me working long hours. A few days away won't be a problem."

Not a problem for Gran or Griff. But for her, spending time with Reese was growing more and more difficult.

"Set it up," he said. "We'll fly down next week. I've got a staff meeting on Tuesday. We'll leave Wednesday morning, come back Friday night at the latest. You'll be home in time to spend the weekend with your son."

Reese and his wife had never had children. She knew he liked kids. Kenzie thought he would have made a good dad.

The limo turned a corner and continued down the street. She usually booked Reese an SUV, but for black-tie occasions, he preferred a stretch. She couldn't help wondering if Andrea would have enjoyed it.

Reggie pulled up in front of her town house, got out to open the rear passenger door. Reese slid out of the car and came around to help Kenzie alight.

"You don't need to walk me to the door," she said. "I can find my own way."

"Tonight you're my date. That doesn't end until you're safely inside your home." His hand rode at her waist as he walked her up the concrete path to the front porch. She couldn't suppress the flutter in her stomach. When Kenzie turned to look at him, his eyes, a fierce cobalt blue, held a trace of something she had never seen before. Heat, she realized, the unmistakable glitter of desire.

He blinked and it was gone.

Or maybe she had only imagined it.

"I know attending a benefit with your assistant wasn't your favorite thing to do," she said. "But it was still a very nice evening."

He took a step back, his face in shadow. In her dream, he had leaned down and kissed her.

"I'm glad you enjoyed it." He moved even farther away. "Good night, Kenzie."

"Good night, Reese."

She watched him walk away, shoulders wide, long strides eating up the ground beneath his black patent shoes. An unexpected yearning moved through her.

Get a grip, Kenzie. You're just an employee. And even if tonight had been a real date, even if she had broken all the rules and kissed him, even seduced him, she would just be another of his women. Reese was never interested in more than a brief affair.

She sighed as she climbed the stairs to her empty bedroom. Tomorrow was another day. Everything would be back to normal.

But as she lay in bed, she thought of Reese and the hot look in his eyes and couldn't fall asleep.

CHAPTER EIGHT

THE TWICE-MONTHLY staff meeting Reese presided over had just come to an end. VPs from every department—Finance, Human Resources, Marketing, Sales, and Promotion—had all presented an update report.

As CEO, it was his job to set the strategy and direction of the company. To do that, he had to know what was going on with their top competitors, which markets to enter, how much capital was needed to expand company profits, and a well of other information. It was challenging, but a job he was good at.

Better than good, when he kept his mind focused on work.

Unfortunately, his thoughts had been scattered since the night of the benefit. It was past time he stopped thinking of Kenzie as a woman, remembering how beautiful she had looked that night. Kenzie was a valued employee, one he admired and respected. That was the way things had to remain.

Since he was a master at controlling his emotions, he knew he could do it. He'd already started distancing himself, getting himself back on track.

Still, as he left the conference room on the way to his office and saw a man in a cheap brown suit handing her a manila envelope, he changed course and headed in that direction.

"What's going on?" he asked, not liking the pale color of her face as she stared at the documents she had taken from inside.

"Good luck, Mrs. Haines," the man in the suit called out. Turning, he walked away. Kenzie looked up at Reese, her expression bleak.

"That was a process server. Lee filed for full custody of Griffin."

Reese clamped down on a surge of anger, disliking Lee Haines more than ever. "On what grounds?"

"Not complying with the terms of the original custody agreement. When we divorced, I was only working part-time. Then the money from the settlement began to run out and I started a full-time job. In March I took the job here, working for Garrett Resources. It's a full work week plus occasional overtime."

"We can figure that out. If you need more time with your family—"

Kenzie shook her head. "That's not it. Not really. You already make concessions most employers wouldn't. The truth is Lee doesn't care how many hours I work. Nor is he interested in actually raising his son. Something's up. I know it. You saw him at the hospital. Lee's barely a father to Griff."

"What is it, then?"

"I'm not sure, but..." She glanced at the sheaf of court documents in her hand. "Lee's brother, Daniel, is a Louisiana state senator. I think Arthur wants Lee to run for the senate here in Texas."

Reese liked Arthur Haines even less than Lee. "What's that got to do with Griff?"

"I remember Arthur talking about it during the divorce. He begged me not to leave his son. Even then Arthur had political ambitions for Lee. Being a divorced man isn't good for a candidate. But a single father raising a young boy would have great voter appeal. Arthur probably believes it'll give Lee the edge he needs to win."

"How's Arthur's relationship with his grandson?"

She sighed. "Griff barely knows him. He isn't a kid kind of guy."

Reese tipped his head toward his office. "Let's go inside where we can talk."

Kenzie walked ahead of him and he closed the door behind them. "I know a good attorney. One of the best in Dallas. He can handle this, make sure you don't lose custody. He's expensive but you don't have to worry, I'll take care of it."

She started shaking her head. "You can't possibly mean to pay for my lawyer."

"You need help. That's what people do. They help each other."

"I can't. People might talk. It might cause problems for you. I'm not willing to take the chance."

"Listen to me, dammit. It's okay to let people in once in a while. It isn't charity. It's just being a friend."

Her pretty golden eyes filled, and his chest tightened. "Griff needs you, Kenzie. Let me help you."

She turned away, walked slowly over to the window and just stood there looking down at the people on the street, the same line of protesters who had been there last week.

With a shuddering breath, she walked back. "Call him. I don't want to lose my son. I don't have any choice."

Reese worked to keep his voice even. "His name's Drew Wilcox. He's with Wilcox, Sullivan, and Boyle. I'll phone him, tell him you'll be in touch. You can set up a meeting in your home. That way he can meet Griff and your grandmother, see where you live."

Resigned, she nodded. "Okay."

"Don't worry. Whatever Lee does, we're not going to let him win."

Kenzie looked up at him and something moved across her features. "Thank you."

"You can thank me when this is over." Heading to his desk, he forced his mind away from Kenzie and her problems, which shouldn't in any way be his yet somehow felt as if they were.

"In the meantime, I need you to set up that trip to Houston. I've given it some thought and since I'll be asking questions that might stir up trouble, I think it would be better if you stayed here."

"Why? Because you're afraid you might have been the target of the crash?"

"That's right, and if someone wants me dead, being with me could put you in danger."

"At this point you don't know if the crash had anything to do with you."

"That's exactly what I need to find out."

"I can help you with that, and until there's a reason to suspect you're the one they were after, there's no reason for me not to go."

She was right. He was jumping to conclusions. If he'd been the target, there likely would have been another attempt on his life by now.

"What about Lee and the situation with Griff?" he asked. "If you need to be here, I can manage on my own."

Her chin firmed. "You need me, so I'm going. I'm not letting Lee ruin my life—or interfere in my work."

Reese felt the pull of a smile. "I guess that settles it, then. Let me know when you get the schedule worked out."

Clutching the custody papers against her chest, Kenzie turned and walked away. When the door closed, Reese realized his pulse was hammering. He was still worked up about the guy in the suit. He was worried about Kenzie. He didn't want anyone hurting her. He didn't want anyone making her cry.

Something he couldn't afford to feel spread through him. Something he was determined to purge from his mind and heart. Sitting down at his desk, he picked up the phone.

THAT NIGHT AND the next, he went out with different women, took them to dinner, then to bed. All he felt the next day was empty. His rigid control was returning. He was putting his lapse of judgment behind him. Everything was smoothing out, getting back to normal.

Then it was Wednesday morning, time to head for Houston. Kenzie was meeting him at the Dallas Executive Airport. They'd be flying down in the company jet, a sleek white Citation CJ4. The jet was an amazing time-saver, well worth the money it had cost.

As he'd packed for the trip, he had again considered leaving Kenzie in Dallas, but with her sharp mind and knack for organization, she would be a real asset.

Still, instead of facing an evening alone with her, he arranged a date with a beautiful redhead named Arial Kaplan, whom he'd spent a few nights with when he'd been working in the Houston office earlier this year. Arial had given him an open invitation to call her whenever he was in town, an invitation that included more than just dinner.

Sleeping with Arial would keep his mind off Kenzie, Reese told himself. He'd be able to concentrate on the investigation and find the man who had sabotaged the chopper.

Or at least find out if someone wanted to stop the Poseidon deal enough to kill him.

A LITTLE OVER an hour after takeoff, the Garrett Resources jet landed at the West Houston Airport, the closest airstrip to the Energy Corridor, where the Houston office was located.

Kenzie smiled. She wasn't a fan of flying, but if you had to travel, a private jet was definitely the way to go.

The plane began its descent. The September day was muggy and overcast, hinting at rain, the landing a little bumpy. Crossing the tarmac, Kenzie walked with Reese toward a pair of black Range Rovers kept at the terminal for out-of-town guests in Houston on Garrett Resources business.

Kenzie sat in the passenger seat as Reese drove the Rover to an apartment building not far away, four units the company leased to accommodate those same people.

Kenzie had been there several times. She knew Reese's private apartment sat at the end of hall, though she had never been inside. She carried her overnight bag into the unit next door, a nicely furnished one-bedroom with a modern kitchen and spacious bath.

Once they were settled, she joined Reese for the drive south from Houston to Galveston, to the Sea Titan Pelican Island heliport. Reese was quiet along the way, as he had been all week, adjusting the volume on the satellite radio to fill the gaps in the conversation.

Reese was CEO of the company. Kenzie had a feeling he regretted his brief lapse in the office on Monday when the process server had appeared and he had allowed his emotions to surface. She knew him well enough to know he had a protective streak when it came to his family, friends, even his employees.

Kenzie was grateful for the distance he was putting between them. She needed to rein herself in, get herself back on track, and Reese-the-CEO, instead of Reese-the-smoking-hot-date, or Reese-the-good-friend, made that a whole lot easier.

She tipped her head back against the headrest as the Rover rolled along I-45. She had accepted Reese's help with the attorney because she'd had no choice, but she never should have let down her guard and allowed herself to think of him as anything more than her employer. She wouldn't let it happen again.

Reese used the control on the steering wheel to turn down the volume on the radio. "I understand you met with Drew Wilcox."

"He called you?"

"Just to let me know he'd talked to you and was taking the case. How did it go?"

"I liked Drew very much and so did Gran. He seemed confident and extremely capable." He also seemed to understand that even with her generous salary, there was never enough money when you had two other people depending on you.

"Have you told Griff his dad wants custody?"

"Not yet. I'm hoping Drew will present my case—a single mother supporting her son and grandmother—and get the court to alter the divorce stipulations and allow me to keep my full-time job."

He nodded. "If that happens, Lee's case will never get off the ground."

"That's what I'm hoping. Drew has submitted some kind of brief that asks the judge for a dismissal. He thinks there's at least a chance of that happening."

"What about Lee?"

"If Lee wants more time with Griff, I don't have any objections, but I doubt that's what he's really after."

The Rover slowed, Reese changed lanes, and through

the heavy morning mist, Galveston appeared on the horizon. The windshield wipers went on, the blades sweeping intermittently across the glass.

"We're almost there," Reese said as he continued through Galveston traffic, then turned onto the Pelican Island Causeway. At the heliport, he parked the Rover, and Kenzie stepped out into the misty sea air. She was glad she had dressed down a little, in brown pants and a blue-and-beige-print blouse, belted at the waist, no jacket, since the temperature was still warm.

Reese had dressed more casually, as well, in crisp, perfectly creased dark blue jeans and a yellow knit pullover. Instead of sneakers, he wore expensive Italian loafers.

He held open the glass door to the main office, and they walked up to the reception desk. A young blond man rose as Reese approached. "May I help you?"

"I'm Reese Garrett. I've got an appointment with Supervisor Brandt."

The name *Ryan* flashed on the young man's gold-plated name tag. "Mr. Brandt is expecting you. If you'll please follow me."

Robert Brandt was in his late forties, with thinning brown hair and a slight paunch over the waistband of his dark brown slacks. He extended his hand, which Reese shook.

"This is my assistant, Kenzie Haines."

"Ms. Haines." Brandt nodded in her direction and turned back to Reese. "I'm glad to see you've recovered from your injuries."

"I was lucky. Two other men weren't. The crash is what I'm here to talk to you about."

Brandt nodded. "Why don't we all have a seat?"

They sat down in sky blue vinyl chairs in front of Brandt's gray metal desk. There were a couple of file cabinets the same bland gray. Framed aerial photos of Sea Titan's offshore platforms lined the walls.

"By now you know the crash wasn't an accident," Reese said, leaning back in his chair.

"That's right. Frank Milburn called me."

"I want to know who was responsible and why it happened. I need the names of all the people onboard that day, including the pilot and copilot. I want the names of the mechanics and anyone who had access to the chopper."

It was information Reese could have pressed for and gotten over the phone, but Kenzie knew he wanted to talk to the people involved in person, see if he could get some answers.

Brandt fell silent.

"If you need to get an approval, I'd suggest you call someone at Sea Titan who can give it to you. It was one of their choppers that went down, and I was on my way to one of their offshore platforms when it happened."

Brandt conceded with a nod and reached for the phone. "I'll make the call, but getting an approval might take a while."

"Keep in mind, a lot more people are going to want the same information—including the FBI."

Brandt's hand stilled. He set the phone back down in its cradle. "You're right. I'll have Ryan get you the information. It shouldn't take long."

Kenzie rose from her chair. "I'll make sure we get what we need."

Reese stood up, too. "I appreciate your help with this," he said to Brandt.

"The pilot, Jake Schofield, was a friend. I was relieved for his family's sake that the crash wasn't entirely his fault. I didn't know Manny Alvarez, the other man who died, but I know he had family. I want the bastard who killed them just as bad as you do."

CHAPTER NINE

WHILE KENZIE STAYED back in the main office and worked with Ryan to collect the information, Reese wandered the area around the heliport. Brandt had given him the names of the two mechanics who had done the most recent maintenance on the chopper.

He glanced up at a noise overhead, watched a helicopter lifting away, the *whop, whop* of the blades loud, then fading into the distance as Reese made his way inside a vast metal hangar. A group of men worked on a big blue-and-white helicopter that held at least twelve passengers plus two pilots. The chopper was typical of the ones that ferried the crew back and forth from offshore platforms, though it had been a smaller, eight-passenger helo that had crashed.

He walked up to one of the mechanics, all of whom wore dark blue overalls. This man was older, with a leonine mane of thick silver hair.

"I'm looking for Fernando Ramirez and Otto Kovacs," Reese said. Kovacs, the lead mechanic, was in charge of the crew here at the Sea Titan terminal.

The mechanic turned and pointed to a bald, barrel-chested guy with arms the size of cannons. "I don't know where Ferdie is at the moment, but that's Otto right over there."

"Thanks." Reese headed in that direction, stopped a few feet away to watch the big guy work.

"What make is it?" Reese asked when Kovacs paused for a breather.

"Airbus H175. Top-of-the-line. Pretty motha', ain't she?"

"That's for sure." His gaze slid from the helicopter back to Otto. "I hear you were the guy in charge of maintenance on the chopper that crashed."

Otto's big bald head came up, his hand tightening around the wrench he was holding. "I worked on it. So did a lot of other guys."

"Any of them good enough to file a piece of metal off one of the gears, crash the helo, and not get caught by the NTSB?"

Otto's jaw hardened. "You better not be saying what I think you are."

"I'll tell you what I'm saying. I'm saying it wasn't just mechanical failure and pilot error. The helicopter was sabotaged. Someone purposely brought it down. From what I hear, you had the skill to do it."

"Who the hell are you?"

"I'm one of the guys lucky enough not to die, and you had better get used to answering questions, because the crash just turned into a homicide investigation. Sooner or later, you'll be talking to the FBI."

Otto's chest puffed out until he looked twice his size. "A smart guy would get the fuck out of here—before I decide to toss you out myself." He was tall, big, and burly, and clearly ready to fight.

"I wouldn't advise it," Reese said blandly.

"You think you can take me, city boy?"

"If you throw that punch you're considering, I guess we'll see."

Otto's mouth drew into a sneer that telegraphed his intentions as he drew back and swung a roundhouse blow that could take a man to his knees.

Reese easily ducked the punch. "I'm telling you to back off, Otto. That's the last warning you're going to get."

Otto waded in swinging. He was the kind of fighter Reese used to be, using his size and strength instead of skill and brains. Reese ducked Otto's powerful fist, sidestepped another attempt, and counterpunched, knocking Otto's head back, then driving a fist into his stomach.

The mechanic was harder than he looked and the fist didn't bury as deeply as it should have. Reese ducked and dodged out of the way as Otto stepped in and swung again, his massive fist clipping Reese's cheek, but sliding away without much damage. Reese bounced back with a solid right that connected with Otto's jaw, driving his head back, threw a couple of left jabs, then another right, followed by a solid left that sent Otto reeling. He hit the wall with a crash and went down hard.

"Stay down, Otto," Reese warned.

"Fuck you!" Accustomed to winning because of his massive size, the man lumbered to his feet. A crowd had begun to gather. Otto looked at them and smiled. Spurred on by their cheers of support, he charged like a bull, head down, big feet thundering across the concrete floor.

Reese used the guy's own momentum against him, turned to the side and gave Otto a shove, followed by a hard kick in the ass as he roared past. He landed on all fours and slid into a metal table, turning it upside down with a clatter. He shook his head like a big wet dog, took a couple of long, deep breaths, and staggered back to his feet.

"All I want, Otto, are the answers to my questions."

A muscle in Otto's jaw worked up and down. His round face was bathed in sweat and he was breathing hard. He took a last ragged breath and blew it out. His shoulders sagged and he nodded. "I didn't sabotage that chopper. I wouldn't do a thing like that."

Reese walked up to him, tipped his head toward a quiet area off to one side of the hangar. "Let's talk."

As THE GROUP of uniformed workmen began to disperse, Kenzie stood in shocked silence in the shadows inside the hangar. She had just watched the CEO of Garrett Resources brawling like a street thug with a man the size of a grizzly bear.

And he had won.

She should have been appalled. Grown men didn't act that way. Not civilized men, at any rate.

Instead, her heart was thundering with excitement and she couldn't stop a twinge of admiration. The memory of Reese moving with the grace of a gazelle and the strength of a tiger was amazing. And sexy. A sweep of unwanted desire still pumped through her veins.

She knew Reese kept himself in good physical condition, knew he practiced with a self-defense coach three early mornings a week. But she had no idea he could handle a bad situation in a way that would make Jack Reacher take notice. No wonder he didn't believe he needed a bodyguard.

He didn't.

He finished talking to the mechanic, spotted her, and headed in her direction. She noticed his knuckles were bruised and there was a faint, darkening spot on his cheek, but aside from that, he looked fine. *Too fine.*

"I…umm, saw what happened with Otto Kovacs."

One of his black eyebrows went up. "We…ahh…worked things out."

"Yes, that was apparent."

"I don't think he had anything to do with sabotaging the engine."

"What about the other guy, Fernando Ramirez?"

"Calls himself Ferdie. Apparently, he's just back from lunch. I'm on my way to talk to him now." Reese started walking and Kenzie fell in beside him, her purse slung over her shoulder.

"You get that passenger list?" he asked.

"It's right here." She pulled it out of her bag and Reese took it from her hand. He took out his cell phone and hit the button for one of his contacts.

"Tabby, it's Reese. I've got those names we talked about." He rattled off the passengers' names and those of the pilots. "I need to know if one of these people was the target. Look for anything in their backgrounds that might have made an enemy willing to take down a helo in order to kill them."

He nodded at something from the other end of the line, then added the names of the last two mechanics to work on the helo before the crash, Ramirez and Kovaks. The call ended and Reese shoved the phone back into the pocket of his jeans.

"One of the detectives from Maximum Security?" she guessed.

"In a way. Computer specialist named Tabitha Love. Technically, Tabby works for Chase and the gang at The Max, but since I'm a Garrett, she puts up with me." A smile touched his lips. She watched the slow, sensuous curve, and her stomach contracted.

"Maybe she'll find something," Kenzie said.

"If anyone can, it's Tabby."

Kenzie paused as Reese came to a halt in front of a dark-skinned Hispanic male as small as Otto was big.

"Ferdie Ramirez?" Reese guessed.

"That's right. What can I do for you?"

Reese identified himself and Kenzie, told Ferdie about the NTSB findings, and asked him about the crash.

"I don't know anything about it, I swear. It's my job to keep the damn things running, not cause them to fall out of the sky."

"You and Otto were the last guys to work on the chopper. The FBI is going to be breathing down your necks. If you two are innocent, who else could have done it?"

Ferdie started shaking his head. He was thin and wiry, his face slightly weathered. "I got no idea who crashed the helo or why the hell they would want to do it." He paused, his eyebrows sliding together. "Wait a minute. I remember something that might be important."

"I'm listening."

"The day before the crash, first thing that morning, one of the guys noticed a window in the back of the shop had been jimmied open. Whoever broke in would have had access to the helo."

"You report the break-in to the police?"

"I reported it to my super and he called the sheriff. Deputy came out and took a look, asked us if anything was missing. We searched but didn't find anything gone. I'm pretty sure the deputy filed a report, but that was the end of it. Until now, it didn't seem important. I mean, we all thought the crash was an accident."

"Thanks, Ferdie." Reese handed him one of his Garrett Resources business cards. "If you think of anything else, I'd appreciate a call."

Ferdie nodded, tucked the card into the breast pocket of his overalls, and walked away.

Kenzie looked at Reese. "You think someone from outside the terminal could have broken in and sabotaged the engine?"

"I don't know, but it's something we need to check out."

They started walking back across the asphalt yard. "I have a feeling you don't think it was Ferdie, either," Kenzie said.

"The break-in changes the dynamics. It makes sense it was someone who wouldn't immediately be a suspect. Someone other than one of the regular mechanics."

"True, but from what you've said, whoever it was had to be an expert, someone who knew how to sabotage the chopper without anyone figuring it out. It's been weeks. Whoever did it almost got away without anyone knowing."

Reese's jaw clenched, but he made no comment.

It was late in the afternoon and they hadn't had anything besides coffee all day.

"We need to eat something," Reese said. "See if you can find us a place close by."

Kenzie took out her cell and brought up restaurants in the area. "There's a place called The Galley. It's on Sea Wolf Parkway. Nothing fancy but the reviews look good."

"Let's go."

The Galley turned out to be a locals' joint with corrugated tin booths and music playing a little too loud. They both ordered catfish po'boys and iced tea.

As they finished the sandwiches, Reese checked the time on his phone. "We need to go to the sheriff's office, but it's getting late. We'll have a better chance of getting the info we want if we go tomorrow morning instead of the end of a long, hot day."

She nodded. It had been a long day, and she was exhausted. She took a drink of iced tea. "I think we made a good start, don't you?"

"Yes, I do. Ferdie was right. Nobody put the break-in together with the crash because everyone thought it was an accident. Now that they know the crash was intentional, the FBI is going to be very interested in finding the intruder."

"Maybe you should leave it to them."

"Maybe. Let's see what Tabby comes up with. Until we know why that particular helicopter was targeted—"

"Until we know for sure it wasn't you they wanted to kill—"

He nodded. "We need to keep going." He paid the bill and slid out of the booth. "Come on, let's go. It's still a ways back to Houston."

After an hour and half of winding his way through traffic, Reese parked the Rover and walked Kenzie to the door of the apartment next to his.

"I've got plans for the evening," he said. "You going to be okay on your own?"

He had plans. Of course he did. "I'll be fine." Aside from the night of the benefit, the only time she had spent an evening with Reese was when he was meeting business associates and needed her there as his assistant. "Actually, I made a note on your calendar that you had blocked out the time. I assumed you had a date."

Something shifted in his features. "That's right. An old friend. I'll knock on your door at nine in the morning. That should give us plenty of time to drive back down to Galveston and talk to the sheriff."

She nodded, but her mind had skipped ahead to the evening he would be spending with another woman—and the night. His delayed departure in the morning said it all. Kenzie even knew the name of his "old friend." Arial Kaplan. She had put it on his schedule. Some masochistic demon had goaded her into looking up the woman's Facebook page. A gorgeous redhead, an attorney who had graduated from Texas A&M.

It shouldn't have bothered her. Reese was single, one of the most eligible bachelors in Dallas. Until the benefit, she had been able to block thoughts of him as anything more than her employer. She'd been able to ignore the attraction and her secret wish that he would notice her as a woman.

It was unrealistic, given who he was, and impossible, considering her highly paid job as his executive assistant.

But lately, after his kindness and concern the day he had driven her to the hospital, combined with the support he had provided in her battle with Lee, her feelings had finally surfaced.

Like a jack-in-the-box springing up from a tightly sealed container, there was no way to push those feelings back down. Now she was forced to examine them.

And what she saw was terrifying.

She realized she was still standing in the hallway staring up at him. "So I guess I'll see you in the morning," she said, though the words seemed to stick in her throat. "Have a nice evening." She walked into the apartment and closed the door, leaned back against it.

Reese was a healthy, extremely virile male. He had needs, she told herself, just like any other man. For the first time it occurred to her that she had needs of her own. She had just buried them when she had divorced Lee.

Since then, she hadn't been with another man, hadn't had the least interest in dating. Now she realized her mistake. She should have made an effort to get her life back on track, should have gone out and socialized, maybe even had an affair.

She closed her eyes and tried to think of a man she might be interested in, someone she at least found attractive. But the only image that came to mind was a tall man with wavy black hair, a brilliant business mind, an amazing body, and the bluest eyes she had ever seen.

She blinked against the sting of tears.

Dear God, what was she going to do?

CHAPTER TEN

REESE SHOWERED AND dressed in slacks, a crisp white shirt and a navy blue blazer. He was ready but found himself reluctant to leave. He thought of Arial Kaplan and the evening ahead, supper at Chez Julienne, then back to Arial's apartment for an after-dinner drink, a brief seduction, and sex.

Arial was beautiful, with the deep red hair and pale complexion of a true redhead, marred not even by a single freckle. She was an attorney, smart, if a little self-absorbed. He told himself the only reason he was hesitant was the work he needed to do. He'd been out of the office all day. He didn't want to get too far behind.

Pulling out his cell, he phoned Arial and postponed their date until tomorrow night, then phoned Derek Stiles, his acquisitions VP, and asked if he was free for dinner.

"Matter of fact, I am," Derek said. "My lady's out of town. Give us a chance to catch up on a few things."

"Fleming's?" Reese suggested, a place not far away they both enjoyed.

"Great, I'll see you there."

Reese hung up the phone, thinking of Arial, wishing he didn't feel such a sense of relief. He just had too much on his mind, he told himself as he stripped off his blazer and rolled up the sleeves of his dress shirt, looking forward to a more casual evening.

Tomorrow night he'd be ready for a little diversion and

Arial was just the woman to provide it. Reese left the apartment and headed for Fleming's Steakhouse.

Unfortunately, the evening didn't go the way he planned. Derek remained concerned about the incidents plaguing the Poseidon. When Reese told him the NTSB had concluded the crash was intentional, Derek went ballistic.

"Dammit, Reese, you realize what that means? That crash has to be connected to the other accidents. If it is, someone wants to destroy this deal bad enough to commit murder."

Reese ignored the unease filtering through him. "Maybe. Or maybe it was about something else altogether, and I just happened to be in the wrong place at the wrong time. Until we get some answers, we can't afford to jump to conclusions."

He went on to fill Derek in on the actions he was taking, what he'd learned so far, and his appointment at the sheriff's office in the morning.

"You sure you don't want to call your brothers?" Derek asked. "Arrange some kind of personal protection?"

"I should know more in a day or two. My instincts say there's something else going on here. If it looks like the threat is real, I'll take care of it."

He wouldn't have brought Kenzie with him if he'd believed he was putting her in danger. But he worked faster and more efficiently with her helping him sort things out and stay on track. "In the meantime, I won't take any unnecessary risks."

INSTEAD OF FEELING refreshed after a night away from work, Reese felt tired and out of sorts the next morning. He was driving back to Galveston, Kenzie in the passenger seat of the Rover, looking nearly as tired as he felt, but still so beautiful his mouth went dry every time he glanced in her direction.

The attraction he felt for her was growing stronger. He should have slept with Arial last night. The distraction would have at least kept him sane this morning instead of aching for a woman he couldn't have. He'd make up for it tonight. Take Arial until he was too tired and sated to think of Kenzie even for a moment.

He turned off Broadway Avenue, headed toward his destination. The sheriff's department on 54th Street off Highway 87 wasn't far from the Sea Titan heliport on Pelican Island. A white, green-striped sheriff's pickup sat in front of an unimposing white concrete block structure.

Kenzie got out of the Rover and her soft perfume teased his senses as she walked past. Gritting his teeth against the blood that began to flow south, Reese silently cursed. At the front counter, he spoke to a dark-haired female deputy whose name tag read M. Orlando, introduced himself and Kenzie.

"I called earlier. Sheriff Martinez arranged for me to speak to Deputy Hollenbeck." Like a lot of people, the sheriff had been impressed by Reese's position as Garrett Resources CEO. He needed information. He would use whatever leverage he could get.

"I'll tell Deputy Hollenbeck you're here." Threading her way around several men in dark green uniforms, Deputy Orlando headed for the rear of the building, then returned a few minutes later followed by a tall guy with a square jaw and sandy hair combed straight back from a wide forehead.

"You're Garrett?" he asked.

"That's right. And this is my assistant, McKenzie Haines."

"I'm Deputy Hollenbeck. Sheriff Martinez said you wanted to talk to me about the break-in at the heliport."

"That's right. Anyplace we can speak in private?"

Hollenbeck's gaze went to Kenzie, slid over her in a way that made Reese's jaw go tight. "Follow me."

The deputy led them into a small, multipurpose room with a TV monitor on the wall and a rectangular walnut conference table that seated six.

Hollenbeck sat down at one end. Reese seated Kenzie, then took a chair between her and the deputy.

"I'd like to know how it went down," Reese said. "What you found when you answered the call."

The deputy studied his notes. "It was a little after eight that morning when dispatch got the call. Apparently, one of the mechanics noticed the open window and discovered it had been pried open sometime during the night."

"So there was evidence of forced entry."

"That's right. Probably a crowbar. Window's big enough for a guy to crawl through without much problem."

"You check for prints?"

He nodded. "Standard procedure on a possible burglary. Didn't find anything usable, just a bunch of smudges on the windowsill. Nothing that could help us find the intruder."

"Any video cameras on the premises?"

"Not in there."

"So someone broke in, but nothing was stolen."

"No, not according to the mechanics on duty that morning."

"Any chance the window could have been jimmied from the inside? Just made to look like a break-in?"

Hollenbeck stiffened, his ego cranked at the idea he might not have done his job as well as he should have.

"No. It was a metal-sashed window, bent inward around the edges then shoved open. No way the break-in was faked."

"What about other break-ins on Pelican Island?" Kenzie asked. "Something that was reported before or after that morning? Or something that happened in the surrounding area?"

Good question, Reese thought. She'd been quiet since they'd left Houston. Clearly she hadn't slept, either. He hoped Lee Haines wasn't giving her more problems.

Hollenbeck cut her a glance that slid like grease over her breasts. "I can check it out for you. Maybe you could give me a call this afternoon."

Reese clenched his jaw. No way was she calling the bastard. "If nothing was missing, what was the intruder after?"

Hollenbeck's mouth flattened out. "How the hell should I know?"

Reese controlled his temper. "Since the crash was just upgraded to a homicide, you might want to give it some thought—before the FBI arrives to ask you the same question."

"Homicide? Someone brought that chopper down on purpose?"

"That's right."

Color surfaced in Hollenbeck's neck and crept into his face. "I hadn't heard."

"The helo gears were tampered with," Reese continued. "The break-in means someone besides the regular crew had access. You got anything that could point us toward who might have broken in that night?"

Hollenbeck shook his head. "Like I said, I can look at other break-ins and burglaries in the area. Maybe that'll turn up something."

The tension in Reese's jaw eased. The deputy's attitude had definitely improved. Amazing what tossing around the letters *FBI* could do. "I appreciate your time and any help you can give us." Reese handed him a card and rose from the chair.

Kenzie rose, as well. She was wearing black slacks and a dove-gray V-neck blouse in a soft fabric that curved over her full breasts. It was modest by any measure, shouldn't have looked sexy, but did, which Hollenbeck clearly noticed.

Reese tamped down the irritation he had no right to feel. "I'd appreciate a call if you come up with anything."

The deputy nodded.

They were on their way back to the Range Rover when Reese's cell phone rang. He pulled it out and checked the screen.

He paused next to Kenzie on the sidewalk and accepted the call. "Hey, Tab, tell me you've got something."

"Couple of things, actually."

"Hold a minute. My assistant, Kenzie Haines, is helping me with this. Let me put you on speaker." They moved into the shade of a nearby tree and Reese held the phone so Kenzie could hear. "Go ahead."

"I ran the names you gave me, got a couple of interesting hits. Manual Alvarez, the guy off the Poseidon who died in the crash, had a nice little side business going. He worked a typical shift, two weeks on, two off, which gave him plenty of time to deal drugs with his brother, Rico, in Houston."

Reese smiled. "I know better than to ask how you managed to find this out."

Tabby laughed. "I had a little help from a mutual friend. I saw where Rico Alvarez was arrested the week before the crash, so I asked Hawk Maddox to look into it, see if there was a chance Rico's brother, Manuel, was working with him. Sure enough, from what Hawk found out, Manuel and Rico worked as a team and both of them had enemies. Apparently, the money from a couple of recent cocaine deliveries went missing. The guys higher up the food chain weren't happy about it. Hawk says Rico was lucky he got arrested or he might be as dead as his brother."

"Hawk thinks they sabotaged the chopper to get to Manuel?"

"He doesn't know but he says it's possible."

"Thanks, Tabby, appreciate the help."

"You said there were a couple of things," Kenzie put in. "Was there something else?" She had a way of keeping him focused, one of the reasons he considered her such a valuable asset.

"Not about Manuel, but Hawk made a few more calls and guess what? Turns out, the copilot on the flight, Craig Bigelow, is sleeping with the wife of one of the mechanics who had access to the chopper. You need to call Hawk. He can fill you in."

Reese nodded. "Will do."

"I'll let you know if I come up with anything else."

Reese ended the call and turned to Kenzie. "It's lunchtime. There's a place to eat just down the block. I can call Hawk from there."

They made their way into a small café called the Sunbonnet and slid into a booth at the back. Pretty, wide-brimmed straw hats banded with silk flowers hung on the walls. The booths were upholstered in bright yellow vinyl, and yellow flowers in small glass vases sat in the middle of the tables.

"Hawk Maddox," Kenzie said as she picked up a menu. "He's one of the guys at The Max, right? You've mentioned his name a couple of times."

"Jason Maddox. Everyone calls him Hawk. He's a bounty hunter, one of the best in the trade. He's got a network of informants all over the country. You want to know what's happening in the underbelly of a city, Hawk's your man."

A little waitress with a bouncy blond ponytail arrived to take their orders: grilled chicken salad for Kenzie, a pastrami sandwich for Reese. While they waited for the food, Reese phoned Hawk.

"I been expecting your call," Maddox said, his deep baritone rumbling over the line clear enough for Kenzie to hear. He was a big guy, former spec-ops marine, six foot four inches of solid muscle. He was recently married and extremely happy about it.

"I understand you've got information for me," Reese said. "I'm putting you on speaker so my assistant can hear."

"Kenzie, right? Chase mentioned you were with her at some fundraiser he and Harper went to."

"My date canceled at the last minute and Kenzie filled in for her."

"I hear she's a real stunner."

Reese's glance strayed toward her. Impossible to deny it. Kenzie was beautiful. "She's sitting right here, you know. She can hear what you're saying."

"Hi, Hawk," Kenzie said with a smile so warm he felt a little pinch in his chest.

"Nice to meet you, Kenzie," Hawk said.

"You mind if we get back to business?" Reese grumbled, mildly irritated and not quite sure why.

"You know about Rico and Manuel Alvarez?" Hawk asked.

"Tabby brought me up to speed on the brothers. She says you have info on the copilot."

"That's right. One of the mechanics who works on Pelican Island is a guy named Tex Lovell. Wife's name is Suzy. Word is Suzy gets around. Lately she's been sleeping with Craig Bigelow, the copilot on the chopper that went down."

Bigelow's name was on his list. He cast Kenzie a glance

and could tell she understood the ramifications, that maybe Bigelow was the target, not him.

"So aside from a dead drug dealer with some serious enemies, we've got a possible jealous husband who could have jimmied the gears in order to kill his rival."

"That's about it," Hawk said.

"Anything else?"

"Not at the moment, but I've put the word out. I'll let you know if something turns up."

"Thanks, Maddox, I owe you."

"No way. As I recall, you were the one who saved my ass last time around."

Reese chuckled at the memory of the night he and Kate Gallagher—now Hawk's wife—had rescued him from a Houston brothel.

The call ended, the food arrived, and they settled in to eat. He had two new leads to follow, both of which put him in the clear as the target of the crash. He looked at Kenzie and felt a little better about bringing her along.

Unfortunately, until he knew for sure what had happened, he had to keep digging. Which meant another night in Houston, another night with Kenzie sleeping in the room next to his.

Reese slid her a glance and thought how pretty she looked surrounded by colorful straw bonnets and bright yellow flowers, her mahogany curls loose around her shoulders.

Inwardly, he groaned.

CHAPTER ELEVEN

AFTER LUNCH, Kenzie and Reese set off for their next destination, an address on San Marino Drive that Tabby had sent him, the residence of Tex and Suzy Lovell. The sky was still dreary, just a few weak rays of sunlight filtering through the layers of overcast, the air still hot, thick, and damp.

Before they had left the café, Kenzie had phoned Supervisor Brandt's assistant, who had helped her before. Ryan had told her Tex Lovell was working at the heliport today. There was no record of him doing maintenance on the chopper, but if he was serious about eliminating his wife's paramour, he could have been the guy who broke in the night before the crash.

Next Kenzie phoned Suzy Lovell and asked if they could stop by. Suzy had agreed. Everyone who worked for Sea Titan on Pelican Island knew about the crash and sympathized with the victims. They wanted answers, wanted to help in any way they could.

As the miles passed, Kenzie's mind went from the upcoming interview with Suzy to the night ahead. Reese had told her he had plans for the evening, so he needed to be back at the hotel no later than six o'clock. Plans, she knew, meant another evening with a woman, either Arial Kaplan or someone else.

Kenzie told herself it was none of her business. Reese was the boss. He could do whatever he pleased.

He pulled the Rover to a stop on Jackson Street in front of a narrow blue house with white trim. The cottage sat on tall stilts with a carport underneath. An upstairs deck accessed the front door.

They climbed the stairs to the deck and Reese knocked. Since infidelity was a tricky subject, Kenzie was taking the lead.

The door opened and a blonde with big hair and even bigger breasts stood in the opening. She was wearing pink flowered yoga pants with high-heeled sandals and a low-cut pink tank that showed everything but her nipples.

She had blue eyes as big as the rest of her assets and they ran over Reese as if she wanted to lick him like a lollipop. He took a step back as if he could feel the impact of that lusty stare.

Kenzie eased a little in front of him. "Hello, Suzy. I'm McKenzie Haines. We spoke earlier. This is Reese Garrett. He was aboard the Sea Titan chopper that went down."

"Come on in." Suzy stepped back, and they walked into a messy living room with bare wood laminated floors and an overstuffed blue velvet sofa and chairs. An open kitchen at the end of the room showed dirty pots and pans on the counter, but they were neatly stacked.

"You want something to drink?" Suzy asked. "Maybe a beer or a Coke or something?"

"I'm okay, thanks," Kenzie said.

"What about you, handsome?"

Faint color rose beneath Reese's tanned cheeks. It took a lot to unsettle him. Kenzie almost smiled.

"I'm fine," Reese said. "We wanted to talk to you about the crash. We were hoping you might be able to help us."

"Sure. Why don't we all go into the living room? You don't mind if I have that beer, do you?"

"No, not at all," Kenzie said. "You know, now that I think about it, I'll take you up on your offer and join you."

Suzy grinned and seemed to relax, which was exactly Kenzie's goal. She carried two beers into the living room and handed one to Kenzie, who sat on the sofa next to Reese.

"So what can I do for you?"

Kenzie smiled. "We're trying to gather a little information. As I said, Reese was one of the passengers. We're trying to figure out what went wrong. As a Sea Titan mechanic, your husband's name came up."

"Tex doesn't work on the EC135. That was the model that went down. And he wasn't even there the day it happened."

"We just need something to go on," Reese said. "We're exploring different avenues."

"What does the crash have to do with Tex, anyway? Like I said, he wasn't at work. He was off fishing with one of his buddies."

Kenzie took a sip of beer. It was cold and bubbly and tasted better than she expected. "His name surfaced because of Craig Bigelow, the copilot. When Craig's name came up, so did yours."

"Which indirectly connects Craig to Tex," Reese added.

Suzy went silent.

"Craig's a good-looking guy," Kenzie continued, having seen his photo on Facebook. "We thought...kind of wondered if he had ever, you know...come on to you?"

Suzy glanced away. "Craig's married."

Kenzie had also seen Tex Lovell's photo on the net, not big and burly, like the image his name conjured, but slightly built, shorter than average, and wearing thick, black-rimmed glasses.

"Sure, he's got a wife," Kenzie said, "but a lot of married guys have a bad situation at home, you know? They don't get what they need. It's not really their fault they stray. That is, if they meet an attractive woman and she isn't getting what she needs, either."

Suzy shrugged. "Craig might have come on to me a few times. A lot of guys do. I mean, you see what I look like. Guys love blondes with big boobs." She looked at Reese as if she hoped he was one of them, but Reese was a master of self-control and his expression remained bland.

"So what did Tex think about that? I mean, if he knew Craig was hitting on you…?"

Suzy started nodding. "Okay, I see where this is going. You're thinking Tex might have done something to the chopper because he was jealous of Craig."

Suzy was smarter than she looked.

"Is that possible?" Reese asked.

Suzy's gaze shifted back and forth between him and Kenzie. "I can tell you two have a thing, so I'll be honest. My husband likes to watch. He doesn't have a problem with me and another guy. He encourages it. Works for both of us."

Kenzie felt as if her chair had just dropped through the floor. "I…umm…see."

"That it?" Suzy asked.

Kenzie managed to nod. "Yes, I guess it is."

Suzy flashed a smile and rose from her chair. "You two ever get bored with each other, give me a call. Maybe we can work something out."

Kenzie set her beer bottle down on the coffee table and she and Reese both rose from the sofa. "Just so you don't get the wrong idea, Reese is my boss, not my boyfriend."

Suzy's lips curved into a smirk. "Whatever."

Anxious to leave before things got worse, Kenzie crossed the room to the door.

"Thanks for clearing things up," Reese said as he stepped out onto the porch.

Suzy winked at him, flashed him a smile, and closed the door.

They got back in the car and Reese started the engine.

"I don't think it was Tex Lovell," Kenzie said as the Rover pulled into the street.

"Doesn't look that way. Lovell's motive has pretty much disappeared." Clearly Tex wasn't the jealous type, which meant he had no reason to want Craig Bigelow dead. Or at least none they knew about.

"I wonder why Suzy thought we were together," Kenzie couldn't resist asking.

Reese flashed her the same smoldering glance she had seen the night of the benefit, heat and need and something more, a combination that made her stomach lift alarmingly. Then it was gone, replaced by his usual distance and control.

He shrugged those wide shoulders. "Woman like Suzy, who knows."

But Kenzie worried that Suzy Lovell had noticed her attraction to Reese that she worked so hard to hide.

She wondered how much longer she could hide it from Reese.

THEY WERE ON the highway back to Houston when Kenzie phoned home. Reese listened as she spoke to her grandmother, asking about Griff and her grandmother's day.

Florence replied, and Kenzie smiled. "We just finished. We're on our way back to the apartment."

Her grandmother said something. Reese caught the blush that rose in Kenzie's cheeks and wondered what her grandmother had said.

"I'll be home tomorrow for sure, Gran." She waited a second for Griff to come on the line. "Hi, sweetheart. I've missed you." Griff must have asked about the weekend. "Don't worry," Kenzie answered. "We're all still going to the museum on Saturday, just like we planned."

The love she had for her son was unmistakable, and Reese felt an unexpected longing. He had wanted children badly. After his bitter divorce, that had changed.

"Your dad called?" he heard Kenzie say. The color leached from her face. "It was nice of him to ask, but you have a playdate with Tommy, remember? His mom invited us over to use their pool."

Griff must have agreed because she relaxed back in her seat. "I'll call your dad, explain why you can't make it. Maybe you can see him next weekend." Griff said something. "All right, have fun. I love you, honey. See you soon."

Kenzie hung up and tipped her head back against the seat.

"I take it your ex wanted to spend Sunday with your son."

She sighed. "I'll have to tell Griff about the custody suit—or Lee will."

"How will Griff take it?"

"I don't know. He hasn't spent much time with his dad since the divorce. Not much before that, either, if you want the truth. I know he wouldn't want to live with his father full-time."

"He won't have to." Reese changed lanes, passing an SUV traveling slower than the rest of the traffic. "Wilcox will make sure it doesn't happen."

"I hope so."

Drew Wilcox was the best family lawyer in Dallas. Reese was fairly certain he could win Kenzie's case and she would be able to maintain custody, but nothing was ever certain.

His gaze slid toward her, settled on her mouth. He imagined the feel of those soft pink lips under his, and heat burned through him. He needed a drink, he thought, or a woman. Anything that would send his thoughts in a different direction.

If it weren't for the stop he planned to make in the morning at the Harris County Jail, he'd have the jet fly down early, take them back to Dallas tonight. But he needed to follow this last lead to its conclusion.

He wearily rubbed the back of his neck as the apartment building appeared ahead. Pulling into the driveway, he parked and turned off the engine, breathed a sigh of relief that the long day had finally come to an end.

CHAPTER TWELVE

KENZIE SAT ON the sofa in the living room of the Houston apartment. It was 7:00 p.m. The long day over, she had changed into a soft yellow, loose-fitting knit top and a pair of dark brown yoga pants, slid her feet into a pair of kidskin slippers. She poured herself a glass of the white wine she'd found in the refrigerator and took several badly needed sips.

She should have relaxed. Instead, she sat on the sofa like a statue, listening to Reese as he moved around in his apartment, getting ready for the evening he had planned. With every minute that passed, her nerves stretched tighter.

She was good at her job. Better than good, and she loved it. But there was only so much she could take and today she realized that she had reached her limit.

Sure, the job paid a top-notch salary, but she could always find another place to work. She likely wouldn't earn as much, but there were adjustments she could make to the way they lived, and she had a little savings to tide her over until she found another position. If she had to, she could find a cheaper place to live in Griff's same school district.

Reese's footsteps sounded on the carpet and she imagined him in his crisp white shirt and perfectly tailored designer suit, imagined how handsome he would look and what his date would think when she saw him.

She thought of them enjoying a meal together in an elegant restaurant, then Reese taking her home. Her throat tightened. She imagined him kissing her, the woman kissing him back.

She blocked the rest, the part she couldn't bear to think about.

With a deep, fortifying breath, she rose from the sofa. She wasn't a masochist. She had done her best to subdue her emotions, but she had failed. She had feelings for Reese and there was no longer any way she could ignore them. It wasn't fair to Reese—or to her. Her ambivalence finally over, her mind made up, she resolved to do what she should have done sooner. It was time for her to quit.

Her hand shook as she set her wineglass down on the coffee table and started across the room. She couldn't wait any longer. Not another minute. It had to be now, before her courage failed.

Her legs felt unsteady as she marched out into the hall, down the corridor, and stopped in front of Reese's door. Her heart was throbbing, her chest squeezed tight. She ran her fingers through her hair, shoving it back from her face, taking a moment to steady her nerves. With a last deep breath, she knocked on the door.

If Reese had delayed, she might have weakened, turned around and run back the way she had come, but all of a sudden he was standing there looking down at her from his superior height, which, without her heels, made her nearly a foot shorter than he was. He was dressed exactly as she had imagined, except his suit coat was gone, the sleeves of his white dress shirt rolled up, revealing his muscular, tanned forearms.

"Kenzie." His intense blue gaze swept over her, noting the pallor of her face or the pulse hammering at the base of her throat, maybe both. "What is it? What's happened?"

"I need to talk to you."

"Come in." He stepped back and she caught the scent

of Paco Rabanne, the cologne he favored, a combination of cinnamon, wood, and leather.

"Your color doesn't look good," he said. "There's a wet bar behind the paneling. Sit down and I'll get you a drink."

"I'm… I'm fine. I just need to get this over with."

His features shifted from concerned to wary. "All right. Tell me what's going on."

She swallowed, gripped her hands together in front of her to keep them from trembling. "I'm quitting, Reese. I'm giving you my two-week notice. I won't just abandon you, of course. I'd never do that. I'll come in whenever you need me until you find a replacement, but I'm quitting. I'm going back to Dallas tonight."

"What are you talking about? You can't just quit and leave. You don't even have a ride to the airport." He urged her over to the sofa, but she didn't sit down.

"The jet's picking us up in the morning," he continued reasonably. "If something's happened—if you have a problem at home—I can get the plane to fly in for us tonight."

Her throat tightened. "There isn't a problem at home. The problem is me, Reese. I'm the problem."

"What is it, Kenzie? Tell me."

Her eyes burned, began to fill with tears. She drew in a ragged breath. "I have feelings for you, Reese. I've done everything in my power to ignore them. I've managed until now, but I can't go on any longer." She shook her head. "It isn't your fault. You've never done or said a single thing that wasn't absolutely professional. The problem is mine, and as hard as I've worked to deny it, I can't pretend anymore."

Reese didn't move, just stood frozen, staring at her as if she'd turned into another woman, someone he had never seen before.

Embarrassment slid through her, but she refused to stop

until there was no way she could possibly turn back. Until this moment, she hadn't realized how deeply she had come to care for him, how totally impossible it would be to continue working for him.

"I don't know how it happened," she rambled on. "Little by little it just did." The tears in her eyes slid down her cheeks. "I'm sorry, but I can't keep pretending it doesn't bother me when you look at me without the least bit of emotion, like I'm a piece of furniture that just takes up space in the room. I can't arrange your dates for you then imagine the two of you together. I can't go on this way any longer."

Reese's beautiful blue eyes seemed to burn right through her. Suntanned hands reached out and caught her shoulders.

"I can't believe this. I can't believe you're standing here saying the exact same words I've wanted to say to you. You can't pretend anymore, Kenzie? Well, neither can I."

And then he pulled her into his arms and his mouth came down over hers.

For several seconds, shock held her immobile. When a rush of heat slid through her, desperation, longing, and a coil of hungry need all poured into the scorching kiss she returned.

Reese groaned. Cupping her face in his hands, he deepened the kiss, turning it hotter and wilder, and somehow unexpectedly sweet.

"Reese…" The whispered word came out on a sigh when he broke the kiss long enough to press his mouth to the side of her neck.

"I have feelings for you, too, Kenzie. I know I shouldn't, but dammit, I do, and I'm tired of pretending those feelings don't exist."

Reese kissed her again, ravaging her mouth, his lips softer than she had imagined and at the same time firm enough to take complete control. The kiss was everything she had yearned for and more. But she hadn't forgotten this was Reese. To him she was just another woman, another conquest.

Trembling, she pulled away. "Are you…are you sure you want to do this? What…what about your date? She must be expecting you."

"I canceled." His eyes remained on her face. "Last night, too. You're the woman I want, Kenzie. It took me a while, but I finally figured out no other woman is going to erase you from my mind." He took her mouth again, plundered it, drew her to the length of his long, hard frame.

Kenzie moaned. No other man was going to erase Reese from her mind, either. She craved him, hungered for him in a way she had never known before. She reminded herself this was Reese and whatever he felt for her wouldn't last.

It didn't matter.

Not tonight.

Making love with Reese was the only thing that could set her free. The only thing that could purge him from her heart and mind. Maybe afterward, she could move on.

"I didn't know," Reese said, pressing soft butterfly kisses to the corners of her mouth. "You never gave a single indication I meant anything more to you than just your employer."

He meant more. Too much more. She went up on her toes and kissed him, a wet, hot, searing kiss that told him how much she wanted him. Her fingers were unsteady as she unbuttoned the front of his starched white shirt and pulled it free of his slacks, ran her hands over his six-pack abs and the lean bands of muscle on his chest.

"Reese…oh, God. I've wanted to touch you this way for so long."

Hard muscle bunched beneath her fingers. Reese kissed her again, briefly this time, caught her hands and held them immobile in both of his.

"We don't have to do this now, Kenzie. We can start over, take things slow and easy, get to know each other."

But Kenzie already knew Reese. She knew he was a man of honor, knew how much he loved his family, how well he treated his employees, even his competitors. She knew that although he dated a lot of women, he was always up-front with them and never took advantage.

Now he was worried he was taking advantage of her.

"There'll be consequences," he continued. "We'll need to figure things out. There are no guarantees—you and I both know that."

They both had failed marriages. People changed, things didn't always go the way you planned.

"There's no way to know how this will work out," he said, "but I promise you, I won't let you and your family get hurt."

Fresh tears filled her eyes. He was being up-front with her, telling her the truth, preparing her for the inevitable. It didn't change things, didn't make her want him any less. She swayed toward him, slid her fingers into the silky black hair at the nape of his neck, went up on her toes, and very softly kissed him.

"I know you, Reese. And I've wanted you for so long. Please…give me this one night."

Those incredible blue eyes turned smoky. "Kenzie, honey. Are you sure?"

"I need this, Reese. I need you."

He ran a long, suntanned finger down her cheek, tipped her head back, and his mouth claimed hers. For several long moments, he nibbled and tasted, altered his kisses between soft and sweet, and hot, long, and deep. She slid the white shirt off his shoulders and ran her hands over his naked chest.

Hard, lean muscle flexed and tightened. She thought of the beautiful tattoo on his back, imagined tracing the intriguing lines, imagined pressing her lips against his hot skin.

Reese pulled her soft yellow top over her head, unhooked her bra and tossed it away, and his hands closed over her breasts. Fresh need poured through her and a noise that sounded like a plea slipped from her throat.

"Reese…"

His mouth replaced his hands and she felt a tug on her nipple that made her knees go weak. Desire pulsed like a drumbeat in her core.

Reese gently kissed her. "We don't have to do this now," he repeated, cupping her face between his palms and looking deep into her eyes. "I don't want to rush you. I want to make this good for you. I want to make it right for both of us."

She thought of the problems they would be facing when they got back to Dallas, the helicopter crash, the accidents that had been plaguing the Poseidon. She thought of Griff and the custody battle she would be fighting in the days to come.

She thought of Reese returning to his office, resuming his duties as CEO. Would he still want her? Or would he come to his senses and realize what a mistake it would be to get involved with one of his employees? Would he simply replace her with someone else?

She couldn't continue the way she had been. She needed to get on with her life, and ending her obsession with Reese was the key.

"Do you want me, Reese?"

His eyes found hers. He took her hand and pressed it against the fly of his slacks. He was big and hard. A little thrill shot through her at the power she held. "I want you, Kenzie. So much."

Desire curled like smoke through her veins. Leaning toward him, she pressed her mouth against his chest over his heart, and Reese hissed in a breath. When she looked up at him, his expression darkened. In a heartbeat, his careful control vanished. One of his hands slid into her hair to hold her in place as his mouth crushed down over hers.

Hot, wet kisses followed, his hands on her breasts, his body hard against hers. Kenzie clung to his neck as he walked her backward till her shoulders came up against the wall, and his mouth claimed hers. Long fingers moved over her body, touching, stroking, setting her on fire.

"Stop me, Kenzie," he whispered, his teeth grazing the side of her neck. "At least tell me to slow down."

"Don't stop," she said. "Please don't slow down." She was burning for him. She wanted everything, all he could give her. "I need you, Reese. I need you so much."

Reese didn't wait for more, just stripped off her stretch pants and the tiny white thong she wore underneath. His belt buckle jangled. She heard the buzz of his zipper. He paused for a moment to dig out his wallet, then he was lifting her up, wrapping her legs around his waist.

"I need you, too," he said. His hands gripped her bottom to hold her in place as he buried himself deep inside.

The heat of his body engulfed her and a whimper escaped her throat. Dear God, nothing had ever felt so good. She clung to his neck as he drove into her, out and then in, pushing her toward the brink. She could feel his pulse thrumming beneath her fingers, the hot dampness of his skin.

Faster, deeper, harder, driving into her, taking her until her womb tightened around him and everything inside her broke apart. She was flying, repeating his name over and over like the chorus of a song. Pleasure tore through her, seemed to go on forever.

Reese didn't stop. Just kept kissing her and moving inside her, driving her up again, then once more over the edge before he gave in to his own powerful release.

Long seconds passed. Little by little, her pulse began to slow and awareness returned.

Reese softly kissed her. "Kenzie? Honey, are you okay?"

She wanted to laugh. She wanted to sing. She wanted to weep. She knew the consequences of what she had done and yet she couldn't regret it. She looked up at Reese and managed to smile.

"I'm fine. Better than fine." Reese set her back on her feet and left to deal with the condom she had barely noticed him putting on. He returned as she was picking up her clothes, preparing to dress and return to her own apartment.

Reese snagged the clothes out of her hand and tossed them up onto the sofa. "You won't be needing those," he said with the sweetest smile she had ever seen. "At least not until morning." Then he scooped her up in his arms, carried her into his bedroom, and firmly closed the door.

They made love twice more, once with hungry abandon, then tenderly. Exhausted, she finally fell asleep hoping he would wake her one last time before morning. She would have stayed awake all night if she could have. She didn't want to face the dawn, face the consequences of what she had done.

In the end, she'd woken to warm rays of sunlight filtering through the window curtains. But as she had feared, when her hand went to the other side of the bed, she found it empty. Reese was already gone.

CHAPTER THIRTEEN

FRIDAY WAS STILL muggy and damp in Houston. Reese parked the Land Rover in a space in front of the Harris County Jail. He had pulled some strings and managed to get in on a special visitor's pass to see Rico Alvarez, who had consented to the visit. Apparently Rico preferred conversation to sitting in his cell.

As he got out of the vehicle, his mind strayed to the hours he'd spent last night with Kenzie and a smile softened his lips. The sex had been better than any of the fantasies he had worked so hard to keep out of his head.

Kenzie had been married before and she had been outspoken in her desire for him. Yet there was a sweetness, a naivety he hadn't expected. He'd decided to take things slowly, let her get used to him. He didn't want to frighten her away.

For months, he'd spent at least five days a week with her, had grown to admire her business savvy and work ethic, to say nothing of the physical beauty that appealed to him on every level.

In the beginning, he'd been able to ignore her feminine attributes and focus on her job skills, her value to the company and to him personally as CEO. But little by little, the way she always seemed to be there when he needed her, her insight into helping him solve the problems he occasionally ran past her, combined with the love and devotion she felt for her family, forced him to see her as a woman and not just an employee.

Never once had he considered the attraction might be mutual. Apparently, Kenzie was as good at hiding her emotions as he was.

As he crossed the sidewalk toward the double front doors of the nine-story redbrick building on San Jacinto, his smile slowly faded. All hell was going to break loose when his relationship with Kenzie came to light. It wasn't PC to date your executive assistant, to say the least.

Hypothetically, it could lead to all sorts of accusations and legal hassles that could cost him, personally, or Garrett Resources a whole lot of money. Not to mention the bad publicity.

Reese was willing to take the chance. He hadn't felt such a strong attraction to a woman in years, maybe ever. His bitter divorce had made him even more wary. If things didn't work out, he would face the problem then.

In the meantime, he wasn't going to deny he was seeing her. And he wasn't giving her up.

As he pushed through the front door, Reese forced his mind back to the puzzle he was trying to solve. Following the instructions he had been given, he checked in with a prison guard in black uniform pants and a short-sleeved white shirt with an embroidered patch on the sleeve. The guard led him down a hall and passed him to another guard, a Black woman with cornrows and a smile that put him a little more at ease.

"Rico's waiting for you," she said. "If you'll just follow me." She led him down another long hall and opened a door into a room with a series of partitioned glass windows. Stools sat on both sides of the window. Rico Alvarez sat on one of them, the only person in the room.

"You've got twenty minutes," the female guard said. Still smiling, she closed the door.

Reese sat down across from Alvarez, who was short, his muscular arms covered with prison tats where they showed below the half sleeve of his orange jumpsuit. The lower portion of his head was shaved, the top longer, a bowl cut that reminded Reese of Moe in the old Three Stooges re-runs he'd watched as a kid on TV.

Alvarez's black eyes followed his movements and he straightened on the stool. "I figured I must know you but I don't. Who the fuck are you, and what do you want?"

"I'm Reese Garrett. I was a passenger on the helicopter that crashed and killed your brother."

Alvarez glanced away, but not before Reese caught a flash of grief in his eyes.

"I'm sorry for your loss," Reese said.

Alvarez's attention swung back to him. "So what do you want?"

"I came to tell you the crash wasn't an accident. I fig-ured you'd want to know. Someone sabotaged the helo."

Alvarez's black eyes narrowed. "You're shittin' me."

"I'm telling you the truth. The thing is, you're locked up in here. It goes without saying, you've got enemies. The question is, did you piss someone off bad enough to get your brother killed?"

Alvarez shot up from his stool. "What the hell are you talkin' about?"

"Word on the street is you pissed off some of the big boys. Some kind of drug deal that went sideways. Maybe they took the chopper down and killed your brother to get even."

Alvarez sank down heavily on the stool. He dropped his head into his hands and shook his head. "No way. They didn't want Manny dead. They wanted both of us to keep on producing. We worked things out. Paying back the money they got coming wasn't a problem. We just needed a little more time."

"And you got them to agree?"

"Yeah."

"Before or after the crash?"

"Before." He looked up at Reese, his jaw tight. "You lookin' to find out who did it?"

"I am."

"You let me know who it is, eh, homie? I take care of them for you. No one kills Rico Alvarez's brother and gets away with it."

Satisfied Rico was telling the truth, Reese rose from the stool, fairly certain now that Manny Alvarez hadn't been the target. The question remained, who was?

"Thanks for the conversation," Reese said.

"Don't forget what I told you, eh?" A guard appeared next to Rico. Rising from his stool, he let the man lead him away.

As far as Reese was concerned, he had hit another dead end. He needed answers. He wasn't quitting until he had them. He wished he knew which rock to turn over next.

IGNORING THE TIGHTNESS in her chest, Kenzie stepped out of the shower, once more back in the apartment next door to Reese's. Hurriedly, she dressed and prepared for their return trip to Dallas. It was still early. She had no idea where Reese was or what she should say to him when he returned. A dozen different scenarios ran through her head, but she cast them away. She had no idea what to say the morning after a night of passionate sex with her boss, no idea what he would say to her.

In the end, she opted to let Reese set the tone.

One thing was certain, Monday morning she would start looking for another job. As she'd promised, she wouldn't leave Reese high and dry. She would stay long enough to help him find a replacement, which was only fair since she was the one who had seduced him.

Sighing as she padded toward the kitchen desperate for a cup of coffee, she gasped at the sight of a tall, handsome man standing at the kitchen counter with a bouquet of roses in his hand.

"Good morning." Reese held up a key. "I've got the master," he said, smiling. Which explained how he'd gotten in.

He handed her the bouquet, leaned down, and softly kissed her. "I was hoping you'd still be in bed when I got back, but I should have remembered you like to get an early start on the day."

She looked down at the roses and her eyes stung. She wondered if they were a parting gift, if he gave all the women he slept with roses the morning after.

"Thank you." She clutched the beautiful roses to her breast. "They're beautiful."

He must have read something in her face. "What's the matter? You aren't regretting last night, are you?"

She managed to smile. "I'll never regret last night, Reese. It was special. At least for me."

Reese took the roses from her hand and set them on the kitchen counter, gently took her shoulders, urging her to look at him. "Tell me what's going on in that beautiful head of yours. If you don't regret last night, what's wrong?"

She sighed. "Nothing's wrong. I understood what would happen when I spent the night with you. Now I'm ready to face the consequences. I'll start looking for someone to take my place as soon as we get back."

Reese frowned. "I thought you understood. What happened between us last night has nothing to do with your job. You're my executive assistant. The most competent one I've ever worked with. I don't expect you to quit because we're seeing each other."

Seeing each other? "You aren't serious. There's no way we could possibly keep a relationship between us secret."

"I don't intend to. There's no rule about employees dating. If I weren't CEO, it wouldn't be a problem. Other couples in the office have relationships."

Couples? Relationships? Had Reese just used those words?

"We talked about this last night," he continued. "We both know it might not work out, but I assumed you thought it was worth the risk."

"You *are* serious."

He smiled but for the first time looked uncertain. "I want to see where this goes. I thought you'd want that, too."

She wanted it. She wanted it so much she ached with it. "I don't know... I... I hadn't thought that far ahead. It seemed so impossible, I never really considered it."

Reese leaned down and kissed her. "How about this weekend? Dinner on Saturday night?"

Kenzie shook her head, still off balance and slightly dazed. "I can't, Reese. I'd love to go, but I have plans with Griff and Gran for the whole weekend. I'm sorry. I wasn't prepared for this to happen. I hope you understand."

"Of course I understand. You have a family to consider. I'll give you some time, whatever you need. We'll work things out when I see you next week." He gave her one of his rare, beautiful smiles. "You're my executive assistant. I'm sure you can find time in my busy schedule for us to be together."

Her heart pinched. Surely this attraction they were feeling could never work out. Or could it? Was she willing to take the chance?

With all the doubts swirling around in her head, she gave him the best smile she could muster. "I'll take care of it," she said.

CHAPTER FOURTEEN

REESE SPENT THE weekend working, mostly to keep his mind off Kenzie. He had always been so sure of her, always counted on her for whatever he needed.

This was different. Personal. She had stirred him up, then left him treading water, uncertain which way to swim. He needed to see her again, get his bearings, figure things out.

He'd decided not to call her. She clearly needed time to sort through her emotions. He just hoped she would come to the same conclusions he had.

It was Sunday evening. Currently, he was living in a penthouse condominium in the Design District, but he was getting tired of the hustle and bustle of the city. After Chase and Harper had bought a home, he'd started thinking about selling and begun to check out different locations. He wasn't in a hurry, but the idea intrigued him.

The intercom buzzed. The guard in the lobby. "Someone to see you, Mr. Garrett. FBI special agent Quinn Taggart."

Reese knew the name. Several years ago, Taggart had worked with a former Maximum Security female detective named Cassidy Jones. Though they'd never met, Taggart had a reputation for being competent and tough but fair.

"Send him up." Reese had been expecting to hear from the feds sooner or later. They were investigating the crash. They were bound to have questions.

The doors to his private elevator opened and Taggart

stepped out. "Sorry to bother you on the weekend," the agent said, flipping open his badge holder, then tucking it neatly back into the inside pocket of his dark brown suit coat. "Special Agent Quinn Taggart." He extended a hand Reese shook. "I've got a few questions I need to ask."

"Actually, I've been expecting you." It might take a while for the federal wheels to start turning, but once they did, they ran full speed ahead. "Come on in."

Taggart was a big man, square-jawed, with a blond buzz cut. He wore a yellow striped tie and pale yellow button-down shirt under his coat. Polished brown wing tips housed a pair of big feet.

Reese led the way into his study, which was furnished in sienna leather and warm shades of mahogany, the only room he had designed himself. He walked over to the wet bar. "I don't suppose you're allowed to have a drink while you're on duty."

"A soda would be good. Whatever you've got will work."

Reese opened a Coke, poured it on the rocks, and handed it to Taggart. He poured himself a Macallan single malt, neat, and carried the drinks over to the sofa and chairs in front of the gas fireplace.

Taggart sat down on the leather sofa. Reese took the chair. "How can I help you?"

Taggart drank some of his Coke, set the glass down on the sleek mahogany coffee table. "I understand you've been digging around, trying to come up with information on the helicopter crash."

"It's not a secret. I was in the helo when it went down. I want to know what happened."

"So do we. We've interviewed the people you've made contact with, as well as a number of others. We know pretty much everything you know, and of course we can access data and information you can't."

"I'm sure that's true." *Or maybe not.* He had Tabitha Love, which tended to even things up.

"You're the CEO of a billion-dollar company," Agent Taggart continued. "People in positions of power have enemies. We figured, once you knew the helicopter had been purposely brought down, you'd start trying to find out if you were the target."

Reese leaned back in his deep leather chair. "I admit the thought has crossed my mind."

"One of the first things we looked at was the passenger list. We checked out the people on board, same as you. Nothing turned up, but a couple of days ago, we got new information. Turns out you weren't listed on the original manifest."

Reese's interest sharpened.

"Apparently there was a last-minute change. Most days, Sea Titan uses a twelve-passenger chopper, an Airbus H-175, to transport passengers and crew back and forth to the offshore rigs. That day, the chopper you'd been assigned was needed elsewhere. The computer randomly picked your name and moved you to the smaller helo. Some of the other passengers were also reassigned. No one knew ahead of time you would be aboard the EC135."

"You sure it wasn't some kind of setup? Someone purposely had me moved onto that chopper?"

"We put our best computer guys on it. They're absolutely sure the change was random. Just a case of wrong place, wrong time."

Relief trickled through him. No need for a bodyguard or to worry about Kenzie's safety. His relief didn't last long.

"If I wasn't the target, who was?"

"We don't know yet. According to the people we've talked to, even with the mechanical problems, the chopper should have been able to autorotate down. That's where pilot error comes in. Jake Schofield made a crucial misjudgment. If he hadn't, there might have been injuries, but odds are, no one would have been killed."

Silence fell as Reese processed the information. He wasn't the reason the chopper went down and whoever did it hadn't necessarily meant to kill anyone.

"Anything else I should know?"

"Just one thing. From now on, it'd be better for you if you left the investigation to the FBI."

The warning came through loud and clear. Interfering in a federal investigation was a serious offense. "I'll keep that in mind."

Taggart set his unfinished cola down on the coffee table and stood up. "At some point, we may have a few more questions for you."

Reese walked him back to the elevator. "You know where to find me."

The agent left and Reese's mind went back to what he had learned. If the crash wasn't meant to kill anyone, maybe it was just supposed to be another accident involving the Poseidon. The more problems, the more chance Garrett Resources would pull the plug on the deal.

So who the hell was willing to go to that much trouble? And why?

FBI warning or not, Reese intended to find out. On Monday, he'd call Derek Stiles, bring him up to speed and get his reaction, see if there'd been any more problems in the last few days.

At least now he knew no one was trying to kill him.

Still, when he finally shut down his computer and went

to bed, he had too much on his mind to sleep. Instead, he thought of the problems with the Poseidon deal, thought of Kenzie, and slid into an erotic dream that didn't last nearly long enough, then shifted in and out of a restless half slumber. A little before dawn, he gave up and rolled out of bed, weary and out of sorts.

After a quick shower and getting dressed in a dark gray pinstripe suit and white shirt, he poured himself a travel cup of coffee and headed for the office. Kenzie usually arrived around seven thirty, but it was a quarter to eight when a knock sounded on his office door. His pulse kicked up in anticipation as he pulled it open.

Instead of Kenzie, Dallas police detective Heath Ford, a longtime friend of Chase's, stood in the doorway, along with two police officers in crisp black DPD uniforms.

"Heath," Reese said. "What's going on?"

"I know it's early, but I need to talk to you about one of your employees."

Reese opened the door wider. "Come on in."

Ford, a good-looking, dark-haired cop in his late forties, was one of the best homicide detectives in the department. It didn't bode well that a murder cop was standing in his office.

The detective turned to the two uniformed officers. "Wait here. I'll be out in a minute."

Reese closed the door behind him. "What's this about, Detective?"

"You know a man by the name of Lee Haines?"

An icy chill slid down his spine. "I do. His ex-wife is my executive assistant."

"That's the reason I'm here. Lee Haines was found dead this morning. Two bullets to the chest, one in the thigh, fired from a .38 caliber revolver."

Reese thought of Griff. Haines wasn't a great dad, but now the boy would grow up without a father. "When was he killed?"

"Saturday night. ME gives a tentative time of death around midnight. Housekeeper found him on the floor of his bedroom this morning."

"I assume you're here to inform Kenzie of her ex-husband's death."

"I'm here to ask Ms. Haines some questions in regard to the murder. Do you know anything about her relationship with her ex?"

Reese's instincts went on alert. Ford was clearly there as more than just the bearer of bad news. "The divorce wasn't friendly, but then most of them aren't, including mine."

"Did you know Lee Haines had filed for full custody of his son, Griffin?"

"I knew," Reese admitted.

"You knew she was fighting it?"

"She's my assistant," Reese reminded him carefully. "I knew she loved her son. She mentioned Lee had filed a suit for full custody. There was never any doubt she would fight it."

"But she doesn't have to fight it now, does she? Lee Haines is dead."

His temper rose. He was famous for his control, but for some reason where Kenzie was concerned, it was a struggle. Reese took a moment to settle himself. "What's going on, Detective?"

Before he had time to answer, there was a rap on the door. Reese beckoned, and Kenzie walked into the office. She flicked a glance at Reese but her gaze went straight to Heath.

"Detective Ford? One of the officers outside said you wanted to see me."

"That's right. I'm sorry to bring you bad news, Ms. Haines, but your ex-husband, Lee Haines, was found murdered in his bedroom this morning."

"Oh, my God." Kenzie swayed and Reese reached out to steady her. He eased her down into one of the leather chairs in front of his desk, then crossed to the wet bar behind the paneling. He poured her a glass of water, returned, and pressed it into her hand.

"Thank you." She took a sip, her hands shaking. "It's just such a shock."

"I understand," Ford said. "However, as I was telling Reese, at least now you don't have to worry about losing custody of your son."

She looked up. "What?"

"Where were you Saturday night, Ms. Haines?"

"I was home."

"Were you alone or was someone else with you?"

Her hands shook. "I was alone. Earlier that day we had all gone to the museum, my son, my grandmother Florence Spencer, and I. After we got back, my grandmother went to see a friend. It was Saturday evening. Sometimes they share a bottle of wine. If that happens, she spends the night instead of driving home."

"And your son?"

"Griff was at a sleepover with his best friend, Tommy Caruthers."

"So there isn't anyone who can verify your alibi?"

"My *alibi*? Why would I need an alibi?" The rest of the color leached out of her face. "You don't…you don't think I killed Lee?"

Standing a few feet away, the detective looked down

at her. "A pistol registered in your name was found in a dumpster just a block from the murder scene. There's a good chance ballistics will confirm the gun was the weapon used to murder Lee Haines. Since you don't have an alibi for that night, I'm afraid you'll have to come down to the station and answer a few more questions."

Kenzie's gaze shot to Reese and he read her fear. Her face was as white as the paper on his desk.

"I didn't kill Lee."

Ford reached down and took the water glass from her shaking hand and set it aside, caught her arm, and eased her up from the chair. "Let's go."

"You're…you're arresting me?"

"Not at this time. But it would be best if you cooperated and came willingly."

Kenzie started trembling and Reese's control slipped another notch. No way had she killed her bastard ex-husband. One thing he knew for sure—Kenzie wasn't a murderer.

"Let her go, Detective." Ford's attention swung to Reese. "Kenzie couldn't have killed Lee Haines on Saturday night because she was with me."

Kenzie's gasp echoed across the office. "Reese, don't!"

The detective's eyes darkened as they zeroed in on Reese's face. "Are you sure about that? You're a well-respected businessman, Reese. You have a reputation as the kind of guy who doesn't mix business with pleasure."

Normally, he wouldn't. Kenzie was different. Since they had actually spent Thursday night together, he told himself it wasn't that much of a lie. And it would give them time to gather the information they needed to prove her innocence.

"I'm sure," Reese said. "Ask Kenzie about the little mole she has on the inside of her thigh."

Tears welled in her eyes as Ford's gaze swung back to

her. "So your relationship is more than just professional? The two of you are sleeping together?"

"Not…not exactly," Kenzie said.

"Yes," Reese countered.

Ford's jaw hardened. Clearly, he suspected Reese was lying. "Looks like I'm done here—for now. If anything else comes up, you can be sure I'll be in touch." Ford strode out of the office without closing the door. Both uniformed officers fell in behind him as he crossed to the executive-floor elevator and disappeared inside.

KENZIE SANK BACK down into the chair, trapping her hands between her knees to keep them from shaking. Reese closed the office door, then returned and stood directly in front of her.

"Are you okay?"

Her eyes flooded with tears she'd managed to hold back until now. "Oh, my God, Reese. What have you done?"

His jaw firmed, his usual control back in place. "Did you kill your ex-husband?"

Kenzie wildly shook her head. "No! Of course not!"

"Then I bought us some time."

"Time? Time for what?"

"Time to figure things out."

"Like what?"

"Like how to prove you're innocent of murder and who the hell killed your ex-husband."

"You lied to a police detective, Reese. You could be arrested. You're the CEO of Garrett Resources. Your job could be in jeopardy. You could even be thrown in jail."

"I'll clear things up once we get rolling. I'll talk to the police, tell them I got the dates mixed up. That we were together Thursday night not Saturday."

She brushed away the wetness on her cheeks. "And you think they'll actually believe you? They'll accept your word you just made a mistake?" She swiped at another errant tear. "I can't believe you did that. I can't believe you would risk yourself that way."

Gripping her shoulders, Reese eased her up from her chair. "You don't think you're worth it?"

She swallowed, her heart squeezing at the look on his face. "I didn't kill Lee."

"I know, honey. We'll figure it out, but we're going to need some help. Why don't you go wash your face while I call my brother?"

Her throat ached. She still couldn't believe Reese had lied for her. He had stepped completely out of line for her. It made her feel warm all over.

Since she didn't have any idea what else to do, she turned and headed out the door. As she walked toward the hallway, she saw Louise standing next to her desk, her eyes wide and worried.

"The police were here when I got to the office," the older woman said. "Is Griff okay?"

"Griff's fine. Unfortunately, Saturday night his father was killed."

"Killed? You mean in a car accident or something?"

"Lee was murdered, Louise. The police are trying to find out who did it."

Louise's eyes widened. She looked at Kenzie with concern. "Oh, dear. Poor Griff."

"I don't know how to tell him. He and his dad were never close, but still… Lee was his father."

"Do the police have any idea who did it?"

Kenzie pressed her lips together and glanced away.

"Wait a minute. Surely they don't think you had anything to do with it?"

Kenzie sighed. "It's complicated, Louise." She shoved her dark hair back from her face. "I'm afraid you'll have to excuse me. I need to use the ladies' room."

Leaving her assistant staring after her, Kenzie headed down the hall. In the last few days, her life had been turned upside down. First, Griff had landed in the hospital. Then the custody suit. Then she had seduced her employer, a man she respected and admired, putting both of their jobs at risk. Now Lee was dead, she was a suspect in his murder, and Reese had lied to give her an alibi.

Kenzie was afraid to imagine what would happen next.

CHAPTER FIFTEEN

THE AFTERNOON TURNED STORMY, dark clouds on the horizon, the wind blowing like a bitch. Reese was meeting Chase in his office at Maximum Security, one of the top detective agencies in Dallas.

Briefly, he'd filled his brother in on Lee Haines's murder and the ongoing investigation. But Chase wanted details. Reese dreaded the confrontation. Hell, he didn't know that much about it himself.

Shoving open the glass front door, he walked into the single-story redbrick building on Blackburn Street.

"Chase is expecting me," he said to Mindy Stewart, the receptionist. The petite brunette sat behind a big oak desk that matched the Western decor of the office.

"He told me you were coming in," she said, pushing her round tortoiseshell glasses up on her nose. "I cleared his calendar for the afternoon."

Good news and bad. Plenty of time for his older brother to rail at him for what he'd done, one of the few people Reese allowed to get away with it.

He waved at Jason Maddox as he strode across the open area where oak desks sat in a line of neat rows. Since he was short on time, he didn't stop to chat. He'd call Hawk later to thank him for his help with Rico Alvarez and ask him to keep his ears open for anything that might help him find Lee Haines's killer.

With a light rap on the door, he walked into Chase's office. His brother rose behind his wide oak desk, his dark blond hair slightly mussed, a scowl on his face. Reese was surprised to see Brandon sprawled on the brown leather sofa, sipping a bottle of beer.

Resigned, Reese headed in that direction while Chase rounded the desk to join them.

"I talked to Heath Ford," Chase said. "He told me as much as he could. What the hell have you done?"

"I'm helping a friend, all right? I'll straighten things out in a couple of days. I just needed to buy a little time to get things started."

"Tell me you aren't really sleeping with her," Chase said. "You just made that up to help her out of a jam."

Reese clenched his jaw. "Who I'm sleeping with is none of your business."

Brandon rose from the sofa to stare him in the face. "It is when she's your employee, bro. You know how dangerous that is. The company belongs to all of us. That woman could ruin you and cause us endless grief."

His jaw went even harder. "It's a chance I'm willing to take."

"Kenzie is a suspect in a homicide," Chase said.

"She didn't kill her no-good ex-husband," Reese replied.

"How can you be sure?" Chase asked.

Reese's temper inched up. "Because I know her. I've worked with her five days a week for the last six months."

"What about the gun the cops found a few blocks away?" Bran asked. "It belongs to her, right?"

"Ford said it was registered to her. We haven't had time to talk about it."

"Well, you damned well better make time," Chase said.

Bran's gaze, a lighter shade of blue than Reese's, pinned

him where he stood. "You ever consider she might be play-ing you, bro? She could have set you up so she could off her ex old man and you'd take the bait, give her the alibi she needed. Could have been a lot more was going on be-tween them than what you know."

Reese shook his head. "I don't believe it. Kenzie isn't a murderer."

"You've only known her six months," Chase said. "How long have the two of you been sleeping together?"

Reese forced himself not to glance away. "We've only spent one night together." And it had been Kenzie's idea. He clamped down on the thought, refusing to let his broth-er's suspicions get to him.

Chase drilled him with a glare. "Why her, for godsake? You've got half the women in Dallas falling at your feet. You won't give any of them a second glance. Why take the chance with this one?"

Reese's control snapped. "Because she's special, dam-mit! Because I want her and she wants me!"

His brothers fell silent, their glances going back and forth as if each knew what the other was thinking. Reese wished like hell they'd tell him what it was.

"Okay, then," Chase said. "Now that we've got things settled, let's sit down and figure this out."

Reese's throat constricted. They might argue, as kids even punched it out. But he could always count on his broth-ers when he needed them. "Fine."

For the next half hour, they discussed the murder and how to proceed. No one mentioned his relationship with Kenzie again. Reese was grateful for that. He had no real idea where he stood with her and no notion how she had become so important to him.

"I'll give Ford another call," Chase said. "Get him to keep me updated as much as possible on the investigation."

"I'll start digging," Bran offered. "Look into Lee Haines's background, see what turns up."

"See what you can find out about Arthur Haines, too," Reese suggested. "According to Kenzie, he's always played a big role in his son's life."

"Arthur Haines…" Bran repeated. "He's Black Sand Oil and Gas, right?"

"That's right."

"How did the daughter-in-law of our biggest competitor end up working for you?"

"*Ex*-daughter-in-law," Reese corrected. "When I hired her, she was a single mother raising a son. Her résumé was outstanding, and I was more interested in finding a competent executive assistant than digging into her past."

"I'll check it out," Bran said, but Reese could see the suspicion that had crept back into his younger brother's eyes.

Finally, the meeting came to a close and the men rose from their deep leather seats.

"You need to stay away from her," Chase said. "At least until this is over."

Reese just shook his head. "Not happening. Kenzie needs me right now and I'm going to be there for her."

Bran's features darkened. "Once the press finds out she's your employee and the two of you are involved in a sexual relationship, it's going to make things a whole lot worse."

"Would you stay away from Jessie if she needed you?" Reese looked at Chase. "Or Harper?"

His brothers exchanged more glances. "Fine," Chase said. "We'll work it out."

Holding back a sigh of relief, Reese headed for the door, anxious to be away from his family. He loved them, but they had a way of making him feel like the delinquent kid he'd been when he had moved in with them in high school.

He preferred the control he felt in the business world.

Which reminded him to phone Derek Stiles as soon as he got back to the office. He'd already called Nathan Temple, one of the best criminal attorneys in Dallas, and convinced him to represent Kenzie. Reese had spent a year in juvenile detention. He knew from experience how law enforcement worked. Where Kenzie was concerned, he wasn't taking any chances.

In the meantime, he had a company to run. He was still involved in a major acquisition that had done nothing but go sideways from the start.

He needed answers. For himself, his company, and for Kenzie.

It was time to go to work.

CHAPTER SIXTEEN

KENZIE PARKED HER Subaru compact SUV in front of the school auditorium and turned off the engine. She had phoned the nurse's office and told them there was a family emergency. Not the details, just enough to get them to release him early.

She spotted Griff crossing the newly mown grass and could have sworn he'd grown an inch taller since that morning. He cracked the car door and slid into the passenger seat, raked a hand through his thick, reddish-brown hair, making it stand on end.

"What's going on, Mom?" He was wearing his favorite pair of ripped jeans, a Dallas Cowboys T-shirt, and a pair of red high-tops. She wanted to reach over and hug him.

"We need to talk but not in the car." She started the engine and drove two blocks to a quiet little park sprinkled with shady live oaks. The clouds had rolled off toward the east and though it was still breezy, patches of sunlight peeked through the overcast that remained.

She reached for Griff's hand as they walked toward a small pond where mallard pairs swam and occasionally waddled up on shore. She led him to one of the benches facing the water and both of them sat down.

"You're scaring me, Mom."

She reached down and brushed back a lock of Griff's

hair. "I'm sorry, sweetheart. I don't know how to say this. It's not something I ever thought I'd have to do."

"What is it, Mom?"

"It's your dad, Griff. He was killed. I'm really sorry." She leaned over and pulled him into a hug, but Griff drew away, his eyes huge and uncertain.

"Dad's dead?"

She nodded. "I'm so sorry."

"Wh-what happened?"

"Someone shot him, Griff. It happened Saturday night. The housekeeper found him this morning."

Griff's amber eyes filled. "He can't be dead. We were going to spend this weekend together. He promised to take me to the movies."

Kenzie's heart twisted. Lee rarely had time for Griff. Though Griff seldom complained, Kenzie knew he yearned for his father's attention. Kenzie figured Lee's sudden interest in his son was probably just a way to strengthen his custody case.

"I'm know, honey. It's a shock for all of us."

Griff cried for a while and she held him. Then he pulled away and just sat quietly beside her. Kenzie didn't rush him. There was more he needed to know, but now wasn't the time.

Eventually, they walked back to the car and she drove home. Kenzie had phoned Gran earlier to tell her about Lee. She wasn't surprised when the smell of cinnamon and apples greeted them at the town house door. Gran's solution to every problem, no matter how large or small, was a slice of warm homemade apple pie.

Griff ran to her, wrapped his arms around her waist, and started crying. Gran gave him a fierce, comforting hug, then led him up the stairs to his bedroom.

Kenzie breathed a grateful sigh once they were out of sight. Her grandmother was a miracle. She always knew exactly what to do in any situation. Her son was in good hands.

As she started for the kitchen, the doorbell rang. Praying it wasn't more trouble, she checked the peephole and was surprised to see Reese standing on the porch, amazingly handsome in the pinstriped suit he'd been wearing that morning.

A mixture of emotions swept through her. Gratitude for the risk he had taken to help her, sexual awareness as her mind replayed the night they had spent together, something deeper she couldn't explain. Her hand went to her diaphragm as she drew in a steadying breath and opened the door.

She managed to smile. "I'm surprised to see you. I know how busy you are. Come on in."

"How's Griff?" Reese glanced around in search of him. "Have you talked to him yet?"

She nodded. "He's taking it hard. He didn't know his father well enough to know the kind of man he really was and I'm not going to destroy his illusions."

"Where is he?"

"Upstairs in his room. Gran's with him. Would you like a glass of iced tea or something?"

He nodded. "Iced tea sounds good. I know the timing's rotten, but we need to talk."

"I know." They headed for the kitchen and Reese sat down at the round white pedestal table while she went to the refrigerator and took out a pitcher of tea. Even in his expensive suit, he didn't look the least bit out of place in her compact kitchen.

Or maybe that was just wishful thinking.

Kenzie set two tall, frosty glasses on the table and took a seat across from him. Since she had no idea what to say, she took a sip of tea.

Reese's beautiful blue eyes settled on her face. "I need to know about the gun," he said softly.

Kenzie wasn't surprised. Reese had risked himself to help her, but in return he wanted answers. And he wouldn't settle for anything but the truth.

"As odd as it sounds, Lee had my revolver in his house. I bought it for self-defense after I graduated from college and got my first job. The neighborhood I was living in wasn't that great. My dad had always had firearms, so he taught me to shoot it."

"Are your parents still alive?"

"My dad died a few years back. Mom remarried and moved to Arizona. I don't see her very often… We never really got along. I'm more like my grandmother." She was rattling. Being with Reese in a situation other than business was new and unnerving.

"So how did Lee get the gun?"

Old memories crowded in and her mouth went dry. She took a sip of tea. "It was during the divorce. He was furious at me for leaving him. He had always been…difficult. After I left him, he would constantly accuse me of being a bad mother. He must have remembered I had the gun. One day he came over and demanded I give it to him. He said it was too dangerous with a child in the house."

"So you just handed it over?"

She glanced away. She wasn't ready to talk about the past. She had just begun to know Reese on a personal level. She wasn't sure what he would think of her if he knew the truth.

"Griff was going to be home any minute. It wasn't worth an argument."

Reese leaned back in his chair. "So Lee had the gun. That means whoever killed him must have known it was in the house when they went inside."

"Or maybe whoever it was didn't plan to kill him. Maybe they got into an argument or something. The killer saw the gun, picked it up, and fired."

"It's possible. You know where Lee kept it?"

She thought of how paranoid Lee could be. He had probably kept it somewhere he could get to it quickly. Maybe that was even the reason he had taken it away from her in the first place. He'd wanted it for his own protection and it was easier than getting one for himself.

"I could make a guess, but I don't know for sure."

Reese was watching her closely. She wondered if he noticed her hesitation. There was a lot he didn't know, a lot she didn't want to tell him. He thought so highly of her. She wondered if that would change if he knew the truth.

"Make a guess," he said, his eyes on her face. There was something in them, a hint of distrust that hadn't been there before. It made her ache inside.

"Lee had enemies. Or at least believed he did. He had clients who'd lost money in one of his many schemes, husbands of women he'd been involved with. At times he was paranoid. He might have wanted the gun because he thought someone was after him. If that was the case, he would have kept it somewhere he could get to it easily."

"He was killed in his bedroom, so maybe it was in his nightstand."

"Maybe."

"What about Griff? You said Lee was worried about having a gun around the boy."

"Griff was rarely there. Lee could have put the gun in his safe while Griff was visiting." She raked a hand through her hair, shoving it back from her face. "I really don't know."

Reese stood up, drew her out of her chair and into his arms. "It's okay. There's no way you can know what your ex-husband was doing that night. I've spoken to Nathan Temple. He's a criminal attorney, one of the best in the city. He's expecting us in his office first thing tomorrow morning."

Kenzie shook her head. "Reese, no. It's too much. You don't have to take on my troubles. You've already done more than enough."

"I'm going to help you, Kenzie. You might as well resign yourself."

He was taking control. It was his way of handling a situation. She wanted to ask him why he would go to so much trouble. But she knew him, knew how protective he could be. This was Reese, the man she was already half in love with.

Standing together in the kitchen, Kenzie leaned into him, rested her head on his shoulder. "This isn't what you signed on for when you took me to bed."

Reese tipped her face up and softly kissed her. "Don't worry. The paybacks I have in mind will make up for all the trouble."

The corners of her mouth tipped into a smile at the humor in his voice. It was the best she had felt all day. The sound of a door opening and footfalls on the stairs ended the conversation.

Kenzie stepped away as Gran and Griff walked into the kitchen. Griff's eyes were red and swollen, his face puffy.

"I'm sorry about your dad, Griff," Reese said.

Fresh tears welled. "Me, too."

Gran mustered a credible smile. "I know just the thing we need to cheer us up. Anyone ready for a piece of hot apple pie?"

Kenzie felt a rush of gratitude. "Sounds perfect," she said.

But catching Reese's worried expression, thinking of Lee's murder and the accusations against her, she knew *perfect* was exactly the wrong word.

REESE WAS JUST about to leave for work the next morning, when Detective Heath Ford showed up at his apartment.

"Thanks for seeing me," Ford said as he stepped out of the private elevator into the high-ceilinged entry. "This is an unofficial visit. I came to talk to you off the record. It'll only take a few minutes."

"I was just heading out," Reese said, not inviting him farther into the room. "What is it?"

"We both know you didn't spend Saturday night with Kenzie Haines."

Reese lounged back against the wall, crossing his arms over his chest. "That right? How do you know?"

"Because you never left your apartment that night. I checked with the guard in the lobby. He said you were home all weekend. No visitors."

Reese shrugged. "You just came up in my private elevator. Maybe I slipped out without him seeing me. Better if no one knows I'm dating an employee."

"I guess it's possible. In that case, maybe I should add you to our suspect list. You're dating Haines's ex-wife, which gives you access to her pistol, and you have no confirmed alibi."

"You're reaching, Detective."

"Maybe. What was your relationship with Lee Haines?"

"I didn't have one."

"But you do have one with his ex-wife."

"That's right."

"How far would you go to protect her?"

Reese's jaw tightened. "She didn't kill Haines, Detective."

Ford reached up and rubbed the back of his neck. He looked tired, as if he'd been putting a lot of overtime into the case. Reese hoped he was. He trusted the detective to eventually find the truth.

"I came here to tell you ballistics confirmed Kenzie's revolver was the murder weapon. I thought you should also know there was no forced entry the night of the murder. Do you know if Kenzie has a key to her husband's home?"

"I doubt it. They're divorced."

"They share custody of her son. Or they did before he wound up dead. Why don't you ask her?"

"I don't need to ask her. I know she didn't kill her ex-husband."

"I want to talk to her again, Reese. You can bring her down to the station sometime today, or I can have her picked up. I can hold her up to forty-eight hours without filing charges."

After a year in detention, Reese knew exactly what the police could do. "Fine. We'll be there as soon as I can make the arrangements. Nathan Temple is her attorney. He'll be with her when she comes in."

"She might want to think about cooperating instead of lawyering up. Just makes her look guilty."

"Bullshit. She needs someone to stand up for her. That's what Temple is paid to do."

"Be careful, Reese. You've already stuck your neck way out for this woman. You don't want this coming back to bite you on the ass."

"You finished?"

"Don't say I didn't warn you."

As soon as Ford was gone, Reese called Nate Temple. The attorney agreed to meet him and Kenzie at police headquarters. Then he phoned Kenzie at the office.

"I need you to clear my schedule for the next couple of hours. And clear your own. We're meeting Nathan Temple at police headquarters. I'm on my way to pick you up."

Since the protesters were still in front of the building, Reggie Porter was waiting in a black SUV limo downstairs. With everything else that was happening, not driving his own car had begun to seem like a minor imposition.

"All right," Kenzie said, but Reese heard the sound of distress she made as she hung up the phone.

CHAPTER SEVENTEEN

THE DALLAS POLICE DEPARTMENT downtown on South Lamar was a recently remodeled five-story red-and-beige structure. Kenzie imagined it was supposed to look welcoming, a symbol of stability in the Dallas community. It just looked daunting to her.

Reese walked beside her as they pushed through the front doors. An attractive man with silver-threaded light brown hair came forward as they approached.

"Nate." Reese extended his hand. "Appreciate your coming on such short notice."

"No problem." In an expensive black three-piece suit, Nathan Temple oozed dignity and class, and there was an air of confidence about him that Kenzie found comforting.

"This is McKenzie Haines," Reese said.

"A pleasure, Ms. Haines," Nate said.

"It's just Kenzie. Thank you for helping."

They exchanged a few pleasantries, then Temple led her down a long corridor to where Detective Ford waited. They went into a stark white interview room with a mirror on one wall—two-way glass, she imagined, just like in the movies. It was chilly in the room. Kenzie shivered as she sat down in a metal chair across from Detective Ford. She felt Reese's coat drape around her shoulders before he sat down.

"We'll take it slow and easy," the detective said. "As long as you tell the truth, you have nothing to worry about."

She nodded. "All right."

"Tell me about the gun."

Kenzie sat up straighter. "The last I knew of it, Lee had the gun. He took it from me during the divorce." She went on to tell him the same story she had told Reese. The detective made notes, though he had told her it was being recorded.

"When was the last time you saw your ex-husband?"

"Not since he came to the hospital to check on Griff the day he fell off his bicycle."

"Speaking of hospitals." Ford got up and walked away. He returned with a manila envelope he set on the table, reached in and pulled out a set of photographs he spread open for her to see. Kenzie's stomach clenched seeing the pictures from when she was married, the photos taken at the hospital, pictures of her body, covered with bruises on her arms, legs, and torso.

"What the hell?" Reese said, his gaze slamming into hers. Kenzie glanced away.

"Your ex-husband had a history of abusing you," Ford said. "Is that correct?"

She couldn't look at Reese. "It only happened two times and it was over a period of several years."

"You came into the emergency room on both those occasions. I have other photos if you need to see them. The second incident mentions fractured ribs."

"I assure you, I haven't forgotten." She flicked a glance at Reese, whose jaw looked hard as stone.

"What about your son?" Ford asked. "Was Lee also abusive to Griffin?"

"No. In his own, self-centered way, he loved his son. Lee never touched him. I was the one he blamed for whatever problems he was having."

"Why didn't you leave the bastard?" Reese asked harshly.

Her face burned with humiliation. She hated that she had been so weak. "I stayed for Griff. I had no money. I couldn't afford a decent place for us to live. So I stayed."

"What changed?" the detective asked.

"I convinced Lee to let me take classes at the community college. I told him I was bored. I needed something to do, and because he didn't want me working, he agreed. I got a friend to sit with Griff while I was at school, and I was always home by the time Lee got there at the end of the day."

"You completed the courses?" Ford asked.

Kenzie nodded. "After I got my degree, I got a part-time job. Like before, I was always home when Lee arrived, so he mostly didn't mind."

"Mostly," Ford repeated. "He didn't like you working. Is that the reason he beat you?"

She shook her head, her dark curls sliding around her shoulders. "It wasn't that. The times he hit me, he was drunk or had some kind of upset at work. Except for those two occasions, he usually just called me names. As soon as I'd saved enough money, I packed up, left, and filed for divorce. In the settlement I got enough to rent a place to live. My grandmother came to stay with us and after that things got better."

"Did you kill him because you were afraid that if he got custody he might abuse your son? If so that would mitigate the circumstances of the murder. Is that want happened?"

"No. I had nothing to do with Lee's death."

"So you never resented the beatings your ex-husband gave you?" Ford asked.

Temple reached across the table and gently caught her arm. "You don't have to answer that, Kenzie. I'm sure Detective Ford is smart enough to understand you've been past that kind of thinking for some time. You've been looking forward, not backward since then."

It was true, she thought. She'd never forgiven Lee for the way he'd treated her, but she'd moved on. He was still Griff's father. She hadn't wanted him dead.

Ford shoved the hospital photos back into the manila folder. "Do you have a key to your ex-husband's home, Ms. Haines?"

"No."

"What about your son? Does he have a key?"

Kenzie moistened her lips and reminded herself it was better to tell the truth. "Lee gave Griff a key in case he ever needed it."

"So you had access?"

She looked up. "I would never go into Lee's house without permission."

"There was no forced entry, Ms. Haines. No shattered windows, no broken locks. Someone just opened the door, walked right in, and shot him."

Her temper heated. "Well, it wasn't me."

Reese leaned toward the detective. "There are a lot of ways of getting into a house without a key. A good set of lock picks will do the trick."

Ford turned his hard gaze on Reese. "You're saying you could do it?"

Ford was a friend of Chase's. He probably knew at least a little about Reese's past. Kenzie knew Reese was involved in Teen Challenge and several other outreach groups for troubled teens. In magazine interviews he talked about his problems as a youth—hard as it was for Kenzie to imagine. He wasn't proud of his past, but he never denied it.

Reese kept his eyes on the detective's face. "I could. But I didn't."

Nathan Temple rose from the table. "I read the report, Detective. You have no fingerprints, no DNA, no gunshot residue, and aside from the fact that the pistol was registered to Ms. Haines, no way to connect her to the murder. You'll need a lot more than that if you expect to bring charges against her."

Kenzie prayed the attorney was right. But aside from her amazing son, since the day she'd met Lee, he had never brought her anything but grief.

The detective rose from the table. "We may have more questions. In the meantime, don't leave town." He flicked a glance at Reese. "That applies to both of you."

CHAPTER EIGHTEEN

IT WAS GETTING dark outside, the evening slipping away. Arthur Haines sat in the study of his Turtle Creek home, elbows on his polished mahogany desk, his head tipped forward into his hands.

"I'm sorry for your loss." Troy Graves sat across from him in a high-backed rose velvet wingback chair, a leg crossed over his knee. The only son of Arthur's late partner, William Graves, Troy had inherited his father's half of the company, making him co-owner of Black Sand Oil and Gas.

Arthur straightened. "I appreciate your condolences, but you didn't come here tonight to talk about my son's murder."

"No, I didn't. Though I sincerely regret the pain Lee's death has caused you."

The kid had no idea. Lee was dead because of him. Because of the mistakes Arthur had made. Mistakes he desperately needed to remedy before someone else got killed.

Troy's hand slid over the straight black hair he slicked back with pomade, and Arthur bit back a laugh. Who did the kid think he was? Fucking Elvis Presley?

Troy had his mother's pretty face, but a weak chin and devious eyes. When it came to women, his old man's money made up for it.

"I need to talk to you about the latest developments in the Poseidon deal," Troy said.

"What about them?"

"Surely you can see this whole thing has gotten out of hand. The helo crash was only supposed to be another accident. No one was supposed to get killed. Garrett wasn't even supposed to be aboard. For God's sake, his brother's a detective. His whole family's connected to law enforcement in some way. All hell would have broken loose if he'd been the guy who took a chunk of rotor blade between the eyes."

Arthur leaned back in his chair, making the springs squeak. He was forty pounds overweight and had a heart condition. Too bad the guy who'd killed his son hadn't shot him instead—saved everybody a lot of trouble.

"You're the one who came up with the idea," Arthur reminded him.

"True, but—"

"You and Reese Garrett have a history, as I recall. You went to college together. According to your dad, Reese beat your ass at pretty much everything you competed at, including women."

"I don't like the bastard. That wasn't the reason I suggested we try to take over the deal."

"No?"

"Dammit, we need that platform. Our market share is in the toilet. First those North Texas wells fizzled out, then we hit a couple of expensive dry holes. We're on the verge of bankruptcy. We have to do something to save the company."

"We are doing something. Soon as Garrett pulls out, we'll be taking over the purchase of the rig."

"We should have bought the Poseidon when it first came up for sale." The rig was the best deal to come up on the secondary market, located just ninety miles off the coast and a good, steady producer.

"We didn't know it was going to sell so cheap," Arthur reminded him. "Now, with all the accidents, it's worth even

less than it was then. If we take over Garrett Resources'
position, we'll be able to raise the capital we need to close
the sale. Once we own the platform, we can expand even
further into offshore drilling. Our market share will go
back up and the company will be worth something again."

Troy fell silent. Until recently, the kid was used to living the high life: trendy designer clothes, accounts at the
finest restaurants, a silver Porsche Carrera. With business
way off, he had to be worried as hell.

Arthur shifted in the leather chair behind his desk. "I
say we keep at it awhile longer. Garrett is good at his job.
All the problems with the rig, he's bound to be thinking
of cutting his losses. Once he backs out, we step in and
close the sale."

Troy nodded, the hint of a satisfied smile on his face.
Arthur had a feeling he was doing exactly what the kid had
intended from the start.

"I don't like it," Troy said. "But I guess we've got no
choice. I've got a couple more things already lined up. We
can move forward with those, but if Garrett still doesn't
back out, we need to try something else."

"Agreed," Arthur said. But there wasn't anything else
to try. He had already exhausted every avenue he could
think of before his new *partner* had talked him into this
crazy scheme.

He glanced at Troy, saw something dark in his eyes. The
kid was far more ruthless than his father, something Arthur had only recently discovered. A real wolf in sheep's
clothing and used to getting his way.

Nothing Arthur could do about it, and he had his own
problems to solve. He only had one more son. Daniel was
the best thing he had ever done is his misbegotten life.

Arthur didn't want to lose that son, too.

Reese sat at his desk the following morning. He hadn't slept well again last night. After his meeting at police head-quarters, he and Kenzie had returned to the office. Im-mersed in an important budget meeting, he'd had no time to talk to her. The abuse she'd suffered at Lee Haines's hands was just one of the things they needed to discuss.

As CEO, juggling his busy schedule, keeping all the balls in the air was never easy. Now he was in the middle of a murder investigation. And there was Kenzie. Every-thing about his attraction to her screamed wrong place, wrong time.

Wrong person.

Still, when he'd seen her first thing that morning, he'd felt the same kick, the same fierce pull of attraction that had drawn him to her from the start. He'd wanted to take her right there in his office, forget his problems and satisfy the hunger he felt just looking at her. He'd wanted to drag her down on top of his desk and bury himself as deep as he could possibly get.

He'd wanted just to hold her.

For the past few hours, he'd managed to force thoughts of her from his mind and concentrate on work. Then her familiar rap again came at his door, the door opened, and she walked into his office.

"Derek Stiles is on the line." The color was back in her cheeks, her shoulders squared. Just the sound of her voice made him hard. "He's calling about the Poseidon. He says it's important."

She was wearing a peach knit skirt suit with a perky lit-tle peach-and-blue print scarf. She was back on her game, he could tell, ready to face whatever lay ahead. Her resil-ience was one of the things that attracted him so strongly.

"Put the call through." Forcing himself to ignore the

lust he shouldn't be feeling, he slid the Poseidon file out of the stack of folders on his desk. It was all on his computer, of course, but he liked to have the actual paperwork in front of him.

He flipped open the file and looked up at Kenzie. "I'd like you to sit in on the conversation."

She nodded, sat down in her usual chair across from him, smoothing her skirt as she crossed her legs. He thought of those pretty legs wrapped around his hips, and his groin tightened.

He hit the speaker button. "What's going on, Derek?"

"Sorry to start your day off on a sour note, but we've got another problem with the rig."

The way things had been going, he wasn't surprised. "What is it this time?"

"Gas leak in one of the platform pipes."

He flicked a glance at Kenzie, saw her make a note on her iPad. "How serious is it?"

"They found the leak and repaired it, but the foreman says it shouldn't have happened in the first place."

Reese shoved back his chair and rose, paced a few feet away, then back. "I need to get out there. I want to talk to the foreman and some of the crew, get their opinion on what's been happening and why."

"Maybe it's time to think about cutting our losses. I know we'd lose money, but taking over a rig with this many problems might end up being worse in the long run."

"I've thought about it, believe me. I just don't like the idea that someone might be playing us. This rig represents all kinds of opportunities. If Sea Titan wasn't making some major internal changes, they never would have put it up for sale."

"Yeah, and certainly not at that price."

"We'll hold awhile longer. I'll have Kenzie set up the trip."

"You want me to go with you?" Derek asked.

"I need you to stay in Houston, keep things running on your end."

"I can handle that." Derek was a navy vet, former jet fighter pilot. He was one of the company's most valuable employees. The call ended and Reese sat back down in his chair.

"I want you to take me with you," Kenzie said, catching him off guard.

"Why?"

"First, because I think I could be useful. Also because of this." She set a folded copy of a newspaper on top of his desk and smoothed it open. The *Spectator* was a tabloid full of splashy headlines, candid photos, and gossip, most of it total BS.

On the cover of the weekly issue was a picture of him and Kenzie getting out of the stretch limo in front of the Adolphus the night of the benefit. "Dallas's Most Eligible Bachelor, Reese Garrett, and His Executive Assistant, McKenzie Haines."

In smaller print, "Sexual Favors Part of the Job at Garrett Resources?"

Reese cursed under his breath. "I was hoping this wouldn't happen."

"I can't imagine what the papers will say when they find out I'm a suspect in my ex-husband's murder—and you're my alibi."

"I don't care what they say." Rising, he rounded the desk, caught her shoulders, leaned down, and kissed her. For an instant, Kenzie stiffened. Then her mouth softened under his, and she returned the kiss, a small sigh of pleasure slipping from her throat.

"I want to see you," he said. "I don't care what the tab-loids say. What about dinner tonight?"

"You have no idea how much I want to be with you. But you need to think about the consequences, Reese."

He thought of his brothers and what they would say when they found out about the article. He thought about the people who worked for him, people he liked and respected. People who respected him.

"All right. We'll leave town for a couple of days, fly back down to Houston, spend the night, and make that trip out to the rig the next day. You're my assistant. You go where I need you. Fuck them if they don't like it."

Her mouth twitched. He wanted to kiss her again, feel the satiny glide of his tongue over those soft pink lips.

"I can't leave tomorrow," she said. "Lee's funeral is to-morrow afternoon. I'm keeping Griff out of school. I can set up the trip for Friday and we can come back on Sunday."

He thought about it. As much as he wanted to be with her, he knew it wouldn't be fair to Griff. The boy needed his mom right now.

"Set it up for next week. We'll fly down Tuesday morn-ing, go out to the rig on Tuesday, come back Wednesday morning. That gives us a couple of days together, and you'll still have the weekend with your son."

He caught the flash of emotion in her eyes. He knew she was worried about Griff. From what she'd said, the boy had taken his father's death harder than she'd expected. Lee's murder had been all over the news. Griff was waiting for the police to find the killer. He wanted justice for his dad.

So far he didn't know his mother was the number one suspect.

"I'll set it up," Kenzie said. "But until we can get out of

the city, we need to be careful. You have your job to think of, and I have Griff."

He nodded. She had a family to consider. Why the hell did everything have to be so complicated?

They worked till lunch, had a quick meal sent in to his office, then Kenzie returned to her desk to finish out the day. She was gone by the time he cleared his desk and left for home.

Reese was sitting in the back of the black SUV, Reggie Porter behind the wheel, when his cell phone rang. Chase's name popped up on the screen. With a sigh of resignation, he pressed the phone against his ear.

"So I guess you saw the paper," Reese said.

"I didn't see it. Mindy did." Chase's receptionist. "Not a surprise. We knew it could happen. That's not the reason I'm calling. I've got something for you. I'd rather talk in person. I'm at the office, but I can meet you wherever."

"After the day I've had, I could use a drink. How about Clancy's?" The Irish pub just down the block from Chase's office, a place The Max crew hung out.

"That'll work."

"I was on my way home. I'll have Reggie swing by and drop me off." Fifteen minutes later, he walked past the old-fashioned etched glass windows and strode into Clancy's. The interior of the pub was all dark wood, with wooden booths and tables in the dining area and a long oak bar with at least twenty different beers on tap.

Chase waved as he approached, a bottle of Lone Star already sitting in front of him. Reese took off his suit coat, hung it on the brass hook at the end of the booth, and slid onto the seat across from his brother. Seconds later, a waitress with short curly blond hair arrived to take his order.

"Jameson," Reese said. "Neat."

The blonde flashed him a smile. "I'll be right back."

Stretching his legs out in front of him, he leaned against the back of the booth. "What's up?"

"Aside from your fame in the tabloids?"

He grunted. "Yeah."

Chase took a drink of his beer. "So how are things going with you and Kenzie?"

"I have no idea. In the office, she's all business, which is good because it keeps me focused. We haven't been anywhere together except the police station since this began."

"If you're seriously interested in her, you need to fix that."

He sighed. "I know." Were his feelings for Kenzie serious? She already meant more to him than any woman he could recall, but until he spent more personal time with her, he couldn't be sure.

"Haines's funeral is tomorrow," Reese said. "I haven't talked to Kenzie about it, but I'm planning to go. We won't be together, but at least she'll know I'm there."

Chase nodded.

Reese's drink arrived and he took a grateful sip, felt the burn of the alcohol loosen his muscles and joints. "So why are we here?"

Chase set his beer bottle down on the table. "Hawk called. He's out of town. Got a lead on a skip he's been hunting, so he gave me the info he had, figured I could follow up."

"And?"

"Nobody knows anything about Haines's murder. No rumors, no speculation, nothing. According to what I could get out of Heath Ford, the cops don't have jack, either. No prints, no blood evidence, absolutely nothing left at the crime scene. The only thing they have is the murder weapon, registered to Kenzie, found two blocks away. It was wiped completely clean. Other than that, zero, zip, nada."

Reese sipped his scotch. "And this helps us…how?"

"According to Hawk—and I agree—the murder had to be a hit. And it had to have been done by a real pro."

Reese frowned. "So not a fight that got out of hand or a crime of passion?"

"No way."

Reese felt a rush of relief. He'd always believed in Kenzie's innocence, but he didn't like the uncertainty that crept in once in a while. "Hawk have any ideas who might have done it?"

"Several, actually. His personal favorite is a guy who works for the mob in Louisiana. He's a real ghost. No one even knows his name."

"What makes Hawk think he's the guy?"

"Apparently, the shooter's known for getting the job done without leaving any trace evidence. He's meticulous in his research and planning. Knows the target inside and out. What the subject does, where he lives, who's in his bed. He formulates a plan, eliminates his quarry, and does whatever it takes to divert attention away from himself."

"Like using the gun that was in Lee's house, then tossing it for the cops to find."

Chase nodded. "He probably knew Haines had the pistol and where he kept it. The shooter might even have known it was registered to his ex."

"If the guy was that good, why did it take him three bullets to put Haines away?"

"Probably the same reason he used Haines's gun then planted it. To make it look like an amateur instead of a pro."

Reese sipped his scotch. "Why would a Louisiana mob hit man want to kill Lee Haines?"

"No idea. But I'll keep working on it. Unfortunately, Bran's headed back to Colorado. He's got to finish getting the new office set up by the end of the week. He didn't want to leave but I told him we could handle things here."

Bran's wife, Jessie, loved the city, and he was always up for a new challenge.

"Bran's going to keep digging," Chase said. "He'll let us know if he comes across anything useful."

Reese sipped his whiskey. "I remember Kenzie mentioning Lee's brother is a Louisiana state senator."

"Could be something."

"Next time I see Kenzie, I'll ask her about it."

Chase nodded, finished the last of his beer, and slid out of the booth. "Your drink's on my tab. I've got a pretty wife waiting at home. I'll let you know if I turn up anything new."

As his brother left, Reese felt a pang of envy. Once he had wanted the kind of life his brothers now had. After his divorce, that had changed. Marriage to Sandra had soured him. He wasn't sure he would ever try it again.

Kenzie's image popped into his head and arousal slipped through him. There was no doubt he wanted her. More than that? He needed time to find out.

CHAPTER NINETEEN

GRAN FIXED HAM and green beans for supper. While the ham was baking, Griff finished his homework. Since Kenzie was upstairs helping him, she and Gran hadn't had time to talk, but Kenzie knew her grandmother had seen the article in the *Spectator*. Maybe now she was beginning to understand what Kenzie had tried to explain about the problems of an office romance.

"Dad's funeral is tomorrow," Griff said glumly as he sat at the desk in his bedroom. It was decorated in navy blue and white, a sailing theme because Griff loved the water so much. "I wish it was already over."

Kenzie ran a hand over his dark hair and pulled him in for a hug. "So do I, sweetheart. But funerals are a way for people to show their respect for the person who died. And they come to be supportive of the family."

He closed his notebook. "I saw on TV where sometimes the killer shows up. The cops come so they can see who's there, then they can check them out, get evidence, and arrest them."

"It's not exactly like the movies, sweetie."

"I'm going to watch for anyone who looks suspicious. Maybe we can catch him ourselves."

She bent down to his level and cupped his cheek. "You need to leave the detective work to the police."

Griff didn't argue, but she could tell by the mutinous

look in his eyes he'd be watchful during the service. Maybe a distraction would help lessen his grief.

Homework finished, they went down to supper. Afterward Griff helped Kenzie clear the dishes then went back up to his room. She was watching him climb the stairs when her cell phone rang. She didn't recognize the number, but it was local, so she took the call.

"Kenzie, this is Martin Bales, Lee's attorney. I'm sorry to call you at home, but I needed a little more time to go over things. I wanted to be sure I had everything correct."

"What's this about, Martin?"

"I wanted to let you know Griffin is the beneficiary of Lee's life insurance policy."

Surprise filtered through her. "I didn't know he had a policy, but it's good to know Lee was thinking of his son."

In his own way, Lee had loved Griff. He'd just been too selfish to ever have time for him. Which was probably good considering his abusive behavior. She hadn't considered using the information against him in the custody battle, but if he hadn't been killed she might have been forced to. Except she didn't want Griff to know.

Unease slipped through her. Protecting Griff gave her a motive for the crime, exactly what the police were probably thinking.

"It's quite a large sum, Kenzie," Bales continued, returning her attention to the call. "Three million dollars."

"What?"

"That's right. As his mother, you're his guardian. Lee also named you Griffin's custodian, which means you'll be managing his money until he reaches his majority at age eighteen."

A three-million-dollar life insurance policy—and I'm in

charge of the money. Her hand tightened on the phone. "No, Martin, I can't do it. You have to appoint someone else."

"It's too late for that, Kenzie. You need to think about what's best for Griff. You're a smart businesswoman. You'll make good choices for your son. No matter what happened between you and Lee, he trusted you. He knew you'd take care of Griff."

Kenzie fell silent, her mind spinning with the ramifications of what this would mean.

"I'd like you to come down to my office as soon as possible," Martin said. "We can go over the details and I'll explain things."

She didn't answer.

"Kenzie?"

"Yes, all right. I'll come down to your office."

"Call my secretary in the morning and set up a time. I'll see you at the funeral. Good night."

The line went dead. She turned to see her grandmother watching her. "More trouble?" Gran asked.

"Lee had a life insurance policy, Gran. Three million dollars." Her chest tightened. "Griff's the beneficiary, and I'm in charge of the money." She swallowed and turned away. "I have to go. I need to see Reese."

Her grandmother dried her hands on the dish towel she was holding. "I'll put Griff to bed. You do whatever you need to, honey."

Kenzie grabbed her purse off the breakfast bar, paused long enough to kiss Gran's cheek, and headed for the garage. A few minutes later, she pulled her Subaru into a visitors' parking space in front of Reese's condominium building. She had never been there. In today's business world, it was too risky for an employer to entertain a female employee in his home.

Too late to worry about that now.

A uniformed guard in the lobby, thick silver hair, slightly overweight, rose from his seat behind the counter. "May I help you?"

"I need to see Reese Garrett. Can you let him know Kenzie Haines is here?"

"Of course, Ms. Haines." The guard made the call and gave Reese her name. "You can go right on up," he said. "His elevator is the one on the right. He'll enter the code."

She hurried in that direction. As she stepped inside and the doors closed, it occurred to her that Reese might have a woman in his apartment, something she had failed to consider. Surely he wouldn't allow her to come up if he had someone there.

On the other hand, they hadn't established any rules. Kenzie had no interest in seeing anyone else, but what about Reese?

She prayed he was alone as the private car swept up to the top floor of the high-rise building. The moment the doors opened and she stepped into the entry, Reese pulled her into his arms.

"Reese…" Her eyes closed in relief. She was shaking, she realized, as she slid her arms around his neck. With a sigh, she pressed herself against him and just hung on.

"It's all right, baby. I'm right here. Whatever's going on, it's going to be okay."

She felt his hand running up and down her back, reassuring her. Just being with him settled her nerves. She held on a little longer, then let go.

"I should have called first," she said. "But I… I wasn't thinking. I just… I had to see you."

He led her farther into the apartment and eased her down onto the sofa in the living room, an elegant space with lots of glass and polished dark wood floors, a sleekly modern, high-ceilinged interior done in white and silver with cool aqua accents.

It was as beautiful and remote as Reese was on the outside, giving no hint of the warm, caring man he was on the inside. She was sure someone else had done the design with little input from Reese.

"Tell me what's happened," he said, looking down at her from his superior height. He was wearing faded jeans and a soft white cotton T-shirt that hugged his powerful chest. She had never seen him dressed in such casual clothes, but he looked good. So incredibly good.

Kenzie swallowed. "I got a call after supper. It was Lee's attorney, Martin Bales. According to Bales, Lee had a life insurance policy. Three million dollars, Reese. And Griff is the beneficiary." Nerves slid through her. "Worse than that, Lee named me custodian. That means I have control of the funds until Griff turns eighteen. Oh, God." She pressed her fingers over her trembling lips. "The police are going to be sure I killed Lee to get the money. Reese, I'm so scared."

He sat down beside her, eased her down beside him and into his arms. "It's okay, baby. The money Griff inherited has nothing to do with you. Every man wants to insure his son's future. Even Lee Haines."

She should have anticipated Lee doing something like this. He was always talking about his son being his legacy. And because he had been just thirty-five, Lee's death benefit policy wouldn't have been that expensive.

"Maybe there's a way to prove I didn't know anything about it," she said.

"Maybe. You have the best criminal attorney in Dallas working for you, along with my brothers, both top-notch detectives. We'll figure it out."

Some of her tension eased. She could feel the heat of his body beside her, incredibly solid and strong. The muscles in his biceps flexed and desire slipped through her. It was completely unexpected and totally out of place. She pressed her knees together, but it only made it worse.

"I know I shouldn't have come," she said. "But I wanted you to hear it from me. I needed you to know the truth, and…"

"And what?" His beautiful blue eyes searched her face.

"And I just needed to see you."

His gaze didn't waver and Kenzie couldn't look away. He must have read the desire she was trying so hard to hide because his pupils flared. Her heart skittered an instant before he tipped her chin up and settled his mouth over hers.

Hunger hit her full force. Kenzie clutched his shoulders and Reese deepened the kiss, turning it hot, wet, and intense, completely swamping her senses. It went on and on until her skin felt flushed, her body damp and throbbing. She could feel Reese's arousal, hard against her thigh.

"I needed to see you, too," he said pressing soft kisses to the corners of her mouth. "Being with you again like this is all I've thought about since we were together. Holding you. Kissing you. Being inside you."

"Reese…"

He pulled back a little. "I'm sorry. I know you didn't come here for this, but—"

Kenzie captured his face between her hands and silenced him with a kiss. He was right. She hadn't come here for this—or maybe she had. She kept on kissing him, aching for him with a desperation even greater than before.

Reese unbuttoned her simple cotton blouse and slid it off her shoulders, unhooked her plain white cotton bra and tossed it away. She hadn't dressed for seduction, hadn't thought that far ahead.

"Such pretty breasts," he said, thumbing her nipple, turning it hard, then settling his mouth there, tugging until she moaned.

He kissed her as he stripped away her clothes, then shed his own. The time he spent keeping himself in shape showed in his solid biceps and six-pack abs. She ran her fingers over his tanned chest and amazing pecs, ringed a flat copper nipple, and heard him groan.

"I want you," he said, caressing her breasts as he eased her back onto the sofa and settled himself between her legs. "I need this so much, Kenzie. I need you."

"I need you, too, Reese."

Reese kissed his way down her body, kissed the inside of her thighs. She was trembling when he began to pleasure her with his mouth and his hands, bringing her to a shattering climax. Then he came up over her and slid deep inside, kissed her as he began to move.

Kenzie thought that she had never known what sex really was until she'd made love with Reese. As his strong, deep thrusts carried her higher, driving her toward the peak again, Kenzie squirmed beneath him, silently begging for more.

"Not yet," he said, drawing her hands above her head and locking her wrists together. "Not until it's time." In and out, fast and then slow, setting up a rhythm so delicious she began to moan.

She started pleading, saying his name over and over. It embarrassed her—and it turned her on.

"You want more?" he asked, pausing.

"Yes, oh, God, Reese, please don't stop..."

He kissed the side of her neck, then took her mouth, let

go of her wrists as he began to move faster, deeper, harder. Pleasure tore through her, stretched into what seemed eternity. For the second time, she was flying, tears in her eyes, her heart filled with emotion.

Afterward, Reese just held her. "You okay? I was a little rough. It wasn't too much?"

A soft sigh whispered out. She reached up and touched his cheek, felt the dark bristles along his jaw. "You were perfect." This time it was exactly the right word.

CHAPTER TWENTY

Kenzie curled up next to Reese on the sofa beneath the lightweight throw he'd tossed over them. Pulling her close, he slid an arm around her and Kenzie leaned against him. They were quiet for a while.

"I need to tell you about what happened with Lee," she finally said, braving a subject she dreaded. "I should have told you sooner, but I was embarrassed. I didn't want you to be disappointed in me."

Reese caught her chin, forcing her to look at him. "You could never disappoint me, Kenzie. You stayed because you felt you had to for Griff. I understand that. I don't like that it happened. But Lee's dead. There's nothing either one of us can do about it now."

There was no mistaking the hard note that had crept into his voice. It occurred to her that in one way or another, he would have made Lee pay.

"I should have left sooner," she said. "There are places that help women in trouble. But more than a year passed between the first incident and the second. By then, I was sure it wouldn't happen again. Still, that terrible first time made me realize how dependent I was on him. I started making plans just in case. Then one night he came home and I could see the anger in his face. He didn't hit me that night, but if I had pushed him the least bit, he would have.

I was grateful Griff was having a sleepover with one of his friends that night."

"I saw the way Lee treated you at the hospital. Maybe he knew Griff wouldn't be there so he could deal with you the way he wanted."

"Maybe. I don't know. After that, I knew I had to leave. A few weeks later, he came home early and caught me packing. That was the second time it happened. I moved out a week later."

Reese released a slow breath. She realized he was working to summon his usually unshakable control. He leaned down and softly kissed her. "I'm sorry for what Lee did to you. But I'm glad you ended up working for me."

She smiled at him. "So am I." She sighed. "Unfortunately, Lee's abusive behavior is just one more thing that makes me look guilty."

Reese squeezed her hand and sat up straighter on the sofa. "I talked to Chase this afternoon."

"About the tabloid article?"

"About the murder. Chase and Hawk both think Lee's killer was a professional, someone good enough to murder him and not leave any evidence—or at least none he didn't plant."

She frowned. "You aren't talking about a hit man of some kind?"

"It's a possibility. Hawk thinks it could be a guy who works for the Louisiana mob. He's looking for a connection."

Unease filtered through her. "Lee's brother, Daniel, is a Louisiana state senator."

He nodded. "I remember you saying that."

"As far as I know, Daniel's a really good guy. I can't believe he'd have anything to do with murder." She had met

Lee's older brother and his wife only a couple of times, but she had liked them both.

"Lee said Daniel was as straight as an arrow. According to Lee, he'd always been his father's favorite. In Arthur's eyes, Lee could never quite measure up. I don't think Daniel would associate with criminals."

"In Louisiana, the mob is heavy into the casino business," Reese said. "Was Lee a gambler? The riverboats in Shreveport are only a few hours away."

"Lee didn't gamble. He didn't like to lose at anything. Same reason he didn't play golf."

"I'll dig into it, see what I can find out." He reached for her hand and brought it to his lips, pressed a soft kiss into her palm. He rose from the sofa, magnificently naked. "In the meantime, let's go to bed."

She thought of the falcon tattoo on his back and a fresh rush of desire slipped through her. With regret, she shook her head. "It's a school night. I have to get home."

"You sure you can't stay, at least for a while?" At the heat in those amazing blue eyes, her abdomen contracted. Her mouth dried up while the rest of her body went soft and damp.

"I guess I could stay…for a while."

Reese leaned down and scooped her up into his arms. "We'll worry about tomorrow when it comes." Striding down the hall, he carried her into his bedroom. "In the meantime, we deserve a little time to forget."

Reese made sure that happened.

THE NIGHT WAS jet-black, no stars, no moon as Troy Graves turned into a deserted street in the warehouse district. Driving through the gate of an empty metal building surrounded by a chain-link fence, he braked his silver Porsche, slowed to a stop in the shadows, and turned off the engine.

It wasn't the first time he'd been there. He'd met the same man in the same deserted spot before. He cracked open the car door, eased out, and started walking, his thousand-dollar Balenciaga sneakers crunching on the gravel.

Up ahead, he could just make out the man's shadowy figure, and rage burned through him. Reaching into the pocket of his windbreaker, he wrapped his fingers around the ivory grip of his Glock 19 semiauto. The gun felt good in his hand.

He'd inherited the weapon from his dad, just like the power he held as half owner of Black Sand Oil and Gas. His father had never fired the weapon, but Troy had. You never knew when you might need to protect yourself.

Just like tonight.

The shadowy figure came into focus as the man came closer. "You bring the money?"

His jaw tightened. "You bring the recording?"

"I said I would, didn't I? You get the flash drive, I get the cash, and no one's the wiser."

"You were well paid for what you did. Now you expect to get paid again, just to keep your mouth shut."

In the thin rays of moonlight shifting through the clouds, Troy saw the man shrug.

"Things heated up. I had to leave town, start over somewhere else. That takes money, more than you paid me the first time."

"How do I know the conversation we had hasn't been copied onto more than one flash drive?"

Another shrug. "Guess that's just a chance you'll have to take."

"Put the flash drive on the ground and back away."

The man set the flash drive on the asphalt. "Now the money," he said.

Troy pulled the pistol out of his pocket. "Sorry, I don't think so." They were standing about ten feet apart, the perfect kill zone, even for a guy with his lack of experience.

"What the hell?" The clouds parted and more light streamed down, illuminating the white circles of the man's dark eyes.

"You shouldn't have come to Dallas," Troy said. "You should have stayed wherever the hell you went." Troy pulled the trigger, once, twice, three times. The guy hit the ground before the shots finished echoing off the metal walls of the buildings.

In seconds he had the flash drive in hand and was driving his car back through the gate. The night closed around him as he continued along the roadway back to the city. He wondered how long it would take before the man's body was found. It didn't matter. There was no way to connect him to any of this.

Troy smiled. Maybe he'd stop by Heather's place, celebrate a little. Heather was a good piece of ass, and after the way he'd handled things tonight, he deserved a reward. Troy stepped on the gas.

CHAPTER TWENTY-ONE

THERE WAS A shift in the mood at the office when Reese walked in the next morning a few minutes later than usual after so little sleep last night. Stepping out of the executive-floor elevator, he couldn't stop a faint smile as he thought of Kenzie.

They were good together in bed, their sexual appetites, likes, and dislikes pretty much the same. It was one more reason they seemed to fit.

"Good morning, Louise." He paused next to her desk. "You remember Kenzie won't be in today. She's going to her ex-husband's funeral."

"I know. I feel sorry for Griff. Kenzie told me he's taking it pretty hard." The older, gray-haired woman was an asset to the company. She was reliable, did her job well, and never complained.

"I guess they weren't very close," he said. "But your dad's your dad. You only get one."

"I don't know about that," Louise disagreed. "My dad ran out on us when I was a baby. The man who adopted me? He's the best father I ever could have wanted."

Reese's gaze held hers for several seconds. Was there a message in those words? Reese thought of Griff. He was a great kid. A son any man would be proud of.

"I'll be attending the funeral myself," Reese said. "You'll have to cover for both of us."

"No problem. Anything special you need me to do?"

"Not that I can think of at the moment. I'll let you know before I leave." He continued walking, catching sideways glances from several employees as he strode toward his office door. *The tabloid article*, he thought, cursing the bastards who had written it and the insinuations it made.

Turning around, he walked back to Louise's desk. "If anyone wants to know, the answer is yes. I'm seeing Kenzie on a social basis. It's not a secret. We're both adults, both single. She isn't quitting her job and I don't expect her to. Anyone who has something to say about it can say it directly to me."

Louise's eyes went saucer-round. She blinked, then she smiled. "It's about time you two got together."

Some of the anger drained out of him. At least one person was on their side. "Thanks, Louise. I know Kenzie will appreciate your support."

Louise just nodded and Reese continued walking. Now that it was out in the open, somehow he felt better. He wasn't sure Kenzie would feel the same.

Sitting behind his desk, he took a look at his schedule, then picked up the phone. His first call went to Tabby.

"Morning, chief," she said. "Let me guess. You need info on a Louisiana state senator named Daniel Haines, brother of the late Lee Haines."

"That's right. How did you know?"

"Chase called me last night."

That was his brother the detective. Always one step ahead. "You got anything yet?"

"Only the stuff at the top. So far it looks like Daniel Haines is the real deal. A solid citizen. One of the good guys. Of course, that could just be an illusion created by his staff. I'm just getting started. I'll keep you in the loop."

"Thanks, Tab." It was still early. He worked all morning, through the lunch hour, then went down to the parking garage, where Reggie picked him up for the ride to the Sparkman-Hillcrest cemetery in north Dallas, the place Lee Haines's funeral service was being held.

He timed it to come in late, sit in a pew in the back of the chapel. Lee had been a big investor in the real estate market. He knew a lot of people in Dallas and many of them were there.

Reese scanned the room for Kenzie. She was sitting between her grandmother and Griff in the front pew of the chapel. Arthur Haines sat in the front pew on the other side of the aisle. Reese recognized Arthur's handsome blond son, Daniel, and Daniel's matching-bookend pretty blonde wife from photos he'd found on the internet that morning. A dark-haired woman dressed in black sat to Arthur's left, occasionally lifting her veil to dab tears from her eyes.

The service went longer than he'd expected, or maybe it just felt that way to him. Afterward the crowd adjourned to attend the graveside service to follow.

Reese didn't plan to go. He just wanted Griff and Kenzie to know he was there for them if they needed him. He waited on the chapel steps for them to appear, started toward them when the woman in black stopped in front of Kenzie, blocking her way.

"What are you doing here?" the woman demanded. "After what you did, you have no right to be here."

"I'm sorry," Kenzie said. "Do I know you?"

"I'm Lee's fiancée, Delia Parr. Believe me, I know who *you* are. The police came to see me. They told me about the gun that killed Lee—your gun. You murdered him! You were afraid he'd get custody of his son, so you killed him!"

"Mom, what does she mean?"

Kenzie's arm went protectively around Griff's shoulders. "She's just upset." Kenzie turned and started leading her son away. Reese stepped in front of the woman so she couldn't follow and his eyes met Kenzie's for an instant.

"Go on," he said. "I'll take care of this."

Kenzie gave him a look of such gratitude his chest went tight. She turned and continued walking, leading Griff and her grandmother on down the steps.

"Get out of my way." Delia tried to brush past him, but Reese stood firm.

"Kenzie had nothing to do with Lee's murder. The police are investigating. They'll find the man who killed him. You need to let them do their job."

"Reese is right, Delia." Arthur Haines's voice rang from beside him. "This is not the time or place for wild accusations." He was as tall as Reese, silver-haired, with an appearance of dignified propriety, an illusion that had worked well for him over the years.

But Arthur Haines was a shrewd and cunning businessman with few moral ethics. He would do whatever it took to make money.

After his partner, William Graves, had died and Bill's son, Troy, had inherited half the company, Reese had begun to hear rumors that the business was in trouble. He frowned as a thought occurred, jotting a mental note to see if Black Sand Oil and Gas had made any attempts to purchase the Poseidon platform. Was it possible they had some connection to the problems with the rig?

Delia walked away in a huff, her snug black dress shifting back and forth over a round behind she was clearly proud of. Arthur remained, his gaze following Kenzie and his grandson across the wide expanse of manicured lawn.

"So it's true," Arthur said, his attention returning to Reese. "You and my ex-daughter-in-law are involved? Delia mentioned she saw your photos on the front page of the newspaper at the grocery store. I didn't believe it at the time."

"We're both single. We're seeing each other—not that it's any of your business."

"Tsk-tsk, my friend. It's not exactly appropriate to be dating one of your employees. Not in your position."

It was true. He should have stayed away from Kenzie. For six months, he'd done his best, then, like a wrecking ball swinging out of control, he couldn't ignore his feelings any longer. He wasn't sorry. Kenzie was worth the risk. "I'm willing to take my chances."

Arthur just smiled.

Reese continued on down the steps, crossing the lawn beneath a cloudy sky that signaled rain, deciding he would go to the graveside service after all. He'd stay at the back of the crowd, but if anyone gave Kenzie trouble, he would be there for her.

From now on, that was the way it was going to be.

IT WAS EARLY EVENING, a light rain beginning to fall. It was still hot in mid-September, the evenings warm and muggy.

Arthur sat in his favorite leather chair in front of the TV in his study, a plate of chicken casserole unfinished on the coffee table. His housekeeper had left for the day. Betty would be back in the morning to tidy things up and fix his meals, more reliable than his dead ex-wife ever had been.

And unlike Judith, who had constantly poked her nose into his business, Betty knew her place, which meant he rarely saw her. If she'd been thirty years younger and willing to service him once in a while, she would have been perfect. On another day, Arthur might have smiled at his own humor.

But today he had buried his youngest son. He didn't have much to smile about.

A noise reached him from somewhere in the house. A jolt of fear hit him as he recognized the sound of breaking glass. Arthur shot to his feet as two men walked into the study, one big and wide, a pleasant face if not for the scowl digging lines into his forehead. The other man was short but muscular, with curly black hair and dark eyes a little too close together.

"What are you doing in my house? Get out this instant!"

"Put your shoes back on, Mr. Haines," the bigger man said calmly. "You're going for a ride."

"A ride? What are you talking about?"

"Mr. DeMarco wants to see you. You need to come with us."

When Arthur started to shake his head, the short guy with the attitude reached beneath his windbreaker and pulled out a heavy black pistol. "You're going—with or without your shoes."

Trying to hide his fear, Arthur sat back down and did as he was told. "You can put the gun away. You've made your point."

Their car sat out front, an innocuous four-door brown sedan. The big guy got in behind the wheel and the short guy got in back with Arthur. He would have preferred the other way around.

"It's almost three hours to Shreveport," the big man said, looking back over his shoulder. "Maybe you can catch a nap."

Arthur said nothing. Sleeping was the last thing on his mind. He owed Sawyer DeMarco several million dollars. At the moment he had no way to pay him.

Still, after the first two uncomfortable hours, he began to nod off, his head slumping down on his chest. The last thing he remembered was the short man calling the big man Nolan. The next thing he knew, pain shot through him as the short guy with the curly black hair elbowed him in the ribs.

"We're here," the short guy said. Nolan opened the rear car door and Arthur and the short man got out. They were parked beneath a green-striped awning in front of a separate entrance into the Pot-of-Gold Resort Casino, the flagship of DeMarco's gambling domain.

In Louisiana, gaming was allowed only on riverboats, which were permanently docked on the water, in this case the muddy Red River that slugged through Shreveport heading south.

"Get going," the man with the black hair said, shoving him forward, enjoying it. "Boss doesn't like to be kept waiting."

Nolan pushed the button on the elevator and it began its ascent to DeMarco's penthouse apartment on the top floor of the club. Arthur wished he had remembered to grab his suit coat as he'd walked out the door. He looked wrinkled and tired after the long drive from Dallas. He hated being at a disadvantage.

DeMarco was waiting when the doors slid open and he stepped into the black-and-white marble entry beneath a huge crystal chandelier. Everything in the penthouse was overdone. Gold and scarlet, white gilded furniture, imitation Greek statues. It reeked of DeMarco's lower-class beginnings, Arthur thought.

"You want a drink?" The words rasped out in DeMarco's smoker's voice. He took a sip of the expensive scotch he favored, making the ice clink in his glass. He was several inches shorter than Arthur, built like a linebacker, with broad shoulders and a thick barrel chest. He had dark brown hair that always needed trimming, black eyes, and a bad complexion. Sawyer DeMarco was not a handsome man.

"Club soda," Arthur said. Getting drunk was not an option.

"Take care of it, Eddie." The black-haired guy headed for the built-in bar, his lips pressed together. Clearly, he didn't like menial tasks.

Eddie returned and handed him the heavy crystal glass. Arthur took a sip, concentrating so his hand wouldn't shake.

"Leave us," DeMarco said, abruptly sending his two henchmen away. He turned back to Arthur. "I hear you're having some problems." DeMarco sipped his scotch.

Arthur said nothing. DeMarco was behind his son's murder. He knew it, had received DeMarco's message loud and clear. And the man wouldn't hesitate to kill again.

"You don't have the money to pay me back, right?"

"Not at this time, but I assure you—"

"Oh, you're going to pay me. We both know that. Unfortunately, you owe me interest as well as principal."

Arthur said nothing, the gruff voice grating on his nerves.

Both still standing, DeMarco wandered casually closer. "Here's the thing. With all the competition from the Indian casinos that have opened in Oklahoma, business is down. We need to expand. We want to locate on the north shore of Lake Pontchartrain and also in the northeast region of Louisiana."

DeMarco took another sip of scotch. "Your son, Daniel, is one of the most influential legislators in Louisiana. Daniel Haines comes out in favor of our proposals, we'll get the approvals we need."

"I'll pay you back," Arthur said. "I just need a little more time. I'll pay what I owe plus interest."

"Oh, I know you will." He patted Arthur on the shoulder hard enough to spill club soda over the rim of his glass. "And I'm going to help you. I'm going to get you that oil rig you've been trying to steal."

A ripple of fear moved down Arthur's spine. "I don't know what you mean."

"The Poseidon. You don't think I know what you've been up to? When I want something, Arthur, I go after it. I get it by whatever means necessary. I need your son's support and you need that drilling platform. So I'm going to get it for you."

Arthur opened his mouth, but no sound came out.

DeMarco just smiled. "I'm going to do what you failed to accomplish. I'm going to force Garrett Resources to pull out of the deal. You're going to buy the rig and get your company back on track so you can pay me the money you owe and move your business forward. In return, you're going to get Daniel to do exactly what I ask."

Arthur's heart was thudding, his mind spinning, fighting to stay in control.

"Daniel's support is the interest payment you owe. I'll even throw in the photos of you and the hooker who tied you up and beat your bare ass with a whip. Does that seem fair?"

His face flushed. He ran his tongue over his dry lips. "It seems fair."

"Good, because if you don't convince Daniel to support our proposals, I'm going to have to find a way to convince him myself. Since you've already lost one son, I don't imagine you want to lose another. Or anyone else in your family."

Arthur felt a wave of nausea as he stared into DeMarco's cold black eyes. Then the door opened and Nolan and Eddie walked back into the room.

"Get him out of here," DeMarco said.

In that instant, Arthur was actually glad to see them.

CHAPTER TWENTY-TWO

KENZIE TOOK FRIDAY off to spend with her son. Reese had called after the funeral and suggested it. He'd spoken to Griff at the graveside service.

"I know it's hard," Reese had said. "I was older than you when my dad died, but it was still rough. He was a businessman like your father, so we didn't get to spend a lot of time together. But I still remember him, remember some of the little things we did together."

"Dad took me out to the lake once," Griff said, fighting back tears. "I wanted him to teach me to water-ski but he said it was too dangerous."

"One of my friends has a boat," Reese said. "Maybe we can go sometime."

Kenzie looked at her son. For the first time that day, something besides sadness shone in Griff's eyes. "Really?"

"If we go and your mom thinks it's okay, I'll teach you."

Gratitude slipped through her. She looked up at Reese, saw the caring in his eyes, and a warm feeling expanded inside her. From that moment on, Kenzie thought the day had somehow seemed brighter.

She couldn't help thinking how different Reese was from Lee. How he actually seemed to take an interest in her son. It scared her to think how deeply she was getting involved with him. She knew what Reese was like, that odds were he'd get bored with her and move on. She told herself she could handle it when the time came.

Friday morning slipped away, drifted into afternoon. The sun was out, the September air still warm after last night's rain.

"Why don't you two go for a swim?" Gran suggested. "Weather's nice today."

Seated at the kitchen table, Griff looked up and his features brightened. "Could we, Mom?"

She smiled, thinking it was a good idea. "I don't see why not." Griff started for the stairs to change, Kenzie close behind him when the doorbell rang. She turned to the door, checked the peephole, and her stomach knotted.

Griff continued up the stairs while Kenzie opened the door. "Detective Ford. I'm surprised to see you." She didn't invite him in. She had no idea what he wanted but it couldn't be good.

"I've got a couple of questions I need to ask. They won't take long."

She had seen him at the funeral yesterday, standing at the back of the crowd. Griff had recognized him from a news broadcast on TV and wanted to ask him about his progress on the murder case. Fortunately, the detective was gone by the time the service was over.

"What do you want to know?"

A cynical smile curved his mouth. He'd be a good-looking man if he weren't always scowling, trying to prove her guilty of murder.

"Turns out you're quite a good shot, Kenzie. You never mentioned your shooting skills. You didn't tell us your father belonged to the Dallas Trap Shooting Club. Or that the two of you went there together often. Why, you've even won trophies."

Her heart was pounding. She wished Reese were there. "I told you my father taught me to shoot."

"You said you bought the pistol for self-defense. You didn't say you were a crack marksman."

She lifted her chin. "Do I need to call my attorney?" It was what Nate Temple would advise her to say.

"What happened the night of the murder? Reese says you were with him but we both know that isn't true. Did you go to your ex-husband's house in order to kill him, or did the two of you get into an argument and things just got out of hand? Maybe you were frightened. After the beatings he gave you, maybe you just reacted. Or you were concerned for Griff's safety. If that's what happened—"

"That isn't what happened. No matter what he did to me, I don't believe Lee would ever have hurt his son, and I was nowhere near Lee's house the night he was killed. I think you had better leave, Detective."

"You might want to think about Reese. I know the two of you are involved. Giving false evidence, interfering in a police investigation—he could be facing some very serious charges."

"Please leave."

Ford took a step back and handed her a business card, which she accepted with a trembling hand. "If you change your mind, give me a call."

The detective walked out of the house. Kenzie closed the door and leaned against it.

"Mom?" Griff stood at the bottom of the stairs, dressed and ready for a swim. "Was that the detective who was on TV? He's the one trying to find Dad's killer."

"That's right."

"He…he doesn't think you did it, does he?"

Oh, God. "He's just doing his job, honey. The police

ask everyone questions. I wasn't anywhere near your dad's house that night."

She saw the fear in his eyes as he walked toward her. "If the cops think you did it, they could arrest you."

She drew him in for a hug. "They aren't going to arrest me, sweetheart. I didn't do anything wrong."

Griff pulled away. "We've got to help them find the bad guy, Mom. If we find the killer, you won't have to worry about the cops. Maybe we could get Reese to help."

The worry in his face made her eyes sting. It wasn't fair that a child his age should be afraid of losing his other parent, too.

"Reese is already helping us, honey. His brothers are detectives. They're looking for clues."

His features brightened. "Really?"

"Yes, they're doing their best to help."

"Okay." He looked up, his shoulders less tense. If Reese was helping, surely everything would be okay. Apparently, she wasn't the only one falling under Reese's spell. "You still want to go swimming?" he asked.

"Sure." She forced a smile, hoping a few laps in the pool would burn off some of the adrenaline still pumping through her system. "I'll change into my suit and be right down."

As she headed up the stairs, she saw Griff wander over to the window and stand there staring out. From the upstairs bedroom, she saw what he was looking at, an unmarked police car parked down the block.

Dear God, when would this nightmare end?

LATE FRIDAY AFTERNOON, Reese got a call from Tabby.

"I took another look at Daniel Haines and this time I went deep. The guy is squeaky-clean and I mean golden.

He isn't up for reelection for two more years, but if the vote were held tomorrow, the guy would win by a landslide."

"An honest politician. A rare commodity. Thanks, Tabby."

"I figured while I was at it, I'd check on Lee."

Reese had already done the basics, but anything he learned could be useful. "And?"

"Born and raised in Dallas. Married Kenzie right after she got out of college. Had a son, divorced five years ago. Considered himself a real estate entrepreneur and he definitely made some money in the business, but there were lawsuits and scandals, endless rumors about his integrity. No wonder Kenzie dumped him."

He thought of the hospital photos he had seen. "Good call on her part."

"You figure out who killed him?"

"Not yet."

"One more thing. Bran called, said he'd been busy getting the office ready, asked me to look into Arthur. From what I could tell, Arthur's a lot like his son—not Daniel, the other one."

"Anything specific?"

"Not yet, but I'm on it."

When the call ended, Reese phoned John Denton, VP of sales and acquisitions at Sea Titan, asked him if Black Sand Oil and Gas had made an offer on the Poseidon. The answer was no.

"You must have had other offers," Reese said.

"We had interest from other companies, but we didn't really put it up for bid. We knew if Garrett Resources bought the rig, the deal would likely go through. I hope nothing's happened to change that."

"You know we've had problems. But we're working them out. I'm just following up, keeping on top of things."

"Let me know if you need my help."

"Thanks, John, I will." So Black Sand hadn't made an offer. But if the company was in trouble, maybe Arthur was having second thoughts. Expanding into offshore drilling could be the answer to his prayers.

Reese needed more information.

A little after 6:00 p.m., he joined Chase at Clancy's, in the same wooden booth as before, sipping the same Irish whiskey.

Chase slid into the booth across from him, rubbed a hand over the close-cropped gold beard along his jaw, and ordered a beer. The waitress with the curly blond hair arrived with a frosty bottle of Lone Star a few minutes later. She flicked Reese a glance as she walked away, but he ignored the not-so-subtle invitation. He had another woman on his mind.

"How was the funeral?" Chase asked, then took a long swallow of beer.

"I felt sorry for Griff. Losing a dad is hard, even if he was a rotten father."

Chase nodded. Bass Garrett had been a powerhouse. A dynamic figure in the oil and gas industry. As a husband and father? Not the best. Still, they'd loved him.

"Arthur Haines was there with his son, Daniel," Reese continued. "And a woman who claimed to be Lee's fiancée."

"I hadn't heard."

"Neither had I. I have heard rumors that Black Sand Oil and Gas is in trouble. I'm trying to find out if it's true. If it is, getting their hands on the Poseidon might be a solution to their problems."

Chase sipped his beer. "You're thinking Arthur might be behind the trouble you've been having?"

"Could be him, could be one of those idiot protesters, could be anyone. But, yeah, I think there's a chance it's him."

"So Arthur Haines, Lee Haines, and Kenzie Haines. Arthur's company may be responsible for the problems on the rig. Lee is dead and Kenzie is a suspect in his murder. I don't know how this all ties together, but I'm not a big believer in coincidence."

Reese frowned. "You aren't thinking Kenzie has anything to do with the Poseidon deal?"

"I'm not sure what to think. I'm wondering if you've considered what role Kenzie might be playing in all of this."

Reese felt a stab of irritation. "She isn't playing any role. She has nothing to do with Lee's murder or anything else. Somehow she just got swept up in all of it."

"You sure? Timing's about right. She came to work for you, what? Six months ago? Isn't that about the time you started negotiating to buy the platform?"

"So what? I was looking for an assistant. Kenzie was looking for a job. She had the right credentials, so I hired her. She's the best I've ever worked with."

"What if she's setting you up? Feeding Arthur Haines information? Bran and I both saw the way you looked at her the night of the banquet. Now she's in your bed."

His temper crept higher. "So I'm attracted to her. So what?"

"It's more than that and you know it. I've never seen you look at a woman the way you look at her."

The hand Reese rested on the table balled into a fist. "Kenzie didn't kill Lee Haines and she isn't in league with Arthur. I thought we'd already settled this."

"That was before you mentioned Arthur's possible involvement in the problems with the rig."

Reese slid out of the booth and stood up. "Kenzie has nothing to do with any of this. I know her. I've worked with her day in and day out for months. She practically ran the company while I was in the hospital after the helicopter crash. She's always there when I need her, and I trust her completely."

Reese stared his brother hard in the face. "I came here to get your input. I never thought the conversation would take this turn. I trust Kenzie. I need to know if I can trust you to stand by a woman I care about. Can you do that?"

Chase's expression subtly altered. He slid out of the booth and they stood face-to-face. "You've always had good instincts, Reese. You wouldn't have made the company as successful as it is without them. If you believe in this woman, then Bran and I will stand with you. With you and with Kenzie. Whatever you need us to do."

Reese's fury ebbed, replaced by a tightness in his chest. When things got tough, Chase and Bran never let him down. "Thank you," he said.

Chase clapped him on the back. "Okay, then." A grim smile touched his lips. "Now all we need to do is figure out what in the hell is going on."

CHAPTER TWENTY-THREE

AFTER WHAT SEEMED a very long weekend, Kenzie arrived at the office early Monday morning. She was anxious to see Reese, not quite sure where they stood.

She glanced up as the elevator doors slid open and Reese walked out, power and confidence in every long stride as he crossed the deep-pile carpet. Heat washed over her just looking at him. When those crystal blue eyes focused on her like twin laser beams, her stomach contracted in blatant sexual desire.

"Good morning," he said, nothing more than those few words, but it seemed as if he reached out and touched her. A memory arose of lying with him, of Reese's mouth on her breasts, of him moving deep inside her.

Ignoring the warmth creeping into her cheeks, she rose from the chair behind her desk. "Are you ready for me?"

He usually just nodded. They always went over his schedule first thing and discussed what needed to be done.

This morning his lips twitched. "I'm definitely ready," he said.

She flushed. She knew exactly what he meant. She was ready for him, too. She had thought of him constantly. It was the reason companies didn't encourage office affairs.

She rose to follow him but turned at the sound of a man's deep voice. Reese was staring over her shoulder, watching a big blond man with a flattop haircut walking toward them. Dressed in a dark brown suit and wingtip shoes, he strode past them, right into Reese's office.

"Well, Special Agent Taggart," Reese said dryly. He motioned for Kenzie to join them, then closed the door. "I hope this means you've found the man responsible for the Sea Titan helicopter crash."

"You could say that. Currently, he's lying on a slab in the morgue."

Reese's glance cut to her. "FBI Special Agent Quinn Taggart, meet my executive assistant, McKenzie Haines."

Taggart dipped his chin in greeting. "Ms. Haines…"

"Special Agent."

"Kenzie's been involved in the investigation since the day the chopper went down, so I'd like her to sit in on our conversation."

Taggart nodded. "That's not a problem. This won't take long."

They moved to the seating area around the dark walnut coffee table. Reese offered the agent something to drink, but he declined.

"Last week," Taggart began, "a mechanic named Louis Kroft was murdered outside a vacant warehouse in Dallas. Took two .45 caliber slugs to the chest, plus a stray bullet that ricocheted off the gravel and lodged in his abdomen. We were able to ID him, track him back to where he was living in Port Arthur. He'd only been working there a few weeks, coincidentally took the job not long after the Sea Titan helicopter went down. Turns out he was an expert on the EC135."

Kenzie remembered the moment she'd heard about the deadly crash and felt a sudden chill.

"You think this is the guy?" Reese asked.

"Looks that way. Before the move, Kroft worked as a helicopter mechanic in Dallas. Quit his job and left town shortly after the crash. We found a couple of big deposits in his bank account, and gas receipts from a station in Galveston. We're still investigating, but there's a good chance it's him."

"So who killed him?"

"That's the question, isn't it? That and the reason he was murdered. Clearly he was working for someone else. That's the person we're looking for now."

"Can you trace the money back to its source?"

Taggart shook his head. "Cash deposits made by Kroft himself." He shoved his big frame up from the sofa. "I figure you're probably still digging around. You hear anything about this guy or anything else, you let me know."

Reese nodded. "I will."

Taggart turned to Kenzie. "Pleasure meeting you, Ms. Haines."

"Agent Taggart." She didn't say it was a pleasure meeting him, too. She'd had enough of law enforcement to last a lifetime. And now the mechanic who had sabotaged the helicopter was dead. Whichever way they turned, murder and mayhem swirled around them.

Reese followed Taggart to the door and closed it behind him. Then he turned back to Kenzie. Surprise jolted through her when he pulled her into his arms and kissed her so thoroughly her knees went weak. She was trembling when he let her go.

"Sorry. I just needed to get that out of my system. I missed you and I've been worried about you."

"We…we can't do that, Reese. I can't concentrate on my job if I'm thinking about you instead of business."

He nodded, a faint, unrepentant smile on his lips. "You're right. I promise it won't happen…often." He actually grinned. "Now we can get to work."

Kenzie laughed. She had never seen this side of him, relaxed and slightly playful. It only made him more attractive.

"Before we get started," she said, "I should probably tell you Detective Ford came by to see me. He questioned me about the shooting skills my dad taught me and warned me I could be dragging you into a lot of trouble."

Reese frowned. "Next time you don't talk to him. You call Nathan."

"I thought about it. Next time I will."

"Good. Now let's go over my schedule for the week—starting with when we'll have time to see each other outside the office. Tonight would be a good start."

Kenzie smiled, the anxiety she'd felt all weekend slipping away. Reese still wanted her. For now, everything was okay.

Except that she was still the primary suspect in her ex-husband's murder. A chill of foreboding crept down her spine. Everything was definitely not okay.

AT THE END of the very long workday, Kenzie looked up to see Reese walking toward her.

"So what time am I picking you up?" he asked.

"I...umm...guess you forgot that meeting you have with the mayor and members of the city council. I should have reminded you earlier, but other things came up. They're expecting you to be there. I don't see any way around it."

Reese softly cursed. "All right, if the meeting doesn't go too late, I'll call you. Maybe I can stop by for a nightcap."

The heat in his eyes said a nightcap would lead exactly where Kenzie wanted to go. "Gran goes to bed early. It's a school night for Griff, so that could work."

She thought he might lean over and kiss her, but fortunately for both of them, at the last minute he came to his senses.

They left the office anticipating their rendezvous later

that night, but fate in the guise of the mayor intervened and Reese's meeting went past midnight. With their trip to Houston scheduled for the next day, Kenzie was able to squelch her disappointment.

Still, worry about Lee's murder, and what the police would do when they discovered the money from his life insurance policy, kept her awake. She was shifting restlessly on the mattress, determined to get some sleep, when an odd sound reached her.

When the noise came again, she grabbed her pink cotton robe off the chair and slipped it on. As she stepped into the hall, she recognized the sound as heavy footfalls on carpet and they seemed to be coming from Griff's bedroom at the end of the hall.

Her pulse kicked up and her mouth went dry. With her pistol gone, she had no weapon to fend off an intruder, and no time to go in search of one. Not when Griff could be in danger.

Hurrying back to her bedroom, she grabbed her keys out of her purse, laced the jagged metal between her fingers as her dad had taught her to do, and stepped back out into the hall. As she approached Griff's room, she could hear men's voices, and the taste of fear filled her mouth.

Moving quietly, she turned the knob and silently opened the door. Moonlight steaming in through the open bedroom window illuminated a man lifting her son over a thick shoulder in a fireman's carry.

"Griff!" She lunged toward him, spotted another man, shorter, with curly black hair, an instant too late. His fist slammed into her jaw, spinning her into the wall, but she kept her grip on the keys.

"Griff!" Struggling to regain her balance, she charged, punching, kicking, raking the keys down his cheek.

"Bitch!" Blood erupted, ran down his face in scarlet rivulets. He reached for her, but she was already racing toward the bigger man holding her son. Griff was unconscious, she realized, his wrists and ankles bound.

Terror struck. "Let him go!" Lashing out with the keys, she fought like a wild thing, screaming for help, praying Gran would hear her in her bedroom downstairs and call the police. Fury and desperation drove her even as the man with the curly black hair jerked her away and punched her in the stomach, then hit her in the face.

Shouting Griff's name, Kenzie gripped the keys, used them to slice one of his arms, and tried to knee him in the groin.

Still unconscious, Griff never stirred, but the bigger man kept moving, ducking through the bedroom window, descending a ladder propped against the side of the town house.

The man with the curly black hair punched her so hard she hit the wall and slid down to the bedroom floor. Her head spun and her vision dimmed as she flashed in and out of consciousness.

"No cops." The man grabbed her chin and tilted her head back. "You hear me, lady? You want your kid to live, you keep quiet and do what they tell you. You got it?"

When she didn't answer soon enough, he slapped her face. "You got it? Say it?"

She swallowed. "No…police."

"That's right. You'll be hearing from us. Till then, keep your mouth shut."

Kenzie tried to get up, but he hit her again. "And tell your boyfriend he had better keep his fucking brothers out of it."

Her eyes slid closed. It was the last thing she remembered until Gran opened the door, saw her lying on the floor covered in blood, and screamed.

CHAPTER TWENTY-FOUR

REESE WAS DEAD asleep when the phone rang. His meeting had run longer than he'd expected and he'd gotten home late. With a weary sigh, he rolled over to grab his cell phone off the nightstand, read the digital numbers on the clock: 4:01 a.m.

Since nothing good happened at four o'clock in the morning, his heart rate jolted from sluggish into high gear. Recognizing Kenzie's cell number sent his pulse rate up another notch. "Kenzie?"

"Reese, it…it's Florence." Her voice shook. "Kenzie's hurt. Men took Griff and they told her not to call the police." Florence sobbed into the phone. "I didn't know who else to call. Please help us, Reese."

But Reese was already up and moving, trying to wrap his head around another disaster, trying not to imagine what terrible thing might have happened to Kenzie. "Does she need an ambulance? How badly is she hurt?"

"She won't go to the hospital. Please come, Reese."

"Listen to me, Flo. I'm on my way right now. I'm calling a doctor. He'll meet us there."

"No police. She just keeps saying it over and over."

"No police, Flo. This man is a friend. He'll help her and there won't be any police involved. Just tell her to hang on until I get there." He swallowed, fought for control. "Both of you. Just hang on."

Florence made a sound in her throat. Then she took a shaky breath. "We'll be okay. I'll take care of her till you get here. Thank you."

Reese ended the call. He didn't want thanks. Kenzie was hurt. He needed to get to her. It occurred to him that nothing in the world could stop him.

Dressing quickly, he made a brief pause in his study to retrieve the Nighthawk semiauto in his safe. He kept the gun for protection. His juvenile records were sealed, which allowed him to get a permit. He had learned the hard way there were bad people in the world.

Minutes later, he was behind the wheel of the Jaguar, roaring out of the garage. As the vehicle fishtailed onto the deserted street, Reese fought to steady himself. It was time to shut down his emotions and regain control.

He voice-dialed Dr. Charles Chandler, a longtime Garrett family friend, and the doctor agreed to meet him at Kenzie's town house on Gilbert Street.

Reese stepped on the gas, sliding around corners, accelerating, rolling through stop signs at intersections. *No police*, he reminded himself, and slowed the Jag enough so he wouldn't get stopped. Still, he made the trip in record time. As he got out of the car and raced up the sidewalk, Florence opened the door.

"Thank God," she said.

"The doctor should be here any minute. Where's Kenzie?"

"Upstairs in Griff's room."

Reese raced past her up the stairs, Florence hurrying to catch up. The door to the bedroom stood open. A lamp burned on the bedside table, casting shadowy light around the room. Aside from the nightstand, the room was in shambles, as if a bomb had exploded, curtains torn down, photos and trophies on top of the dresser broken and strewn all over the floor.

Kenzie sat on the edge of Griff's bed, her head hanging forward, dark hair hiding her face. Bruises began to darken the back of her neck and her arms below the short sleeves of her pink cotton robe. Kenzie sobbed into Griff's Dallas Cowboys jersey, which she hugged against her chest.

For an instant, Reese stood frozen, blinding rage pouring through him. Clamping down hard on his emotions, he crouched on the floor in front of Kenzie. Reaching out, he gently caught hold of her hand.

"It's okay, baby. I'm here now. Everything's going to be okay."

She looked up at him, her eyes stricken with fear and grief. Tears tracked down her cheeks. "Reese…oh, God." She leaned forward, put her head on his shoulder, and kept sobbing. Reese gently held her that way, terrified he would hurt her. He didn't know how badly she was injured. He didn't want to make it worse.

Wiping tears from her cheeks, Kenzie sat up on the edge of the bed. "They took him, Reese. They took Griff. They came right…right into our home and kidnapped my little boy."

He took her hand. It felt icy cold. He saw the bruises on her knuckles and pressed his lips there. "We're going to get him back. I promise you. Right now, I need to see how badly you're hurt."

She didn't protest when he opened her robe. His jaw tightened as he studied the darkening bruises on her pretty breasts and torso, did a quick check for broken bones, didn't find any, but she sucked in a breath when he touched her ribs. Her eyes were puffy, her jaw bruised, her plump bottom lip cut and swollen. Fresh rage welled inside him. It took all his will to battle it down.

"I need you to tell me exactly what happened," he said softly. "Can you do that, honey?"

Tear-filled eyes fixed on his face. She took a steadying breath and nodded. "It…it was late. I tried to sleep but I had too much on my mind. I was lying there, thinking about Lee's murder, thinking about what the police might do, when I heard a noise. I wasn't sure what it was, so I got… got up to check. I heard voices in Griff's bedroom and when I opened the door, I saw… I saw a man carrying him over his shoulders toward the open window." Her voice broke.

"It's okay, baby, just take your time." *Where the hell is that doctor?* He ground his teeth in frustration but kept his emotions locked down tight.

"Griff was… Griff was bound hand and foot and I… I realized he was unconscious. I tried to stop the man who was taking him. I didn't see the second man until…until he hit me."

Reese clamped down on a shot of fury, managed to hang on to his temper by a thread. "Go on."

"We fought. I had my keys between my fingers like my dad taught me and I raked them down his face. He was bleeding and he was furious. That's why he kept hitting me." She glanced toward the window as if she thought Griff might reappear.

"What happened then?"

"The first man disappeared out the window with Griff over his shoulders, but the second man stayed to warn me not to call the police." She covered her lips with a trembling hand and blood smeared her fingers. "He said…" She swallowed. "He said I would be hearing from them.

He said to tell my…my boyfriend to keep his brothers out of it. Oh, God, Reese."

He wanted to pull her into his arms and hold on tight, but he didn't dare. Not until the doctor checked her injuries.

Instead, he held on to her trembling hand. "Listen to me, honey. Those men kidnapped Griff for a reason. They're probably planning to ransom him back to you. If it's money they want, I've got plenty. More than enough. We'll get him back, no matter what it takes. I promise you."

Her eyes met his, hers glazed with tears. He had no idea what she was thinking. But the fact that they knew who he was put an extra layer of intrigue over the abduction. He had to find out what the hell was going on.

"You said there were two men. Can you tell me what they looked like?"

She swallowed, sat up a little straighter, winced at the movement. "Everything happened so fast it's all…it's all kind of a blur."

She closed her eyes, taking time to recall. "I don't remember much about the first man. He was as tall as you, I guess, only thicker in the chest and shoulders. Not muscular, just bigger. The other man had curly black hair. He had kind of a homely, dish-shaped face and he was a lot shorter. I remember the first man handled Griff carefully while the other man… I… I think that man could have killed me and it wouldn't have bothered him at all."

Emotion seared Reese's chest. He clamped down to stay in control.

A sound in the hall caught his attention. He glanced up to see an imposing silver-haired man standing in the doorway, medical bag in hand.

Reese pushed to his feet. "Charles. Thank you so much

for coming." He turned. "Kenzie, this is Dr. Chandler. He's a friend. He's going to take care of you."

Her gaze went to the doctor and fear flashed in her eyes. "You won't tell the police?"

"I'm here to help you. That's all." His gaze swung to Reese. "Give me a moment with my patient, will you, Reese?"

He didn't want to leave. He wanted to stay in case Kenzie needed him. He forced a smile in her direction. "I'll be right outside if you need me."

Reese stepped into the hall and closed the door, careful to keep his emotions in check, trying to work out his next move. *No police.* That left out FBI agent Quinn Taggart, or Detective Heath Ford. But they needed help, needed information. Bran was in Colorado. He had to call Chase. No other choice but to take the risk.

Florence stood in the hall a few feet away, staring worriedly at the bedroom door.

"I need to borrow your cell phone, Flo. They might be tracking mine."

Her eyes flashed to his, fresh worry in them. She pulled her phone out of the pocket of the robe she was wearing and handed it to Reese.

It occurred to him that Chase might see the kidnapping as another way of setting him up. He might think Kenzie was in on the abduction as a way to extort money from him. But the battered, devastated mother he had seen in the bedroom wasn't pulling any kind of con.

Not recognizing the number, Chase didn't pick up. Reese texted him, then dialed again, and his brother answered on the first ring.

"More trouble?" Chase asked.

"Big trouble. Two men broke into Kenzie's town house

and kidnapped her son. They warned her not to call the police or involve you or Bran, but I can't do this alone. And don't tell me this could be part of a setup because if you could see the beating Kenzie took trying to save her boy you would know she would never do anything to hurt him."

Silence fell as Chase assessed the information. "She okay?"

"She refused to go to the hospital. Doc Chandler is with her now."

"Charlie's good. He'll make sure she's all right."

"She must have put up a helluva fight. The room is completely destroyed and not all the blood in there is hers."

Chase grunted. "It's a wonder they didn't kill her."

His stomach knotted. He'd thought the same thing.

"We can't let them know you're involved," Reese said. "We need to meet somewhere safe."

"Where are you?"

"Her town house on Gilbert in Oaklawn."

"How about that little place near Turtle Creek Park? Mel's Diner. It opens at 6:00 a.m."

"That'll work. I'll meet you there."

"Try not to corrupt the crime scene," Chase said. "Maybe we can get some fingerprints, something to help us run these guys down. I'll bring a forensics kit, whatever else we need."

Reese nodded. "Thanks."

"Disable your phone and make sure you aren't tailed."

Advice he didn't need. The hard lessons he'd learned as a member of a teenage gang were buried but not forgotten. What he hadn't told Griff the day of his father's funeral was that Bass Garrett's constant absence and the lack of any parental guidance had resulted in a year in juvenile detention.

That and a deadly car accident not even his brothers

knew about had changed Reese's life. As bad as those days had been, there were occasions like this he was grateful for the skills he had learned.

Dr. Chandler finished examining Kenzie, gave Reese a rundown on her condition, and suggested she return to her own room to lie down. Kenzie refused.

"There's no way I can sleep. Not when my son is in danger." She sounded stronger, only a faint tremor remaining in her voice. "I'm sure Gran has coffee made. It's almost daylight. I'm going to put on some clothes and go downstairs."

Reese felt a rush of admiration. Kenzie was a strong woman. She had fought the men who took her son and she was ready to do it again. She swayed as she rose from the edge of the bed and Reese slid an arm around her waist to steady her.

"You're in pretty rough shape. You sure about this?"

"My son has been kidnapped. Those men are going to call, and when they do, I need to be ready."

He clenched his jaw. They'd taken Griff for a reason. They'd call—sooner or later. He needed to be prepared when they did.

Kenzie leaned against him as he guided her down the hall into her bedroom, helped her sit down on the edge of the bed.

"I've got to go out for a while," he said. "I won't be gone long and I'll explain everything when I get back. Till then, just take it easy, okay?" He leaned down and kissed the corner of her mouth, where he was sure he wouldn't hurt her. Even battered and bruised she looked beautiful. Reese felt a twinge of desire that under the circumstances embarrassed him.

"I don't think they'll call for a while. They'll want to get everything in place. But if they do, just tell them we'll pay

whatever they ask, then we'll figure out our next move. In
the meantime, I'll send your grandmother in to help you
get dressed."

In the hall, he stopped Florence as she approached. "You
need to leave Griff's room the way it is for now. There
might be fingerprints, DNA, other clues that will tell us
who these men are."

"Kenzie said they were both wearing gloves. I guess I
should have mentioned that before."

"It's all right. We still might find something. Take care
of her till I get back. Lock the doors and don't let anyone
in except me."

Florence nodded. Her short silver hair was unkempt and
circles darkened the skin beneath her pale blue eyes. She
looked ten years older than she had the last time he had
seen her.

"We'll get him back," Reese told her, his voice a little
gruff.

Florence said nothing. Reese prayed he could keep his
word.

CHAPTER TWENTY-FIVE

MEL'S DINER LOOKED like an old railroad car, chrome with bright red trim. It sat beneath a cluster of live oaks next to a little stream. As Reese pushed through the door, he spotted Chase's dark gold hair at a booth at the back. Reese made his way down the aisle and slid onto the red vinyl seat across from him.

"How's she doing?" Chase turned over the china mug on Reese's side of the table and motioned for a dark-skinned waitress with corkscrew curls to fill it up.

"Those bastards beat the hell out of her," Reese said as the woman finished pouring and walked away. "She fought them, sliced one of them up pretty good with her house keys. Still wound up with bruised ribs, a split lip, and a black eye. Doc says she's got a slight concussion but it could have been a lot worse."

Just saying it had his hand tightening around the handle of the mug.

"What about mentally? She ready for what's coming?"

"Kenzie's strong. But she's scared, Chase. She loves her son with everything inside her, and she's terrified what might be happening to him."

"She give you a description?"

"It's pretty basic. One my height only heavier. The other short and homely, with curly black hair. She may remember more once the shock wears off."

Chase grabbed a black canvas bag off the seat beside him and set it on top of the Formica table.

Reese took a sip of his coffee, needing it, glad it was black and strong.

"There's a fingerprint kit in here," Chase said. "Bags for any trace evidence you find. If Kenzie cut one of them, see if you can get a blood smear for DNA."

Reese nodded. "Apparently, they were wearing gloves, but there's definitely blood in the room that isn't hers."

"I brought you a couple of throwaway phones. I've already programmed my cell number into each of them. We can stay in touch and not have to worry about them tracking us."

"Good idea." He should have thought of that. At least he had disabled his cell. His worry for Kenzie and Griff had left his mind a little fuzzy, but his focus was returning. Soon he'd be able to proceed with his usual unshakable control.

"There's no way to know where this is headed," Chase said. "I assume you've got your own weapon, but there's an S&W .380 in the bag you might want for backup."

Reese pulled back the navy blue windbreaker he was wearing with jeans and a dark blue T-shirt, flashing the Nighthawk .45 holstered on his belt. "I'm armed, but a spare piece might come in handy."

He was an extremely good shot. This wasn't the first time he was glad he had taken the classes for a concealed-carry permit.

Chase took a drink of his coffee. "I'm going to say this right up front. Even if you give the kidnappers what they want, there's still a chance they'll kill the boy."

His stomach clenched. He knew it. Didn't want to believe it, but he knew it was true. "We have to find them, go in, and get Griff out ourselves."

"That's right. Once they call, you need to draw out the negotiations as long as possible, give us time to find out where they've got him stashed. Make sure you ask for proof of life and make sure they understand the boy can't be harmed in any way or they don't get the money."

Reese nodded. His brother had to know the money would be coming from him. Chase didn't mention it. A child's life was at stake.

"You need to call Tabby," Chase said, taking a drink of his coffee. "Have her set Kenzie's phone up to track the ransom call when it comes in. Once you're back at her house, enable your phone and do the same in case they contact you directly."

He nodded, anxious to get back to the town house. He didn't like leaving Kenzie alone. "Anything else?"

"I'll put the word out. Hawk's back in town. I'll talk to him, see what he can find out. Lissa's in Denver, but I'll bring Jax and Wolfe up to speed, make sure they keep their eyes and ears open." Detectives who worked at The Max. "If there's word on the street of anything going down, we'll know about it."

Reese rose from the booth, tossed money on the table to pay for their coffee and a generous tip. "I'll see what I can find in Griff's bedroom." It would take some time to get the results from the lab Chase used, but the information could be crucial.

"Keep in touch," Chase said, also rising.

Worried about Kenzie, Reese grabbed the canvas satchel and headed out the door.

KENZIE SAT AT the breakfast table, holding a plastic bag of frozen peas against the side of her face. Her cell phone rested on the table in front of her. She had no idea when the men would call. She just prayed that they would. Prayed that wherever Griff was, he was okay and the men hadn't hurt him.

The thought sent a shaft of pain straight into her heart. Griff was just a little boy. By now he was probably awake and terrified. Maybe afraid something horrible had happened to her and Gran. He had no way of knowing.

Silently, she willed him not to fight the men. Just hold on until she could bring him home. A sob caught in her throat but she forced it away. She couldn't afford to break down. She had to be strong for Griff.

"Reese should be back soon," Gran said, pulling Kenzie's mind out of the dark place it had wandered.

She set the bag of frozen peas on the table. "Maybe Reese decided he doesn't want to get any more deeply involved. Maybe he figured we've brought him enough trouble already."

One of her grandmother's silver eyebrows arched up. "You think he'd abandon you?"

Her throat tightened. She couldn't believe she had said the words out loud. "No. Reese wouldn't do that."

"I know he wouldn't. The man has real feelings for you, honey. It's in his eyes every time he looks at you."

Kenzie leaned back in her chair, her body aching, every muscle moving as if she were wrapped in chains. "Even if he cares for me, he's not interested in a long-term relationship. A couple of months, then he'll be looking for someone new and he'll want us to just go back to being colleagues."

Which his other women seemed able to do, but not Kenzie. She was in too deep. Her days as his assistant were limited. But she trusted him to help her get settled somewhere else. The thought sent fresh pain into her already battered heart.

"You don't know that's what's going to happen," her grandmother said.

"I'm his assistant, Gran. I know how he thinks. For heaven's sake, I arranged his dates for him."

Her mind flashed back to Arial Kaplan and the list of beautiful women Reese had dated. None of them had lasted long. At the moment, thoughts of losing Reese where wildly overshadowed by worry for her son. What was happening to Griff? Where had they taken him?

An insistent knock came at the door, and nerves shot up her spine. Would the men come back? Would they be bold enough to knock on her front door?

"It's probably Reese," Gran said, reading her fear. "I'll be sure and check before I let him in."

He appeared in the kitchen a few seconds later, tall and imposing, like a man who could conquer the world. He was carrying a black canvas satchel, which he set on the counter, then he bent down and gently kissed her lips.

"How are you holding up?"

Her throat constricted. "I feel like my world has collapsed around me."

"He's going to be okay. You have to believe that."

She nodded. "I know."

"No phone calls?"

"Not yet."

He unzipped the bag and set a disposable cell phone on the table in front of her. "From now on, any calls you make, use this phone. Yours has been set up to track incoming calls. With any luck we can figure out where they're coming from. Mine's set up the same way."

"Your friend Tabby?"

"That's right. She'll help us any way she can."

"You think they want money?"

"Most likely."

"I don't have the kind of money they're going to want." She glanced up. "Maybe they know about the life insurance policy. The three million dollars coming to Griff."

"It's possible."

"Oh, God, if that's what they're after, it won't work. I went to see Lee's attorney on my lunch hour yesterday. The money belongs to Griff, but not until he turns eighteen. In the meantime, I have to submit a monthly budget. There's no way I can get the full amount even in an emergency."

"Griff's grandfather owns half of Black Sand Oil and Gas. Maybe they figure you can get the money from him."

She pressed her lips together. "I don't know if Arthur would be willing to pay. It would probably depend on how much they want." She looked up at him. "Should I call him? Maybe I should call him."

"You aren't calling Arthur. He'll want to take control and you can't let that happen."

Kenzie raked back her hair. Her hands were shaking. She clamped them between her knees under the table. "I wish they'd call. Why don't they call?"

Reese caught her chin, forcing her to look up at him. "Listen to me, honey. Getting the ransom money isn't a problem. I can take care of it. The problem is that even if we pay them, they might not let Griff go."

She straightened. "What do you mean?"

"We need to find Griff ourselves. That's the only way we can be sure he'll get home safely."

She started shaking her head. "No. No, no, no, no, no. We have to give the kidnappers what they want. Then they'll let Griff go."

Reese just stared at her, those piercing blue eyes willing her to understand. She wanted to put her head down on the table and weep. She wanted to scream out her terror. Instead she steeled herself. "You really believe they might... they might kill him?"

"If he sees their faces, he'll be able to identify them. Even if he doesn't, letting him go poses all sorts of problems."

"What...what are we going to do?"

"Do you trust me?"

With everything but her heart. "You know I do."

"Then we'll work together to bring him home, figure things out as we go. In the meantime, I'm going upstairs, see what kind of evidence those two scumbags left behind."

She stood up from the chair. "I need to do something. Let me help."

Reese reached out and took her hand, wrapped his warm fingers around it. "All right. It's going to take both of us to make this work. Let's go."

CHAPTER TWENTY-SIX

REESE KNEW HOW to use a fingerprint kit. You didn't have brothers, uncles, aunts, and friends all in law enforcement and not know the basics of how things like that worked. But Kenzie was sure the men had worn latex gloves, so their best hope was blood DNA.

His smile turned wolfish. There was blood on her keys and on the carpet, blood on her robe. She'd made them hurt and good for her. Unfortunately, Kenzie had showered off the blood and skin under her fingernails. His jaw hardened. She had fought them hard. Reese wanted to send both the bastards straight to hell.

Instead, he swabbed blood samples and bagged them, bagged the robe Kenzie had been wearing, then they went outside to see what else they could find.

"They must have carried the ladder in through the back gate and left the same way," Kenzie said, her gaze going around the small enclosed patio.

Reese looked up at the window, still open, the curtain fluttering in the faint, moist breeze. "Takes a good-sized ladder to get up that high. They must have been driving a van or a pickup."

"Maybe one of the neighbors saw something."

"Maybe. But until we know what's going on, we can't risk asking too many questions."

"Mrs. Landsdale has frequent insomnia. She's our neighbor across the street. She's a nice old lady but she's nosy. Maybe she saw something that could help us."

He nodded. "Let's finish this and get it off to the lab. If we still haven't gotten a call, maybe you can talk to her."

As soon as they were back in the house, Reese called the office and spoke to his executive VP, Vincent Salvador. Reese told Vince he had a family emergency and was taking time off, asked him to take the helm until further notice.

"Anything I can do to help?" Vince was smart, ambitious, and good at his job.

"Yeah," Reese said. "Keep everything running smoothly. If you have a problem, call my private number." Reese gave him the disposable number. "But it better be important."

"I'll handle things, Reese. Don't worry."

Next he spoke to Louise, told her roughly the same story, gave her the same number, and added that Kenzie would be helping him until the situation was resolved.

"Let me know if there's anything I can do," Louise said.

"I will. Thanks."

Next he called for a messenger to pick up the evidence he had bagged at Kenzie's house. The package was to be delivered to Dallas Diagnostic Services, a private DNA testing lab that Chase used, a business primarily involved in determining paternity.

In this case, once the results were back, they'd be run through DNA databases in search of a match. Nothing they found would stand up in court, and without law enforcement, getting results could be tricky, but Reese figured Chase or Tabby could get it done.

Unfortunately, it was going to take time.

The messenger left with the package but still no word from the kidnappers. Gran was keeping herself busy working in the kitchen. She was diligently making soup and sandwiches, though it was unlikely anyone was in the mood to eat. When the plates sat untouched on the table, she went into her room and closed the door. Reese had a feeling she was crying and didn't want anyone to see.

Kenzie sat stiffly at the kitchen table, Reese across from her, both of them edgy, neither of them good at waiting.

"Why won't they call?" Kenzie asked, pushing up from her chair, pacing over to the window to stare outside at nothing in particular. Her face was pale beneath the darkening bruises, her hair, pulled into a messy ponytail, was still damp from the shower. She looked younger, fragile, and more vulnerable than he had ever seen her. Her heartbreak touched feelings inside him that Reese had believed long dead.

"They haven't called because they're letting us know who's in control," he said. "It's a negotiating tactic." One he had used himself, though the stakes had never been life and death.

He saw Kenzie's lips moving, knew she was saying a prayer for Griff's safety.

"These guys had this well planned," he said when she returned to the table, trembling as she sat back down. He wished there was something he could do, something besides just sit and wait.

"They knew which room was his," he continued. "They brought their own ladder, probably used chloroform or something similar to subdue him. They've thought this through, which means they probably know we're going to want proof of life. They aren't going to do anything to harm Griff until they get what they want. He should be okay until then."

She made a sound in her throat. "Until then? Until we pay them? And then what? Then they kill him?"

The tears glistening in her eyes drove him up from his chair. He pulled her into his arms. "That's not going to happen. We're going to find him and bring him home." He caught her chin, tipped her head up, and softly kissed her. "Do you believe me?"

A resigned sigh whispered out. "I have to believe you. I can't allow myself to imagine the alternative."

The ringing of a cell phone ended the moment and Reese let her go. Kenzie's worried eyes flashed to his. He nodded and she picked up the phone, held it so he could hear.

"This is Kenzie."

"I believe I have something you want." The voice was unrecognizable, completely distorted by some kind of device. It sounded like a steel guitar string turned into words.

"Let me talk to my son," Kenzie said. "I need to know he's all right."

"All in due course," the eerie metallic voice answered. "Is your boyfriend there? I imagine you called him first thing."

He caught a flash of fear in her face, then it was gone. "You didn't tell me not to. You said not to call the police."

"Don't worry, I'm glad he's there. You see, it's going to be up to Reese whether your son lives or dies."

Kenzie swayed. Reese reached out to steady her as he battled the fury sweeping through him. He took the phone from Kenzie's trembling hand, set it down on the table, and hit the speaker button. "How much do you want? Whatever it is, you won't get a dime until we know Griff's all right."

"You don't understand," the metallic voice said. "It isn't your money I want. Money won't buy the return of the boy."

He flicked a glance at Kenzie, read the shock on her face. "What, then? What do you want?"

"I want you to give up the Poseidon. I want you to pull out of the deal."

Icy calm replaced his fury. "That's what this is about? You kidnapped an innocent child to force my company to give up a business venture?"

"It isn't quite as simple as you make it sound. There are ramifications you wouldn't understand, but yes. That's what it will take for the boy to be returned to his mother."

Reese's mind was spinning, going back to what his brother had said. *Give them what they want and they might kill the boy, anyway.* He thought of everything that had happened. The accidents. The helicopter crash leaving two men dead. The mechanic responsible found murdered.

It was a ruthless pattern he couldn't ignore.

"Reese…?" Kenzie's terrified voice snapped him back to the moment.

"I'll abandon our position in the deal if that's what you want, but it's going to take some time. There are papers to file, lawyers on both sides. They'll have to negotiate the terms of the cancellation. Nothing happens quickly when that kind of money is involved. Before I do anything, I need to know the boy is okay. Put him on the phone."

Kenzie moved closer to the table. There was a shuffling sound and Griff's voice came over the line.

"Mom? Is that you?"

"Griff." Tears sprang into her eyes. "Oh, baby, are you okay? They haven't hurt you?"

"I'm locked in a room someplace but I don't know where it is. They wear ski masks whenever they come in. I'm scared, Mom."

"We're going to bring you home, Griff," Reese said firmly. "Just do what they tell you until we can make that happen."

Kenzie leaned toward the phone as if she wanted to get closer to her son. "I love you, sweetheart."

"I love—"

The phone jerked away and the metallic voice resumed. "As you heard, the boy is fine. He'll stay that way as long as you keep your end of the bargain."

"We'll expect to talk to him again before I sign the papers."

"Fine. You've got three days. Get it done by close of business on Thursday or the kid dies."

As soon as the call came to an end, Reese grabbed the disposable and hit Tabby's contact number. "The kidnappers just called. You able to get a trace?"

"I'm on it, but so far it's pinging all over the country. I'll keep after it. It might take a while."

"Keep me posted." The line went dead.

KENZIE COLLAPSED INTO a chair, tears streaking down her cheeks. She wiped them away and looked up at Reese. "I can't believe this is happening. I can't believe they kidnapped Griff to force you to back out of a business deal."

Reese's eyes, a hard, icy blue, lashed into hers. His jaw was set, his features grim. She had never seen such controlled fury in his face.

"They're going to wish they hadn't touched him," Reese said. "They're going to wish they had never set their sights on that oil rig."

"That's what's been going on all along," Kenzie said. "The accidents, the crash. More accidents. Then they killed the mechanic who sabotaged the helicopter."

Reese seemed to force his fury back inside. "Probably to keep him quiet. They've been escalating, growing more and more determined to get what they want."

He looked down at her and she read the guilt he was feeling. "I'm sorry this happened to you," he said. "To Griff. I feel responsible. Derek Stiles tried to convince me to back out of the purchase, but I wouldn't do it. Now these men have your son."

"It's not your fault, Reese. You had no way of knowing this would happen."

"Maybe not, but I'm going to fix it." He reached into his pocket and pulled out the disposable phone, hit a number in the contacts.

"Who are you calling?" she asked.

"My brother."

Renewed fear hit her. The men had warned her not to involve Reese's brothers. But the truth was they couldn't do this alone. They had to trust someone and Reese trusted Chase.

Kenzie grabbed his arm, her fingers digging into his biceps. "I want to hear what he says."

Reese pushed the speaker button, set the phone on the table. "They called," he said when Chase answered. "They want me to back out of the Poseidon deal."

"For Chrissake, that's what this is about? The accidents? The chopper crash? They want the rig that badly?"

"It's more than that, apparently. Whatever's going on, it's linked to something bigger."

For a moment, Chase fell silent. "Lee Haines's murder. It has to be part of this. Linked in some way. Too much going on for his death to just be coincidence."

"I didn't kill him," Kenzie said. "I swear I didn't."

She could hear Chase shifting the phone from one ear to the other. "Reese believed you from the start. Now your innocence is becoming more and more apparent. They've got your boy. Murder and kidnapping? Whatever's going on, it's big. You just need to believe that no matter what happens, we're going to figure it out."

"We're going to get your son back," Reese promised.

"For that to happen," Chase said, "we need to make plans."

Kenzie didn't argue. She trusted the men to help her. But she refused to stand idle. She would do whatever was necessary to help her son.

The brothers talked, laid out some sort of strategy, but Kenzie's mind was on Griff and the terror she had heard in his voice. She imagined him locked in a dark room, men in ski masks standing guard over him.

Her throat closed up. Everything inside her felt icy cold.

When Gran appeared in the kitchen, Kenzie walked over and hugged her. Gran hugged her back, both of them holding on longer than they usually did. With a shaky breath, she explained the phone call, told her grandmother that she had spoken to Griff and that he was all right. Gran nodded dully. She looked haggard and pale, as brittle as a fallen leaf.

"We're going to get him back," Kenzie told her. "Reese and his brother are working on it. He's going to be okay."

Gran said nothing. Kenzie closed her eyes and tried to convince herself to believe it.

CHAPTER TWENTY-SEVEN

REESE PHONED THE Garrett Resources contract lawyers and set the wheels in motion to cancel the deal. But he wasn't ready to contact Sea Titan yet. Giving the kidnappers what they wanted could be a death sentence for Griff.

It was afternoon when Tabby called on Reese's disposable phone. They were back at the kitchen table, Gran holed up in her room.

"I'm with Kenzie," Reese said. "I'm putting you on speaker." Whatever happened, Kenzie deserved to be kept in the loop. Plus, he was sure there was no way in hell she was letting him do this alone. He set the phone on the table.

"A couple of things," Tabby said. "First, I'm still working on that trace. These guys are good. I haven't got anything yet, but I'll keep at it."

"Thanks, Tab."

"Also, I've been looking into Black Sand Oil and Gas."

"And?"

"The company has definitely been slipping in and out of the red. They need a way to infuse money into their coffers or they're going to be in serious trouble."

So his suspicions were confirmed. Black Sand needed the Poseidon. The question was, what lengths would they go to in order to get it? Murder? Kidnapping? Griff was Arthur's grandson, his own flesh and blood. Was he willing to put the boy in danger to save his failing business?

"Anything else?" Reese asked.

"Hawk talked to one of his informants, picked up some info on Arthur Haines. Turns out Lee Haines wasn't a gambler, but his father is. According to Hawk, Arthur keeps it strictly on the down-low, only sits in on the most exclusive card games, but word is he fancies himself a highly skilled player and he isn't interested in anything but very high stakes."

Reese cast a glance at Kenzie, caught a spark of anger in her eyes. She was making the same connection he was. It was looking more and more like Arthur was involved.

"Where does Arthur gamble?" Kenzie asked.

"With a company to run in Dallas," Reese added, "it may not be Vegas. Good chance it's somewhere closer to home."

"I took a look at his credit card receipts," Tabby said. "As a high-dollar player, his hotel stays, food, and alcohol would be comped. They'd give him pretty much anything he wanted. But I found gas receipts along the route to Louisiana."

"Louisiana," Reese repeated. "That connection keeps cropping up."

"It looks like Shreveport was his destination. There are half a dozen casinos along the river."

"Can you tell which club he plays in?" Kenzie asked.

"There are a few miscellaneous charges in the area around the Pot-of-Gold Resort Casino. A Mexican restaurant and a little bakery, both within walking distance. But Sam's Town isn't much farther away. For now that's all I've got."

"Thank you so much, Tabby," Kenzie said.

"Stay safe, you two."

Reese shoved the phone into his pocket. "Hawk thinks Lee was killed by a shooter connected to the Louisiana mob. They run the casinos. Now we find a link between Arthur and the Shreveport clubs."

"I can't believe Arthur would harm his own grandson," Kenzie said.

"If he's gambling in high-stakes games, he might owe the casino more money than he can pay. Those guys don't mess around. A couple of broken legs would be less than nothing to them. Big losses? Could be a whole lot worse."

Kenzie picked up her mug, the coffee long grown cold. Instead of taking a sip, her hands shook as she set the mug back down on the table. Reese wished he could convince her to eat something, but so far she hadn't had a bit of food all day.

His disposable rang again. It was Hawk. Reese hit the speaker button.

"You talk to Tabby?" Hawk asked.

"She called, brought us to speed."

"According to Tab, Black Sand Oil and Gas is in financial trouble. Maybe Arthur owes the casino boys money he can't repay."

"Same thought we had," Reese said. "Could be, getting the company back on track is the only way to generate the capital he needs to repay his debt. Black Sand Oil and Gas never made an offer on the Poseidon, but owning it would be a real game changer."

"Makes sense—which is why I'm on my way to Shreveport. I've got connections there. Might be able to find out if Haines owes money to the mob. If he does, good chance he's involved in everything that's been going on. I'll let you know what I come up with."

"We really appreciate your help," Kenzie said, tears creeping back into her voice.

Hawk's deep voice softened. "Try to stay positive till I get back to you, okay, Kenzie?"

She swallowed. "Okay." The line went dead and she wiped tears from her cheeks. Pushing wearily up from her chair, she paced restlessly around the kitchen. "We need to talk to Arthur. Force him to tell us what's going on."

"It's risky," Reese said. Though he could imagine putting his hands around Arthur's neck and squeezing the information out of him. "If Arthur's involved in the kidnapping, it could put Griff's life in danger."

Kenzie turned, looked him straight in the face. "You're right. We can't trust Arthur. But Lee's dead and now Griff's been kidnapped. Arthur has to be the key. We have to talk to him. We don't have any choice."

Reese scrubbed a hand over his face, feeling the rough growth along his unshaven jaw. He was tired, yet worry kept his adrenaline pumping. Kenzie was right. Griff's time was running out. Arthur could have the answers they so desperately needed. There was no other choice.

"All right," he said. "We'll see what Arthur has to say."

GRIFF CURLED UP on the king-size bed. He was lying on a fancy spread, silky and kind of smooth, but the curtains were drawn, so he couldn't tell the color. He could move around a little, but one of his wrists was handcuffed to the headboard so he couldn't get far.

He didn't remember how he got there. He didn't remember anything about last night. Just going to bed, then waking up in this room. His eyes burned but he had already cried too much when the men weren't around.

He checked the digital clock on the nightstand. Every hour, one of them came in to check on him. They brought him food or took him to the bathroom, which was also fancy, with lots of mirrors and one of those big Jacuzzi tubs.

The men wore black ski masks so he couldn't see their faces, but one of them turned on the TV and set it to the Disney channel, which was better than just staring at the walls. He had a feeling he was in some fancy hotel. He didn't know where, but he hoped it was in Dallas so it wouldn't take long for him to get home.

His throat tightened as fear slithered through him. So far the men were treating him okay, but the short one was constantly bitching about having to babysit a kid. The bigger one was nicer, but he could tell the man didn't really want to be there.

Neither did he. Even school was better than being locked up in some weird place with no idea when they would let him go.

His throat ached. What if they killed him instead of letting him go? It seemed like it would be a lot easier and they wouldn't have to worry about getting caught.

He reminded himself that Reese was with his mom. Reese had said they were going to bring him home. It was like a promise. Reese was rich and smart, and Griff could tell Reese liked his mom a lot. If the men wanted money, he was sure Reese would give it to them.

He hung on to the thought as he waited for another hour to pass. Reese and his mom would give the men what they wanted and they would let him go.

In the meantime, he wasn't a baby. He wasn't going to cry in front of them. No way was he letting them see how scared he really was.

As he glanced at the clock, he thought of his mom and Gran and how much he wanted to go home. One of the men would be coming in soon. He wondered what Reese would do if he'd been kidnapped. It was the first time the thought had actually formed in his head.

He was pretty sure he knew what Reese would do.

Reese would try to escape.

As THE MOTHER of Arthur's grandchild, Kenzie calling Arthur's office wasn't out of the ordinary. She identified herself, and his assistant, a young man named Jonathan O'Neill, informed her that his boss wasn't feeling well and had taken the day off.

"Mr. Haines is home recovering," Jonathan said. "If you need him, you should be able to reach him there."

"I have that number. Thanks for your help." Kenzie wondered if he'd heard the rumors that she was responsible for Arthur's son's murder, though his tone betrayed nothing.

Kenzie turned to Reese, who sat next to her at the kitchen table. "Arthur's at home. His assistant said he took the day off."

"Better for us," Reese said, a hard edge in his voice. "No witnesses."

Kenzie cut him a sharp glance but he was already out of his chair and moving toward the door.

"I need to check around the area before we leave," he said. "Make sure no one is watching. Hang on till I get back."

He returned a few minutes later, certain the town house wasn't under surveillance. They climbed into his shiny black Jag and Kenzie gave him directions to Arthur's mansion on Deloache Avenue in Old Preston Hollow. As they pulled up in front of the house, which resembled a French château, Kenzie noticed a for-sale sign in the yard.

"Looks like Tabby was right," she said. "Arthur loves this place. There's no way he would sell it unless he had to."

"Let's go see what he has to say." Reese got out of the Jag and they walked together up to the porch. As Reese rang the doorbell, Kenzie noticed the drapes were drawn in Arthur's study and several rooms upstairs.

It took a few minutes before the door swung open and Arthur's housekeeper, Betty Vernon, a stout, older woman who had worked for Arthur for years, stood in the opening.

"Hello, Betty," Kenzie said, casting Reese a warning glance. There would be at least one witness to whatever he might have planned. "It's nice to see you again."

Betty looked nervous, her gaze going from Kenzie to Reese and back. She had definitely heard the rumors that Kenzie was responsible for Lee's death.

"I'm afraid Mr. Haines is a little under the weather," the housekeeper said. "In fact, I was just about to leave. Mr. Haines gave me the rest of the day off so he could have the house to himself."

Kenzie reached out and touched the woman's arm. "We need to talk to him, Betty. It's about his grandson."

"It's important," Reese added.

Betty hesitated, clearly uncertain. "All right, I'll just go up and tell him you're here."

"You don't need to worry." Kenzie smiled. "We'll check on him, make sure he's okay." Kenzie hoped her concern appeared at least half-genuine, though she had never been much of an actress. "You go ahead. We promise not to stay too long."

Reese gave her one of his most charming smiles. "Thanks, Betty. Enjoy your day off."

Not surprisingly, Betty returned his smile and stepped back to let them in. They climbed the sweeping staircase, holding on to the ornate wrought-iron banister. Though the sun was shining outside, the gilded wall sconces were burn-

ing, necessary with the bedroom doors all closed, blocking the sunlight. The master suite sat at the end of the hall,
the door also closed. Was Arthur that ill? Or was he hiding
from something? Or someone?

Kenzie rapped lightly. "Arthur? It's Kenzie. I need to
talk to you."

A brief pause ensued. "I'm not feeling well. You'll have
to come back another time."

Instead Reese opened the door and they walked into the
huge master suite. A big four-poster bed dominated the
room, a pair of suitcases sitting open on top of the peach
silk counterpane. One of the bags was full, Arthur busily
throwing clothes into the other.

"Going somewhere?" Reese drawled, the coolness in his
tone disguising the anger Kenzie read in his face.

Arthur just stood there, his gaze darting around the room
in search of a way to escape.

"How can you be part of this, Arthur?" Kenzie's temper rose. "Lee is dead. Griff's been kidnapped. Are you
that desperate?"

Arthur's thick silver eyebrows pulled together in a frown.
His shoulders slumped as if lead bars weighed them down.
He looked ten years older. "What are you talking about?"

"We're not fools," Reese said. "We know you're involved
in this. Tell us where the boy is and you can fly off to wherever the hell you want."

The color drained out of Arthur's face. "The boy? You
don't mean Griff? Are you…are you saying someone has
kidnapped my grandson?"

"You know they have," Kenzie said, fighting to stay in
control. "You wanted the Poseidon. The kidnappers are
demanding Reese back out of the purchase in exchange
for Griff's release."

Arthur swayed. He might have fallen if Reese hadn't gripped his shoulder, dragged him over to a nearby chair, and shoved him down into the seat.

"Mother of God," he said. "I didn't know, I swear. I owe them money. They said they'd get the rig for me so I could pay them back, but…but…"

Reese stared down at him. "But what, Arthur?"

Arthur said nothing.

"By now your housekeeper is gone and we're all alone in this big house," Reese said. "On most occasions, I'm a civilized man, but I can promise you I'll do whatever it takes to wring the information out of you." A muscle worked in his jaw. "I'll do what I have to—and enjoy every minute of it."

Arthur just sat there shaking his head. "I didn't know about Griff until you just told me. They said they'd get me the platform. They never told me how." His eyes, a pale shade of blue, found Kenzie's across the bedroom. "I'm sorry, my dear. So sorry. I'd never do anything to hurt the boy."

"Who's behind this, Arthur?" Reese pressed. "Give me a name."

For a moment, Arthur's eyes slid closed. He dragged in a shaky breath of air.

"Now, Arthur," Reese demanded.

"His name is Sawyer DeMarco. He owns the Pot-of-Gold casino, among other clubs in the state. I owe him several million dollars."

"Keep talking," Reese commanded.

"DeMarco says the Oklahoma casinos are cutting into his profits, costing him a lot of money. He wants to build clubs in northern Louisiana to make up for the losses. He needs me to convince Daniel to help him. He knows if Daniel supports the proposal, the legislature will fall into line and the state will grant him the permits he needs." Arthur looked at Kenzie with regret-filled eyes. "More casinos mean more money. That's what this is all about."

"What does Daniel think of this?" Reese asked. "He willing to go along with DeMarco's plans?"

Arthur shook his head. "I went to see him over the weekend. He refused to even consider DeMarco's request."

Kenzie's throat tightened. She just wanted her son to come home. "Please, Arthur, if you have any idea where they might have taken Griff—"

"I don't know!" He shot up from the chair and his gaze jerked to Reese. "DeMarco killed Lee!" He swallowed. "He murdered my son and now Daniel is also in danger! I'd tell you where the boy is if I knew!"

The anguish etched into his face said it was the truth. Reese flicked a glance at Kenzie. "Let's go." As they stepped out into the hall, he turned back and pinned Arthur with a glare.

"We were never here. You understand that, Haines? Because you open your mouth about any of this and Sawyer DeMarco won't be the only one you'll have to deal with. I can personally guarantee, you won't walk away in one piece."

CHAPTER TWENTY-EIGHT

THEY WERE BACK in the town house, Reese making phone calls to bring everyone up to speed while Kenzie paced back and forth across the kitchen floor and Flo distracted herself at the sink, dicing vegetables for a fresh pot of soup.

In the last twenty minutes, Reese had watched Kenzie go from shocked disbelief, to grief, then anger.

She turned toward him and something shifted in her face and posture, a subtle change as her shoulders squared and her back straightened. The worry lines across her forehead smoothed out, and resolve hardened her expression.

"We've got less than three days. We know who's responsible for all of this. We can be in Shreveport in less than three hours. We need to go there ourselves, see what we can find out."

Admiration stirred emotions Reese couldn't afford to feel. Her courage and strength impressed him more every day. With admiration and respect came arousal, which he firmly tamped down, but it didn't make him want her any less. Even with the bruise on her jaw and the skin turning purple around one eye, she was beautiful. And she was determined. She wouldn't give up until she brought her son home.

Reese had never known a woman like her. Not the tough girls he'd dated when he'd been a teenage delinquent, nor the debutantes after he'd reformed. Certainly not his wife, whom he'd married because he'd wanted a home and family only to discover Sandra's reasons for marrying him were exactly the opposite.

His mother had been a strong, self-reliant woman. Perhaps that was where he had learned to appreciate those qualities.

One thing he knew, Kenzie was different. Special. It made him determined to protect her no matter the cost and even more determined to find her boy and bring him home.

"Hawk is there," she continued to argue doggedly, though so far he hadn't said a word. "By the time we get there, he might have new information. If DeMarco's behind the kidnapping, there's even a chance the men are holding Griff somewhere right in Shreveport. Maybe even the casino."

It was a definite possibility. Of course, the kidnappers could also be in Dallas or anywhere else on the planet.

"I saw the men who took Griff," she reminded him. "If they work for DeMarco, they might be in the club. Maybe I'll recognize one of them."

He scrubbed a hand over his face. "Unfortunately, the kidnappers know who we are. Christ, our photos have been all over the tabloids. They'd spot us the minute we walked through the door."

Kenzie's chin firmed. "So we change our appearance, make ourselves unrecognizable."

Reese just shook his head. It was a crazy idea. Kenzie was battered and bruised and terrified for her son. A half-baked undercover scheme was dangerous at best. "It's not a good idea."

Kenzie pinned him with a glare. "I'll admit my plan isn't perfect, but we can't just sit here and wait for something to happen. If we want to find Griff, we have to *make* something happen." She clamped her hands on her hips. "I'm going to Shreveport—with or without you."

Reese's temper flared. No way was he letting Kenzie put herself in danger. On the other hand, few people had the courage it took to go head-to-head with him. He gave her points for that.

And if the boy was actually there…

A grim look settled over his features. "Fine. Go upstairs and pack your things. As soon as you're ready, we're going to Shreveport."

TAKING ACTION—no matter what it was—filled Kenzie with renewed strength, fresh hope, and iron-hard determination. At worst, she was sure they would glean useful information. Maybe Tabby would call with an exact location for the kidnappers. Maybe it would even turn out to be Shreveport. Or maybe she would spot one of the kidnappers.

She pulled herself together in a way she hadn't been able to since her son had been abducted. She could do this. It was far better than waiting for hours, maybe days till she heard from the men again.

Before they'd gone to see Arthur, Kenzie had applied makeup to cover the bruises on her face. Now she went through her wardrobe, choosing dark blue skinny jeans and a pair of strappy high heels, adding a white midriff top and big hoop earrings. She threw a spare change of clothes into an overnight bag, grabbed a couple of recent photos of Griff, and she was ready.

So was Reese. Now that he had decided to go along with her idea, he settled in to do it right.

They left the town house, headed for Reese's apartment so he could pack what he needed. On the way, he pulled into a costume shop, where he bought Kenzie a curly blond wig.

With Halloween coming up the end of next month, the shop also carried colored contact lenses, mostly red or neon yellow, but also brown, blue, and green. Reese bought a pair in dark brown. They were going as a rural couple, they decided, from Pleasant Hill, a town east of Dallas they both knew.

At Reese's apartment, he disappeared into his bedroom while Kenzie put on the wig. In the beveled mirror in the entry, in her tight jeans and high heels, she looked a little like Olivia Newton-John in the movie version of *Grease*.

She wasn't sure why Reese was taking so long until he appeared in worn jeans, a pair of battered cowboy boots, and a snug-fitting sleeveless black T-shirt. His eyes, no longer an intense shade of blue, were a deep dark brown. He had buzzed his hair short around the back and on the sides. Combined with the rough, day-old beard along his jaw, it gave him an edgy, youthful vibe.

He settled a battered straw cowboy hat on his head and tugged it low on his forehead. The handsome executive was gone, replaced by a Southern country boy. He should have looked ridiculous. Instead he just looked *hot*.

As difficult as things were, as terrified as she was for her son, a wave of heat washed through her that had nothing to do with the near ninety-degree weather outside. It lasted only an instant, followed by a shot of guilt, then fear, when she thought of Griff and what he might be suffering.

Kenzie forced the fear away. If she wanted to find her son, she had to stay focused. Had to keep her mind on the job she was determined to do.

Reese's deep brown eyes ran over her head to foot. "You look amazing. Considering the reason you're dressed that way, I'm glad you can't read my mind."

She almost smiled. "I can't believe you cut your hair."

He shrugged, moving the black T-shirt that hugged his sculpted chest and revealed mouthwatering biceps. "Not a great job," he said, "but it'll grow back, and I don't think anyone's going to recognize either of us now."

"Where'd you get the hat and boots?"

Reese just smiled. "Actually, they're mine. I was wearing them the last time I came back from the ranch." A place he and his brothers owned in the Hill Country, though Reese didn't go there often.

"Maybe when this is over," he said, "the three of us can fly down and I'll teach Griff to ride."

Her throat tightened. Would they really be together that long? "He'd love that."

Serious again, Reese tipped his head toward the door. "We need to get going. We still have to pick up the rental car."

A black Ford F-150 pickup. Top-of-the-line, with a powerful engine and fancy chrome wheels. It fit their image but wouldn't really stand out in a town like Shreveport.

Reese turned to grab the overnight bag he had set on the floor and she caught a glimpse of the falcon's head on his spine, barely visible above the neck of the T-shirt. The tips of the bird's wings appeared on his shoulders. He looked good. Better than good. But not the least like Reese Garrett, CEO of a billion-dollar corporation.

An hour later the pickup was on its way to Shreveport. Tabby still hadn't phoned with a location for the origin of the kidnappers' call, but Kenzie remained hopeful.

And Hawk was there. She hadn't met Jason "Hawk" Maddox, just talked to him on the phone, but Reese trusted him, and Kenzie trusted Reese.

She leaned back in the seat of the truck and said a prayer that they would find her son.

THERE WERE HALF a dozen major casinos in Shreveport, plus Harrah's Louisiana Downs, a casino and racetrack on the east side of town.

ID was required for a hotel room these days and unlike in his criminal youth, Reese no longer had a fake ID. So instead of staying at the casino hotel, he'd made online reservations for a one-bedroom family suite at the Holiday Inn downtown, fairly close to the Pot-of-Gold. He was just turning into the parking lot when his burner phone rang. Chase was on the line.

"What's up?" Reese asked.

"Heath Ford came to see me. He's looking for you. Wasn't able to find you at your office or on your cell." *Big surprise.*

"What's he want?"

"He wants to talk to Kenzie. She's not home and her grandmother isn't coughing up her whereabouts. He figures she's with you. He says if you don't bring her to the station, he's putting a BOLO out on both of you."

"Fuck." Reese pulled into a parking space and turned off the engine, put the phone on speaker.

"My guess," Chase said, "Heath's found out about the life insurance policy—the three million dollars that goes to Griff."

"Christ, more trouble we don't need."

"It was only a matter of time."

"Can you talk to him?" Reese asked. "Get him to hold off a couple of days?" When Kenzie looked at him with those big golden-brown eyes, everything inside him tightened. "Kenzie has family in Dallas. She isn't going to run away."

"Where are you?" Chase asked.

"Shreveport. Hawk's in town. Guy named Sawyer De-Marco is behind the kidnapping. Owns the Pot-of-Gold casino. Arthur Haines owes DeMarco big money." He went on to explain how it all fit together, Lee Haines's murder, the extortion, Daniel Haines, and the gaming permits.

"The mob involvement ratchets up the danger," Chase said. "You should have called."

He'd planned to. Things were moving way too fast. "We're talking now. I'll call if we come up with something new."

"Kenzie's with you?"

"She's here."

"I'll try to get Ford to hold off as long as possible. I'm not far away if you need my help. Both of you stay safe." The line went dead.

"Let's go." Reese checked them into the hotel and they carried their bags and laptops up to room 310. The third-floor suite was high enough for protection and close to the stairs in case they needed to leave without being seen. As soon as they were settled, he phoned Hawk and gave him their location.

"Haven't heard anything more from the kidnappers. Figured if we're here, there's a chance we'd learn something useful."

"Could turn out to be a good idea," Hawk said. "With DeMarco involved, it's possible the kidnappers are holding the boy somewhere in the area."

Kenzie stood so close, Reese could feel the jolt of hope that ran through her body. Sliding an arm around her waist, he eased her against his side and kissed her cheek.

"Anything new on the shooter?" Reese asked. "After talking to Arthur, it's clear Haines's killer must work for the mob, just like you figured."

"I've got a meet with one of my informants later tonight. He's got something. I'll let you know what I find out."

"I'll leave a key for you at the front desk. We're in suite 310. There's a sofa in the living room if you need a place to crash."

"Thanks."

The call ended and Kenzie went to the window to stare off toward the river. Reese tried not to think how sexy she looked in her tight jeans and blond wig. But he was a man and he wanted her. Add to that, this was Kenzie, and everything about her appealed to him.

His groin swelled. It wasn't the right time, but his body didn't seem to care. He forced himself not to glance at the bedroom door.

"Come on," Reese said. "Time to go to work." Setting a hand at her waist, he urged her out of the hotel room.

They made their way into the warm, humid night and loaded into the pickup, Reese stashing his .45 in the glove box. The big Ford engine fired up, and he pulled out of the lot. The casino wasn't far, but they were driving instead of walking, keeping their options open in case they needed to leave in a hurry.

It was dark as he drove down Texas Street toward the river. Up ahead, the Pot-of-Gold sat to the left on the water's edge, the casino shaped like an old-fashioned riverboat docked near the bank. The hotel tower next to it was twenty stories high. The entire property glowed with neon lights—crimson, emerald green, electric blue, all reflected on the surface of the river, creating a stunning rainbow of temptation for hopeful gamblers.

Reese parked the truck, locked the glove box, and helped Kenzie down. As he pushed through the front door of the club, the sound of bells ringing and the whirl of slots greeted them.

"You play blackjack?" Reese asked.

"I like to play, but I haven't gambled much. I can't afford to lose."

Reese took his wallet out of his back pocket. "You can tonight." Taking her hand, he pressed a wad of bills into her palm.

Kenzie shook her head, moving the heavy blond curls that hung past her shoulders. "I can't take your money." She tried to give it back. "If I play, I'll just lose. I've never been a lucky gambler."

Reese inwardly smiled. He'd never known a woman who refused to take his money. "Consider it the cost of information. With two of us gambling, we can cover more ground."

She hesitated a moment more.

"Think of Griff," he said, and her fingers closed around the bills.

"Let's head for the blackjack tables. We'll play together for a while, then split up and you can wander the floor, see if you can spot either of the men who took Griff."

The plan was simple: gather information but don't be obvious about it. He was trusting Kenzie to handle her part of the job. Considering the possible danger and being the controlling bastard he was, it wasn't that easy to do.

Especially not as he sat at the blackjack table next to her and watched the other three men at the table ogling her pretty breasts. The bare midriff and tight jeans showed off her curves, and every time she moved, he caught a glimpse of cleavage. So did the men.

Reese managed to play a few decent hands. Kenzie seemed to get the hang of it fairly quickly and he smiled at her growing stack of chips. The female dealer fanned the cards faceup on the table and left on a break, and a new dealer arrived, a man this time.

"I want to try my luck somewhere else," Kenzie said,

casting Reese a meaningful glance. Time to wander the floor, keep an eye out for the kidnappers while digging for information.

The fat man on the end stool eyed her lewdly. "Don't go, sweet thing. You're my lucky charm. I've been winning ever since you sat down."

Reese's jaw tightened as Kenzie slid off the stool.

"Sorry, big guy." She flashed him a phony smile. "Gotta use the ladies' room." She batted her lashes at the men at the table. "Maybe I'll see y'all later."

Reese pulled her close. "Stay out of trouble, darlin'." The words came out with the soft Texas drawl he'd been born with but long ago discarded.

Kenzie flashed him a smile. "See ya later, honey lamb."

Reese couldn't stop a grin. When Kenzie leaned down and kissed him full on the mouth, he felt a rush of heat that slid all the way into his groin. The woman was his Achilles' heel. He still wasn't sure what to do about it.

He watched the sexy sway of her hips as she walked away, then played a couple more hands, collected his chips, and left the game. He told himself to let her do her job while he did his, but she hadn't been gone ten minutes before he began to worry. What if she spotted one of the kidnappers and the wig wouldn't be enough to keep the guy from recognizing her?

Reese began a calculated wander of the casino floor in search of her.

CHAPTER TWENTY-NINE

KENZIE CIRCLED THE main casino floor, pausing to play blackjack or put money into a slot machine. So far she hadn't seen anyone familiar. She had purposely chosen a seat at a blackjack table with no other players, giving her a chance to chat with the dealer, a heavyset woman in her thirties with bleached blond hair curled under around her shoulders.

Her name was Shirley, divorced and raising two kids.

"I'm a single mother, too," Kenzie said. "I'm raising a son on my own, so I know how tough it can be."

"My ex-husband was a real loser." Shirley slid cards out of a six-deck shoe and pushed them across the green felt table. "Cleaned out the checking account and just disappeared. Me and the kids have been fending for ourselves ever since."

Kenzie picked up the hand she'd been dealt. "I divorced my ex-husband two years ago. Unfortunately, he came back a couple of days ago, beat the crap out of me, and stole our son." Her eyes teared, the story too close to the truth.

Sympathy reflected in Shirley's round face. "You call the police?"

"I did." *Sort of.* Law enforcement in the form of Chase Garrett and the guys at The Max. She wiped a tear from her cheek. "So far they haven't come up with anything."

"So I guess that's how you got the shiner."

Kenzie touched the bruise next to her eye. Every time she moved, her body ached from the fight with Griff's abductor. "I was hoping I'd covered it up."

Shirley grunted. "I've had enough beatings to know a black eye when I see one."

A memory of the short man with the curly black hair flashed in her head, but she pushed it away. "I don't think Ray would hurt our son," she said, making up a name. "But there's no way to know for sure. I'm worried sick about him."

Shirley dealt herself a twenty-one and Kenzie tossed in her cards.

"Men," the dealer growled, raking in Kenzie's chips. "They're all bastards. Some just worse than others."

Kenzie made no reply. A new hand of cards arrived. She tapped for a hit, then turned over her hand when she busted.

"That's the real reason I'm here," she said as the dealer swept in the bet. "My ex is a gambler. He used to come to the Pot-of-Gold all the time. He always lost way more than he ever won, but that didn't stop him. I think he might be here with my son."

Shirley began to shuffle all six decks in the shoe, breaking them into small stacks, shuffling until all of the cards were rearranged, then stacking them back in the box.

She slid Kenzie's cards across the green felt table. "I'm about to take a break. I've got a couple of friends who work in housekeeping. Not many kids in a club like this one. How old is he?"

"Griff's nine."

Shirley nodded. "I'll ask them to put the word out, see if any of the maids have seen a nine-year-old boy upstairs in one of the rooms."

"That would be so great." She placed a new bet as she

took a photo out of her purse, wrote her cell number on the back, and handed it to Shirley.

"That's Griff," she said. "My cell number's on the back."

Shirley slid the photo into the pocket of her black slacks. "I hope I can help. Us gals gotta stick together." She spread her hands on the table and walked away as a new dealer, a young Asian woman, appeared to take her place.

Kenzie played a few more hands, but her winning streak had died long ago and she was anxious to talk to Reese. She winced as she slid down from the stool, turned and spotted him seated at a slot machine a few feet away. In his battered straw hat and snug black T-shirt, he looked like a country girl's dream. She had a hunch he'd been there awhile, keeping watch over her. Kenzie felt a rush of longing.

"I saw you talking to the dealer," he said as she approached. "Find out anything?"

"No, but she's going to ask around, see if any of the housekeeping staff has seen a nine-year-old boy."

Reese's black brows drew into a frown as he punched the spin button on the slot machine.

"I know it's dangerous," Kenzie said, reading the look on his face. "But if there's a chance he's here, we need to know."

Reese's sigh held a hint of resignation. "You're right. Let's wander some more, then we'll head over to the casino steakhouse and get some supper. That'll give us more time in the club. Maybe you'll spot one of the men or your dealer will call."

There was only a very slim chance either of those things would happen, but as they prowled the casino floor, Kenzie clung to the thin shred of hope.

GRIFF STARED AT the clock. It was almost time for one of the men to check on him. He could feel his heart thumping as fast as when he stole third base, and his hands were sweating. For the last hour, he had been planning, figuring a way to escape.

He had heard the men talking, knew their voices, knew the short guy's name was Eddie. The other guy, Nolan, had left a while ago. He'd be back when it was his turn, he'd said. Which meant there was only one of them in there now.

Griff heard footsteps on the carpet, watched the door swing open and Eddie walk in. Both men always wore ski masks but there was just something creepy about Eddie. The guy was a scary dude.

Griff wished he could wait for the other guy, even though he was bigger, but he didn't stand a chance against both of them. He had to go for it now.

"You need to take a piss?" Eddie asked harshly.

Griff managed to nod. "Yeah."

Eddie walked over and unfastened the handcuff. "Behave yourself and I'll leave it off. You can get a good night's sleep. Fuck with me and you'll be sorry."

Griff's mouth dried up. Did he really have the nerve to do this? "Okay," he said.

Sliding off the bed, he hurried into the bathroom, closed the door, and just stood there, dragging in deep breaths of air, trying to work up his courage. There was no window in the bathroom. He had to get past Eddie to escape. The only possible weapon he could find was the toilet brush next to the john.

He grabbed it, walked out by the tub where there was room to swing it a few times and see how it felt in his hands.

"Hurry the fuck up in there."

Griff quietly opened the bathroom door. Eddie stood across the room, facing away from him, his cell phone pressed to his ear. It was now or never.

Slipping silently out of the bathroom, he gripped the toilet brush like a bat and swung it with all his strength. He played Little League ball and he was pretty good. He cracked Eddie in the side of the head so hard the handle on the brush broke and flew off in pieces. The guy staggered sideways and Griff streaked past him out of the bedroom into the living room and raced for the door.

"Son of a bitch!" Eddie's footfalls thundered behind him and icy fear slid into his stomach. Griff fumbled with the lock and jerked the door open but Eddie slammed it shut. Griff whirled and tried to punch him, managed to grab the ski mask and jerk it off over his head.

Rage turned Eddie's expression demonic. He punched Griff hard enough to split his lip, then hit him again. His head spun as he slammed into the wall and slid down onto the carpet.

"Little motherfucker. You're lucky I don't kill you." Eddie kicked him in the ribs, and he groaned.

"Get up and get back in the bedroom."

Griff swayed as he climbed to his feet and Eddie followed, shoving him across the carpet toward the bed. The handcuff locked into place around his wrist. Eddie went over and turned off the TV.

"And you can forget about food or water or anything else until I say so. You got it?"

Griff nodded. His eyes burned. He blinked to fight back tears he refused to let fall.

The last thing he heard was Eddie on his cell phone.

"Kid saw my face," he said. "We need to get rid of him."

The person on the other end of the phone said something Griff couldn't hear.

"Yeah, well, we'll get rid of his mother, too. Tie up loose ends."

Griff's stomach rolled and he clenched his teeth to keep from puking. He'd failed. Even worse, trying to escape might get both him and his mom killed. The tears he'd been fighting spilled over and slid silently down his cheeks.

JASON "HAWK" MADDOX sat at a table in the corner of a bar called the Blue Cypress, a block off the water at Cross Lake. The place wasn't much more than an overgrown shack with a long bar and scattered tables, but it had video poker and pool tables, and the locals loved it.

Jase had been there half an hour, sipping a cold bottle of Red River beer, waiting for a guy named Long Bailey. Long was even taller than Jase, who stood six-four, but unlike his two-hundred-twenty-pound frame, Long was thin as a rake. He was half Cajun, with wrinkled cocoa skin and a toothy smile.

Hawk had known him for years, always paid Long well for whatever information he gleaned, and they'd become friends of a sort.

Long pushed through the front door, spotted Hawk at the back of the room, and sauntered in that direction, pausing at the bar to order himself a bottle of beer and carry it over to the table.

The men shook hands, and Long sat down across from him.

"Sorry I'm late. Wanted ta be sure I got here clean of a tail. These are some bad boys you're a dealin' with, Hawk."

"I gathered that from the dead guy, Lee Haines, they killed in Dallas. You able to get the shooter's name?"

Long nodded. "Name's Jeremy Bolt. One of the best in the biz-ness. Got a reputation of walking away clean, no evidence, nothin'—leastways not unless he left it there apurpose."

"Looks like he set up Haines's ex-wife to take the fall for the murder."

"Sounds like Bolt."

"You know where I can find him?"

Long sipped his beer. "Can't help ya there. Bolt likes to gamble, hangs around the casinos. That's all I know."

"Anything else?" Jase asked, sliding a crisp hundred-dollar bill across the table.

"I get sump-un, I know how to find y'all." Long picked up the money, shoved back his chair, and stood up.

"Good to see you, Long," Hawk said. "Thanks for the help."

Long just nodded and sauntered back toward the door.

Hawk finished his last swallow of beer, set the bottle on the table, and followed. As he walked out into the night, he spotted Long's thin frame beneath an overhead parking light, sauntering toward his old beater Chevy pickup. Just as Long stepped off the porch, Hawk caught a flash of metal in the dense shrubbery at the edge of the lot.

"Gun!" he shouted an instant before a rifle shot echoed in the darkness. Hawk pulled his Kimber semiauto and fired as he raced toward his friend. The shooter was running, sprinting through the leafy foliage, rapidly disappearing out of sight. Hawk pulled off a couple more rounds, but his target was nowhere to be seen and Long was down.

Hawk veered off the path and raced toward his friend, lying in a yellow circle of light, his shirt covered with blood. Long's eyes were open and he was breathing.

"How bad is it?" Hawk asked as he knelt beside him, his Kimber still gripped in one hand.

"Shoulder wound. Be dead if it wasn't for you."

"Just hold on." Hawk shoved the Kimber into the holster at his waist and stripped off the denim shirt he was wearing over it. Wadding it up, he took Long's hand and pressed the shirt against the wound. "Keep pressure on it."

He pulled his cell, hit the button for 9-1-1, and spoke to dispatch, reported the shooting and the urgent need for an ambulance.

"Ambulance ain't gonna help," Long said. "Bolt gonna come for me. I'm already a dead man."

Hawk reached down and gripped Long's hand. "I've got friends. You'll have a guard 24/7 at the hospital. In the meantime, I'm going after Bolt. He's the dead man, not you—and that's a promise. Understood?"

Long managed a single nod and closed his eyes. As Hawk waited for the ambulance, he phoned Chase and asked him to set up protection for Long at the hospital.

"I'll make some calls," Chase said. "Consider it done."

"Thanks. I'll stick around the room till your guy shows up. I've got a few things to do after that, then I'm going hunting."

CHAPTER THIRTY

"THAT'S HAWK," REESE SAID, nodding toward the door.

Kenzie turned to see a tall, good-looking man with thick dark brown hair walking into the Vagabond Steakhouse. Hawk had phoned Reese earlier, said he had news. Just finished with supper, Reese suggested they meet in the bar.

The soft notes of a piano and low amber lighting complemented the dark walls and brown leather chairs. Kenzie sat across from Reese at a quiet corner table, both of them sipping after-dinner drinks, a Kahlua and cream for her, a single malt for Reese.

They drank slowly, mostly pretending. What they were doing was dangerous. They couldn't afford to lose their focus.

Hawk slid into one of the round-backed leather chairs at the table.

"Kenzie, this is Jason Maddox," Reese said.

Hawk just nodded. She had imagined a man who smiled more often, but he wasn't smiling tonight.

"Nice to finally meet you," he said.

"You, too, Hawk. I hope you don't mind me calling you that. Seems like everyone else does."

"Don't mind at all. So many people call me that, half the time I think of myself as Hawk instead of Jason." Maddox turned to Reese, apparently not into small talk.

"What's going on?" Reese asked, picking up on the tense vibes coming off his friend in waves.

"Guy who shot Lee Haines? Name's Jeremy Bolt. He's a hit man, one of the best. Had a little run-in with him tonight. No way to prove it was Bolt, but the guy he shot is one of my informants, Long Bailey. Long came to me with intel on Bolt. Twenty minutes later, someone shot him in the parking lot ."

"Oh, my God." Kenzie's heart jerked. "Is he…is he…?"

"Took a round in the shoulder, but he should be okay. Be dead if I hadn't spotted the gun in time to shout a warning. Chase is setting up protection for him at the hospital until I can track Bolt down."

"Bolt is the man who shot Lee," Kenzie said. "Now he shot your friend. I feel as if this is somehow my fault."

Reese turned toward her, a dark look on his face. "It's not your fault. None of this is your fault. Arthur Haines is responsible for all of this."

She shivered. It was true. Arthur and his gambling. Because of him, all of them were in danger, especially her son.

"Keep in mind, you and Griff aren't his only victims," Reese said. "The selfish bastard managed to get his own son killed."

Her throat tightened. Lee was a rotten husband and father, but he didn't deserve to be murdered.

"Long wasn't able to get Bolt's location," Hawk said, "just that he likes to gamble and hangs around the casinos."

It occurred to her that if they could prove Jeremy Bolt had killed Lee, she would no longer be the primary suspect in his murder.

"I'm going to find him," Hawk said. "Long's a friend. He won't be safe until Bolt's dead."

Reese gripped his friend's heavily muscled shoulder. "We need him alive, Hawk. We need proof he killed Lee Haines. It's the only way to prove Kenzie's innocence."

Hawk's gaze swung back to her, held for several seconds. "Locked up or dead. Either way works for me."

REESE CHECKED HIS WATCH. It was two o'clock in the morning and all of them were exhausted.

"There's nothing more we can do here tonight," he said. "We'll start searching for Griff again in the morning."

Kenzie wearily nodded.

"I'm heading back to the hospital to check on Long," Hawk said. "He should be out of surgery by now."

"That Holiday Inn's just a few blocks away." Reese slid his key card out of his wallet and handed it to Hawk, who tucked it into his pocket.

"I'll see you back in the room," Hawk said.

Maddox headed in one direction and Reese and Kenzie went the other, making their way out of the casino to the parking lot, then heading back to the hotel. Kenzie also had a key card, so they went directly up to their third-floor suite.

Pistol in hand, Reese checked the interior, but the room was empty and nothing seemed out of place.

"Let's get some sleep," he said. "If something breaks tomorrow, we need to be ready."

Kenzie said nothing, just wandered into the bedroom and started stripping off her clothes. There was just enough light coming through the crack in the curtains to illuminate her body in a pretty pink neon glow. She pulled on an oversize cotton T-shirt that shouldn't have been sexy but was and climbed into bed.

Reese sighed into the darkness. No way was he getting any sleep tonight, not when he was already aroused. And with Hawk coming in later, he couldn't sleep on the sofa. He always slept naked, but tonight he left on his boxer briefs, walked over, and slid beneath the covers, staying as far from Kenzie as possible.

"Get some sleep, baby." Turning on his side, he faced away from her and willed himself to fall sleep, not that he actually thought he would.

"Aren't…aren't you going to kiss me good night?"

Reese closed his eyes and clenched his jaw, fighting for control. Rolling onto his back, he stared up at the ceiling. "I'm afraid to, honey. I'm already hard just watching you undress. I've wanted you for days. Even with everything that's happened, that hasn't changed."

"I'm sorry I put you through all of this." Her voice sounded shaky, vulnerable as she rarely let show.

Reese turned toward her. "It's just life, baby. Sometimes it gets in the way." He leaned over and kissed her forehead. "Go to sleep."

An hour passed. Reese was still wide-awake, and though she hadn't made a sound, he knew Kenzie was awake, too.

"You can't sleep, either?" he asked, breaking into the silence.

She sighed. "I wish I could. I feel like my body is plugged into an electric socket. My mind keeps spinning, replaying the scene in Griff's room, seeing it in different ways. Was there something I could have done? Some way I could have saved him?" Her voice broke. "I don't know."

Reese came up over her. "You fought like a wild thing, honey. You did your best against two hardened men. There was nothing more you could have done."

Her eyes glistened. Tears leaked from the corners and rolled down her cheeks. "I need you to kiss me, Reese. I need you to touch me, make love to me. Please, Reese. Make me forget what might be happening to my son."

His chest clamped down. He knew it was selfish, knew

he should find another way to help her sleep, but he wanted her, and tonight she needed him.

He leaned over and kissed her, softly at first, then deeper, drawing it out, nibbling and tasting until he felt her body soften and she started kissing him back with the same urgency he was feeling.

He nipped an earlobe, pressed his mouth against the side of her neck. "I'll make you forget, baby. At least for tonight." He kissed her temple, kissed the pulse throbbing at the base of her throat, moved lower, felt her body heating, responding as she gave herself over to him.

He shoved the covers aside and moved down to her beautiful breasts, suckling and tasting, trailing kisses over her soft skin, ringing her navel. He was hard and aching, his pulse pounding as need burned through him. But tonight was for Kenzie. As much as he wanted her, tonight her needs were more important than his.

He parted her legs and settled himself between them, kissed her abdomen and felt the brush of her fingers in his newly shorn hair. His arousal strengthened. He kissed the inside of her thighs and felt her tremble.

She cried out as he began to pleasure her, driving her up, keeping her on the edge until she was clutching the sheets. Her body quivered and tightened. He knew what to do, how to please her, knew she was near the brink. She cried his name as a powerful climax struck, and slowly she began to spiral down.

Relaxed at last, her eyes drifted closed and Reese kissed her softly. When he started to roll away, she clutched his shoulders.

"No…please, Reese. Not yet. I want to feel you inside me. I need more… I want you to finish this."

He wanted to. Jesus God, he wanted to bury himself so

deep he wouldn't know where one of them stopped and the other started.

"Are you sure?"

When she leaned up and kissed him, he felt the wetness of tears on her cheeks. "Please."

There was no turning back now and Reese didn't want to. His mouth found hers and he savored the sweetness, a taste that belonged to Kenzie alone. He retrieved a condom and began to kiss her again, turned his attention to her pretty breasts, making them pucker and tighten.

He was a skillful lover and he used that skill to drive her toward the edge once more, then he buried himself deep and started moving, setting up a rhythm her body urgently matched. Kenzie arched beneath him, her fingers digging into his shoulders, a cry escaping as she reached release once more.

Reese's iron control shattered. His mind shut down and pure male instinct took over. Thrusting hard and deep, taking what he so desperately needed, his body went rigid as he followed her to a wild, earth-shattering climax.

Long seconds passed. Easing off her, he settled down on the bed beside her and drew her into his arms, unexpected emotion moving through him. He felt as if she belonged to him, as if he had claimed her in some primal way. He had never felt that way about a woman before.

Shaking off the feeling, he rose to deal with the condom and returned to find Kenzie fighting to hold back tears.

Sliding into the bed beside her, Reese smoothed damp hair back from her forehead. "Don't cry, honey. We're going to find him. We're going to bring him home."

Kenzie looked up at him. "Thank you for being here. No matter what happens between us, I'll never forget what you've done."

Reese fell silent. *No matter what happens.* The words

burned a hole in his chest. They hadn't had time to think of the future. Until this was over, there was nothing he could say or do. All that mattered was finding a way to bring Griff safely back to his mother.

Reese vowed he would do whatever it took to see it done.

WHEN KENZIE WALKED into the living room the next morning, she found two men standing at the counter in the open galley kitchen. Hawk was only a little taller than Reese, but he was brawny, with powerful arms, a thick neck and shoulders. Reese's lean muscles were more sculpted, his biceps sinewy instead of bulky, but he was just as solidly built. Both of them were sex personified.

A thought that sent a shaft of guilt straight into her heart, remorse for the pleasure she had received while her son was suffering, terrified he would never get home.

Her throat tightened. She had needed Reese last night and as always he had been there for her. After his intense lovemaking, she had fallen into a bone-deep slumber, free of the constant fear that threatened to paralyze her completely.

He walked toward her, tall and dark and so incredibly handsome. Kenzie glanced away, afraid her feelings for him would show in her eyes.

"I'm glad you got some sleep," he said, a soft note in his voice she rarely heard, along with a hint of male pride. He pressed a mug of hot coffee into her hand. "We've got work to do and you'll be more help now that you're rested."

She flushed at the memory of last night and wrapped her fingers around the mug, grateful for the soothing warmth. "Thanks." She took a sip and was surprised how good it tasted.

"I need to call the office, make sure things are running smoothly. It's time to speak to our attorneys, see how they're coming with the cancellation documents. I also need to call Derek Stiles, let him know what's going on."

Kenzie had talked to Gran earlier. Her grandmother was worried sick but holding it together. Kenzie retrieved her laptop, pulled it out of its case, and set it on the kitchen table.

"I'll call Louise," she said. "She'll be in near-panic mode. I'll see what I can do to help." She could also check her email, see if there was anything important.

Hawk set his coffee mug down on the kitchen counter. "I'm headed back to the hospital. Soon as I'm sure Long's okay, I'll start hunting Bolt."

"Keep in touch," Reese said as he picked up his phone.

"And be careful," Kenzie added.

Hawk smiled. "Same thing my wife said when I talked to her this morning. I reminded her I'm always careful." Hawk grabbed his gear bag and turned back to Kenzie. "Can you shoot?"

"A little too well, according to the police."

He pulled out a .38 revolver and set it on the counter, turned, and headed out the door.

They made the necessary calls and worked on the internet. Over an hour slipped past. Kenzie poured herself another cup of coffee just as her cell phone rang. Her pulse took a leap. Thinking it was the kidnappers, she glanced at Reese, who moved up beside her.

"Hello." Her hands shook as she held the phone so he could hear.

"It's Shirley," the blackjack dealer said in a gruff voice. "Is this Kenzie?"

"It's Kenzie. Hi, Shirley. Did you…did you find him?"

"No way to know if it's your boy, but one of the cleaning gals has a boyfriend who works room service. Said he's been bringing kiddie meals to room 1806. It's a suite on the eighteenth floor. Said he could hear cartoons playing on the TV in the bedroom."

Kenzie's pulse speeded.

"Doesn't mean it's him," Shirley warned. "But the boyfriend said there were two guys in the room and neither of them looked much like a daddy."

"Thank you, Shirley, thank you so much. I really appreciate your help."

"Be good if you kept my name out of it."

"I will, I promise."

Reese phoned Hawk. "We got a lead on the boy. There's a chance they've got him stashed in the casino hotel."

"A suite on the eighteenth floor," Kenzie added in the background. "We have to go find out."

Reese put the phone on speaker.

"Take it easy," Hawk said. "You can't just go storming in with no idea what you're facing. We need intel. We need to be certain the boy's actually in the room and if he is, who's in there with him. If he's there, we need a plan to get him out."

Kenzie's worried glance flashed to Reese. She wanted to rush back to the hotel, pound on the door of the suite, and demand the men let Griff go. But they needed to be prepared or something could go wrong and Griff would be in terrible danger.

"Hawk's right, honey," Reese said. "We have to be prepared."

She nodded. "I know."

"I need to find Bolt," Hawk said. "But your son comes first. I'll head over to the hotel and keep an eye on the room until you get there. What's the number?"

"It's 1806," Reese said.

"Arm yourselves and meet me there."

CHAPTER THIRTY-ONE

REESE WAS ANXIOUS to get back to the casino, but before they left the room, he called Chase.

"Two things," Reese said. "Hawk was right. Haines's killer is a mob hit man named Jeremy Bolt. But maybe you know that already."

"Hawk called, brought me up to speed. What's the second thing?"

"We may have found the boy. It's far from certain, but it's possible they've stashed him in a suite in the Pot-of-Gold casino."

"DeMarco's club?"

"That's right."

"Which means he's got a small army at his disposal. What's your plan?"

"We're working on it. We need more information. Once we confirm Griff's there, we can move forward."

"I'm coming to Shreveport. Four of us are better than three."

"It might be a wasted trip," Reese warned.

"I'll fly. Won't take as long to get there."

"Take the jet. Kenzie can set it up. Flight takes less than an hour."

"Good idea."

"I'll stay in touch, keep you abreast of what's going on."

Thirty minutes later, they were armed and ready, Reese's Nighthawk holstered at his waist beneath a lightweight black nylon windbreaker, plus the .380 ankle gun Chase had loaned him. Kenzie had the .38 revolver Hawk had left her in the purse slung over her shoulder.

But they couldn't act until they had intel. They needed to be sure Griff was there. They needed to know if there was a guard outside the room, needed to size up the exits, figure the best way in and out.

They arrived at the hotel, texted Hawk, and headed for the elevator. Hawk was already upstairs, somewhere out of sight. Reese and Kenzie crowded into the car with a group of tourists, who slowed the ride by getting off at half a dozen different floors.

Finally, the elevator doors slid open on the eighteenth floor, and Reese and Kenzie exited, just a couple heading back to their room to change or take a break from playing the slot machines. Reese wore his boots and straw cowboy hat, Kenzie her curly blond wig.

Reese had tried to talk her into waiting downstairs till they had more information, but he had known from the start the effort would be futile.

"Griff's my son," she'd said. "I have to be there."

Since he'd feel exactly the same if his own son were in danger, he'd grumbled his displeasure and simply nodded.

Suite 1806 loomed ahead. As he walked next to her down what seemed like an endless hallway, the loud, orange-and-pink floral-patterned carpet rubbed on his nerves. No guards outside the door, no one around when they arrived. They moved close enough to the door to listen for noises coming from inside and heard the sound of voices. It didn't take long to figure out it was just the TV.

No one went in, no one came out. At the warning ding of the elevator doors sliding open, Reese pushed Kenzie up against the wall and kissed her. A man and woman engaged in a little harmless foreplay in the hallway outside their room wasn't an unusual sight in a casino.

It didn't bother the older couple walking past, but it bothered the hell out of Reese. He was hard, seriously aroused, and wishing he could drag Kenzie into one of the empty rooms and take her, pound into her until both of them were sated.

Not going to happen. Last night had been an anomaly. Kenzie had been exhausted and desperately in need of sleep. He was glad he'd been able to give her what she needed.

The older couple moved past, turned the corner, and disappeared. No sign of Hawk. Reese knew he was there somewhere but didn't really expect to see him.

Another sound reached them. Along with the guest elevators, a service elevator at the end of the hall rumbled up and down the tower. The doors slid open and Reese caught the rattle of a food cart moving toward them along the passage.

Kenzie moved before he did, pulling his head down and kissing him, hiding both their faces and their motive. Reese felt an immediate rush of heat. He couldn't help wondering if Kenzie felt any of the arousal sweeping through him, caught the little sound she made in her throat, and thought that maybe she did.

The cart passed by, pushed by a waiter in black slacks and a short white jacket who disappeared into a room at the end of the hall.

Reluctantly Reese broke the kiss and took Kenzie's hand. "Come on, baby. There's something we need to do." Pulling her along beside him, he stopped for a moment to text Hawk his plan, then continued toward the service elevator.

"What are we doing?" Kenzie asked as the doors slid open and he pulled her inside.

"I know how we can get into the room. But there's something we need first."

"What's that?"

"A waiter's jacket." Reese pushed the button for the first floor. "And I know just the place to find one."

Twenty minutes later, they were back on the eighteenth floor, Reese dressed in the black slacks and a short white jacket he had bought from a waiter for more than the guy's last paycheck. The pants were a little too short, the jacket a little snug in the shoulders, but it was the best he could do.

His feet were too big for the waiter's shoes, so he still wore his scuffed leather boots. He prayed no one would notice. His hat and the rest of his clothes were out in the pickup, where he had hastily changed while Hawk kept an eye on the suite.

It was almost noon. Reese gripped the handle of the food cart that rattled along in front of him, covered by a white linen cloth and a couple of domed silver platters. The smell of fried chicken and mashed potatoes drifted up from beneath the lids.

As they approached room 1806, Hawk strode around the corner.

"Go," Reese said to Kenzie, who hurried toward Hawk down the passage. Hawk pulled her behind him, and the two of them eased back against the wall out of sight. Nobody spoke as Reese pushed the cart up to the door and pressed the buzzer.

The TV still played softly. Good chance no one was in the room, but they had to know for sure. He knocked again. The sound of footsteps padding across the carpet was unexpected, the first evidence of an actual human being inside.

His pulse kicked up.

"Who is it?"

"Room service."

"You got the wrong room. I didn't order any food."

"You sure? I got two orders of fried chicken and mashed potatoes. Says here it's for suite 1806."

"I told you—I didn't order it."

"Yeah, well, if it wasn't you, I'll have to take it back. I do that, it'll just get thrown out. You might as well have it. No charge."

There was a moment's hesitation. Then the door opened as far as the end of the security chain, enough for the guy inside to look into the hall. The black slacks and short white waiter's jacket did the trick. The chain slid off, the door opened, and a short, muscular man with curly black hair stepped back to let him in.

Reese pushed the cart through the door, jamming it open with the wheels as he pulled the pistol beneath his white jacket. "Hands up! Do it now!"

The guy's hands shot into the air, and Reese moved farther into the room, forcing the guy backward. Behind him, Hawk pushed the cart farther inside and followed, holding the guy at gunpoint while Reese sprinted for the bedroom.

The bedroom door stood open. He panned the room with the pistol in a two-handed grip, checked the bathroom, and returned to the bedroom. The bed was unmade, the covers messy and tossed aside, but the room was empty.

He looked up to see Kenzie running into the bedroom. He holstered his weapon and pulled her into his arms. "He's not here, honey."

Her eyes filled. "Are you sure? That man in there—he... he's one of the kidnappers."

Reese began to search the bedroom, looking for any sign Griff had been there. A single sock lay half exposed at the foot of the bed.

"Is this Griff's?" He held up a white athletic sock way too small for a full-grown man. There were red and blue strips around the calf.

"Oh, God, Reese." Kenzie took the sock and held it

against her heart. "Texas Ranger team colors. Griff wore them to bed sometimes."

Reese looked at Kenzie's grief-stricken face, and rage burned through him. "Griff isn't here now, but he was." He urged her back into the living room, over to where Hawk held the kidnapper at gunpoint.

"He's one of them," Kenzie repeated. "He's the one who hit me."

The scabbed-over scratches on the side of the man's face reminded Reese of what he'd done and how hard Kenzie had fought him. Reese clamped down on a wave of fury that threatened to break through his iron control.

"He's going to wish he'd never touched you." Moving closer, Reese backhanded the guy across the mouth hard enough to split his lip and send a spray of blood into the air. "Where's the boy?"

"Guy's name is Eddie Fontaine," Hawk said. "He's one of DeMarco's enforcers. I made a couple of calls on my way over, asked a friend in law enforcement for the names of the guys in Sawyer DeMarco's inner circle. He gave me names and texted me photos. Eddie's picture was among them. According to my source, he usually works with a guy named Nolan Webb."

Reese grabbed the front of Eddie's shirt, jerked him up on his toes, and slammed him back against the wall. "I asked you a question. Where's the boy?"

Eddie wiped blood off his mouth. "Go fuck yourself."

Reese fought down a fresh rush of fury. He drew back and punched Eddie square in the face. Blood flew and Eddie slammed backward into the wall. Reese grabbed him again, dragged him over to a chair, and heaved him into the seat.

"You're going to tell me where he is." He flexed his

hand, ignored the scraped knuckles, and clenched his fist. "It's just a matter of time."

"And if he gets tired of hitting you," Hawk added, "I'm happy to take his place."

"Where's the boy?" Reese pressed, his expression leaving no doubt what would happen if Eddie failed to answer again. He glanced at Kenzie, who was staring at him as if he were a man she had never seen before.

Reese ignored her. "You really want to do this, Eddie? Because every time I hit you, I'm going to think about the beating you gave Kenzie and feel really good."

Eddie's jaw jutted out. His gaze went from Reese's furious expression to Hawk's hard-edged, determined one.

He let out a defeated sigh. "God's truth, I don't know where the kid is. Nolan and a couple of the boys came and got him early this morning. No idea where they were taking him. Wasn't my problem anymore."

Reese punched him hard enough to knock the chair over backward, spilling Eddie onto the floor, his head hitting with a melon-like thump.

"That one was for Griff." He and Hawk righted the chair and Eddie slumped back in the seat, blood trickling from his nose and mouth.

"So you don't know where they took the boy," Reese drawled, a hint of Texas slipping out.

"No."

"Make a guess," Hawk commanded.

Eddie managed to shrug, but Reese could see the fear in his small black eyes. "On my mother's grave, I don't know. DeMarco owns property all over the state. Could be anywhere."

Reese dug into the front pocket of Eddie's jeans and

pulled out his cell phone. Looking into the contacts, he spotted Nolan's name.

"I'm going to call Nolan and you're going to ask him where he took the boy. Say anything else and I shoot you dead. Understand?"

Eddie nodded.

Reese hit the dial button and put the call on speaker. He pulled out his .45, racked the slide, and pressed it against Eddie's temple.

The phone went straight to voice mail. Reese hit the button again, same thing.

"Phone must be turned off," Hawk said.

Reese tossed the phone to Kenzie, who caught it and tucked it into her purse. While Hawk used zip ties to bind Eddie's hands and feet, Reese went into the bathroom and grabbed a washcloth, returned, and stuffed it into Eddie's mouth. Two zip ties around his head held the gag in place.

Reese and Hawk dragged Eddie into the bedroom closet, dumped him on the floor, and closed the door.

"They won't find him for a while," Hawk said darkly. "With any luck, not until tomorrow."

"Let's hope it's long enough for us to find Griff."

Time was running out. Reese was surprised a call hadn't already come in from DeMarco or one of his henchmen to check on the progress Reese was making with the rig. Knowing he couldn't hold off much longer, this morning Reese had phoned Derek Stiles.

"The lawyers are almost finished with the documents," Reese had said. "Get hold of Sea Titan and give them the bad news. Tell them we want the deal canceled ASAP."

"Are you sure you want to do this now? The troubles with the Poseidon have really been smoothing out. I think we're back on track to get everything done and close the purchase."

"Another problem's come up. Canceling is the only way to solve it. Get everything ready, but don't pull the plug yet, not before closing time on Thursday night. Got it?"

"You're the boss. Whatever you say."

Clearly Derek wasn't happy. But a little boy's life was at stake. Even backing out of the purchase might not bring Griff home.

He thought of what could happen to the boy, and worry churned through him. He forced himself to concentrate. Now was not the time.

Reese stripped off his waiter's jacket, leaving him in his black T-shirt and borrowed black slacks, set a hand at Kenzie's waist, and urged her toward the door. "Let's get out of here."

No one spoke as they left the suite. Not as the three of them rode the elevator down to the bottom floor and crossed the casino on their way to the parking lot.

They stepped out into the afternoon heat but as Hawk set off for his black Yukon, Kenzie stopped Reese with a hand on his chest. "I've seen you fight. I watched you with that big mechanic. But what happened up in that room… that was different."

Reese made no comment.

"There was something in your eyes. I think you could have killed that man."

He didn't deny it. When he was younger, there'd been a time he'd been close to committing murder more than once. That time was over. The man he was then was dead and buried.

Except that he wasn't. Not completely. Kenzie had no idea the lengths he would go to in order to protect the people he cared about, a group that now included Kenzie and her family.

"He hurt you," Reese said. "He won't do it again."

Kenzie fell silent. They crossed to the pickup and Reese helped her inside, then slid behind the wheel and fired the engine, setting the air conditioner in motion.

"I need Eddie's cell phone," he said as they idled in the parking lot.

Kenzie handed over the phone and Reese pulled up Recents and scanned the list. A call had come in at eight o'clock that morning, caller ID *Nolan*.

As the truck continued to run, cooling the interior, Reese phoned Tabby. "I got one of the kidnapper's cell phones, Tab. There's a number on it I need you to ping. Belongs to a guy named Nolan Webb." He explained that they'd found Griff's location, but by the time they'd arrived, the boy had already been moved.

"Webb was with him when the men picked him up. I'm hoping they're still together at the new location." Reese was counting on DeMarco keeping Griff alive at least as long as the Poseidon deal was still in motion.

"You have Webb's number?" Tabby asked.

Reese checked the screen and rattled off the digits, which started with Shreveport area code 318. "I tried calling him earlier, but the call went straight to voice mail. Hoping you can do something that will help."

"I'll get back to you as soon as can. It might take a while."

"Thanks, Tab." Reese tossed Eddie's phone back to Kenzie.

"You think there's a chance this will work?" she asked, tucking the phone back into her purse.

Reese put the truck in gear and drove out of the parking lot. "Let's hope so." Because they didn't have much of anything else. "Maybe we'll get lucky."

But if something didn't break soon, their luck was going to run out.

CHAPTER THIRTY-TWO

GRIFF SHIVERED. There was no air conditioning and though it was burning hot in the tiny, airless bedroom, he couldn't seem to get warm.

His eyes stung with tears. He wasn't in the fancy hotel room anymore, that was for sure. Just a dirty old wooden shack out in the swamp.

At least he was still alive. He thought he'd be dead by now.

Just before the sun came up, Nolan had come into the room with two other men, big burly dudes who liked kids even less than Eddie. They had jerked his arms in front of him and bound his wrists together with plastic ties, tied his ankles, and stuffed a gag in his mouth. They'd put a bag over his head, lifted him off the bed, and dumped him into a laundry cart.

A rattling elevator took him down to the bottom floor. The next thing he knew they were loading him into the trunk of a car and slamming the lid.

He'd started crying then. Last night, he had pulled off Eddie's ski mask and seen his butt-ugly face. When Nolan and his creepy friends showed up, they didn't bother with disguises. He knew what they looked like. That was how Griff knew they were going to kill him.

He'd thought it would be over by now.

Instead, after what seemed forever but was probably less than an hour, the car pulled off the highway onto a bumpy road. He was sweating inside the trunk, so scared he was afraid he would wet his pants and embarrass himself. He could feel the car turning this way and that, following some kind of curvy lane. Out in the boonies, he figured, where they could dump his body and no one would ever find him.

Not even his mom and Reese.

His throat clogged up and his eyes watered.

During the uncomfortable ride, he'd managed to spit out the gag and scrape the hood off his head, but it was too dark in the trunk to see. When the car braked and finally stopped, he took a deep breath and gathered his courage. He wasn't going to die crying and begging. *No way.*

Then the trunk lid popped open and he was surprised to see a dilapidated old cabin among the trees, mostly hidden by tall grass and thick green leafy foliage. The ground was wet and swampy, so the cabin sat on stilts a couple of feet off the ground. Through the undergrowth, he caught a glimpse of water slugging its way along an overgrown creek.

The two men lifted him out of the trunk. They were wearing guns but they didn't shoot him, just carted him into the cabin, into a tiny bedroom that smelled like a dead rat or something worse, and tossed him up onto a saggy bed with a rusted iron headboard and creaky springs.

They didn't say a word. He flinched when Nolan pulled his pocketknife, but the guy just leaned down and cut the plastic tie around his ankles and the one biting into his wrists.

"There's no way out, so you can forget trying to escape. Even if you managed to do it, there's nowhere to go."

Griff glanced around. There were windows, but they were all boarded up. The only way out was the old plank door they'd come in through.

"Sooner or later, someone will show up with food," Nolan said. "You need to take a piss, use the bucket in the corner." Nolan walked out of the room and closed the door, latching it behind him.

So here he was, still alive. He wasn't sure why until he heard Nolan say they needed him for something called *proof of life* during a phone call tomorrow morning. After that, they could get rid of him.

Griff closed his eyes, trying to hold back more tears. He figured they wouldn't want blood all over the cabin, so they would probably take him out into the woods to shoot him.

He thought about what might happen once he was out of the cabin, but instead of getting more scared, his eyes popped open. It was thick and swampy out there. If they didn't tie his hands and feet, maybe he could find a way to escape. He was a Boy Scout. He'd been camping more than once, and he wasn't afraid of snakes. Well, maybe the poisonous kind. But he could figure that out as he went along.

If there was any chance at all, he had to take it.

It was better than just dying.

KENZIE AND REESE went back to the Holiday Inn to wait for Tabby's call. As they approached the door to the room, Kenzie heard voices inside. Hawk would be meeting them there, but there was more than one person speaking.

Reese eased her behind him and pulled his weapon. It surprised her how naturally it fit in his hand, as if he had held it dozens of times. After watching him with Eddie, everything she'd thought she knew about Reese had changed. He was harder, tougher, less forgiving. And yet he was still Reese, the man she was so desperately trying not to love.

Using his key card, Reese turned the knob and shoved

the hotel room door open with his boot, taking a shooting stance as he surged into the living room.

Three semiautos drew down on him at the same time.

"So I guess we're all a little on edge," Chase drawled as he holstered his weapon. Hawk did the same.

Kenzie recognized the third man as Brandon Garrett, youngest of the brothers. Dark brown hair and eyes a lighter shade of blue than Reese's, his complexion less swarthy, though his carved features were no less handsome. Reese had once mentioned that Bran was a highly decorated former special operations soldier.

Seeing the dark look on his face and the hard line of his jaw as he holstered his weapon, Kenzie didn't doubt it.

Then he grinned and the impression vanished as if it were never there.

"I thought you were in Denver," Reese said to him, gripping his brother's shoulder in greeting. "What are you doing here?"

"Chase has been keeping me up to speed. The way things were going, I figured you might need some help. Got to Dallas just in time to catch the jet." He walked over and pulled Kenzie in for a quick, hard hug.

"It's going to be okay," Bran said. "We're all here now. We're going to find your boy."

Her eyes burned. "Thank you for coming," she managed.

Brandon grinned. "Are you kidding? Stay in Denver and let these guys get all the glory?"

The words made her smile, his confidence easing some of the fear inside her. Reese looked at his brothers and emotion surfaced in his face. Then it was gone, his control back in place.

He drew Kenzie against his side, an arm possessively

around her waist. "We're waiting to hear from Tabby. There's a chance she'll come up with Griff's location."

Reese went on to give them the kidnapper's names and explain what had happened at the casino. He told them about Eddie's cell phone and that Tabby was trying to ping Nolan Webb's location.

"We're working on the assumption Webb is still with Griff. If he is, we may be able to find him."

"Amen to that," Chase said.

The men began to mill impatiently around the room, waiting for a call that could still be some time away—if it came at all.

Then Hawk's phone started playing some country tune. He stepped away to take the call, and the lines of his face turned grim. He said something Kenzie didn't catch and the call ended.

Hawk turned toward them. "That was a guy named Buddy Brackett, one of my informants. I put word out it was worth big money for info on Jeremy Bolt. Buddy says he knows where to find him, but I need to get there now."

"Bolt's our ticket to proving Kenzie's innocence," Reese said. "Add to that, he shot your friend. If you've got a line on him—"

"Go," Chase finished, his gaze going to Bran and Reese. "We've got this covered."

The edge of Hawk's hard mouth curved up. "Yeah, looks that way." He turned to Kenzie. "With luck, I'll solve at least one of your problems."

"Be careful," Kenzie said as she had before.

Hawk smiled. "Yes, ma'am." Pulling his pistol, he dropped the magazine to check the load, shoved it in with the flat of his big hand, and slid the gun back into the holster at his waist. "If you need my help, just call."

"We'll keep you posted," Chase said. "You do the same."

As Hawk's big, muscular frame disappeared out the door, Reese kissed the top of Kenzie's head, which didn't go unnoticed by the men. "Anybody else here hungry?" he asked. "Because I'm calling room service and ordering something to eat."

"Count me in," Bran said.

Chase went to the desk and picked up the room service menu. "Pastrami on rye or burgers?"

"Both," Reese said.

Kenzie realized food was just something for the guys to do to break up the waiting.

"I've got an idea." She headed for the kitchen table, where she'd set up her laptop. "Eddie said DeMarco owns property all over the state. County tax parcel records are public. I'll call the Houston office. Rick Holloway and his people in acquisitions deal with that stuff every day. He can get us a list of all the property DeMarco owns."

Reese nodded. "Good idea. Real estate, oil well leases, Rick knows how to find out who they belong to. Even if DeMarco owns the land in the name of a corporation, Rick should be able to track it down."

"It won't give us an exact location," Chase said, "but at least it will narrow the possibilities."

The atmosphere in the room subtly altered as everyone got moving. Hawk was hunting Bolt. Food was on the way, and Kenzie had found a means of tracking down DeMarco's property. If nothing else, it gave them something to do.

When the sandwiches arrived, there was plenty to eat, but the thought of food made Kenzie slightly nauseous. Reese must have noticed her reluctance. Opening one of the burgers, he put it on a plate and brought it over to where she was sat behind the computer.

"I know you're too worried to eat, but you've got to keep up your strength."

"I'm just… I'm not hungry."

"Do it for me." He held the burger out to her, and since she would do just about anything for Reese, she took a bite. It tasted wonderful and she found herself eating more, drinking some of the Coke he had ordered for her—the real thing instead of Diet because he said she needed the sugar. She managed to finish most of the burger and had to admit she felt better now that she had eaten.

The guys were just cleaning up their trash when Reese's disposable rang. He picked it up and checked the screen.

"It's Tabby." He put the phone on speaker and Chase and Bran clustered around the table beside them.

"I got a partial location," Tabby said. "No calls after the one to Eddie's phone this morning but I was able to ping the tower closest to that call. It's in the middle of nowhere, only limited cell service. There's nothing around, no town, not even a gas station."

"That's probably why we couldn't reach him earlier," Reese said.

"He's somewhere with no cell service," Kenzie added.

"Or maybe Webb got antsy," Bran said. "Destroyed the phone so he couldn't be tracked."

"It's a possibility," Tabby agreed. "But he could also be out there somewhere. It's thousands of acres. Without service, there's just no way to track him."

"Send me the cell tower coordinates," Reese said.

"Will do. The tower's located southeast of Shreveport in an area called Loggy Bayou. You can find it on Google Maps. That's all I've got."

"Loggy Bayou. Thanks, Tab."

"I'll keep an eye on Webb's phone. Let you know if his location changes. Good luck." Tabby ended the call.

Kenzie's heart was pumping with hope. There was a chance they'd found some connection that would lead them to Griff.

Reese's intense blue eyes locked on her face. "You get anything from Rick Holloway yet?"

"Let me check." Kenzie hurriedly checked her email, found an incoming message from Rick that included an attachment. "I've got something."

"Now that we know the location of the tower," Bran said. "Maybe Holloway's intel can pinpoint a parcel DeMarco owns in the area."

She clicked the attachment and Reese walked around to look over her shoulder. "Rick sent a list of properties the tax rolls show in DeMarco's name. He's working on the corporate info. He's says it'll take a while."

"Tell him to keep at it," Reese said. "Top priority. And we need tax assessor's maps to locate the parcels he's already found."

"Hold on, I think that's here." Kenzie opened a second attachment, which included county maps of property in Louisiana that matched the parcels owned personally in Sawyer DeMarco's name.

"Anything in Loggy Bayou?" Reese asked.

"Let's see where it is." She went to Google Maps, typed in the location, and the area popped right up. Amazing what satellite imagery could do. "There's a lot of land out there. Tabby was right. It's thousands of acres."

She checked the property maps for anything DeMarco owned southeast of the city near the cell tower, and her hope deflated. "I don't see anything he owns in that direction, nothing in Loggy Bayou."

"Get back to Rick. Tell him to focus specifically in that area. Maybe DeMarco owns something in a corporate name."

She nodded, sent Rick an email, which he answered right away.

I'm on it, his message read.

"What do we do now?" she asked.

Bran grunted. "My least favorite thing."

"We sit back and wait," Chase finished for him.

"Unless Hawk calls and needs help with Jeremy Bolt," Bran said hopefully.

Reese stared at his younger brother and just shook his head.

CHAPTER THIRTY-THREE

REESE HATED WAITING almost as much as Bran. Forty minutes had passed and still no email from Rick. Then Kenzie's cell phone started ringing, not the disposable, which meant it could be DeMarco or one of his men.

Kenzie checked the caller ID. "Blocked," she said, pressing the phone against her ear. Reese moved into position beside her.

"This is Kenzie."

"So I guess you two don't like following orders. Or maybe you just want me to put a gun to the kid's head and pull the trigger."

"No!" Kenzie started shaking. "No, please. Please don't hurt him."

This time the call was not distorted. It was a man's voice, deep and raspy, like a smoker. Reese took the phone out of Kenzie's hand, put it on the table, and hit the speaker button. "I've set everything in motion just the way you wanted. The deal will be canceled before your deadline."

"Why are you in Shreveport? By the way, Eddie says hello."

Reese softly cursed. He glanced at his brothers. Chase looked resigned. Bran's features had gone iron hard.

"I asked you a question," the caller said. "Why are you in Shreveport. Who'd you talk to that led you here?"

Reese considered his answer. Best to stay as close to the

truth as possible. "Griff is Arthur Haines's grandson. We figured Haines had the most to gain from taking over the Poseidon deal. We looked into his background and figured he owned you a big-ass gambling debt, thought maybe you were the guy in charge. Which meant you probably had the boy stashed somewhere in Shreveport. We wanted to be close by when you let him go."

DeMarco chuckled, a grating sound that zipped up Reese's spine. "If you think I'm buying that, you're dumber than I thought. Who's the big guy? I warned you not to drag your brothers into this."

Hawk. "He isn't my brother. Just a friend who owed me a favor."

"All right, here's the deal. Now that you've figured all of this out, you may as well assign your position in the purchase directly over to Black Sand Oil and Gas. And since you decided to play detective, you've got a new deadline. Get this done by ten o'clock tomorrow morning you get the kid back alive. Fuck up again, he's dead."

Kenzie's face went bone white. Reese held on to his control by a thread. "Fine, we'll do whatever you want. But we'll still need proof of life before I sign the final documents."

"One more phone call. You talk to the kid, but if the deal isn't closed, the kid disappears without a trace and there's no way to prove who killed him. You understand?"

Reese's hand tightened into a fist. "I understand."

"You'd better." The line went dead.

Kenzie walked away from the phone into the bedroom and Reese could hear her crying. He wanted to go to her, tell her everything would be okay, but it was a promise he wasn't sure he could keep.

"It was a fairly long phone call," he said. "Think Tabby can trace it?"

"No point," Chase said. "He'll be using a disposable and we already know where to find him."

A penthouse apartment above the casino. It was common knowledge in Shreveport.

"You're right," Reese said. "It's Griff's location we need to find."

"Wherever Griff is," Bran said, "now that DeMarco knows Reese is in Shreveport, he'll beef up security around the boy. We'll be going up against a small army."

Reese flicked a glance toward the bedroom, saw Kenzie wiping tears from her cheeks. He forced himself to focus. He phoned Derek Stiles and told him what he needed him to do. Black Sand Oil and Gas would be substituted in the contract, taking over the purchase of the platform. Whatever it took, the deal needed to be completed by tomorrow morning.

Derek wasn't happy, but he would do what Reese asked.

When the call ended, he checked Kenzie's computer screen, felt a rush when he spotted an email from Rick Holloway.

Did a little digging. Found a piece of property in Loggy Bayou owned by DeMarco's grandfather. Attaching an assessor's plat map and deed description. Hope this is what you're looking for.

Reese clicked open the attachment and examined the map. He felt Kenzie moving up behind him, caught her hand, and gave it a reassuring squeeze. "Holloway found a piece of property in Loggy Bayou owned by DeMarco's granddad. Got to be where they're holding Griff." A least he hoped so.

He felt Kenzie's pulse accelerate, pounding in the delicate bones in her wrist. She looked down at him and managed a worried smile. "Let me in there. I'm better at this than you are."

Reese smiled back and felt a sense of longing. How had this woman managed to get through his carefully guarded defenses?

"You're right," he said. "You *are* better." He slid out of the chair. "Help us figure out what we're up against."

THIS WAS KENZIE'S DOMAIN. Handling problems, coming up with solutions. Blocking thoughts of Griff and the kidnappers' new deadline, she brought up Loggy Bayou, overlaying parcel map details with the angles of meandering streams and what looked like dirt lanes. She cross-checked, using the legal description on the deed, along with longitude and latitude coordinates on Google Earth.

Finally satisfied, she leaned back in her chair. "There it is, guys. I'll bring up the satellite image."

Bran and Chase moved closer to Reese, who looked over her shoulder. The bayou landscape was forbidding, nothing but green for miles, a huge mass of swampy land cut by overgrown creeks, heavy thickets of trees, and dense, leafy foliage.

Kenzie went to Google Earth and zoomed north and south around the property. It was mostly a sea of green.

"Looks like a big bunch of nothing," Bran grumbled.

"The map shows a couple of hunting camps in the area," Kenzie said. "You can see a few buildings here and there, but none of them are near DeMarco's property." She zoomed in as close as possible.

"Looks like there's some kind of structure on the land," Reese said. "But it can't be very big."

"You mentioned hunting camps," Chase said. "Maybe that's what this is."

Bran started nodding. "A cabin the old man built for hunting. Got to be plenty of game out there."

"White tail deer, otter, turkeys, skunks, turtles, bobcats, opossums, and just about everything else," Chase said.

"Not to mention alligators and snakes," Bran added glumly.

Kenzie suppressed a shiver. "How can we be sure that's where they're holding Griff?"

"Nolan's last call came from a tower in Loggy Bayou," Reese said. "No more calls since then. I think he's there."

Chase and Bran exchanged glances. "Then let's go get him," Bran said.

Kenzie's heart raced. The men were going after Griff.

"We need supplies," Chase said.

"Weapons and clothes," Bran agreed. "We brought most of what we need, but going into Loggy Bayou isn't the same as blasting our way through the halls of a casino."

"We've got tactical vests out in the rented SUV," Chase said. "But we need one for Reese and some miscellaneous outdoor gear. And we could use a couple of pairs of night vision goggles."

"We need an army surplus store." Brandon took out his cell and started searching. "Bob's Army/Navy. That ought to do it. Toss me the car keys."

"I'll go with you," Chase offered. "Might see something else we need." He looked at Reese. "Anything special we can pick up for you?"

"I could use a pair of cargo pants. New boots are a bitch, so I'll make do with the ones I'm wearing. Make sure we've got face paint and plenty of ammo."

"Will do," Chase said. He and Bran disappeared out

the door. Reese walked over to the living room window and stood with his back turned, hands braced on his narrow hips.

Kenzie came up behind him. Sliding her arms around his waist, she rested her cheek against his back. "I know we have to do this, but I'm scared. I'm terrified of losing my son, and the prospect of you being shot or killed—"

Reese turned around, wrapped her in his arms, and silenced her with a kiss. In a matter of heartbeats, it went from a way to make her forget the danger to something hot and desperate. Kenzie wanted the kiss to go on and on, wanted the heat building inside her to push away her terrible fear. She whimpered when Reese pulled away.

"We're getting him out," Reese said, keeping her in the circle of his arms. "And none of us are going to die."

Her eyes welled. "You can't know that."

"Not for sure. Nothing is ever completely certain. But my brothers are both former military. Brandon was a special ops soldier, Chase an army MP. They know what they're doing." He tipped her chin up and softly kissed her lips. "And I'm fairly capable myself."

It was true. She knew he practiced martial arts. She had watched him fight the big burly Sea Titan mechanic, seen the way he'd handled Eddie Fontaine. Reese was in amazing physical condition. He was tough and he was smart.

"You never talk about your past," she said. "You know all about me and my family. About Lee. What happened in the past to make you the way you are?"

His features closed up and his mouth thinned. "You mean cold and insensitive? I know that's what people say."

Her heart melted. She reached up and cupped his cheek, felt the roughness along his jaw that made him look like the hard man she knew he could be. "You aren't cold and insensitive. You're the most caring man I've ever met. For some reason you just don't want people to know."

Reese sighed. He sat down on the sofa and drew her down beside him. "I know I keep most people at a distance. It's good business practice, but it's also a defense mechanism. It's just easier not to let anyone in." He flicked her a sideways glance. "No way for me to get hurt."

Kenzie frowned. "But you always seem so self-assured."

"I know I'm good at what I do. I've got plenty of confidence when it comes to business. It's relationships that give me trouble."

She processed that. They were in a relationship of sorts, but it was mostly brought on by circumstance. Or was it? She wanted to believe it was more. "What about me? Surely you aren't afraid I'll hurt you."

His beautiful blue eyes fixed on her face. "You could," he said softly, surprising her.

She glanced away, afraid of the emotion rising inside her. She didn't want to get hurt, either. "You're close to your brothers," she said, shifting the conversation in a safer direction.

"I owe my brothers everything. When I was a kid I was always in trouble. I got involved in a teenage gang, ended up in juvenile detention. If it hadn't been for my mom and my brothers, I'd probably be dead by now."

Her heart squeezed. "They helped you turn your life around."

Something moved across his features. Clearly there was something more. "They were a big part of it. But something else happened. Something I've never told anyone... not even Chase and Bran."

Kenzie stayed silent, afraid if she spoke he wouldn't go

on. But her gaze held his, urging him to continue, telling him without words he could trust her.

His glance cut away. "I'd just gotten out of detention. Still finding my way, I guess. One of my buddies talked me into going out drinking with him. We were both underage, but that just made it more exciting. We got reeling drunk. I knew Billy shouldn't be driving, but he was more afraid of his dad than having an accident. It was three o'clock in the morning when the front tire blew on his dad's Buick sedan. Billy swerved and hit a tree at sixty miles an hour."

"Oh, Reese."

"Billy died instantly. I wasn't even hurt." He sighed into the quiet. "I checked to be sure he was dead, but his head was split open. There was no doubt. I climbed out of the car and walked away. No one ever knew I was even there. Billy's death was the real reason I changed."

Kenzie slid her arms around his neck and held him. "It wasn't your fault."

Reese blew out a shaky breath. "I shouldn't have been drinking in the first place."

"The tire blew. That wasn't your fault."

"I know. I tried to stop Billy from driving, but he wouldn't listen. In the end, his death made me realize how tenuous life can be. And it made me want to make the most out of mine."

Kenzie's thoughts went to the danger he and his brothers would be facing. "I don't want you to get hurt, Reese. Asking you to go in after Griff—"

Reese caught her chin and softly kissed her. "You aren't asking me to do anything. Your son is in danger. We can't bring in the police or they'll kill him. We're doing what we have to do."

Noises sounded in the hall. There was a two-and-one

rap on the door the instant before it opened and Chase and Brandon strode back into the living room. She noticed they both kept their gun hands free, and each carried a big plastic bag he tossed up onto the sofa.

"Let's get dressed and do a little recon," Chase said. "DeMarco's given you until tomorrow morning. We need to have Griff safe before the deadline."

Reese started pulling stuff out of the bag. He dragged out a pair of camouflage cargo pants and a long-sleeved camo T-shirt. Kenzie didn't have to be a soldier to know the swamp wasn't a friendly place for exposed skin.

He grabbed a couple more items and disappeared into the bedroom. Kenzie followed, giving Chase and Bran privacy to change. She was wearing her skinny jeans with a navy blue T-shirt and black sneakers, her hair pulled into a ponytail. It would have to do.

When she and Reese returned to the living room, Kenzie stood transfixed as she watched the men in action, moving with the same ease of purpose she had noticed in Reese.

Brandon crossed to the hall closet, reached in, and pulled out a couple of canvas bags the men had apparently brought with them. One was big and bulky, another long and narrow with a zipper that ran full length. Bran tossed it up onto the sofa, unzipped it, and pulled out an assault rifle.

"AR-15," he announced. "Converted to full auto." He handed it to Chase, then pulled what looked like another assault rifle out of the bag. "Pneu-Dart G2 X-Caliber. Gas-based remote delivery projector. Otherwise known as a tranq gun."

His blue eyes flashed to Chase, then to her. "I figured my brother wouldn't be happy if I just ended the bastards."

Chase's mouth edged up. "No. At least not unless we have to."

Bran turned to Reese. "You're the man when it comes to handguns. You're carrying your Nighthawk, right?"

"That's right." Reese's mouth curved into a sexy smile. "You got a good look at it when I walked in this morning."

Brandon grinned.

Reese slid the gun out of the holster at his waist, checked the load, then slid it back in with an ease Kenzie still found unsettling. "Where did you learn to handle a gun the way you do?"

"High school. Not that I'm proud of it."

"Maybe not," Chase said. "But at fifty feet, you're the best pistol shot I've ever seen." Chase fetched a canvas bag from behind the sofa, pulled it open, and tossed Reese a second weapon.

"Beretta nine mil," he said. "That .380 I loaned you makes a good ankle gun, but for what we're getting into, you need a backup weapon with some muscle."

Reese nodded. "Thanks." He checked the pistol, made sure the magazine was full, then shoved it into his waistband at the back of his cargo pants.

Chase held up a square black plastic case. "Satellite phone." He smiled. "'Don't leave home without one,'" he said, parroting the American Express ad. "And last but not least, there's a little toy out in the SUV your brother was determined to buy."

"What is it?" Reese asked.

Bran flashed a cocky smile. "A drone."

Reese actually grinned. "I like it."

"All right, fine," Chase said, sounding like a typical big brother. "If you two are ready to try out your new toys, let's go see what's out there."

CHAPTER THIRTY-FOUR

THE AFTERNOON WAS nearly gone when Reese drove out of Shreveport in the black Ford pickup, Kenzie riding nervously in the seat beside him. Chase drove in the SUV with Brandon. Better to have two vehicles in case something went wrong.

Which undoubtedly it would. That was just the way the world worked. They had discussed asking Hawk to help, but his sights were set on Jeremy Bolt. They needed him to bring Bolt in, needed a way to prove Bolt had killed Lee Haines.

None of them wanted to return Griff to a home where his mother faced years in prison.

As they left the city, Reese turned onto US 71 and drove southeast about forty minutes toward the area known as Loggy Bayou. They passed through rural farm country before turning down a dirt road leading east into the bayou.

Reese glanced over at Kenzie. With no cell service, she was using maps she had previously downloaded to find the safest route in and out, giving him directions along a lane on the opposite side of the stream that wound through the woods beside the cabin. Which meant they could travel the road without running into one of the kidnappers heading back to the city. Plus the terrain along the riverbank was highly overgrown, shielding the vehicles as they got closer to their objective.

Behind him, Chase had dropped back a little so one vehicle could provide cover for the other. Reese wished Kenzie had stayed at the hotel, but he hadn't even suggested it.

No way was she staying behind while he went after her son. "I can help you," she'd said. "I can do what I do best—take care of the detail work. That will free all of you up to go in after Griff."

She was right. The maps she was using were invaluable. She was also monitoring the sat phone Brandon had brought with him. Once they got there, they would be using handheld two-way radios, which Kenzie would monitor to make sure everyone stayed connected. Though Reese worried about her, she was a real asset. He had to stay focused on that.

"The cabin's about half a mile ahead," Kenzie said.

Reese slowed as she relayed the message to Chase. At a quarter of a mile, he pulled off the dirt road and backed into a thick copse of trees while Chase backed the SUV out of sight a little farther away.

Reese spotted them walking toward the pickup, gear bags slung over their shoulders. Bran was carrying the drone, which he set up on the tailgate of the truck.

"DJI Mavic 2 Pro." Bran held the small device in the palm of his hand. "This one works with a 1000TVL mini FPV camera. We can control it from the pilot's viewpoint and at the same time record the surround as a video file."

"So I guess you don't need cell service or Wi-Fi to run the thing," Reese said.

Bran just grinned. "That's the beauty of it. Kenzie's already downloaded the files necessary to view the drone's progress on her iPad."

"And it's nice and quiet," Chase added. "With any luck, it'll give us the intel we need and won't be spotted."

"We'll make a run with the drone," Bran said. "Then spread out and walk the creek, traverse the area, and find the best place to cross. We'll send the drone out one more time before it gets dark. Once we've got the intel, we map out a plan. Soon as we have what we need, we go in."

Now that the mission was actually under way, Bran had taken charge. He was a former Delta Operator, one of the most elite soldiers in the world. Going into a hostage situation was something he had done a dozen times, probably a lot more. Reese was grateful to have his brother along.

Bran launched the drone, then steered it in the direction of the cabin, careful to keep it at a high altitude. Reese watched the progress on the iPad screen as the drone flew over the clearing in front of the cabin. Three cars appeared, parked haphazardly along the creek—an old Jeep Wrangler, a dirty four-door sedan, and an older Chevy SUV.

The drone flight continued, circling the swampy area from high above. The first man who came into view was rangy, with a mustache and dark brown hair. The second guy was average height, with a stocky build and wearing wraparound sunglasses, his hair hidden beneath a Dallas Cowboys ball cap. The third guy was big and muscular, with mocha skin and long black hair pulled back in a ponytail at the nape of his neck.

None of them looked like they belonged in a suit. This was the hired muscle. They probably only worked for De-Marco when he needed extra manpower. Which meant his regular crew was likely inside the cabin.

Not good.

"Griff has to be inside," Reese said. "These three guys wouldn't be here unless DeMarco was expecting trouble."

"Hard to tell exactly how many we're dealing with," Bran said.

"Nolan Webb's got to be in with Griff," Chase said. "Tabby's keeping an eye on his cell number. She'd call if she'd pinged him in a different location."

"Could be more than just him," Reese said.

Chase shifted his attention back to the screen. "We'll know more after our second drone run. Be interesting to see if anyone leaves or anyone new shows up."

"Roger that," Bran said.

Reese, who wasn't very good at waiting, clenched his jaw. Every instinct for trouble that he had honed in his bad-boy days said Griff was in the cabin. He wanted to go in and bring him out.

But his brothers were right. They needed as much information as they could get before they acted. As CEO of a company involved in hundred-million-dollar business deals, he understood that better than most.

"Let's gear up and check out the area," Bran said. "Reese, you head north. Chase, you go south. We need to find the best place to cross." He eyed his two brothers. "I'm not carrying any anti-venom, so try not to get bitten by a snake."

KENZIE SAT DOWN to wait on a fallen log beneath the high branches of a yellow pine tree. She had spotted an abandoned campsite, a circle of downed logs around a long-dead firepit, and the men had decided to use it as their base of operations. The drone had safely landed to conserve the battery. It would fly once more when the men returned.

Kenzie prayed her son was actually inside the cabin and that Reese and his brothers would be able to bring him out safely. At the thought of Griff being hurt or killed, cold fear slid through her. *Or Reese.* Dear God, what if she lost them both?

Kenzie clamped down on the notion. The men were risking their lives to save her son. She had to believe in them, have faith that they would succeed.

Half an hour slipped past. She had no idea what was happening in the cabin. Or the swamp. The .38 revolver she'd carried in her purse now rode in a holster at her waist. Reese wanted her armed in case of trouble.

Kenzie agreed. When the men went in after Griff, they might need help. She intended to be ready.

A faint noise sounded and she rose as Chase walked back into the makeshift camp, his heavy leather boots sloshing through a puddle as he came toward her. Because this was only a reconnaissance mission, they had maintained radio silence. After the rescue mission was under way, she would be able to monitor communications and know what was going on.

Only a few seconds had passed when the bushes parted and Brandon appeared like a ghost out of thin air. He and Chase glanced around the camp.

"Any sign of Reese?" Chase asked.

Unease slid through her. "No."

"He's only a few minutes late," Chase said, checking his heavy wristwatch. "Not time to worry yet."

"I'll go look for him." Bran disappeared back into the foliage and Kenzie's nerves inched up.

"You don't think something's happened to him?"

Chase shook his head, dark blond hair glinting in the late afternoon sunlight. "He's determined to bring the boy out. My guess, he's doing a little extra recon. Reese never was good at following orders."

No, he was used to being in charge, doing things his own way. Kenzie fought the urge to follow Brandon in search of him, but she wasn't a soldier and her movements might be spotted by the men on the other side of the creek.

Fifteen minutes later, Reese walked into the camp, followed by Bran.

"What happened out there?" Chase asked.

"I got close enough to the cabin to see at least two men inside."

Chase grunted. "Next time stick with the plan. We need to work together if we're going to pull this off."

Reese cast him a mutinous glare. "I saw an opening and took it." Then he sighed. "You're right. Sorry."

Bran slapped him on the shoulder. "You don't win battles by second-guessing yourself. You followed your instincts and brought us some valuable intel. Now we know we're facing at least five men." He grinned. "Just makes it a little more interesting is all."

Kenzie almost smiled. She liked Reese's brothers. And she trusted them—the way she trusted Reese.

She looked over to see him walking toward her, his familiar long strides filled with purpose. Still, it was hard to imagine the man dressed head to foot in camo, his lean face covered in black grease paint, was Reese, CEO of a powerful Dallas corporation.

Or Reese the tender lover. This man was a woman's secret fantasy, a true alpha male. It occurred to her that if things were different and Griff were safely home, she'd like to get to know this Reese, the formidable man he kept locked away.

Arousal slipped through her. What sort of lover would he be if his deeper passions were unleashed?

Kenzie shook the untimely thought away.

"Let's review," Bran said, pulling her back to the moment as he seated himself on one of the logs, clearly in military mode. They all sat down around the empty campfire, Kenzie next to Reese.

"Sit rep," Bran prodded. "Reese?"

"From what I could tell, it looks like the road coming in from the north dead-ends at the cabin. That's the way they came in and their only way out."

"He's right," Chase agreed. "No exit south of the cabin. They can cross the creek on foot and reach the road on our side, but that's it."

"So we've got them bottled up in there," Bran said.

That's one way to look at it, Kenzie thought.

"Anyone find a decent crossing?" Chase asked. "The way I went in isn't any good. Too many hazards."

"Same to the north," Reese agreed.

"I found a route," Bran said. "Had to clear some of the brush and obstacles, but I left it marked with yellow neon reflective tape. It'll work as a way to bring Griff out."

Kenzie's heart began to pound. It wouldn't be long now.

"What about your sniper's nest?" Reese asked Bran.

"Already in place. Tranq gun's loaded and waiting on-site." Bran rose from the log. "Let's fire up the drone and make another pass over the cabin before it's too dark. We can check things out, make sure everything looks good. There's a crescent moon tonight, which will help or hurt, depending on how the situation unfolds. As soon as it's full dark, we go in."

GRIFF SAT ON the edge of the saggy iron bed. The slivers of sunlight that dimly lit the room through cracks in the walls were fading. It was almost dark outside, the evening filled with eerie swamp sounds.

Fear crawled through him. Time was running out. Tomorrow morning, as soon as the call the men were waiting for came in, they were going to kill him.

His stomach churned. Any minute they would be bringing something for supper. For once in his life, Griff wasn't hungry.

He had to find a way to escape. He couldn't afford to wait.

His mind spun with ideas, stuff he'd seen in the movies or read in fantasy novels. But he didn't have a weapon and he didn't really think any of the make-believe stuff would work.

In the end, he decided the best he could do was be ready if an opportunity came along. It worried him that even if he got away, the men might do what they said and come after him and his mom.

Griff closed his eyes and took a deep breath. He would think about that when the time came.

In the meantime, he would be ready.

CHAPTER THIRTY-FIVE

"TWO MINUTES," BRAN SAID. "Check your gear one last time, then we move out."

Reese was more than ready. Had been for what seemed hours. It was heading toward full dark, the night sounds of the bayou beginning to come alive. A coyote howled. Insects rubbed their wings, setting up an eerie rhythm. A bobcat growled in the underbrush not far away.

Reese strode toward Kenzie, reached out, and caught her shoulders. "You going to be okay?"

She managed a passable smile. "I'm terrified, but I'll be all right."

"I know you will." Leaning down, he kissed her, taking it as deep as time allowed. "You've got a radio. You'll be able to hear what we're saying. The keys are in the pickup. If anything goes wrong, take the truck and get out of here."

"I'm not going anywhere without you and Griff, so don't waste your breath." Reese opened his mouth to protest, but Kenzie pressed her fingers over his lips. "Don't argue. Just kiss me one last time and get going."

Reese complied, lingering a few seconds longer than he should have, earning a nudge from Chase.

"Time to go."

"Stay safe," Kenzie called after them.

Reese draped a pair of night-vision binoculars around his neck and adjusted the earbud that connected him to the radio he was carrying. Bran headed in one direction, Reese and Chase in another. The plan was for Brandon to use the tranq gun to take out the men guarding the perimeter. Once they were down, Reese and Chase would drag the men's unconscious bodies out of sight. But it could get dicey.

Whatever it took, they would do what they had to. The men were kidnappers, hired killers. A child's life was at stake. They didn't have a lot of choices.

Reese followed Chase along the path Bran had scouted and marked with yellow glow-in-the-dark tape. The trail sloped onto the bank of the creek. Reese's cowboy boots sank ankle-deep in the mud, then a few more steps and he was sloshing through the water, a slowly moving stream about three feet deep. A beaver slid into the lazy current on his right and suddenly a deer bolted on his left, bounding noisily through the low-hanging branches toward safety.

At the sound, Chase went still in the water ahead of him, waiting, giving the silence a chance to return, followed by the forest sounds that had muffled their movements.

Something cut through the water between them. Reese tensed as he watched a big-bodied snake swimming toward him, head raised just above the surface. Hard to tell what flavor it was, but a poisonous bite out here could be deadly. Reese silently pulled an eight-inch folding knife out of his pocket and flipped the blade open.

The snake kept closing but turned away at the last moment and swam on past, missing him by inches. Reese breathed a sigh of relief. He started moving again, quietly slogging his way toward the opposite shore. Taking a moment to dump the water out of his boots, he dragged them back on and caught up with Chase.

Neither spoke. Chase left the trail and began circling toward the south while Reese headed north. The drone had revealed two doors into the cabin. Chase would go in through the back, Reese the front. Bran would go in through an attic window the drone had spotted, accessible from the roof.

But first they had to deal with the men patrolling the grounds outside.

Careful to stay in the shadows, Reese made his way through the heavy foliage to the north. Using the night-vision binoculars, he scanned the area. The rangy guy with the mustache stood not far away near the bank of the creek. On the other side of the clearing, the guy with the stocky build in the ball cap leaned against the Jeep, smoking a cigarette. The big guy with the ponytail was nowhere in sight, likely behind the cabin. Chase would have him spotted.

The guy with the mustache was farthest from the cabin, probably the easiest target. Bran would take him out first. Reese moved into position behind him, heard his brother's muted shot echo softly through the bayou, and the man went down.

Reese hurried toward him. He was still awake but groggy, his eyes slowly closing as he lost consciousness. After hauling him into the bushes out of sight, satisfied he was no longer a threat, Reese headed for the guy smoking in the shadows next to the Jeep.

A muffled shot sounded from high in the trees. The dart took the stocky man in the side of the neck. A hissing sound came from his throat, the guy pawed at the dart, then slid soundlessly to the ground.

Reese stepped out of the foliage, grabbed the man's limp arms, and dragged him out of sight behind the Jeep.

One to go.

The radio crackled to life. Reese tensed when Kenzie's voice came over his earpiece. "Chase's radio isn't working right. He hasn't been able to reach you or Bran. He says the third perimeter guard went inside the cabin."

Which, from his position, Bran would have seen. Since he hadn't communicated the info, his radio wasn't working, either.

Fuck. "Roger that. Can you reach Bran?"

"I think so. Hang on." Kenzie came back on the radio a few seconds later. "He says it's time for plan B. He says to tell you he's heading into position."

"Got it. Thanks, baby."

Plan B was simple. Everything that could be done at this point had been executed. The third man was out of sight inside. They needed to move in. Bran would be going into the cabin through the attic window. Once he was in position, Chase would breach the back door while Reese went in through the front.

But they couldn't move until Bran had located Griff's whereabouts inside the cabin. And without direct radio contact, everything was going to be more difficult.

He thumbed the mic and spoke to Kenzie. "Make sure Bran and Chase both know you'll be relaying communications."

"Roger that, already done."

Reese smiled. The lady was amazing. He started moving into position, getting closer to the front door, careful not to be seen. Chase would be doing the same while Bran roped up to the attic window from a blind spot on the west side of the cabin.

"Bran's on the roof," Kenzie said, relaying his message. "The window wasn't a problem. He's going inside."

The radio went silent. Time dragged. The porch light went on, giving Reese a jolt, but no one came out. Through the dirty front window, he could see shapes moving around inside the cabin.

"Griff's alone in the bedroom," Kenzie relayed. "Three targets inside. No time to lose. Move into position."

Gripping his .45 two-handed, Reese moved closer. He was twenty yards from the front door, slipping through the shadows, closing the distance when he heard Kenzie's frantic voice through his earpiece.

"Plan C! Plan C!" No way she knew what it was, and he didn't have time to explain. Plan C meant A and B had turned into a serious clusterfuck and each man was on his own, his objective to bring Griff out safely at any cost.

When the front door burst open and Griff bolted out onto the porch, Reese understood. He drew down on the man chasing the boy, but it was too late. A thick arm wrapped around Griff's neck and hauled him backward against a wide barrel chest. A semiauto pressed against the side of Griff's head.

"Get back in the house, you little shit!" It was the big guy with the ponytail.

Reese stepped out of the shadows, his pistol aimed at the gunman's head. "Let him go."

"Reese!" Griff clawed wildly at the man's beefy arm.

"Easy, Griff. Stand down. Everything's going to be okay."

Trusting him, the boy stopped fighting. Shots rang out inside the cabin. Reese figured Bran and Chase had taken care of the other two men.

"Drop the gun or I kill the kid!" the gunman demanded, his arm tightening around Griff's neck as he dragged him across the porch.

"There are three of us," Reese said calmly. "Your friends

are either dead or out of commission. You aren't getting out of here alive unless you let the boy go."

The gunman shook his head, his low ponytail sliding back and forth across his broad back. "No way. The kid's my insurance. He goes with me. When I get to the first gas station, I'll let him go."

"I don't want to go with him, Reese!"

Reese held steady, his hands firm around the pistol grip, the barrel aimed at the gunman's head. "The boy stays here. You let him go and you live. Otherwise, you're a dead man."

Instead, keeping low, using Griff as a shield, the guy forced the boy down the steps, off the raised porch, and began hauling him across the clearing toward the Jeep. Bran and Chase both appeared in the doorway, pistols aimed toward the gunman.

"Let him go," Reese called. "You're outmanned and outgunned. No way you're getting out of here with the boy."

The gunman's hard mouth slanted up on one side. "You've got the men but I've got the kid. That gives me leverage. I take the kid with me, he'll be okay. You try to shoot it out, I'll kill him."

Reese steadied his pistol. He could make the shot—as long as nothing went wrong and he didn't let his emotions get in the way. "I'm done asking."

"Don't be a fool! You shoot, you'll hit the kid!"

"Last chance." Reese tracked the pair with his weapon, sighting down the barrel.

He didn't want to kill the guy. He'd been involved in enough bad stuff in his youth, done everything in his power to leave his past behind. But the gunman had almost reached the Jeep and letting him leave with Griff was not an option. And second by second as the distance increased, the shot was getting tougher.

"Stay cool, Griff," Reese calmly instructed, holding the pistol steady. The boy went stock-still, and Reese pulled the trigger. The gunman's head exploded, and Griff bolted, running full speed toward Reese. Reese caught him hard against him and hung on tight.

"You're okay. It's over. You're safe." He smoothed the boy's reddish hair back from his forehead. "Your mom's here. She's waiting for you on the other side of the creek. Everything's going to be okay."

Griff looked up at him, tears in his eyes. "Thanks for coming to get me."

Reese just nodded, his throat too tight to speak. Pulling the radio out of his pocket, he thumbed the mic. "Griff's out and we're all safe." Kenzie's soft sob came through the speaker as he handed the radio to her son.

"Mom?"

"Griff! Oh, God, Griff, are you okay? They didn't hurt you?"

"Reese came to get me. I'm okay."

"I'm here waiting for you. I love you, sweetheart."

"I love you, too, Mom."

Griff handed back the radio as Bran and Chase walked up.

"You must be Griff," Chase said. "Nice to meet you. This is Brandon. We're Reese's brothers."

Griff's eyes teared. He wiped them with the back of his hand. "Thanks for helping Reese."

Bran smiled. "That's what brothers do."

Reese glanced back at the cabin. "What's the situation inside?"

Chase's gaze followed Reese's. "Location's secure. Two men wounded. Nothing fatal. Unless you want to bring the police into this, we can call for an ambulance from the road."

"You think DeMarco will come after us?"

"I doubt it. For him, this was always just business. His plan didn't work. He'll reassess the situation and come at it from a different angle. Arthur Haines is the guy with the problem now."

And his son, Daniel. Reese didn't like to think what De-Marco might do to Daniel Haines and his family to get his casinos approved.

He looked at Griff. "We need to get across the creek. You up for a swim?"

Griff glanced around. "Where are the other two guys? Are they dead?"

"No. Bran shot them with tranquilizer darts. We need to be gone before they wake up."

"Don't we have to call the police?"

"Not right now. Come on, we can talk about this later. Let's go." Setting a hand on Griff's shoulder, he blocked the boy's view of the carnage as he urged him toward the crossing Brandon had marked. The scant sliver of moon had slipped behind the clouds, making the crossing even more difficult. Bran led the way. When they reached the bank of the stream, Reese turned to Griff, who was eyeing the thick, swampy foliage with obvious apprehension.

"Hop on my back and I'll carry you across."

Griff didn't move. It was clear the boy was torn. He was a strong kid. He didn't want to go into the swamp, but he wanted to prove himself to Reese.

"I'm dressed for this," Reese added, giving him an excuse. "You're barefoot and in your pajamas." He turned his back. "Get on and let's go."

Griff finally hopped on and Reese pulled the kid's legs

around his waist. "Hang on tight." Griff clung to his neck as Reese followed Bran into the murky water. Chase followed, keeping watch behind them.

They were entering the deepest part of the stream when something heavy splashed down from the bank into the creek. Bran's flashlight shined through the mossy, low-hanging branches into a pair of eyes just above the surface of the water moving rapidly toward them.

"Gator!" Bran shouted, pulling his knife as he stepped forward to deal with the threat. Reese increased his pace, moving past Bran into the lead, making his way toward the muddy bank on the opposite side of stream. Loud splashing and cursing split the quiet. Then dead silence.

"Wow," Griff said, straining to see into the darkness. "Your brother killed that big gator with a knife!"

Reese couldn't stop a laugh. "Yeah, Bran can be pretty impressive at times."

Griff sighed. "I wish I had a brother."

Reese's thoughts sidetracked to Kenzie. He wondered what it would be like to have a child, the family he had wanted but thought he would never have. It was the wrong time to consider it. Kenzie was still the prime suspect in her ex-husband's murder. And what would she say when she found out he had killed a man?

The clouds parted as he sloshed up onshore to find her waiting at the top of the muddy bank. Griff slipped off his back and raced toward her.

"Mom! Mom!"

Kenzie caught him in her arms, lifted him off the ground, and just hung on. Reese knew she was fighting not to cry.

"I was so scared," Griff said. His feet back on the ground, he pulled away to look up at her. "I told myself you and Reese would come, and you did." For an instant, his golden-brown eyes filled with tears. "Reese even brought his brothers." He sniffed and steadied himself. "Bran killed an alligator with his knife, Mom. You should have seen it. You think someday I could have a brother?"

For an instant, Kenzie's eyes locked with Reese's. She looked back down at her son. "I don't know. Maybe someday."

But Reese could hear the uncertainty in her voice. After everything he had told her about himself, maybe she didn't want to be with him. Tonight he had killed a man. He should have felt remorse but all he felt was relief that Griff was safe and a sense that justice had been served.

But Griff had seen it and that had to be traumatic. As they headed back to the truck, Reese noticed the boy's buoyant mood had faded, sliding into something darker as the events of the night began to sink in. He'd seen a man's brains blown out right in front of him. He'd need counseling at the very least.

Reese paused to dump the water out of his worn cowboy boots and pull them back on. They collected the gear in their makeshift camp and headed for the vehicles.

Seated in the pickup between Kenzie and Reese, Griff fell asleep before they had reached the highway, his head in his mother's lap. As soon as they were in cell range, Kenzie phoned her grandmother. Chase would be using his disposable to call 9-1-1 and anonymously report the shooting.

After a stop at the Holiday Inn to pick up the bags they'd left behind, Chase and Bran headed for the airport to catch the jet. Preferring not to leave the rented pickup in Shreveport, a possible connection to the dead man at the cabin, Reese drove back to Dallas in the truck. Griff and Kenzie had both stubbornly insisted on going with him.

It was four o'clock in the morning by the time they reached the city.

Unfortunately, a black-and-white patrol car sat waiting in front of the town house when they arrived. Ten minutes after they walked inside, Detective Heath Ford and two uniformed police officers showed up at the door with a warrant for Kenzie's arrest.

CHAPTER THIRTY-SIX

KENZIE LOOKED AT REESE, fresh fear clawing at her insides. Griff had fallen asleep on the ride back to Dallas and Reese had carried him upstairs. Gran had taken over while Griff showered and got ready for bed, though it was almost morning. Fortunately, Griff hadn't seen the patrol car or heard the police arrive.

"What's the charge?" Reese asked as Detective Ford bulled his way into the living room, the officers close behind.

The detective's jaw tightened. "Obstruction of justice for starters. You were both told not to leave the city. Instead, you were spotted crossing the state line into Louisiana." He stared hard at Reese. "At the moment, I'm not bringing you in, Reese, but unless you tell the truth about your whereabouts the night of the murder, you're next on my list."

Reese swore softly.

"All right, I was home by myself that night," Kenzie said, tired of the subterfuge and the unfair strain on Reese. "But I didn't have anything to do with Lee's murder."

"Kenzie," Reese warned.

"No, Reese. It's time for the truth."

Footsteps sounded. Apparently Griff had heard the commotion and come down to see what was happening. When he reached the bottom step and saw the police, he raced to Kenzie.

"You can't arrest my mom! She didn't do anything! She and Reese came to save me from the kidnappers!"

"It's all right, Griff," Reese said. "The police are just doing their job. Everything's going to be okay."

"Don't let them take her away!" Griff's hair was damp and sticking up all over, his face flushed and his eyes wild.

Kenzie's heart clenched.

For the first time, the detective looked uncertain. "I'm beginning to get the impression there's a lot more going on here than I know about. I think it's time you both told me what the hell is going on."

Kenzie pulled Griff in for a hug. "Go back upstairs with Gran, sweetheart. Let Reese and me talk to the police."

Gran stood at the bottom of the staircase. When Griff hesitated, she came forward and slipped an arm around his shoulders. "Come on, honey. Let the adults handle this. You've had more than enough excitement for tonight."

Griff cast Kenzie a last worried glance, then reluctantly, let Gran lead him back up to his room.

"Gran made coffee," Kenzie said, resigned that the time for honesty had arrived. "We can talk in the kitchen."

Reese did not look pleased. "Fine," he growled, "but I'm calling Nate Temple. I need to let him know what's going on."

But all Kenzie wanted was to tell the police the truth and have them believe her. Maybe this time they would.

Detective Ford instructed his men to wait outside and the three of them went into the kitchen. Kenzie poured a cup of coffee for the detective, but after the long trip home, she and Reese were already suffering a caffeine hangover.

"Start from the beginning," Ford said. "Talk nice and slow so even us city boys can understand."

"Very funny," Reese said, taking a seat at the table across from him.

"Who wants to go first?" Ford asked, lounging back in his chair.

"I will," Kenzie said. "But you'll need Reese to fill in the blackmail part of the story."

One of the detective's dark brown eyebrows arched up. "This I can't wait to hear."

Kenzie spent the next half hour laying out the details of the kidnapping, the beating she had taken, the men involved, and why they had abducted her son. Then Reese stepped in to explain about the gambling debt Arthur Haines owed Sawyer DeMarco, a member of the Louisiana mob, and the casino owner's extortion attempt, an effort to gain control of an offshore drilling rig for Arthur's company, Black Sand Oil and Gas, so he could repay his debt.

"I'm with you so far," Ford said. "Griffin was kidnapped and taken to Louisiana to put pressure on Reese. The two of you went there to retrieve him. What happened in Louisiana?"

Kenzie didn't miss Reese's warning glance. "Nothing that has any bearing on why you're here. Suffice it to say, we made a deal with DeMarco and brought Griff back home."

The detective's expression said he knew there was a lot more to the story, but he didn't push it, at least not right then. "The problem remains, we still don't have any proof Lee Haines was killed by someone other than his ex-wife."

"Not yet," Reese said, "but if you'll give us a little more time, we can come up with the proof you need."

Kenzie knew Reese was banking on Hawk Maddox. But anything could happen. Jeremy Bolt could have already disappeared, never to be seen or heard from again.

Ford rose from his chair. "I'll talk to Arthur Haines. If he's involved in a kidnapping, he's got a lot of explaining to do." Ford drank the last of his coffee and set the mug back down on the table. "In the meantime, I'm telling both of you again not to leave the city and this time you'd better listen."

As soon as the detective was gone, Kenzie turned to Reese. "I feel terrible for putting you through all of this."

Something moved across his features and flashed in his eyes. Instead of reaching for her, pulling her into his arms, he remained distant, his careful control back in place. He'd been quiet since they'd left Louisiana.

"We were both targets," he said. "We've been working together from the start, and in the last few days, we've made a lot of headway. Griff's home safe. We know who killed Lee, and Hawk is hunting him. We have to hope something will break."

She looked at his hard, remote expression, and her heart squeezed. With Griff riding between them in the pickup, they hadn't talked about what had happened at the cabin. Griff had been strangely silent, as well. She'd heard the gunshots, but with all of them safely returned, the details hadn't been a priority at the time.

Now they were alone.

"I think it's time you told me what went on at the cabin," she said. "Sooner or later, Griff's going to want to talk about it. I really need to know."

Reese scrubbed a hand over the several days' growth of beard along his jaw and leaned his hips against the kitchen counter. His shuttered expression didn't change.

"You heard some of what was happening on the radio. Bran took out two of the perimeter guards with the tranq gun and we moved into position the way we planned. Then things went to hell when Griff broke free and tried to escape just as we were ready to go in. One of the gunmen caught up with him on the front porch and used him as a shield."

Her stomach knotted. "Oh, my God."

"Bran and Chase followed the plan, went in, and took down the two kidnappers inside. Both men were shot but their wounds weren't fatal. Chase called 911 on the disposable and anonymously reported the incident as soon as we were in cell range."

"So you were…you were out in front?"

"That's right." His eyes seemed bluer, more intense. They never left her face. "I took out the guy who held Griff."

Her heart twisted, began to beat like a bird trapped in her chest. She studied his expression, unable to read his thoughts. "By *took out*, do you…do you mean you killed him?"

"If I'd let him leave with Griff, we might not have been able to find him again. I didn't have any choice."

Her mind spun. She had been so worried about Griff, she hadn't considered what might happen to the kidnappers during the rescue attempt. She had thought about someone dying, but mostly she was worried about Griff and Reese and his brothers. "And Griff saw this?"

Reese just nodded. "I'm sorry. If there had been any other way…"

"No wonder he was so upset."

Reese made no reply.

"He'll need counseling," she said. "Someone he can talk to about what happened."

"I know. Whatever it costs, I can pay—"

"No! Griff's my problem, not yours." She held his gaze. "What happens when Griff tells the doctor you killed one of the kidnappers?"

"It's doctor-patient privilege. Nothing they can do. But it isn't a secret a little boy should be burdened with. When the time is right, I'll tell Ford what happened. Considering the circumstances, I'm sure we can work things out."

Her mind was spinning. She needed time to process the information. "I'll speak to Griff, tell him not to talk about it at school. He won't want to get you in trouble."

Reese fell silent. He glanced down at the floor then back, as if he wanted to say something more, but in the end, he just pushed away from the counter and prepared to leave.

"I'd better go," he finally said. "If you need anything, just call."

Her heart throbbed. She didn't want him to leave. "What about work?"

"Take whatever time you need." He didn't touch her, made no effort to kiss her goodbye, just turned and walked away. Long strides carried him across the living room. Reese pulled open the door. His gaze ran over her one last time. "Good night, Kenzie."

She didn't answer. She didn't want to leave things so uncertain between them, but she needed time to figure things out, time to decide what was best for Griff. This was a different man than the Reese she knew. Harder, tougher. A man who could kill another human being.

She had to think of her son. Had to be sure being with Reese was the right thing for both of them.

And what about Reese? Since they had been together, she had brought him nothing but trouble. Women loved him. Why should he stay with her when he could be with someone else and leave all the problems behind? And what would the police do when he told them he had killed a man?

Kenzie stayed silent as Reese walked out the door.

It was almost dawn, the sun lurking below the horizon, casting the city in an eerie purple glow. Hawk had spent the night digging for information in the underbelly of the city, starting in the seedy hoods of Shreveport, the Downtown Riverfront, then the dive bars of Lakeside and Allendale, coming up without much for his efforts. He knew more about Bolt than before, but not enough to find him.

From what he'd learned, Jeremy Bolt was in his late forties, a shadowy figure reported to have once worked for the CIA. Rumor had it, he lived a double life, one under an alias as the reclusive son of a wealthy entrepreneur who had left him a sizable fortune. The other as a hired killer, one of the best in the trade.

Jase had a lead on Bolt that might pan out, but he'd been up all night. He needed to be at the top of his game to take on a predator like Bolt.

As the first rays of light broke over the city, he checked into a motel with a two-diamond AAA rating on the sign out front, figuring it would at least be clean. The room was small, but most of them felt that way to him. He stretched out on one of the beds to catch a few z's and closed his tired, heavy-lidded eyes.

When he woke up, he would call Kate, mostly just to hear the sound of her voice, but also because he didn't want his wife to worry. As soon as it was dark, he'd start again, pick up Bolt's scent, follow the trail wherever it led. Long Bailey was still in the hospital, still guarded by the protection detail Chase was providing, but soon he'd be released.

Hawk wanted Bolt out of action before that happened. Word was the assassin had a long memory. He wouldn't forget what he considered Long's betrayal.

A grim smile surfaced in the darkness. Before this was over, he wouldn't forget Hawk Maddox, either.

ARTHUR HAINES PULLED into the parking lot of the Pot-of-Gold casino and walked to the separate hotel entrance that led up to the penthouse suite.

DeMarco didn't go out a lot. Odds were good he'd be home. Arthur pushed the intercom button next to the private elevator.

One of DeMarco's no-necks answered. "Yeah, who is it?"

"Arthur Haines. I need to speak to Mr. DeMarco."

"Hold on. I'll see if he's here." Mob speak for whether or not DeMarco would see him.

The man's voice came back on. "Mr. De Marco says you can come on up."

Arthur stepped into the elevator and pushed the button. The carriage didn't move till a code was keyed in from the penthouse.

The elevator began to rise and Arthur's hand shook as he reached in his jacket and wrapped his fingers around the revolver in his pocket.

The gun wasn't fancy, not one of those big semiautomatic pistols in all the gangster movies. It was just a weapon he'd bought years ago for protection. You didn't have to be a marksman to use it. Just aim the gun and pull the trigger. If he got close enough, it wouldn't matter that he had only fired the pistol a couple of times before he'd locked it in his safe years ago.

The elevator doors opened and he stepped out onto the black and white marble floors in the garishly over-decorated penthouse suite. DeMarco ambled toward him, shorter than Arthur, his barrel chest puffed out, a heavy crystal glass of expensive scotch in his hand.

"You look tired, Arthur." DeMarco's raspy voice always grated on his nerves. "By now you must know that your grandson has been rescued. That means you aren't getting that drilling platform you wanted so badly, and you still owe me several million dollars. So why are you here?"

Two of DeMarco's dim-witted bodyguards stood at the

back of the room. Arthur had purposely chosen an ill-fitting worn tweed jacket and a pair of scuffed shoes. Nothing threatening about him. By the time they figured it out, it would be too late.

"I didn't know my grandson was safe. But I'm thankful for it. That isn't why I came."

"No? Enlighten me."

"Would you mind if I poured myself a drink?"

DeMarco snapped his fingers and one of the bodyguards came forward. "A scotch for my guest."

When the bodyguard started for the bar, Arthur headed in that direction, which brought him closer to DeMarco. His hand went into his pocket. If he hesitated, he'd lose his nerve. He pulled the pistol, aimed, and fired from no more than three feet away.

The stunned expression on Sawyer DeMarco's face the instant before blood gushed from the hole in his throat was worth the hail of gunfire that slammed into Arthur's chest. As he hit the cold marble floor, his last thought was of Daniel.

At least his precious son was safe.

CHAPTER THIRTY-SEVEN

AFTER LEAVING KENZIE'S town house, Reese went home and made a brief attempt to sleep. When the effort failed, he rolled out of bed, showered, dressed, and went into the office. It was early Thursday morning. He filled the day with meetings and appointments, then worked late that night.

Anything to keep his mind off Kenzie.

The office felt empty without her. He'd grown used to her presence, her willingness to help with any problem that came up, used to the warmth she exuded just being near.

But Kenzie needed time with her son. She was doing her best to help Griff through an extremely traumatic experience. Since their return to Dallas, Reese had talked to her only once. Neither of them had mentioned their relationship—or lack thereof.

He'd asked about Griff, and Kenzie had told him she'd made an appointment that day with a child psychologist named Margaret Stone. Reese had checked Stone's credentials and found the woman was considered one of the best in Dallas.

He was sitting behind his desk Friday morning, going over company financials and checking in with some of his VPs, when the intercom buzzed.

Louise's voice came over the line. "Detective Ford is calling, sir."

His pulse kicked up. He intended to talk to Ford about

the shooting, but there were other matters to take care of
first. Maybe this was the break they'd been hoping for.

"Put him through." Reese picked up the phone and settled back in his chair, the receiver notched against his shoulder. "What can I do for you, Detective?"

"Arthur Haines is dead."

"What?" Reese shot forward.

"That's right. So is Sawyer DeMarco. Shreveport Police
got a 9-1-1 call from the Pot-of-Gold hotel. Apparently, Arthur Haines showed up looking for DeMarco and made it
up to his penthouse suite. I guess it never occurred to De-
Marco that Haines might try to kill him. Arthur put a slug
in DeMarco's throat before his bodyguards took him out."

"Jesus."

"Yeah. This thing just keeps escalating. I'm beginning
to believe your Ms. Haines could be telling the truth."

"She was set up, Heath. Haines was killed by a mob hit
man." He didn't mention Bolt's name. Hawk was tracking
Bolt, putting himself at risk. Police interference could make
the danger even greater.

"Assuming you're right," Ford said, "why would the mob
hit Lee Haines?"

"I asked Arthur about it before we went to Shreveport.
He said DeMarco arranged the hit on his son as a warning.
Apparently, the debt he owed was substantial. Lee's death
was a way of convincing Arthur to repay the money." He
didn't mention the gaming permits. Too much information
might be worse than not enough.

"If DeMarco ordered the hit, maybe Arthur thought his
son Daniel was also in danger."

"I'd say that's exactly right. Arthur killed the guy to
protect his other son."

The detective went silent. Then a sigh whispered over

the line. "Unfortunately, Kenzie's still the prime suspect in her ex-husband's murder. Nothing we can do until something turns up that clears her name."

"I'm working on it."

"I'll stay on it, too. If I find anything, you'll be the first to know. Good luck, Reese. And I appreciate the cooperation."

Reese hung up the phone. He needed to talk to Kenzie. And to Griff. The boy had just lost his dad. Now his grandfather was dead. Griff had been the victim of a brutal kidnapping and seen a man killed right in front of him. The boy trusted Reese, and Reese wasn't going to let him down.

He called the garage and had his car brought up to the valet stand, then grabbed his suit jacket off the coatrack and slung it over one shoulder. Kenzie might not want to see him. Clearly, she was having second thoughts about them after the shooting. But he wanted—needed—to see her.

Kenzie was important to him. More important than he could have imagined. He wanted her, and not just in his bed. Every day he grew more certain of his feelings, more certain she was the right woman for him. And deep down, he believed Kenzie felt the same.

Reese wasn't the kind of man who gave up when the going got tough. No matter what he'd done to protect her son, he was a different man now than he had been all those years ago. He just had to find a way to prove it.

He walked out of his office, over to Louise's desk. "Clear my schedule for the rest of the day, Louise. If something important comes up, you can reach me on my cell."

The older woman looked up at him. "Mr. Stiles called while you were on the line. He said it was in regard to the Poseidon deal. He was hoping to talk to you right away."

"I'll call him. Thanks, Louise."

Reese walked into the elevator and hit the button for the parking garage. As the doors slid open, he pressed Derek's contact number.

"What's going on?" Reese asked when Derek picked up.

"I wanted to give you a heads-up on where we are in the deal."

"I'm just heading for my car. Go ahead."

"I talked to Sea Titan after your last phone call and we're back in business. I explained that a problem had come up on our end, but you managed to resolve it. The last of the permits have been approved. If we want this done, we need to act."

Reese had explained to Derek why he'd changed his mind—again—and decided *not* to back out of the deal. He'd resolved the problems that had come up on his end— not mentioning the rescue of a kidnapped child—and was ready to move forward. He'd hoped Sea Titan wouldn't get nervous and refuse. Apparently that hadn't happened.

"So far everything is moving along smoothly," Derek said. "No more accidents."

"Good. Stay on top of it, make sure everything's in order for the closing, and keep me posted."

"You still want to go out to the rig?"

With all that had happened, he needed to focus. Touring the rig, talking to the people who worked there, was something he had been trying to do from the start. "As a matter of fact, yes. I'll handle the arrangements from this end."

"Great. Let me know if there's anything you need."

"Will do." Reese ended the call.

The valet had his black Jag up and running. Reese slid behind the wheel and pulled the car out into the street.

The protesters were gone. A big storm had blown in last night and it was still cloudy and raining off and on. The group had already dwindled to around ten people. Now the last of the stragglers where gone. Turned out, protesting was a lot more work than people believed.

Which made him think of the accidents DeMarco had arranged to stop Garrett Resources from purchasing the rig. Reese had been working with the installation supervisor on the platform to identify the person or persons responsible, so far without results. Eventually, they'd find the guy and throw his ass in jail. At least with Haines and DeMarco both dead, the trouble on the rig was over.

And Griff and Kenzie were no longer in danger.

He started to pick up the phone to call so she'd know he was coming, but what if she refused to see him?

Reese kept driving. She was still his executive assistant. If he just showed up, she'd be hard-pressed not to let him in.

Reese pulled up in front of her town house and turned off the engine, then just sat there. What was it about McKenzie Haines that set her apart from every other woman he had dated?

The thought had kept him awake more nights than he could count. Then he remembered telling her about Billy Curtis, the boy who'd been killed in the car wreck when Reese was seventeen. He'd been at least partly to blame. He'd never told anyone what a devastating, life-altering event Billy's death had been.

But Kenzie had a way of reaching through the iron control he wore like armor around him. He'd let her in and she'd revived a part of him that had died that night with Billy. Kenzie had brought him into the light, restored his hopes and dreams, and taught him how to love.

He loved her, he silently admitted. He'd tried to deny it, but it was true. He loved her and he wasn't letting her go without a fight.

Unfortunately, when he finally got out of the car and knocked on the front door, it was Florence who answered.

"I'm sorry, Reese, Kenzie's not here. She took Griff to see that psychologist, Dr. Stone. I'm not sure when they'll be back, but you're welcome to come in and wait."

Reese just shook his head. "I can't. I've got too much to do at the office."

"At least come in for a glass of iced tea. I haven't had a chance to thank you for saving my grandson."

He weakened. He liked Florence Spencer. When she held open the screen door, he walked inside and followed her into the kitchen.

"Griff might be safe," he said, "but I don't think Kenzie approves of my methods."

"She told me about it. Sometimes bad things happen and there's nothing we can do. She'll figure it out. She's just worried about her son." Flo poured two glasses of tea, and they sat down at the kitchen table. "She worries about you, too, you know."

He knew in some way it was true. She was his assistant. It was her job to care of him, do whatever he needed to help him keep the company running smoothly. But that wasn't the same as loving him.

"I need to talk to her, but it never seems to be the right time."

"My advice? Make time."

But with everything going on, that was easier said than done.

"Detective Ford came by to tell her about Arthur. He was a lot more pleasant this time. I think he's finally starting to believe she's innocent."

Reese set his glass down on the table. "Heath Ford's a

good cop. He's looking for the truth. We just have to help him find it."

"Arthur's the reason Kenzie took Griff back to see Dr. Stone. She was afraid his grandfather's death on top of everything else would be too much for Griff to handle."

"How's he doing?"

"Griff's a strong boy. He'll be okay, but it's going to take some time."

"Yeah." Reese finished his iced tea and rose from the table. "Tell Kenzie… Tell her I'm sorry I missed her."

"I'll tell her." Flo walked him to the door. "Don't give up on them, Reese. In time, everything will get back to normal."

Reese just nodded. He'd given up on normal a long time ago.

CHAPTER THIRTY-EIGHT

KENZIE SPENT A miserable weekend thinking about Reese, wishing she had handled things differently. He'd called her twice on Friday, but she had missed both calls and hadn't called him back.

She wasn't sure what to say. She had no idea what he was thinking after the way she had treated him. Reese had saved her son's life—at great risk to his own—and she had practically tossed him out in the street.

She knew he'd come by the house to see her, but again, fate had intervened and she had missed him. Reese hadn't tried to contact her again.

Choosing a very businesslike navy-and-white skirt suit, she drove to the office Monday morning. Until Reese fired her or she quit, she still had a job to do. She arrived early and so did Louise, but Reese hadn't come in yet.

"Boy, am I glad to see you," Louise said. "I don't know how you keep up with that man. He's a handful, I swear."

"I know he can be demanding."

"That, dear girl, is an understatement." Louise smiled. "He's different when you're around. You know how to handle him." Her eyes twinkled. "How to soothe the savage beast, so to speak."

Kenzie laughed. "Maybe so. I think the three of us make a pretty good team."

"You're right, we do." The familiar deep voice sent tingles down her spine. "Welcome back, Kenzie. You ready to go to work?"

"I'm… I'm ready."

"Good, let's go." He strode off toward his office without another word, and Kenzie fell in behind him. Her pulse was racing, her mouth paper-dry.

After everything that had happened, she had no idea what to say, so she just closed the door behind her and sat down in her usual chair in front of his desk. She opened her iPad, ready to go over his schedule and make notes on what he needed her to do.

It was still early, the workday not officially started, when Reese looked up at her from behind his desk, his expression unreadable.

"How was your weekend?" he asked.

She opened her mouth to make some bland reply but emotion welled up and unexpected words tumbled out. "Arthur killed DeMarco. Arthur's dead, too." As if the police wouldn't have already told him. Dear God, she needed to get a grip.

His features softened as he rose from his desk and walked toward her. Kenzie rose, as well. Uncertain, she took a hesitant step in his direction. Reese closed the distance and pulled her into his arms.

"I heard the news. I tried to call you. Are you okay? How's Griff?"

A breath trembled out. "Griff's doing fine. We're both all right." Unable to ignore her feelings any longer, she slid her arms around his neck and just hung on. "I missed you. I missed you so much."

A shudder went through his hard frame. "I missed you, too." Reese bent his head and kissed her, softly at first, then deeper.

The kiss lingered, went on and on, neither of them wanting the moment to end. The feel of his mouth over hers sent heat pulsing through her. The kiss went deeper, turned wilder, hotter, burned completely out of control. She wanted to strip him naked, have her way with him on top of his desk. She wanted him inside her so much she ached with it.

"I need you," he said against the side of her neck. "It's all I can do not to take you right here." He kissed her again and every sensible thought flew out of her head.

"We can't…can't do that." Heat flushed her cheeks as she looked up at him. "Can we?"

His gaze went from guarded blue to hot blue flame. "My family owns the company. Hell, the whole damned building belongs to us. As long as it's what you want, too, we can do whatever we damn well please."

Striding to the door, he pushed the lock, walked back, and started kissing her again. The next thing she knew her blouse was unbuttoned, the front hook on her bra undone. Reese filled his hands with her breasts, lowered his head, and took a nipple into his mouth.

Kenzie moaned softly. Sliding her hands into his silky black hair, she arched her back to give him better access. Her heart pounded as desire burned through her. She was panting and on fire.

"I want you," she said. "I ache with wanting you, Reese."

A growl came from his throat. Reese kissed his way down her neck and nipped an earlobe, sending little shivers over her skin.

"We don't have time for this," he said gruffly. "Not enough time for me to do it right."

"I don't care." She trembled. "Please, Reese."

He kissed her again, long, wet, and deep. She felt his hands sliding her skirt up around her waist, then he turned her around and she understood what he wanted, bent over his desk, and felt the snap of her thong as Reese ripped it away.

It was a secret, forbidden fantasy that he would take her this way, claim her in some wild, primitive fashion. He slid into her, touched her as he took her fast and hard, both of them burning out of control. Reaching the edge, she tipped into climax at supersonic speed. Pleasure scorched through her, meshed with the love she felt for him, drawing the moment into what seemed like forever.

As they began to spiral down, Reese adjusted her clothes, turned her into his arms, and just held her. Kissing her softly one last time, he left to deal with the condom he'd dug out of his wallet.

Kenzie used his private bathroom to freshen herself and came out neatly dressed, her hair finger-combed back in place. The only evidence of their misconduct was the flush in her cheeks and Reese's look of male satisfaction.

"We need to talk," he said. "It's been hell not knowing what you're thinking, how you're feeling. I can deal with just about anything, as long as I know where I stand."

She looked up at him and wondered if her feelings showed in her eyes. "I owe you an apology. You've done nothing but try to help me from the start. Things just seemed to get so mixed-up. I've been trying to figure out what's best for Griff. And even though I'm innocent of Lee's murder, I'm still the number one suspect. Dragging you into my problems just isn't fair."

He paced over to the window, stood looking down at the street teeming with people fourteen stories below.

He turned back to her. "You don't owe me anything, Kenzie. In a way I owe you." He sighed. "After everything that's happened, I wasn't expecting to see you today. I set up a meeting tonight with a group of regional managers. Some of them are flying in from out of town. I can try to cancel, but—"

"You can't do that, Reese. Whatever happens, you still have a job to do." She quashed her disappointment. Reese was CEO. He had duties, responsibilities. Accepting those responsibilities made him the man he was, the man she'd fallen in love with.

He shoved his hands into the pockets of his slacks. "I was planning to fly down to Houston in the morning. We'll be closing on the Poseidon deal this week. I need to make that long-overdue trip out to the rig." His eyes found hers. There was something in them. It looked almost like longing.

"If you went with me, we could spend the night together. We could talk things over, figure things out. What do you think?"

Her eyes misted. After all the trouble, he still wanted to be with her. "I'd love to go. Gran is with Griff and it's only one night."

The tension went out of his wide shoulders. He gave her the sweetest smile. "Okay, then. I've got a lot to do before we leave, so we'd better get to work."

Those incredible blue eyes ran over her, heated again. She read their silent message. *Before I think of another way to use my desk.*

Kenzie's blush returned, the idea all too tempting. It was eight o'clock in the morning, the office just open. She flicked him a last amused glance. "I'll get my notepad," she said.

THE MORNING WAS slipping away. Sunlight sliced through the crack in the bedroom curtains, reminding Troy he was overdue at the office, but he made no move to get out of bed. After the best sex of his life, he lay spent and sated among his expensive black satin sheets. Delia Parr curled up on the bed beside him, a red-painted nail toying with the sparse black hair on his chest.

Troy had started seeing Delia after Lee Haines's death. He'd called to comfort her in the loss of her fiancé. He chuckled—and comfort her he had. The woman was completely uninhibited, he'd discovered, and totally insatiable.

She was also a money-hungry bitch.

Which was how Lee Haines had managed to get into her pants.

He reached down and squeezed her plump ass, eliciting a throaty laugh. She was a rounded kind of woman, soft against his thinner, more sinewy frame. In bed, he didn't have the stamina she had, but she suited him just the same.

And in a strange way, he trusted her. Delia was as devious and conniving as he was, ready to do whatever it took to pay for the lavish lifestyle they both enjoyed.

When he'd told Delia about the helicopter mechanic, how the guy had tried to blackmail him and Troy had been forced to kill him, instead of being appalled, she'd been sexually aroused by the story.

Delia traced a line from his chest to his groin, and lust slipped through him.

"What are we going to do about the Poseidon?" she asked, eyeing him from beneath her thick black lashes. She knew about that, too, knew he'd been trying to take over the deal. He wasn't even sure how she'd found out. Arthur, maybe. The old man had secretly had a yen for Delia himself.

"Don't worry, I've got it handled. Just because Arthur managed to fuck everything up doesn't mean I'm willing to let it go."

Between what Arthur had told him and the questions the cops had asked when they'd grilled him about Arthur's death and Sawyer DeMarco, Troy had been able to piece together pretty much what had happened.

"I'm not letting that prick Reese Garrett come out on top again." Troy hated the bastard, had since their college days. Garrett always got what he went after no matter what it took. Troy was as good-looking as Reese, but he didn't have the persistence or the drive. Didn't matter—it galled him just the same.

With Arthur out of the way, Troy had full control of Black Sand Oil and Gas. He planned to make the company a bigger success than ever before. Yesterday, his highly paid inside man, his coconspirator on the platform, had confirmed that Garrett Resources was still planning to go through with the purchase.

Not going to happen.

He also knew Reese was planning a trip out to the rig sometime tomorrow. Hell, he even knew the prick's schedule once he arrived.

As Delia continued to fondle him, Troy smiled. The timing was perfect. He intended to beat Reese Garrett at his own game. Troy was winning this round.

One way or another.

CHAPTER THIRTY-NINE

THE GARRETT CITATION CJ4 landed at the West Houston Airport at ten o'clock the next morning. Reese led Kenzie down the metal stairs over to one of the Land Rovers parked just off the tarmac. Both of them got in and buckled their seat belts.

They hadn't talked much on the plane. Two other Garrett employees had joined them on the flight, scheduled for meetings in the Houston office. To all outward appearances, he was CEO of the company and Kenzie was his executive assistant. For their relationship to work, they had to separate their personal lives from their jobs.

It wasn't easy for either of them. There were things he needed to say, questions he wanted to ask, things he hoped Kenzie would want to hear. Things he hoped she would say to him.

All of that would happen tonight. He had carefully planned the evening: an intimate supper in his Houston apartment catered by Chez Julienne, one of the finest restaurants in Houston, then snuggling together on the sofa, where they could talk before he carried her to bed.

His groin tightened just thinking about making love to her. He had it all worked out, just prayed things would go as he planned.

Once things were straightened out between them, he

could concentrate on finding the evidence they needed to prove Kenzie innocent of murder.

Instead of stopping at his Houston apartment, Reese drove straight from the airport south on I-45 to Galveston and the Sea Titan Pelican Island terminal. The helicopter was waiting when they arrived, an EC155 this time, a chopper big enough to hold thirteen passengers plus a two-man crew.

This was a modified version, designed for Sea Titan's top executives, a plush, roomier interior that carried only eight people. An attempt, Reese figured, to make up for the disastrous flight he had barely survived before.

He glanced at Kenzie as they crossed the tarmac toward the aircraft. She looked luscious in a pair of snug-fitting jeans and a pale blue short-sleeve sweater that hugged her pretty breasts, while Reese wore crisp blue jeans and a white button-down shirt with the sleeves rolled up.

A salty ocean breeze whipped the navy blue windbreaker with *POSEIDON* in bold white letters on the back he'd been given when they arrived.

As the blades began to spin up, Reese felt the first twinge of nerves. He'd been expecting it, had tried to prepare himself, but as he settled in the buttercream leather seat next to Kenzie, his pulse kicked up and his mouth went dry.

He was gripping the armrest, he realized, when he felt the brush of her hand as her fingers twined with his. She knew what was going through his head, knew part of him was replaying the crash that had killed two men and put him in the hospital. Kenzie always seemed to understand.

He squeezed her fingers. "I'm okay. Just a little nervous after what happened before."

She cast him a knowing glance. "If it makes you feel any

better, I'm a little nervous myself. I've never been crazy about helicopters."

Reese smiled. "Maybe the company should buy one of its own. Then we can make sure everything is maintained the way it should be."

Her golden eyes sparkled. "Your brothers would probably approve. Especially Brandon. He seems to be up for just about anything."

Reese chuckled. "I think Bran might have had enough of helicopter flying in the army."

She grinned. "You could be right."

The chopper had already lifted away, Reese realized, and was winging a path over the heliport and out over the ocean. He held on to Kenzie's hand and began to relax.

Less than an hour later, he spotted the platform, rising like a metal giant out of the sea. Four pillars pushed the Poseidon nearly two hundred feet above the surface of the water. As the chopper circled, Reese took in the twenty-story structure that produced a hundred-thousand barrels of oil a day, and housed the eighty-plus employees who lived and worked on the rig.

The chopper continued its descent, its wheels settling lightly on the helo pad angled out over the ocean, and the blades began to slow. The doors slid open. They ducked as they ran across the pad to join the three men waiting to greet them, including Dave Pierce, Poseidon's installation manager.

"Welcome aboard," Dave said, the stiff wind ruffling his thick red hair. The chopper engine made it hard to hear. Reese shook Pierce's hand and introduced Kenzie, and Dave introduced the other two guys who would be showing them around.

"Let's get inside where it's not so noisy and I'll show you what goes on around here."

KENZIE AND REESE followed Pierce and his men down a set of metal stairs into what appeared to be one of the data control centers.

Five men and one woman, dressed in the yellow coveralls worn by the Poseidon crew, sat in front of a bank of dials and gauges, watching production levels and God only knew what else.

They went from one room to another, one level to the next, Dave Pierce or one of the other men rattling off complicated explanations of the different work done by the massive drilling equipment.

They talked about blowout valves, cement-lined casings, and all the other important safety precautions in place. Reese asked poignant questions and seemed to comprehend most of what was being said, but the lengthy discussion of machinery and equipment was putting Kenzie to sleep. Which Reese seemed to sense.

When they reached the cafeteria, he pulled her aside. "We'll be coming back here to eat when the tour is over. In the meantime I'd like to get your take on employee morale, what their workdays are like, their family life, that kind of thing. I think it would be more productive for you to talk to some of the crew while I finish the tour of the rig."

Relieved, Kenzie smiled and nodded. "I can handle that." Reese left with the men and Kenzie pushed through the doors leading into the cafeteria. She paused next to a heavyset man with thinning gray hair and asked how to get a cup of coffee.

"Just head in that direction, ma'am." He pointed toward a line of thermal containers and stacks of paper cups against the wall. "They never run out. With twenty-four-hour shifts seven days a week, coffee is the lifeblood of this place."

"I can understand that. Thanks." Kenzie headed across the room and poured a cup of coffee from the container of French roast next to the decaf, then walked over to speak to one of the few women she had seen among the crew.

Introducing herself and explaining her interest, she sat down at the table with a safety engineer named Marty De-Salvo.

"I've been wondering what it's like to work here." Kenzie sipped her coffee, which was fresh and hot and strong.

"It's not an easy lifestyle, that's for sure." Marty, a small woman with heavy black hair and a pretty face, explained that there were few women on the rig because it was difficult for them to be separated from their children for two weeks at a time.

"For me and my husband, it works. We don't have any kids and he's a salesman, so he sets his own schedule. My two weeks off gives us a chance to travel, something we both really enjoy."

Kenzie spoke to a few of the men and got similar answers. Leaving home every two weeks wasn't easy, but having two weeks off all at once had its advantages, and the pay was good.

A guy named Joe Wickersham warned her that rig life wasn't for everyone. "There ain't no windows in your room, you know? So you got a problem with enclosed spaces, this ain't the job for you."

She was beginning to understand that. The cafeteria was big, with plenty of lighting, lots of tables, and room to move around, but you couldn't see outside. In a lot of ways, the rig was like a giant submarine. She would be glad when they were headed back home.

Her gaze went to the door as Reese walked in. The man with him was taller, more muscular, with a thick barrel chest. But it was Reese who dominated the space, clearly the man in control.

Her pulse kicked up the way it always did. As he strode toward her, she felt the same spike of awareness that hit her every morning when he walked into the office.

"How's it going?" he asked.

"Great. It's an interesting life. It's not for me, that's for sure, but the people who work here seem happy with their jobs."

He nodded. "Good to hear." He glanced around the room, taking note of available tables. "Let's get something to eat." They went through a line that offered a variety of food, everything from lettuce wraps to enchiladas to good old American standards like burgers and chili.

Good food was important on a rig.

"There's a supply ship on the way," Reese said as they sat down across from Dave Pierce and the big guy he had walked in with, Tony Sandini. "We're scheduled to go for a ride, take a look at the rig from the water. You like the ocean, right? You don't get seasick or anything?"

"Nope."

"Good. Soon as we've finished our boat ride, we'll take off back to Houston." His gaze heated. "I've got plans for us tonight."

Kenzie's stomach contracted. He just had to look at her the way he was now and she wanted him. She swallowed and nodded. "Okay."

The supply boat was a red-and-white affair sixty feet long. The platform produced its own power and water, but food supplies, all sorts of products that were needed on a daily basis, arrived by boats out of Galveston.

Kenzie stepped onto the deck and immediately lost her balance as a heavy wave lifted the vessel several feet into the air. Reese's strong hand wrapped around her waist to steady her, and she smiled. "Thanks."

"My pleasure." His hot glance said his mind was already on the night ahead. Kenzie felt a rush of heat, but Reese's attention had returned to the job at hand.

He followed Tony along the deck toward the bow of the boat, where a big metal crane was offloading supplies to a deck that circled the base of the rig. An elevator lifted the goods to the various decks, where they were unloaded.

Reese was busy asking questions, but as the boat pulled away from the lower deck to circle the four massive pillars supporting the rig, Kenzie was absorbed by the beautiful day, the clear blue sky, and foamy white waves breaking against the hull.

She watched a seagull circling above her and smiled at the warmth of the sun on her face. She noticed Reese moving farther away as Tony explained something about the crane.

It took a moment to realize something in the atmosphere had shifted. She turned at the sound of shouting and running feet. The engine stalled and a wave washed over the bow. Then the big boat shuddered and erupted in a fierce explosion, pieces and parts flying into the air with murderous force.

"Kenzie!" Reese raced toward her. He was still several yards away when a second explosion ripped through the air, lifting the center of the boat out of the sea and flipping the deck onto its side.

Kenzie screamed as she hit the cold water, the shock taking her breath away. Kicking her legs, she pushed toward the surface, broke through, and dragged in a deep breath of air. The sea was littered with huge chunks of wood and pieces of plastic, some of them on fire, but the boat itself seemed to be holding together in some kind of tenuous bond. But where was Reese?

Treading water, she turned in a circle, madly searching for him, determined not to panic, fighting to stay calm until she found him. He had been farther away, somewhere past the crane on the bow of the boat. Half the crane remained on the deck, but the rest had been blown apart. A huge piece of metal attached to a slab of wood floated in the ocean a few yards away.

"Reese!" More and more frantic, she swam toward the bow but saw no sign of him. She'd been the best swimmer on her high school swim team and she used that skill now, diving beneath the surface again and again. Still, no sign of him.

Her pulse was pounding, hard and fast, and fear threatened to overwhelm her. She dived again, swam toward the bow, and dived again.

Her heart jerked when she spotted him, ten feet below the surface, struggling to free himself from the heavy piece of metal holding him under the sea.

Kenzie went up, took a deep breath, and scissored through the water, swimming back down as fast as she could. She came up beside him, reached out, and touched him as he struggled to free himself. His eyes met hers and she read the resignation. He didn't believe she could free him. He thought he was going to die.

Terror hit her so hard, her mind spun. Her eyes burned and it wasn't from the salty water. No way was she letting him die!

Her throat tightened and her chest clamped down as she

tugged on the rough strip of metal pinning his leg against the heavy submerged chunk of wood. It didn't budge.

His eyes were closed now and she saw the breath he'd been holding drifting in small bubbles toward the surface. Kenzie yanked frantically on the metal strip, but there was no give. Reese had kicked off his sneakers in an effort to free himself, but his pant leg had snagged and was caught tight.

Her air was gone. She shot to the surface, dragged in a quick breath, and dived again. Forcing herself to concentrate, to find a solution to the problem, she spotted a smaller piece of metal sticking out of the wood and managed to pull it free. It was sharp on one edge, perfect to use as a blade. She began sawing back and forth, trying to cut through the denim pant leg trapping below the surface.

Her breath was almost gone when she realized the whole section of wood and metal was slowly sinking, pulling both of them down. In moments, it would be too far to the surface for either of them to reach.

Griff's sweet face appeared in her mind. She couldn't die. She had to think of Griff! A few more seconds were all they had. Chest burning, she reached for Reese, pulled as hard as she could, and the last of his pant leg tore free.

Determined now, kicking as hard as she could toward the murky sunlight, she was almost there when two bodies surged into the water beside her. One of them pushed Reese to the surface, the other grabbed her arm and pulled her up beside him. She broke through the surface and dragged in a lifesaving breath of air.

"Reese!" Coughing and sputtering, she felt herself lifted into a lifeboat and saw Reese lying on the bottom, one of the rescuers giving him artificial respiration.

She started to shiver. Her eyes burned. "Please, God,

don't let him die." A blanket wrapped around her shoulders as she knelt beside him, reached out, and touched his cheek. "I love you, Reese," she said. "Please come back to me."

They worked over him for several more terrifying minutes before he coughed, coughed some more, dragged in a breath, and expelled what seemed like gallons of seawater.

"Reese..." His name came out on a whisper of air and the tears she'd been fighting slid down her cheeks.

"He's gonna be all right," Tony said with the widest smile she had ever seen. "He's gonna be okay."

Kenzie started crying.

After that, everything seemed to blur. A Coast Guard chopper arrived and airlifted Reese and two other injured men out of the lifeboat. Reese refused to go unless they took her with them.

Inside the chopper, he held on to her hand, his eyes on her face. "I remember some of it, not all. Did I imagine you swimming underwater toward me? Was it real or some kind of delusion?"

She could still recall her terrible fear. "I couldn't find you. I kept swimming. Then I saw you—trapped by a piece of the crane."

"So it *was* you. I knew it." He gave her one of his sweet smiles. "My pant leg was caught and I couldn't get free. I was almost out of air. I didn't think you could get me free in time, but..." His beautiful blue eyes glistened. "You saved my life."

Kenzie tried to smile, but her chest was hurting and everything inside her wanted to weep with relief. She wiped away a drop of wetness on her cheek. *He's alive*, she reminded herself, and a real smile finally surfaced.

"I told you I was on the swim team. I didn't tell you I was captain."

A soft laugh escaped, then Reese started coughing.

Kenzie squeezed his hand. "You need to rest. Just relax and take it easy, okay?"

His eyes darkened. "This wasn't an accident."

She didn't argue. Too many bad things had happened.

Reese's features hardened. "Sawyer DeMarco is dead. So is Arthur Haines. I thought the trouble was over. What the hell is going on?"

As the chopper flew toward Houston, Kenzie shivered.

CHAPTER FORTY

NIGHT HAD SETTLED IN, warm and humid, the hum of insects the only sound in the quiet. Hawk stood in the shadows outside the house, a big two-story structure behind wrought-iron gates sitting on several acres in a rural part of Crosslake. Jeremy Bolt's private retreat.

Or in this case, the home of Martel Ames, the reclusive, wealthy son of the late Collin Ames, a successful entrepreneur who had lived in Atlanta.

The address on North Lakeshore Drive was surrounded by open space, with the added advantage of a boat dock, a water escape should the need arise. Though the property was fenced, it wasn't electrified.

Wearing a pair of latex gloves, Hawk used the skills he'd learned as a spec ops marine to disarm the digital perimeter alarm system, which wasn't particularly sophisticated. Clearly Bolt didn't expect to be tracked to his residence. And if trouble managed to find him, he trusted his skills to handle it.

Not this time.

Hawk disabled the system on the house with the same ease as the fence, pried off a screen on one of the downstairs bedrooms, and slipped inside. He had spotted Bolt sitting in front of the TV in the family room. Hadn't seen anyone else in the residence.

Approaching the open bedroom door, he quickly stepped back out of sight at the sound of footsteps coming down the hall. Bolt walked passed him; average height, with a lean frame and neatly trimmed brown hair, completely unremarkable in jeans and sneakers and a New Orleans Saints T-shirt. A man perfectly suited to blend in, to kill and disappear.

Pulling his Kimber, Hawk peeked into the hall and saw Bolt disappear into a room farther down the corridor. Moving quickly, he followed, flattening himself against the wall, peering in to see Bolt reaching for something beneath a nightstand. Then the far bedroom wall began to move, sliding open to reveal a hidden room on the opposite side.

Holding his pistol in a two-handed grip, Hawk leveled the weapon at Bolt's back and stepped into the bedroom. "Don't move. Hands in the air or you're a dead man." He meant it. Jeremy Bolt was one of most dangerous men in the country. Odds were he wouldn't give up without a fight.

Bolt slowly raised his hands.

"Easy, now. No sudden moves."

"How did you get in?"

"Your security system could definitely use an upgrade."

"If it's money you're after, I'll open the safe and you can take what's inside."

Hawk shook his head. "I don't think so. What I want is for you and me to take a little ride down to the police station, where you're going to tell the cops who you really are and what you do for a living. You're also going to confess that you murdered Lee Haines and set his wife up to take the fall."

Bolt laughed. It was a harsh, high-pitched sound that sent a chill down Hawk's spine.

"Hands behind your back. Slowly. You don't want to make me nervous."

As Bolt moved to comply, Hawk pulled a zip tie out of his pocket. "Move an inch and I pull the trigger."

Bolt stood stock-still. Hawk looped the zip tie around the

man's wrists, but before he could pull it tight, Bolt whirled and kicked, and the gun went flying. Hawk grabbed Bolt by the front of his T-shirt and swung a blow that sent him crashing into the nightstand. An instant later, the drawer was open and Bolt had a gun in his hand. Hawk dived toward Bolt and gripped his wrist, forcing the barrel into the air.

A shot rang out, then another, raining plaster down from the ceiling. They struggled, fighting for control of the weapon. Hawk was bigger, but Bolt was wiry and in prime physical condition.

The gun wavered, the barrel just inches from Hawk's throat. Time had run out. Hawk forced the pistol toward Bolt and pulled the trigger, the shot exploding through his neck beneath his jaw, blowing off the top of his head.

Jeremy Bolt lay dead beneath him, blood soaking into the carpet.

Fuck.

He'd wanted Bolt alive. Unfortunately, he'd had no choice. Not if he'd wanted to remain among the living.

As Jase shoved to his feet, he glanced toward the room hidden behind the wall and started in that direction. He stepped through the entrance and froze, unable to believe his eyes.

Evidence was one of the reasons he had come. A guy like Bolt, every kill perfectly planned, no clues left behind—kept a room full of them.

Hawk holstered his Kimber and walked inside. Photos lined the walls, Bolt's targets as he'd tracked them, then a souvenir of each kill. A trophy to relive his successes.

He spotted Lee Haines's picture, pinned on the cork board next to a photo of Kenzie. There was a bullet neatly displayed in a small glass bottle, undoubtedly from the revolver he had used to kill Haines and left for the police to find. From the start, he had planned for Kenzie to take the blame.

Hawk had found what he'd come for. Now he had to get the evidence to the police without incriminating himself.

Ten minutes later, he pulled off the road and used his burner phone to call the crime desk at the Shreveport *Times*. The call went to a reporter on the night desk.

"This is Joe Murphy. What can I do for you?"

"I've got a story for you, Joe. Be one of the biggest to break in the country this year. If you're interested, go to 7845 North Lakeshore Drive. You'll find the body of a hit man named Jeremy Bolt. Uses the alias Martel Ames."

"Who is this?"

"You'll also find a room filled with trophies Bolt kept of the kills he made."

"I need to know who this is. Give me your—"

Hawk hung up the phone. A little ways father down the road, he pulled over again and tossed the disposable into the lake. With any luck, the reporter would do his job and the cops would find evidence that would clear Kenzie's name.

Equally important, the police would be so busy following up on Bolt's kills, they wouldn't spend much time trying to find the guy who had ended him.

And Long Bailey would be safe.

Hawk turned the Yukon toward Dallas. His wife would be waiting. He smiled. It was time to go home.

IT WAS GETTING LATE. Kenzie sat next to Reese's hospital bed. The doctor had insisted on keeping him overnight for observation. Reese had grumbled and protested, but finally agreed. She had phoned Gran and also talked to Griff, made sure they knew she and Reese were both okay.

While the doctors were examining him, Kenzie phoned

Chase, who called Brandon. Less than twenty minutes later, an armed guard arrived and positioned himself in the hall outside Reese's door.

"Chase is on his way," the guard said, a big African American named Otis Poole. "He was out of town, but he's heading back to Dallas. Soon as he gets there, he and his wife are flying down."

That had been several hours ago. Bran had called and spoken to Reese, who told his brother there was no reason for him to fly all the way from Denver since he was being released in the morning. Bran had reluctantly agreed.

But Chase was closer. Kenzie rose as the door quietly opened and the oldest Garrett brother's blond head appeared. He walked in with Harper and each of them came over and hugged her.

"Sorry it took me so long to get here," Chase said. "I was in Austin, meeting with a client. How's he doing?"

"The doctor says he's going to be fine. But a piece of wood or metal hit him in the head when the boat exploded." She had told him some of this on the phone. "They ran a few more tests. He suffered a mild concussion, along with all the salt water that went into his lungs. The doctor wants to make sure there aren't any complications, but he doesn't expect there will be."

Harper reached down and took hold of Kenzie's hand. "How about you? Are you doing okay?"

"I'm good. Just so grateful Reese is going to be all right."

"I did some digging after I got your call," Chase said to her. "You didn't mention you were the one who pulled him to the surface. Word is you saved my brother's life."

Her throat tightened. She blocked the memory of how close Reese had come to dying, the heart-stopping moments of terror. Instead, she managed to smile. "I used to be on the swim team."

Chase's hard mouth curved up. "Lucky for Reese."

"You must have been terrified," Harper added with such sympathy Kenzie's eyes filled.

She wiped away a tear with the tip of her finger. "I couldn't bear to lose him."

Harper's gaze shot to Chase and a look passed between them. "Why don't we go get a cup of coffee?" Harper suggested. "Maybe something to eat. Chase can stay with Reese while we're gone."

She didn't want to leave him. She wanted to be there in case he needed her. But she hadn't eaten for hours and she was beginning to feel light-headed. "All right, I could use a little food."

"We won't be gone long," Harper said to Chase as she and Kenzie left the room.

In the cafeteria, Kenzie ordered a bowl of chicken soup and a cup of coffee while Harper just ordered a glass of iced tea.

"Chase is afraid Reese was the target of the explosion," Harper said, once they were seated. "That's the reason for the guard. What do you think?"

Kenzie shook her head. "I don't know. The FBI is certain Reese was aboard the chopper that crashed purely by chance. But this is the second time he's almost been killed, and both times the incidents were related to the Poseidon."

"Maybe Reese will have some idea what's going on when he wakes up," Harper said.

"I'm staying with him tonight. I don't want him to wake up alone."

Harper reached across the table and covered Kenzie's

hand. "It's clear how much you care about him. I think he cares a great deal for you, too."

She glanced away. "I'm not sure what Reese feels for me, but he's Reese, so it probably doesn't matter. In time, he'll be looking for someone new."

"Just because he's been that way in the past doesn't mean—"

"It's all right. I've known from the start what would happen. I just want him safe."

Harper fell silent. Kenzie finished her soup and they started back. Visiting hours were long over, but Chase was family and law enforcement had cleared it. Reese was awake when she and Kenzie walked back into the room.

"So who wants you dead?" Chase asked him bluntly.

"I don't know. But you can be sure I'm going to find out."

"You need personal security until you do."

Kenzie spoke before Reese could protest. "Don't you dare argue. Your brother just wants you safe."

Reese smiled. "Why do I need a bodyguard when I've got my own personal guardian angel?"

Kenzie blocked the memory of Reese's body hanging limply in the water. "Next time I might not be there when something happens," she said softly.

Reese's gaze met hers and there was something in his eyes that made her heart squeeze.

His attention returned to Chase. "All right, fine. A bodyguard—for now."

Chase and Harper stayed until the nurse finally shooed them out. Then, satisfied Reese was going to be okay, they prepared to return to the airport, where Chase's twin Baron waited to return them to Dallas.

Reese tried to talk Kenzie into going with them, but she refused. Since he seemed to like having her with him, he hadn't put up much of a fight. They would return on the jet tomorrow.

By noon, the doctor had signed the release papers and a big male nurse escorted Reese, in the mandatory wheelchair, down to the lobby. The other two men injured in the explosion were still there, but their conditions were reported as stable.

In the lobby, a good-looking, heavily muscled man with short dark hair Reese introduced as Jaxon Ryker, a former navy SEAL who worked at The Max, waited next to the elevator.

Jax would be acting as Reese's bodyguard. The man looked as if he could handle the job.

"I appreciate this, Jax," Reese said. "Though it's probably not necessary. Sometimes my brother can be a little overprotective."

Jax grunted. "Better safe than sorry, I always say."

Kenzie firmly agreed.

Ryker stayed close but somehow remained unobtrusive. He drove them to the airport, where they boarded the Garrett jet and settled into their seats.

Reese was quiet as they waited for the pilot to go through the checklist, and the engines roared to life. The jet taxied down the runway and rolled to a stop, waiting for permission to take off.

Kenzie's gaze moved over Reese, whose pallor was fading, his color returning. "You're awfully quiet. Are you all right?"

He sighed. "Just trying to make some sense of all this. I've had plenty of time to think in the last twenty-four hours, and we both know that explosion wasn't an accident. It's only a matter of time until the authorities figure that out. But what the hell was the motive? Now that Arthur Haines is dead, even if Sawyer DeMarco were still alive, he'd have no reason to press for control of the rig. So who else wants it?"

"Maybe the explosion had nothing to do with taking over the deal," Kenzie said. "Maybe whoever was responsible was after you personally. That's what your brother is worried about. That's why Jax is here."

"I don't deny it's a possibility. But if someone wanted me dead, they could have done it a dozen different times. Instead, each time was connected to the Poseidon."

"You need to make a list of your enemies, Reese, people who dislike you enough to want you dead."

He grumbled something about the hazards of being a CEO, then fell silent as the jet began to rumble down the airstrip, gathered speed, and pushed into the air. As the flight smoothed out and the jet leveled off, his head came up as if an idea had struck.

"What if there was someone who wanted the rig, but also disliked me enough to kill me? Or maybe just didn't care if I died as long as he got what he wanted?"

Kenzie turned toward him. "Who are you talking about?"

"Troy Graves."

"Arthur's partner?"

"That's right. Troy and I met in college. From the start, we never got along." Reese went on to explain how they had competed against each other in everything from sports to women, and Troy always managed to come out the loser. "In the years since then, we've been anything but friendly."

"With Arthur dead, Troy's now in control of Black Sand Oil and Gas," Kenzie said. "That puts him in a position to get even for whatever grievances he might hold against you."

"That's right. If Black Sand winds up with the Poseidon, the company gets a badly needed boost, and maybe in the process, Troy gets rid of the competition—for good."

CHAPTER FORTY-ONE

THE JET LANDED at the Dallas Executive Airport late in the afternoon. Reese's cell phone started ringing as he descended the metal stairs onto the tarmac. Hawk's name appeared on the screen.

"Good news," Hawk said. "Good for Kenzie. Not so good for Jeremy Bolt."

"What's going on?"

"Bolt's dead. Better yet, the narcissistic bastard left a room full of trophies, one for each of his kills. He had Lee Haines's photo, a photo of Kenzie, and a spent shell casing from Kenzie's pistol that he used to kill the guy. All we have to do is wait for the cops to find it, which hopefully has already happened. It shouldn't take too long for Kenzie's name to be cleared."

"I can hardly believe it. That's really good work. Thanks, Hawk. If there's anything you ever need—and I mean anything—you call me. Okay?"

"I'll keep it in mind. I heard what happened on the boat. You okay?"

"Fine, considering how much seawater I drank. Kenzie saved my life. And from what I've been told, she damned near died trying to do it."

"She's a keeper, bro."

"I know," Reese said gruffly. The call ended and he caught up with Kenzie near where Reggie stood next to an

SUV limo. "That was Hawk. He took care of your problem. The cops have to work things out, but it shouldn't take long before your name is cleared."

"Oh, my God, really? Are you sure?"

"Bolt's dead, but he left plenty of evidence behind, trophies of the kills he made—including Lee Haines. If it goes down the way Hawk thinks, it won't take long."

Kenzie threw her arms around his neck. "You did it! Thank you! Reese, I'll never be able to thank you enough."

Reese's drew her snugly against him. "You're welcome, but you should be thanking Hawk."

"True, but if it weren't for you, I never would have met him, and I'd probably be in jail."

The notion chilled him. *I love you, baby*, he thought. *I love you and I'm not letting you go.*

He wanted to say the words, but he wasn't sure what Kenzie would say when he did. And with Ryker walking a few feet behind, now was not the time.

Add to that, there was his old nemesis, Troy Graves. If he was right and Graves was behind the accidents—including the two that had very nearly killed him—the bastard was going down.

From the airport, Reggie drove the limo toward Kenzie's town house. He hated to leave her, but she had been through enough, and he had Graves to deal with. There was no evidence, just his suspicions, but deep down his certainty was growing.

He considered confronting Troy in his office, getting it all out in the open, hearing what the guy had to say. But as CEO of Black Sand, Troy would have too much control in the workplace. Employees, clients, security people—better to catch him off guard somewhere else.

"I'm heading in to work," Reese said as the limo pulled

out to pass a slower vehicle. "I can shower and change in my office. I've got a couple of things I need to do."

"You're recovering from a concussion," Kenzie reminded him, as if the headache throbbing at his temple wasn't enough. "You shouldn't be going to work. You need to stay home and rest."

"The doctor said the head injury was mild, and I won't stay long." Just long enough to dig up as much information as he could on Graves. He needed something to connect Troy to the Poseidon. With luck and Tabby Love, he might be able to find it. "I promise to call as soon as I get free."

She flicked him a sideways glance. She knew him well enough to know there was more going on than what he was telling her.

"If you're going in, so am I," she said. "I've got as much work to do as you. I assume Jax will be going with us."

He tried to keep it light, smiled at the back of Ryker's head where he sat up front with Reggie. "Sure. Got to keep my brother happy."

Kenzie cast him another skeptical glance as the limo pulled up in front of her town house. Reese carried her overnight bag inside and while she ran upstairs to change, he chatted with Flo. Griff was in school. Reese was happy the boy seemed to be moving forward without too many scars from the trauma he suffered.

From Kenzie's, the limo took them to the office.

"We've got plenty of security," Reese assured Jax as they walked into the multistory lobby. "The executive floor isn't even accessible without signing in at the desk, so there's no need for you to stay. Why don't you come back at closing, make sure we get home safely?"

Amusement touched Jax's lips. "I don't think that's what

Chase had in mind, but I promise to be discreet. You won't even know I'm here."

Reese felt a trickle of irritation. He'd been taking care of himself since he was fifteen. He studied Jax's determined features and a sigh of resignation whispered out. As Kenzie had said, his brother just wanted him safe.

"Okay, fine, whatever. We're headed upstairs. I'll be in my office."

Jax nodded, rode up with them to the executive floor, then disappeared, presumably to check out building security.

Looking forward to getting out of the clothes Kenzie had scrounged from his Houston apartment that morning and brought to the hospital, Reese showered in his private bath and changed into a white shirt and navy blue suit.

While Kenzie worked on his schedule for the coming week, Reese spent the afternoon digging into Troy Graves, his lifestyle, groups he belonged to, articles written about him or Black Sand Oil and Gas, everything he could find on the internet.

He learned the basics, but nothing that could help him. Reese phoned Tabitha Love. "Tab, it's Reese. I need a little more help."

"Sure, chief. What can I do for you?"

Reese filled her in on his suspicions about Graves, and half an hour later, Tabby called back.

"What have you got?" Reese asked.

"Just some small stuff so far, but you never know what might help."

"I'm listening."

She ran through his biography, born and raised in Dallas, went to Texas University, where Reese had originally met him. "Never married," Tabby said. "No kids. Inherited half ownership of Black Sand Oil and Gas from his father."

Nothing new there. "What else?"

"After his dad died, Troy moved into his father's house, a palatial residence in Bluffview. Two days after his partner, Arthur Haines, was killed, he turned in his old Porsche and leased a new one. Oh, and he's seeing a woman named Delia Parr, the late Lee Haines's fiancée."

Delia Parr. Reese remembered her. *Didn't take her long to get back in the game*, he thought. From his impression at the funeral, he wasn't surprised.

"What about Graves's finances?"

"Troy's not the best credit risk. In the last six months, he's developed a habit of being late on his bills. His mortgage is a couple of months behind. For a while, his spending slowed down, but recently there's been an uptick. He must think he's going to have money coming in from somewhere."

"Yeah, and I think I know where. Anything else?"

"I can dig deeper if you want."

"That's enough for now. Thanks, Tabby." Reese hung up the phone. It was almost closing time. He hadn't made much progress but tomorrow he'd start again. He was tired, his headache returning, but he was looking forward to his evening with Kenzie.

He was thinking about the things he wanted to say when his intercom buzzed.

"Troy Graves is here to see you, Reese." He could hear the tension in Kenzie's voice, felt the same tension settle between his shoulders.

He'd tossed his Nighthawk after the shooting in Shreveport. The Beretta he'd used as backup was in his right-hand top desk drawer.

He reached over and unlocked it. "Send him in."

The door opened and Kenzie walked into his office, personally escorting Troy into the room. She closed the door behind her, gave him a look that dared him to send her away. She wanted to be there, wanted to hear what Graves had to say. He didn't like it. He had no idea what Troy might do. But she had saved his life. He figured he owed her that much.

Reese rose behind his desk. "I'm surprised to see you here. You know my assistant, McKenzie Haines. I'd like her to sit in on our meeting."

Troy's dark eyes ran over her, took in her stunning figure and softly curling mahogany hair. A knowing smirk lifted the corners of his mouth. "Same old Reese."

Reese clamped down on a surge of temper. "Maybe. Maybe not. Either way, unfortunately for you I'm still alive."

Troy's pupils flared an instant before his expression hardened. "I came to talk to you. Figure things out, you know? CEO to CEO. That's what we do, right?"

Wariness slipped through him. Men were dead. Graves was involved. How far was Troy willing to go to get what he wanted? "Sometimes."

Troy's glance strayed to Kenzie and returned. "You always win, don't you?"

A sound came from Kenzie's throat as Troy reached beneath his suit coat and pulled out a semiautomatic pistol, aimed it at Reese's chest.

Rage burned through him. "I thought you just wanted to talk."

"It's past time for that." Troy kept the gun leveled at Reese, then turned it toward Kenzie. "Get over by the window. You, too, Reese."

Neither of them moved. Reese considered the gun in his desk. If he could distract Troy long enough, he could reach it.

"Are you sure you want to do this? I can still sign the

platform over to Black Sand Oil and Gas. You'd get the rig, and we could pretend none of this ever happened."

Troy chuckled. "So I guess you haven't heard. My inside man got busted. The fool kept the money I've been sending him under his goddamn bed. I don't know what the idiot did to get caught, but whatever it was, he promptly spilled his guts. Coast Guard picked him up. They transported him from the Poseidon to the Galveston sheriff's station. By now there's a good chance the cops are looking for me."

"How did you find out?" Reese asked.

"It's always better to have one spy keeping track of another. The second guy's job was to keep me informed." He zeroed in on Reese. "I won't be needing either one of them anymore."

Reese glanced at Kenzie. She knew the Beretta was in his desk drawer. As long as he kept Troy talking, he could probably reach it, but he had already killed one man and he was determined not to do it again. If he did, he might lose the only woman he had ever loved.

Kenzie's eyes questioned him as he ignored the pistol and rounded the desk, putting him closer to Troy.

Troy's gun hand wavered. "What are you doing?" His grip tightened. "I told you to get over by the window."

"There's still time to talk," Reese said calmly. "You're an important man in Dallas. With a good attorney—" Reese lunged and Kenzie screamed as the two men flew through the air and landed hard on the floor. Reese gripped Troy's wrist, fighting for control of the pistol, and Troy pulled the trigger, sending shock waves across the room.

Reese squeezed harder, banging Troy's wrist on the floor until the gun fell from Troy's hand, but Troy jerked free and rolled to his feet. Reese followed, kicking the gun out of Troy's reach.

The door swung open as they faced each other, circling now, taking each other's measure. Jax stood in the opening, gun drawn, but Reese just shook his head.

Troy moved in and swung a blow Reese ducked, then straightened and hit him with a left-right combination. Reese counterpunched, hitting Troy hard in the jaw, but Troy stayed on his feet.

"Looks like your skills have improved since college," Reese said.

"It's all about motivation." Troy flashed a feral smile. "I've always wanted to kick your ass."

Reese's jaw clenched. "Come and get me."

Taking the bait, Troy stepped into the trap Reese had set. Troy swung, Reese ducked and threw a series of punches that drove Troy back against the wall. A framed photo of Reese with his brothers hit the floor and glass shattered as he moved in to finish Troy off, knocking his head back again and again, then throwing a last hard punch that rang Troy's bell and sent him crashing into a table, knocking it over. He landed unconscious on the plush gray carpet.

Ryker rushed into the office and in seconds, Troy was cuffed and sitting on the floor, his back against the wood-paneled wall.

"Cops are on the way," Jax said.

But Reese was already walking toward Kenzie, then pulling her into his arms. "I'm not the same man," he said to her. "I hope you believe that."

Kenzie looked up at him, emotion in her face. "You're the best man I've ever known, Reese Garrett, and I love you."

The last of the ice in his heart melted away. "I love you, too," he said. And then he kissed her, in front of half the staff clustered at the door. And his bodyguard.

CHAPTER FORTY-TWO

KENZIE SAT ON the sofa in Reese's living room. It was late. They had spent hours with the Dallas police. Troy Graves, who had only been wanted for questioning in regard to the Poseidon, was now in police custody and facing charges of attempted murder, among a long list of others.

Two of the Poseidon crew had been arrested on an array of charges that included discharging an explosive device on a marine vessel, resulting in grave personal injury. People were going to jail. Kenzie thought the sentences they would receive were well-deserved.

Her gaze went to Reese, who stood at the wet bar opening a bottle of vintage Cristal champagne. She wasn't exactly sure of the occasion. Maybe just that both of them were still alive.

He carried the champagne over, filled two crystal flutes, and set the bottle in the silver ice bucket on the coffee table.

"What are we celebrating?" Kenzie asked as he touched his glass to hers and took a drink.

"Actually, I'm just trying to work up the courage to say what I've been wanting to say for a while now."

Her stomach curled. After the incident with Troy in the office, Reese had said he loved her. She knew he cared for her. He had proven it again and again. But there were different kinds of love.

From the start, she had been waiting for the time he

would end things, try to return the relationship merely to friendship. As he had always done with the women he dated.

She took a big sip of champagne. Maybe that time had come.

"Go ahead," she said. "Tell me what you're thinking."

He looked nervous. Reese was never nervous. Her stomach tightened into a knot.

He took a drink of champagne. "After the way I kissed you at the office, the gossip is going to spread like wildfire."

Her heart squeezed. She took a deep breath and tried to prepare herself. "You're right, it is."

"There's a way we can fix that."

Her eyes burned, filled with tears. She loved him. She would make it easy for him. "What do you want me to do?"

Shock hit her as he went down on one knee in front of the sofa, reached into his pocket, and pulled out a blue velvet box.

"I want you to marry me. I love you, Kenzie. With everything inside me." He opened the box and a diamond solitaire sparkled in the lamplight. "I've never felt this way about a woman before. I never will again. Say you'll marry me and I'll do everything in my power to make you happy."

For an instant, she couldn't breathe. Then she threw her arms around his neck, nearly knocking him over. "Reese." She hung on tighter. "Reese, I love you so much."

He eased her back enough to look at her, his amazing blue eyes filled with love. "Is that a yes?"

"Of course it's a yes. I love you. Griff loves you. Gran loves you. If you'll have all of us, then yes, yes, a thousand times yes." She went back into his arms.

"I want us to be a family," he said, nuzzling the side of

her neck. "I want us to have more kids. If…if that's what you want, too."

She smiled at him through her tears. "I do, I absolutely, do. Griff wants a brother. We can give him one."

The last of his tension slipped away. "Or a baby sister who looks just like you."

Kenzie brushed away tears. "I feel like I'm dreaming."

"If you're dreaming, we both are, and it's a beautiful dream. You're everything I ever wanted, baby. I can't wait to start a life with you." Reese slid the ring onto her finger and very thoroughly kissed her.

IT WAS LATE morning now, the sun well up. Kenzie had been awake for a while watching Reese sleep. He was lying on his stomach, dozing softly beside her. Her gaze ran over the beautiful tattooed wings stretching across his wide shoulders. She traced one of the feathers with the tip of her finger, then shrieked when Reese erupted beneath her, laughing as he turned over, bringing her with him, setting her on top of him.

"Good morning," he said, grinning. He was aroused, she realized, and a rush of desire slipped through her.

She smiled down at him. "After making love all night, I can't believe you're thinking about sex."

Reese cupped her breast and gently caressed her. "And you're not?"

She laughed, her body softening beneath his touch. "I'm thinking about it now." She leaned forward, her long dark hair cocooning them as she lifted a little and eased him inside her.

Reese groaned as she took control, setting up a rhythm he quickly matched. Gripping her hips to hold her in place, he drove into her, heightening the pleasure. Demanding and giving, they took from each other, took and gave until there was no holding back. Pleasure erupted, fierce and sweet, carrying her over the edge. Reese followed a few moments later.

"I love you," he said as he curled her against his side and settled an arm around her. "I can't wait to marry you." He gave her a last brief kiss. "In fact, I bought you an early wedding present."

"You did?"

"If you don't like it, we can sell it and buy something else, but I've been looking at the property for a while now. It's a big two-story home, with plenty of room for all of us. Maybe I was thinking of marrying you even before I figured it out."

"Oh, Reese, that's a wonderful present. I can't wait to see it. Thank you."

"Don't thank me yet. We're just getting started."

Kenzie thought of the family they would make together, trusting him with her heart as she hadn't been able to do before.

Kenzie smiled. As Reese had said, they were just getting started.

EPILOGUE

Eight months later

REESE MANNED THE ski boat he had bought as a family Christmas present, a bright red MasterCraft ProStar. His wife and newly adopted son were both water sprites. Griff had taken to skiing as if he'd been born to it, already single skiing and jumping waves.

A lot had happened in the last eight months. Kenzie had been cleared as a suspect in Lee Haines's murder, thanks to evidence uncovered in Shreveport. No mention was ever made of how the evidence was found.

The DNA samples Reese had collected at Kenzie's town house after the kidnapping was a match to Eddie Fontaine. Fontaine was arrested, and, not knowing the evidence wouldn't hold up in court, immediately rolled on Nolan Webb. Neither mentioned Sawyer DeMarco, but it didn't really matter since DeMarco was dead.

Reese had gone to Heath Ford about the shooting in Loggy Bayou. Turned out the man Reese had killed was wanted for murder. Given the circumstances—the rescue of a kidnapped child—no charges were filed.

Troy Graves was rotting in jail. He had taken a plea deal, which had shaved a few years off his sentence, but his actions had cost people their lives and there was no way he was getting off without paying for his crimes.

Delia Parr had skated, but she hadn't really committed a crime. According to the tabloids, she was involved with a real estate mogul old enough to be her grandfather.

In early spring, Reese had agreed to coach Griff's Little League baseball team. He couldn't believe how much fun he was having. He was a family man now, with a son and a grandmother who lived with him in the big house he had purchased in Preston Hollow.

He and Kenzie had talked about kids and were trying to get pregnant. They weren't in a hurry. Reese grinned. Being goal-oriented, he was giving it his very best effort.

And the Poseidon?

The day before the purchase was set to close, Sea Titan had backed out of the deal. Being a superstitious lot, the crew on the rig was close to mutiny, convinced after all the accidents that Reese Garrett and his company were a jinx. No amount of explanation could convince them otherwise.

Reese could have fought it and maybe won, but he'd backed out once himself, and in a way he was relieved. Offshore drilling could be profitable, but that profit came with a good deal of risk. Better to move forward than look back. For now, he was satisfied with the path the company was taking.

He slowed the jet boat engine and the hull settled in the water. Griff swam over and passed his ski to Kenzie, who stowed it and helped him aboard. Time to head back to shore. Flo would have lunch waiting on one of the picnic tables, and he was getting hungry.

"All set back there?" Reese asked.

"Yeah, Dad."

"Kenzie?"

Sitting in the co-captain's chair, she tossed him a sexy

smile. "Definitely ready." She grinned. "I've got plans for you this afternoon."

Reese laughed. Same plans he had. Reese hit the throttle and the boat surged forward, carrying him and his family toward home.

* * * * *

COME MIDNIGHT

CHAPTER ONE

THE SOUND OF a baby's high-pitched, incessant crying put his teeth on edge. Derek Stiles forced himself to relax as he settled back in his wide leather business-class seat. The airplane engines hummed outside the window, dulling the noise a little, but the crying only grew louder.

Derek silently cursed. His trip to Colombia had already gotten off to a rocky start when a crucial meeting in the Houston office of Garrett Resources, where he worked as VP of mergers and acquisitions, ran over and he missed his nonstop flight. Now he'd be connecting in El Salvador, laying over a couple of hours before boarding a plane to Bogotá, not getting to his hotel until well after dark.

He pulled out his laptop and set it on the fold-down table in front of him, ready to turn it on once the 737 was in the air. He usually worked on a flight. He always had plenty to do, but he'd been staying up late every night, so he also needed some sleep. It was important to be at the top of his game first thing in the morning.

The baby's cries grew louder, and his nerves revved up. He hadn't really noticed the woman sitting in the seat beside him until she stood up and turned toward the mother and child in the row behind him.

She jangled her car keys over the back of the seat and smiled. "Look, baby. Look at these. I bet you'd like to play with these, wouldn't you?" The baby's crying slowed, turned to whimpers, then sniffles, then stopped altogether. Glancing over his shoulder, Derek watched a little girl bundled in pink, maybe a year old, reach up for the car keys.

"I never thought of that," the mother said, sounding desperate and making him feel guilty. He didn't have kids, but he could imagine how tough it would be to take a child on an international flight.

The mom, a black-haired woman in her midtwenties, took out her own set of keys and held them up, but the baby ignored them, fascinated by the glittering heart on the end of the other key chain dangling in front of her.

"I hate to ask you this," the mother said, "but is it all right if Sophie plays with your keys for a while?"

"Absolutely," his seatmate said. She was pretty, he realized, with long blond hair and big blue eyes. A little above average height, slender but curvy in all the right places. "Once we're in the air," she continued, "if you want me to hold her, give you a little break, I'd be happy to."

The mother's smile held relief and gratitude. "I might just take you up on that. My name is Carmen, by the way."

"Breanna." Her smile went even brighter, and Derek felt an unexpected kick. He was usually able to leave his libido behind when he was away on business.

"You have a darling baby," Breanna said.

Carmen smiled. "Thank you."

The flight attendant urged Breanna to sit back down so the flight could get underway, and the engines roared, preparing for takeoff.

"So I guess you're a mom," Derek heard himself saying, though he made it a habit of keeping to himself on a flight. He always had too much work to catch up on.

Breanna shifted to turn toward him. "I'd love to have

children someday, but I'm not a mother yet. I work with kids, so I know a few tricks."

"What kind of work do you do?"

"I'm with a nonprofit called Shelter the Children. *Abrego Los Niños* in Spanish. We support an orphanage in a little village outside San Salvador. That's where I'm headed."

"Sounds interesting."

"What about you?"

"I work in the oil business as a VP for Garrett Resources. I'm on my way to Bogotá to explore a possible merger with a Colombian energy company. Missed my flight, so I'm taking the local."

"You work for an oil company?"

"That's right."

Her dark gold eyebrows pinched together. "Don't you worry about the environment?"

Here we go, he thought, wishing he had kept his mouth shut after all. "Actually, I do. My company is heavily invested in green energy research, but until we find a way to supply the needs of seven billion people, we're stuck using fossil fuels."

She glanced away, faint color in her cheeks. "You're right. I wouldn't be able to get to El Salvador without flying, and a jet needs fuel. I just wish the change would happen sooner."

He relaxed and smiled. "So do I." He held out a hand. "Derek Stiles. I know your name is Breanna."

"Yes. Everyone just calls me Bree."

"Nice to meet you, Bree."

"You, too, Derek."

When the flight attendant appeared to take their drink orders, Bree asked for a glass of chardonnay and Derek found himself ordering a scotch. He reminded himself he needed to be working—or sleeping—but as the conversation continued, he discovered he was enjoying himself.

"So you live in Houston?" he asked, intrigued despite himself.

"Dallas. I was in Houston for a charity benefit. It was easier just to fly on down from there."

"A charity benefit. Sounds like you were there to raise money."

"That's right. We do a lot of good for the kids, but it's expensive."

They talked some more. He deserved a little break, he told himself, ignoring his laptop. Everyone said he was a workaholic, and it was true. A few hours on a plane talking to a beautiful, interesting woman wasn't a crime.

At one point, Carmen handed little Sophie over to Bree, and she rocked the baby to sleep.

"You've certainly got a way with kids," he said.

"I know. I like them, and they usually like me."

He was beginning to like her, too. When she handed the baby back to her mother half an hour later, it occurred to him he'd like to see her again after they got back to Texas.

"You know, Dallas isn't that far from Houston. That's where my company is headquartered, so I'm in the city fairly often. Any chance we could get together for a drink or dinner sometime?"

She looked down at his left hand. He had seen her do it before.

He smiled. "Not married, I promise."

"Not living with anyone? No fiancée, no serious relationship, nothing like that?"

He wondered why she was so wary and guessed she had been burned before. "I give you my word—I'm not involved with anyone." He didn't have time to be. "So how about dinner when we get back?"

Her glance went over his expertly tailored navy blue suit and starched white shirt, clothes he hadn't had time to change out of. He was six two, kept himself in shape, and wasn't bad to look at. He wondered if she liked what she saw.

"I don't date very much," she said.

"Good. Then if you say yes, you'll make me feel special."

She laughed. "All right, I'll give you my card. If you still want to get together when you get back to Texas, give me a call."

"Great." They exchanged business cards, and he looked down at her name. Breanna Winters. Director of finance, Renewed Hope Charities. One of his dark eyebrows went up. "Director of finance. Sounds like a big job."

The faint blush returned to her cheeks. "It's a lot of hard work, but it's worth it."

Now he was totally intrigued. He wondered why she didn't date. She wasn't just pretty—she was also intelligent and interesting. He thought he was right about her having been burned. He didn't like the idea. He wondered about the prick who had done it.

They ate their meals, rubber chicken in marsala sauce for him, and a Niçoise salad for her, laughing and talking as the plane winged south.

They were an hour out of San Salvador International Airport when he noticed a commotion at the rear of the cabin. The curtain behind the business-class section flew open, and a lean, black-haired man stood in the aisle, an assault rifle strapped across his chest.

Adrenaline hit him like a punch in the stomach. In a thick Spanish accent, the gunman started shouting orders.

"This plane is now under the control of the *Defensores de Naturaleza de Honduras*. You will all stay calm and keep to your seats. Do exactly as we say and no one will get hurt."

Breanna made a sound in her throat.

"Easy," Derek said softly. He reached for her hand, and she laced her fingers with his. He could feel her trembling. "Whoever they are, they want something. We're their means of getting it. If we do what they say, we should be all right."

He only half believed it himself. But Bree was frightened, and the only way out of this was for everyone to stay calm.

The gunman remained where he was, which, combined with the engine noise, gave them an element of privacy.

"H-how many do you think there are?" Breanna whispered.

"Enough to take control of the plane. There's somewhere around 160 passengers on a 737, plus the crew. One guy in each section. I'd say four or five at least."

"How could they get their guns through the TSA metal detectors?"

"Smuggled them aboard, most likely. Vetting everyone in the airport ground crew at an international airport is nearly impossible."

"If you're right, someone in the flight crew must be involved."

"Yeah, unfortunately."

He felt the tilt of the wings as the plane began making a slow turn, altering its course. Then the captain's voice came over the loud speakers.

"Ladies and gentlemen. By now you know control of the plane has been taken over by outside forces. We are changing direction to land in Honduras. We've been assured that once the group's demands are met, you will all be released. Please stay calm. We should be landing at our new destination within the hour."

"One of them must be in the cockpit," Bree whispered. "I thought the doors were kept locked to prevent this kind of thing."

"Maybe the pilot or copilot is their inside man. Or it could be one of the flight attendants. Looks like they had this well planned."

"What…what do you think they want?"

"*Silencio!*" The gunman strode up the aisle and paused right next to Bree's seat. He had a narrow face, high cheekbones and hollow cheeks. "No more talking!"

The soft little whimper came again. Her hand was shaking. Derek squeezed her fingers.

It seemed half a lifetime had passed instead of only an hour before he felt a subtle shift in the plane's altitude. It was still daylight, but soon dusk would be falling. The plane had been in the air for nearly four hours. The gunman had moved back into position next to the curtain, where he could watch everyone in his section.

"We're starting our descent," Bree said.

"That could be good. Once we're on the ground, they'll get the negotiations underway." Or it could be very bad. But he didn't say that.

"I'm really scared," Bree said.

I'm not feeling too good about this myself, Derek thought. "We'll be okay," he said.

That was when the baby started crying.

CHAPTER TWO

"SILENCIO!"

Bree's stomach curled into a knot. The gunman strode up the aisle and stopped next to Carmen and her baby. An overweight passenger, a red-faced man with thinning brown hair, sat in the aisle seat next to them.

He was sweating profusely, clearly afraid. "Keep that goddamned kid quiet," he demanded.

Next to Bree, Derek stiffened. He was tall enough to turn and look over the back of his seat. "Take it easy, buddy. She's doing the best she can."

Carmen jiggled Sophie on her lap, and the baby finally stopped crying. The plane continued its descent, and the hijacker strode back down the aisle to where he had been standing before. The captain made the usual announcements about tray tables and seatbacks, and the gunman settled himself in one of the flight attendants' seats for the landing.

Derek had taken a chance and opened his laptop, been on it a couple of minutes before the gunman had spotted him and loudly demanded he hand it over. Bree wondered what message he had sent. The plane was equipped with GPS, so by now its altered course would have been charted by the authorities. The hijackers were probably already negotiating for the passengers' release.

Or at least she prayed they were.

She flicked a glance toward the man seated beside her. Unlike the overweight guy next to Carmen, Derek Stiles had stayed cool and collected. At least on the surface. She had a feeling he was seething underneath, furious the men had been able to get past security and take over the plane.

She had noticed him as soon as she'd buckled into her seat: very good-looking and clean shaven, with short, thick, perfectly styled dark brown hair. Broad shouldered, with what appeared to be a lean, solid build, the guy made his expensive, perfectly tailored navy blue suit look way better than it ever could on a rack.

Everything about him shouted successful businessman, a corporate higher-up. Which, apparently, he was. He exuded confidence and control, and she felt better having him beside her. It was probably foolish, but he made her feel safer.

The plane landed smoothly and streaked down the runway, the brakes slowing the aircraft more rapidly than usual.

"Short runway," Derek said as the tires screeched. A puff of dust and smoke rose in the windows, and the plane slowed even more.

Bree looked out the window and saw dense jungle the length of the runway as far as she could see. Mountains heavily covered with tropical trees and vines rose in the distance. "Where do you think we are?"

Derek looked past her out the window. "No idea. Middle of nowhere, that's for sure."

The captain's voice came over the loudspeaker. "We have arrived at our new destination. The authorities have been contacted and are working to resolve the situation. I ask that you all remain calm until that happens."

The plane went silent, and the minutes began to tick past.

"What happens now?" Bree asked. In answer, the hollow-cheeked, hard-faced gunman strode to the front of the plane and turned to face them. His hands curled around the stock of the assault rifle strapped across his chest.

"You will take out your passports and your cell phones. You will place them in the bag being carried down the aisle."

Nausea rolled in Bree's stomach. Handing over her passport was exactly what she'd been afraid of. Dear God, if they realized who she was—

She clamped down on the thought. Maybe they wouldn't recognize her name. Her real name, the one on her passport, not the one on her business cards that she had been using for the last five years.

She told herself there was no reason to panic. She was in a foreign country, away from American newspapers and TV. The men were terrorists with their own agenda. So far it seemed to have nothing to do with her.

Looking back down the aisle, Bree saw a woman—one of the terrorists—in the same black pants, white shirt and lace-up leather boots the male hijacker had been wearing. She had the same sort of assault weapon draped across her chest, too. Her hair was black and thick, pulled back into a severe knot at the nape of her neck. She held a plastic garbage bag in front of her, pausing at each row to collect passports and cell phones from the passengers on each side of the aisle.

Derek pulled the dark blue document out of his inside suit coat pocket and turned to look at Bree as she fumbled to get hers out of her purse. She was shaking so badly she nearly dropped it. Derek reached out and caught her wrist, steadying her hand.

"Easy," he said, and somehow it calmed her. She dropped the passport into the bag, followed by her cell. Derek dropped his in after her, and they settled back in their seats.

"Just think about that fancy dinner I'm going to take you to in Dallas," Derek whispered. "What's the best restaurant in town?"

He was doing his best to distract her. She could have kissed him for it. She managed to smile. "The Mansion at Turtle Creek is one of my favorites."

Derek just shook his head. "Nope. Got to be somewhere special. Somewhere you'd like to go but have never been."

She'd been to every first-class restaurant in Dallas. But there was a place she'd always wanted to go. No one would ever think of taking her there, and she didn't have the courage to go by herself.

"Actually, there is a place I've been wanting to go for a while. How about taking me to the Sagebrush Saloon? Food is simple, but it's supposed to be good. And they have a country-western band there on Friday nights. We could have dinner and go dancing." She cocked an eyebrow. "That is, if you know how to two-step." The words came out as a challenge. They were only playing a game. It would probably never happen.

"You like country music?" he asked. There was something in his face she couldn't read, as if he were looking into the past.

"You don't like country-western?"

He glanced away. "I used to."

"Did you dance?"

He didn't deny it, just shook his head. "It was a long time ago."

Bree smiled. "Dancing's like riding a bicycle. Once you know how, you never forget."

His eyes, a warm golden brown, found hers. She recognized the interest there. "I wouldn't have taken you for the country music type," he said.

Neither would anyone else. "Maybe that's why I like it."

His lips stretched into a reluctant smile. The idea of kissing him was definitely appealing.

"Okay, then," he said. "The Sagebrush Saloon it is. I've got a friend who met his wife there. They still go dancing once in a while."

"All right, it's a date." They just had to stay alive in order to make it happen.

Derek smiled, but the worry in those golden-brown eyes said he knew exactly what she was thinking.

Time dragged on. After the first hour on the ground, the gunman threatened to punish anyone caught talking. Maybe he thought the passengers might hatch a rebellion, but Bree didn't think that was going to happen.

Then the baby started sniffling and began to cry again. When Carmen's attention failed to quiet her, Bree leaned over, took the baby in her arms and settled back in her seat. A few softly crooned words and some gentle rocking and little Sophie quieted again.

"Sooner or later, she's going to get hungry," Carmen said worriedly. "She won't stop crying until she's fed, and there's no way I can warm a bottle for her in here. I thought we'd be home by now."

If Sophie started crying, there was no way to know what the gunman would do. It was like a time bomb ticking down to an explosion.

Hours slipped past. The sleeping baby went back into her mother's arms. The gunman allowed the passengers to use the bathroom one at a time. Bree wondered how long it would be before the toilets were full and it began to smell bad in the cabin.

The air-conditioning had been turned down to conserve power, so cool air barely came in. Night had fallen, which helped the temperature inside, but the next day would be brutal. Derek had stripped off his jacket and rolled up his sleeves, showing tanned, muscular forearms. He had taken off his tie long ago and unbuttoned his shirt collar.

As time crawled past, he had said only a few words, but she could feel his solid presence. Bree was grateful for it. She glanced out the window, into the darkness outside. With the cabin lights off, people began to fall asleep.

"Get some rest if you can," Derek said. "No way to know what's going to happen tomorrow. You'll handle it better if you're rested."

Derek put his seat back a little and closed his eyes. She had a feeling he was used to sleeping just about anywhere. Bree thought she'd be too worried to sleep, but as the hours wore on, fatigue and hunger began to take their toll, and eventually she nodded off.

THE SUN WAS coming up when Bree opened her eyes. She saw that Derek was awake, looking alert and far too appealing, while her mouth was dry and gritty and her makeup was smudged. Derek glanced toward the aisle, and his features tightened. Bree followed his gaze and saw the hollow-cheeked hijacker striding toward them. Her pulse took a frightened leap.

The man stopped right next to Derek's aisle seat, but his gaze was locked on Bree. "You will come with me."

Nausea rolled in her stomach, and for an instant she thought she might throw up. They had found her.

"What do you want with her?" Derek asked. "You've got a plane full of hostages. Leave her here. She's helping take care of the baby." Who was overdue to start crying any minute.

Cold black eyes locked on Derek's face. "You would be

wise to mind your own business, gringo." He looked past Derek to Bree. "You heard what I said. Do not make trouble or others will suffer."

He raised his rifle, pointed it toward Carmen and the baby, but continued to stare Bree down. "You will come with me. Now."

Bree was shaking as she rose from her seat. She looked at Carmen's stricken face and baby Sophie's sleepy smile. Whatever happened, she had no choice but to follow the gunman's orders. She turned sideways and started to ease past Derek, but he rose from his seat, blocking her way.

"If she goes, I go with her," he said, oblivious, it seemed, to the gun barrel aimed at his chest. "That's the deal. She'll do what you want, but I go with her."

"Derek…" His name came out in a frightened whisper.

"Who are you?" the gunman asked in his heavily accented Spanish.

"I'm Derek Stiles. I'm her fiancé. Where she goes, I go."

Oh God, Bree thought. "You don't have to do this," she said softly, gathering a bit of courage as she hoisted the strap of her purse over her shoulder. She wasn't Derek's problem. He barely knew her. He didn't even know her real name.

Derek didn't move.

The gunman's gaze shifted back and forth between them as he tried to make a decision. Then he grabbed Derek's shoulder and hauled him into the aisle, shoved the barrel of the rifle into his back. "*Si*, perhaps it is good you come along. You might prove to be useful."

The hijacker turned to Bree. "You will come with your man." A wolfish grin split his face. "Or I will kill him."

CHAPTER THREE

As THEY CROSSED the tarmac, Derek reached for Bree's hand and pulled her up beside him. The hijacker walked behind them, his rifle pointed at Derek's back. Three other men appeared at the edge of the runway to join them, grim-faced, dark-skinned men with greasy hair and unkempt beards. They were using wireless radios to communicate, clearly in touch with each other and the a-holes on the plane.

Up ahead, a row of metal buildings clustered together on one side of the runway, which was dotted with potholes and patches of bare earth where the asphalt had been worn away. Weeds in search of sunlight grew up through cracks in the pavement. The field was clearly abandoned, dense jungle growing along both sides of the runway, spilling onto the tarmac. High-peaked, jungle-covered mountains rose in the distance, clouds drifting over the crests.

From the looks of the Quonset hut–style buildings, Derek figured the airstrip might have been used by the military at one time. It was abandoned now, and he was fairly certain civilization was a long way away.

"You shouldn't have done that," Bree said to him softly as they neared one of the metal structures, apparently their destination. "You barely know me."

He shrugged. "We're getting married. What choice did I have?"

That made her smile. Derek thought maybe that alone

was worth it. He still hadn't figured out exactly why he'd done it. It was stupid—no doubt about that. But then he thought of the soft look in Bree's eyes as she was holding Carmen's baby. Given the same choice, he would do it again.

Derek surveyed the dense, endless green landscape. He had no idea where they were, but he'd been involved in a number of business deals in Latin America. He'd read the crime rate in Honduras had fallen in the last few years, but violence and death were still everyday occurrences.

From the looks of the hard men and women involved in the hijacking, they wouldn't hesitate to carry out their threats.

He glanced at Bree, who still held onto his hand. He didn't know why they had singled her out, but he had a feeling she wasn't completely surprised. That should have made him wary, but somehow it only made him feel more protective.

The hijacker marched them off the tarmac, across a slab of concrete surrounded by a cluster of dilapidated corrugated buildings. A rusty door opened, and a man stepped out to greet them.

"*Buenos tardes, señor y señorita.*" He was tall and whip-lash lean, with long-fingered, graceful hands. "Welcome to Honduras."

Bree said nothing, just clung to Derek's hand.

"Who are you?" Derek asked. "What do you want?"

"We are *Los Defensores de los Naturaleza.* Defenders of nature. We are fighting to save our beloved country from people like you." His black gaze ran over Derek's expensive suit and shiny black Ferragamo shoes. "It is big corporations and wealthy land owners who are trying to destroy it."

He knew about the environmental movement in Honduras. One of its most prominent leaders, a woman named

Berta Flores, had been assassinated a few years back for her activism against a hydroelectric plant. The hijackers, however, with their leathery skin and knotted hands, looked more like rebels or mercenaries than activists.

But maybe he was wrong.

"I am General Alonso de Leon Batista. From now on, you will be dealing with me." Batista looked different from the others—well dressed in tailored black slacks and a spotless white short-sleeved shirt. When his mouth curved beneath his thin black mustache, he looked almost elegant.

"Put them in the women's quarters," Batista said.

One of the hijackers shoved Derek from behind, and he stumbled forward. He straightened and kept walking, Breanna close beside him. Their footsteps echoed as the gunman marched them down an empty, cement-floored corridor into a room with a row of six narrow beds. A wooden nightstand sat between two bunks, which were covered by thin gray wool blankets. A couple of wooden benches and a battered plank table rested along the wall, a basin and pitcher on top.

Maybe the room had been occupied by female personnel, but it had clearly been out of use for years. Derek figured the lone female hijacker was staying with the men.

"*El baño está allí.*" *The bathroom is there,* the gunman said, gesturing toward a door at the end of the chamber next to a boarded-up window. He was heavyset and unshaven, wearing a red bandanna around his thick neck. "*El agua esta en la jarra.*" *Water is in the pitcher.*

Derek spoke Spanish. It was a necessity during negotiations in foreign countries. It was one of the reasons he'd been hired. He could tell Breanna also understood, but neither of them replied. Better to keep them guessing.

"*Comprende?*" the gunman asked.

Still no reply. The gunman stepped into Derek's space. "I think you understand me very well, eh, gringo? Do not play games with Cisco, or you will be sorry."

Derek clamped down on his temper. Calm control worked better in a situation like this. "I understand what you said," he finally conceded, replying in Spanish.

"*Bueno.* You will stay here until El Defensor sends for you." It meant the Defender. Derek doubted defending the environment was the leader's only motive. With so much manpower, money and planning expended, it was likely more self-serving.

Cisco strolled into the corridor, closed and locked the door. Footfalls sounded as the guard walked away. When Derek turned toward Breanna, she stepped into his arms.

"It's okay," he said, drawing her closer. "Everything's going to be all right." He shouldn't have noticed how good she felt pressed against him, how well they fit together, but he did. "We just need to stay calm till help arrives."

She took a step back and looked up at him. "You shouldn't have done it. You should have stayed on the plane."

"Too late to worry about that now." Derek started moving, making a cursory check of their surroundings, examining the walls, checking under the beds, looking into the bathroom. He climbed up onto the wooden table and pushed up one of the acoustic ceiling tiles to look at the space between the tiles and the roof. He jumped down from the table and brushed the dust off his slacks.

"I'll take a closer look, see what we might be able to use. But I don't think the place is bugged."

"Why did you do it?" Bree asked. "You don't know anything about me. You don't even know my real name."

A trickle of unease slipped through him. He'd known something was off about her. "So you're not Breanna Winters?"

"No."

"Well, then, considering the circumstances, I think you better tell me who you are."

She pressed her lips together. Even with her lipstick gone, they were a pretty shade of pink, and Derek felt an unexpected surge of arousal. Though one look at their surroundings was enough to tamp it down.

"My real name is Breanna Wingate. But I don't use my family name. I haven't for more than five years."

"Wingate," he repeated. "The only Wingate of any consequence I can think of is Jonathan Wingate, the multibillionaire software engineer."

"He's my dad."

And with those words, it all fell together. "So you're the target of the hijacking?"

"I'm not sure. That's the funny part—I don't really think they were after me. I was supposed to be on a flight next week from Dallas, but I changed my mind at the last minute and decided to leave earlier, fly directly out of Houston. I think maybe they just saw my passport and put two and two together."

"So there's a chance you were just a bonus. They collected everyone's passport, or at least those of us flying business or first-class. They checked the names to see who might be useful, and your name popped."

"I think that's a possibility."

"Even if you're right and it was just wrong place, wrong time, it doesn't alter the circumstances."

"I know."

"I don't want to scare you, but in a situation like this, even if they ransom you and your dad agrees to pay, they might not let you go."

Bree's chin angled up. "*Us,*" she corrected. "They might

not let *us* go. Because whatever happens, you risked your life for me, and I'm not leaving here without you."

BREE LOOKED INTO Derek's golden eyes and thought she caught a hint of approval. But he was a difficult man to read, so she couldn't be sure. Oddly, now that the worst had happened, she felt stronger, less afraid. Resigned to the situation, she was ready to face whatever lay ahead.

And Derek was with her. That was an unexpected bonus.

"Do you think there's a guard outside our door?" she asked.

Derek walked over and tried the knob, found the door securely bolted. "The lock is solid, but I think the guard's gone. I'm a guy in a business suit and you're a billionaire's daughter. I don't think they see us as much of a threat. Which actually works in our favor."

"How do you mean?"

"They're underestimating us. They think we'll just sit back and do whatever they say."

Exactly what Breanna planned to do. "My father will pay whatever they ask. He and my mother love me. You don't have to worry about that. We're still very close. I just didn't want to live my life in a fishbowl and back then, that was the way it was."

"I can understand that. Your dad's a world-renowned figure, which put you in the spotlight. I've always been on my own. It's easy to imagine how trapped you felt."

"Once I got out of college, I realized the life my parents wanted for me wasn't what I wanted. I craved independence. I wanted to explore the world, find my own place in it."

"Good for you," Derek said.

She walked over to the boarded-up window, saw nothing but jungle beyond. "I traveled for a while. I had a trust fund, which gave me tremendous freedom, but I've never been the kind of person to sit around and do nothing. So I started a nonprofit, and it felt really good to do something for other people. From there the organization expanded into a number of charities under one umbrella."

"Including the orphanage in the village outside San Salvador?"

"That's right."

Derek came over and stood beside her, peered through the cracks in the boards to see what she had seen—an endless sea of green that was more daunting than a thousand miles of ocean.

He turned to survey their barren quarters, and his mouth curved faintly. "At least we've got indoor plumbing."

Bree almost smiled. "Always a plus."

"There's not much we can do except wait and see how this plays out. Once we know the game plan, we can make some decisions."

She frowned. "Decisions? What sort of decisions? There's a small army out there, Derek. They have automatic weapons, and I would guess they're willing to kill to get what they want. We just have to wait till my dad pays the money and they let us go."

Derek fell silent. He didn't have to speak for her to read his thoughts. Bree shivered as she recalled his words. *Even if he pays, they might not let us go.*

"You think they might kill us even if they get the money, just to keep us quiet."

"Doesn't matter if you were the original target. You're here now, and that changes the dynamics. What happens next depends on who's behind this and what they really want. Once we know that, we can decide what to do."

Her glance went from Derek to the window and back.

"You aren't thinking we should try to escape? Look outside. The jungle would kill us for sure."

"Not necessarily. But it isn't time to worry about that yet."

Not necessarily. She studied his wide-shouldered build and muscular forearms, the strong sinews in the column of his neck. "So what were you before? A soldier of some kind? A SEAL or something?"

"I was navy, but I wasn't a SEAL. I was a fighter jet pilot. Flew off carriers for a while. Mostly I was stationed in Pensacola, Florida. But a pilot has a lot of survival training in case he gets shot down. I had engine trouble once over Colombia and had to punch out. It was an isolated area, and I'd lost my comms. Took me six days to reach a village where I could get help. I was damned glad I knew what to do."

Bree wasn't sure if Derek's training was a plus or minus. No way was she braving the perils of a jungle. She'd rather stay here and fight.

"Like I said, it's too soon to do more than wait," he repeated, "but it never hurts to be prepared." With that he returned to his examination of the room, which was large but mostly empty. He examined the lock on the door, went back into the bathroom and returned.

"No window in there, just a row of rusty showers, sinks and johns. Might be able to use the porcelain lid off one of the commodes as a weapon. I could break the mirror. Piece of shattered glass makes a good knife."

Her heart rate picked up. She wasn't liking the sound of this.

"I still don't think the room is bugged, which supports your theory they weren't expecting you. I can take a bed apart, make a defensive weapon out of one of the wooden slats."

"You're making me nervous, Derek."

"Take it easy, okay? There's a chance this will all go down smoothly. They ask for money. Your dad pays and they release you—*us*," he amended when she opened her mouth to correct him. "And they let the hostages go. But it's always smart to have a contingency plan."

He was right. She had no idea what was going on out there, or what the hijackers planned to do. They needed to be prepared.

"What do you think is happening to the people on the plane?"

His features tightened. "I don't know, but to tell you the truth, I'd rather be here. At least we have some options."

Did they? Because so far she didn't see any. They had no guns and no way to escape, and even if they could get out of the compound, there was no place to go but miles of deadly jungle.

Her nerves returned. She watched Derek slide back under the bed and heard a wrenching sound as he tore off one of the wooden slats holding up the thin mattress. Easing back out, he began to fashion some kind of weapon. Bree ignored the sinking feeling in the pit of her stomach and sat down on the bunk to wait.

CHAPTER FOUR

RAFAEL CASTILLO, EL DEFENSOR, sat at the end of a heavy plank table across from his top aide, Julio Montez.

"God is smiling on us, Raffie," Julio said, using the nickname he had given Rafael when they were boys. "The daughter of Jonathan Wingate, one of the richest men in the world, has fallen smack-dab into our hands." Julio was half American and handsome, with blond hair and blue eyes.

He'd been born in Honduras, attended school with Rafael, then traveled to the States with his mother using the name Jules Martel, his mother's maiden name. He had been educated at Harvard, studying for his master's when he became a suspect in the murder of several young women. Wisely, he had returned to his homeland, where he was once more Julio Montez.

Rafael leaned against the high back of his carved wooden chair. "Yes, it seems quite a stroke of good fortune—a twist of fate that eliminates many of our problems."

"You're talking about the 160 passengers aboard the plane. Things will definitely be easier without them."

Rafael nodded. Unlike his top man, General Batista, with his darkly elegant good looks, Rafael was average in height and build, with thinning brown hair and dull brown eyes. Except for a small scar bisecting his left eyebrow, Rafael was completely unremarkable.

And utterly ruthless, a quality he prided himself upon.

"If all goes well," he said, "we will no longer be burdened with 160 people needing to be fed and cared for and constantly guarded, people who could even now be plotting a rebellion to regain control of the plane."

"Have you made contact with Wingate?" Julio asked.

"*Si*, this morning. I spoke to Jonathan Wingate himself and explained our cause. I told him circumstances have forced us to act to protect the lands and people of our country. Señor Wingate was very sympathetic, though he did not agree with our methods."

"What about the money? Did he agree to pay for the return of his daughter and her fiancé?"

"Wingate seemed to hesitate when I mentioned Derek Stiles, the name on his passport, but in the end Wingate agreed to our terms."

Julio grinned. "Maybe Wingate didn't know his daughter was planning to marry. Or he wants her to marry someone he thinks is better suited."

Rafael ignored the faint gleam in Julio's eyes that appeared whenever he focused on a woman. "It is possible Wingate doesn't approve. Either way, Stiles is part of the deal."

Julio sat forward in his chair. "How much, Raffie? How much did Wingate agree to pay?"

"The same amount I would have demanded from the airline. Five hundred million dollars." An amount most likely to have come from the U.S. government, though they would surely deny any payment of a terrorist demand.

"And Wingate agreed?"

Rafael shrugged. "That is only half of one of his many billions." Rafael smiled. "I think he may have considered it a bargain."

The gleam returned to Julio's blue eyes. "She must be something special to be worth that much money."

"Perhaps she is." Rafael rose from his chair. "Why don't we see?"

DEREK HEARD FOOTSTEPS approaching out in the corridor. He shoved his wooden bat and makeshift knife beneath the mattress and sat down on the bed next to Bree.

The door opened, and two men walked into the room. One was of average height and build, with thin brown hair and a scar cutting his eyebrow. The other was taller, blond and blue-eyed, good-looking in a slick sort of way.

Derek and Bree both rose from the bed. When the brown-haired man spoke, authority rang in his voice. It was clear he was the man in charge.

"I am Rafael Hernandez Castillo. My men call me El Defensor. This is my aide, Julio Montez."

Montez's blue stare went to Bree, ran over her breasts beneath her silky pink floral blouse, slid like grease over the stretch jeans that showed off her curves. The glimmer of heat in his eyes sent a shot of adrenaline into Derek's blood.

Castillo's attention swung to Bree. "Ms. Wingate, you will be relieved to know that I have spoken to your father. Señor Wingate has agreed to pay the ransom for your safe return. As the amount is large, he has asked us to give him three days in which to assemble the necessary funds. Once he has paid the ransom, you and your fiancé will be freed."

"What about the people on the plane?" Bree asked.

"We will allow the plane to continue on to its original destination. The passengers and crew will come to no harm."

"And Ms. Wingate?" Derek asked.

"As I said, once the transaction is completed, you will both be released." Castillo's cold eyes met his. They reminded Derek of a reptile's. "In the meantime, I must ensure my men's safety. The two of you will be transferred from here to a different location."

"A different location," Derek repeated in an effort to keep Castillo talking. The more they knew, the better.

"It is only a precaution, you understand." Castillo's lips curved faintly. "Unfortunately, the accommodations won't be quite as luxurious as these." He turned and started for the door, and Montez fell in behind him.

As Castillo stepped into the corridor, Montez turned and fixed his stare on Bree. "Maybe…after you're settled, I can make things easier for you." His hot gaze ran over her, leaving no doubt as to what he was thinking. "That is, after we get to know each other better." Montez walked out and closed the door, and Derek unclenched his fists.

"They're moving us," Bree said softly.

Derek released a slow, calming breath. "They're changing the game plan. It's a lot easier to control the two of us than a plane full of men, women and children. And in this case, the outcome will be the same."

"My father pays the ransom instead of the airline paying, or the government, or someone else."

"That's right."

She walked over to the boarded-up window, and Derek joined her. Fine rays of sunlight filtered through the cracks between the boards, gleaming on her shiny blond hair. It curled softly in the humidity, framing her face. Derek reached out and wound a silky strand around his finger.

Bree turned to look at him. "Where do you think they'll take us?"

He glanced at the sea of green barely visible through the window. He had a bad feeling he knew where they were going—a place where no one would follow.

"My guess? They've got a camp set up somewhere in the jungle. Why don't you use the head, maybe even take a shower? It might be the last chance you get."

She nodded. Though he could read her uncertainty, she was stronger than he had first believed. Grabbing the big leather purse she had carried off the plane, she disappeared into the ratty bathroom. He heard the thump and gurgle of the toilet being flushed, then the rattle of metal as the shower went on.

An image appeared of Bree standing naked beneath the spray, rivulets of water running over her bare breasts, cascading down the shapely legs defined by the stretch jeans she'd been wearing.

His groin tightened. The last thing he needed was an attraction to a woman at a time when both of them were in danger. Even if they were safely back home, she was way out of his league. If Bree had any idea of his background—or if her father did—she wouldn't give him the time of day.

Now that he knew whom she was, he needed to back off, ignore his little head and keep his big head in the game. Especially now, when staying focused might mean the difference between life and death.

Unfortunately, as the shower continued to run, his body didn't agree.

Derek cursed silently.

Bree emerged a few minutes later, her face clean and shiny, her damp blond hair pulled back in a ponytail. She looked fresher, clear-eyed, ready to deal with what lay ahead. He found this Bree even more attractive than the one he had met before.

She had put a trace of gloss on those plump pink lips, and he imagined what it might be like to kiss her. Lust hit him, and a fresh shot of arousal burned through him. Damn, this wasn't good.

Derek went to use the bathroom and freshen up, but he didn't have a razor, so he couldn't shave, and he didn't take time to shower. He didn't want to leave Bree alone that long. Not when Julio Montez clearly had designs on her. And whatever the prick had in mind, Derek didn't think the man would wait for Bree's permission.

CHAPTER FIVE

IT WAS LATE in the morning by the time the general's men ordered them into the jungle. The authorities knew where the plane had landed. Bree had expected to see soldiers or Honduran police, some sort of law enforcement, when she walked out of the metal hut. She'd assumed they would have followed the plane's GPS to the abandoned airstrip, but no one was there.

Derek believed the hijackers had threatened to kill the passengers, either with a bomb or some other method of mass murder to keep the military and police away.

As the hours slipped past, Bree followed Derek and half a dozen armed men along a narrow, overgrown jungle trail. Five more men and the female hijacker marched behind them, all heavily armed. The man they had met when they first arrived, General Batista, led the group. There was no sign of Castillo or Montez.

The airliner had taken off several hours earlier. Bree remembered the sick feeling in the pit of her stomach as the sound of the jet engines grew fainter and finally disappeared. She prayed Carmen and baby Sophie and all the passengers would arrive in San Salvador safely.

A half-buried root appeared out of nowhere, and she stumbled and nearly fell.

Derek turned to check on her. "You okay?"

The man seemed to have a sixth sense where she was

concerned, his instincts fine-tuned to pick up any shift in her demeanor as she followed the narrow, overgrown path in his wake.

"I'm okay. Just a root I didn't see."

"You need to be careful. No medical facilities. We can't afford any broken bones out here." He turned and continued walking.

Bree concentrated on putting one foot in front of the other. A broken ankle could be fatal as they marched toward God only knew where. As they moved deeper into the jungle, the terrain seemed more and more forbidding. The temperature was rising, the humidity making her pink-flowered blouse stick to her skin.

She had forced herself to put on the long-sleeved cardigan she'd carried on the plane. She certainly didn't need it for warmth out here, but bugs were a definite hazard.

She picked up her pace to keep up with Derek's long strides, though he continued looking back to make sure she was okay. Only a few rays of sun fought their way through the canopy of trees, and the wide green leaves that obscured the trail glistened with drops of morning rain.

Even in the shade, the heat was oppressive, but as they trekked upward, climbing from the flatlands into more mountainous jungle terrain, the temperature was dropping, becoming more bearable.

She lifted the strap of her big leather purse and settled it more comfortably on her shoulder. The heavy bag was her lifeline. Traveling into a third world country, she carried everything from makeup to snacks, bandages to bug spray. She and Derek were both grateful for the latter.

The bag also carried the makeshift knife Derek had fashioned earlier from one of the wooden slats by scraping the ends back and forth across the rough cement floor.

Even if Batista or one of his soldiers found the weapon, odds were they wouldn't hurt her. She was far too valuable.

Bree fixed her gaze on Derek's broad shoulders. He had cautioned her to stay close as he moved up the trail ahead of her, watching for any sign of danger.

"They've got some big cats out here," he'd said. "Puma and jaguar, ocelots, half a dozen smaller species, but they're usually nocturnal and more afraid of you than you are of them. The biggest danger is snakes. There are dozens of poisonous varieties—coral snakes, bushmasters, vipers and big constrictors like pythons."

Bree hated snakes. The thought of being bitten by one was terrifying.

"Stay close and be wary," he said. "And be careful not to injure yourself. Infection is the real killer in the jungle."

Though the orphanage wasn't far outside the city, she'd educated herself on the perils of the jungle. She knew the dangers of infection and was glad she was wearing sneakers instead of the low-heeled pumps she usually wore. She prayed Derek's expensive dress shoes wouldn't rub blisters on his feet.

Her gaze returned to him as the guards marched them down the trail. His white dress shirt stuck to his back, outlining the solid muscles beneath his skin. His hips were narrow, his damp slacks clinging to a pair of muscular thighs.

Bree tore her gaze away and focused on where she was walking. The daily rains made the track slippery, and mud coated her sneakers. It took concentrated effort not to stumble over the roots and fallen logs on the narrow trail.

During a brief stop, Derek had put himself between her and Batista's men while she stepped off the trail to relieve herself. She thanked God again and again that he was there.

The day wore on, and though the guards set a moderate

pace, by midafternoon Bree was exhausted. She worked out at a gym and did yoga to stay in shape, but she wasn't prepared for a trek like this.

She was beginning to feel light-headed when Batista called a halt. After checking for snakes, bugs and the vicious red ants Derek had warned her about, she sank down wearily on a fallen log.

Derek sat down beside her. "You doing okay?"

"I've had better days."

His mouth edged up. "Yeah, that's for sure."

Cisco, the heavyset guy with the red bandanna, walked up and handed each of them a plastic bottle of water. He seemed to be in charge of them. Bree cracked the lid on the water bottle and took a long drink.

Cisco handed them each something to eat. "*Baleada,*" he said, naming the food before he walked away.

Bree examined the makeshift meal, a tortilla stuffed with refried red beans and some kind of crumbled cheese. "Looks like the Honduran version of a burrito." She took another big drink of water.

"You need to conserve that as much as you can," Derek said. "No idea when they'll give us any more."

She put the lid back on the bottle and bit into the tortilla, which tasted surprisingly good. Or maybe it was just that she hadn't eaten any real food for more than twenty-four hours. Mindful of Derek's advice, she ate half the *baleada* and wrapped the other half in a Kleenex she took out of the little packet in her purse.

Derek's smile held approval as he ate half, plucked a big green leaf off a tree and used it to wrap up the other half. He stuffed it into the pocket of his wrinkled navy slacks and glanced at the armed band of men around them before returning his attention to her.

"You're doing great, Bree. You just have to go a little farther. It's too dangerous to travel at night out here, so they'll be making camp soon."

"Maybe we'll reach the new camp by nightfall."

Derek shook his head. "Now that the hostages have been released, the Honduran military will be looking for the men responsible for the hijacking. There'll be soldiers all over the airstrip. Batista has to get his men farther away, somewhere they can't be found."

Her shoulders slumped.

"Sorry, princess. I wish I had better news."

An ache slipped through her at his use of the name. "My dad used to call me that when I was a little girl."

Derek smiled. "I'm not surprised. With your blond hair and those pretty blue eyes, you must have looked like a fairy princess."

Warmth slipped through her at the compliment. "When I got older, I hated the name. I felt like it made me sound pampered and spoiled."

"You're beautiful. And the way you've held up today—whatever happens, you can be proud of yourself."

She glanced away, her eyes suddenly stinging. "I hope I can do as well tomorrow."

Derek took her hand and gave it a reassuring squeeze. "You'll do fine. With any luck, your dad is putting the money together to buy your release. In a day or two, this will all be over."

"If I'm leaving, so are you." She leaned over and kissed him, just a soft brush of lips, but Derek groaned. "That's so you'll remember."

She caught a flash of heat in his golden-brown eyes, which he tried in vain to disguise. At least the attraction wasn't one-sided.

"Vamanos! Pronto! Pronto!" Cisco used the barrel of his rifle to nudge Derek to his feet. He helped Bree up and they set off once more along the trail.

Another hour passed. The sunlight was beginning to fade when Batista halted the march in a clearing beneath a tall canopy of trees.

Bree surveyed the dense grasses and endless jungle around them. It wasn't their final destination. A temporary camp at best. Derek was right—tomorrow was going to be another exhausting day.

CHAPTER SIX

DEREK SAT DOWN next to Bree on a fallen log and heard her tired sigh. She'd been amazing today, never complaining, just keeping her eyes on the trail and placing one weary foot in front of another.

She had surprised him—again. She was a wealthy heiress, daughter of one of the richest, most powerful men in the world, a fact he'd never come close to suspecting. Her sincere, down-to-earth attitude was one of the things that had attracted him to her.

Aside from being beautiful, on the plane she'd been fun and interesting to talk to—and interested in what *he* had to say. He remembered the way she'd helped the woman in the seat behind her. Carmen and her baby were merely fellow passengers, and yet Bree had been eager to lend a hand.

He didn't regret leaving the plane with her. He hoped her name would be enough to keep her safe, but with men like these, there were no guarantees. Whatever happened, he'd do everything in his power to protect her.

He glanced up to see the general moving toward them in his ominously graceful way.

"In the jungle, the sun sets early," Batista said as Derek rose from the log. "We will make camp here." His thin lips curved. "As honored guests, you will have your own sleeping platform. Please follow me."

Bree rose unsteadily, and Derek rested his hand on her

waist to support her. They crossed the clearing to where a group of men were stripping thick tree branches and binding them together to form a makeshift deck several feet off the ground.

"Tomorrow we will reach our destination." The general turned to Bree, a cool smile on his face. "I hope your father has his finances in order. If he wishes to see his daughter again, he will not waste too much time."

Derek said nothing. Neither did Bree. Both of them understood the implication. If Wingate wanted to see her alive, he would pay—and pay promptly.

"Cisco will see to your needs," Batista said. "Sleep well, my friends. Tomorrow will be a long day." As Batista strode away, Bree turned and slid her arms around Derek's waist. She rested her head on his shoulder, and he could feel her trembling.

"It's going to be okay." He smoothed back a lock of blond hair that had escaped her bedraggled ponytail and managed to smile. "At least we'll be sleeping off the ground."

Bree looked up at him, still looking uncertain. "I'm really glad to have you with me, Derek."

Something stirred inside him. Though she was tired and disheveled, her clothes damp and her shoes muddy, she attracted him as no woman had in a very long time.

"Damn, I'd like to kiss you."

Her eyes met his. "I'd like that, too," she said softly, and a jolt of heat went straight to his loins. He started getting hard, clenched his jaw against his growing arousal.

"Not a good idea," he said, surveying the rough men around them. "At least not here."

Bree glanced away. "I know."

Derek let her go as Cisco arrived and handed them each a bottle of water. "You will sleep there." He pointed toward the platform. "Pilar brought clothes. Soon she will bring you food."

The female hijacker. It was the first time Derek had heard one of them call her by name.

There wouldn't be a fire. Too much chance of smoke being spotted from the air.

Cisco left, and Derek helped Bree up on the platform, then spread the bedrolls open on top, both of them cleaner than Derek would have expected. Two sets of neatly folded camouflage fatigues and two pairs of lace-up leather boots sat a few feet away. Another platform, probably for Batista, was barely visible through the foliage thirty yards away.

They sat down on the bedrolls, and each cracked open a bottle of water. They had climbed into the mountains during the day, and the temperature had dropped, making the evening air surprisingly comfortable.

Pilar, a tall, lean woman in her thirties with straight black hair parted in the middle and clipped at her nape, appeared carrying tin plates of food.

"Eat. The march will be long tomorrow." She handed each of them a plate filled with some kind of meat and more *baleadas*. "You will need your strength."

"*Gracias.*" Bree started eating with her fingers. Derek bit into a chunk of cold meat, the strong, gamey taste unfamiliar. He didn't want to know what it was.

"At least it's filling," Bree said.

"Whatever it is, we won't go to bed hungry." But Derek was feeling another kind of hunger. The more time he spent with Bree, the more he wanted her. And he was pretty sure she wanted him.

He wished things were different. Wished she weren't Jonathan Wingate's daughter and he wasn't the trailer trash son of an unknown man who had merely contributed his sperm to the equation. He wished the circumstances were different all around.

Bree ate slowly, making each bite last, saving half of one stuffed tortilla for tomorrow. Derek did the same. It was dark by the time they finished and Pilar picked up their empty tin plates.

As they prepared for bed, Derek took off his shoes and smoothed some of the sanitizer Bree carried in her bag over the sore spots on his feet. She carefully placed a waterproof Band-Aid over the red marks, and he prayed the boots they'd left for him came close to fitting.

"We need to get some sleep," Derek said when he had finished, stretching out on his bedroll. Bree surprised him by moving her bedroll closer to his.

"You don't mind, do you? I've never, you know, slept in a jungle before."

Hell no, he didn't mind. "Darlin,' you can sleep next to me anytime you want."

It was too dark to see her smile, but he was beginning to know her well enough to imagine her pretty lips curving. He could hear the rustle of fabric as she adjusted her clothes to get more comfortable, and tried not to imagine her taking them off altogether and lying down naked beside him.

She settled herself on the bedroll, facing away from him. Derek moved closer so they were snuggled together, spoon fashion. When he draped an arm over her waist, she released a relieved sigh.

"That better?" he asked.

"Much better." But instead of going to sleep, she shifted a little and rolled onto her back. "It's really dark out here." Not even the twinkle of stars could penetrate the thick canopy overhead.

"Yeah."

"Will you kiss me, Derek?"

His groin clenched hard as arousal burned through him, making him start to get hard. *Jesus.* She wanted him to kiss her? Derek wanted that more than his next breath of air—that and a whole lot more. If she had any idea the things he wanted to do, she would probably run screaming into the jungle.

Or maybe not.

Leaning over, he trailed soft kisses across her cheek, then settled his mouth over hers. Bree made a sweet little sound in her throat, and his blood began to pound. He wanted to hear that sound while she was moving beneath him. Wanted to strip away her garments and burying himself as deep as he could get.

Struggling to slow things down, he only managed to take the kiss deeper, delving in to taste her, inhaling the scent of aroused woman and making him hard as stone. Bree whimpered. Her arms went around his neck, and the kiss turned hotter, wetter, wilder. He didn't remember unbuttoning her blouse until his palm filled with her soft bare breast. It perfectly fit his hand, and Derek groaned.

His thumb slid back and forth across her nipple. The small bud went diamond hard, and his erection throbbed with every heartbeat. Unable to resist, he slid his hand over her smooth skin, inside the jeans she'd unzipped for comfort, inside her panties. Curving his palm over her round behind, he lifted her a little, pulling her into him, letting her feel his arousal.

"I want you," he said. "Bree, I want you so much."

Bree softly kissed him. "I want you, too, Derek. Please…" Her whispered words sounded like a plea, and it was the need in her voice that brought him to his senses.

"Jesus, we can't do this." He shook his head and moved

away from her, rolled onto his back and dragged in deep breaths of air. "Not out here." Not with an army of rough, unkempt men ready to take his place the minute they realized what was going on.

"I'm sorry," she said in the darkness, sounding uncertain as she hadn't before. "I'm not usually... I don't do this kind of thing with men I barely know. I just..." She sighed into the darkness. "I just wanted to control my life again, even if it was only for a while."

Derek gathered her into his arms. "Don't be sorry, princess. If we were anywhere but here, I wouldn't let you sleep until morning." He kissed her softly one last time. "Hey, we still have that date at the Sagebrush Saloon, yeah? Afterward, we can finish what we started in the jungle."

He felt her body relax, knew she was smiling again. "Okay."

Derek kissed her forehead. "Get some sleep, darlin'. We have a long walk ahead of us tomorrow."

Bree rolled onto her side and snuggled against him spoon fashion, the way they were before. Derek inwardly groaned. He was still hard as a brick, still aching for her.

It would be a long day for Bree tomorrow.

But it was going to be one hell of a long *night* for him.

CHAPTER SEVEN

BREE WAS SURE she couldn't sleep. Not with the eerie sounds that warned of the terrible danger in the jungle. Big cats screamed in the darkness. Bugs whizzed past so close she could feel the brush of their wings. Crickets, owls and frogs all chimed in to create a menacing cacophony that made the hair on the back of her neck rise.

Then the warmth of Derek's solid body began to seep through her clothes, and she stared to relax. Whatever happened, she wasn't alone. Needing the rest to keep her strength up, and knowing Derek was near, she closed her eyes and eventually drifted off to sleep.

She wasn't sure what time it was when she felt Derek's solid body move away from her. Bree opened her eyes and saw that the moon was up. A few silver rays cutting through the branches of the tree next to the platform gave her enough light to see Derek's big hand wrap around a branch and twist it off to one side, holding it away from his face.

"Don't move," he said softly, sending a chill down her spine.

The clouds shifted, and more moonlight slanted in, giving her a glimpse of a huge snake slithering down the heavy branch that Derek was holding, creating a route for the reptile to travel away from their sleeping platform.

Bree made a sound in her throat as the snake slid over his hand, its forked tongue sliding in and out of its wide, predatory mouth. Her heart was pounding, her blood pumping so hard she could hear every thick beat.

She didn't move. She didn't think she could. She watched in terrified silence as the snake continued along the detour Derek had fashioned, along the branch into a different tree, winding its big body around the trunk on its way to the ground.

A breath whooshed out. "Oh my God."

Derek let go of the branch, turned and pulled her into his arms. "It's okay. It won't bother us now. It was a python—a constrictor, not a venomous snake." He didn't mention that a python that size could crush your ribs, drive the air out of your lungs and suffocate you to death.

Bree burrowed into him, trying not to tremble. "What if you hadn't been here?"

"I am here," he said. "That's all that counts."

She wanted him to lay her back on the bedroll and kiss her again, wanted to feel the heat of his mouth moving hotly over hers. Wanted him to touch her, continue where he had left off.

"Get some sleep," he said instead. "I'll be right here."

"What about you?"

"I'll sleep once we reach the camp."

She didn't argue. She was pretty sure it wouldn't do any good. She stretched out beside him and closed her eyes, but it was hours before she fell asleep and only a few minutes later that the female hijacker roused them.

"Get dressed," Pilar said. "I will bring food."

Derek was already wearing the cargo pants that had been set out for him, Bree saw as she sat up rubbing her eyes. The pants fit perfectly over his rounded, muscular behind, looking nearly as tailored as his expensive suit. When he turned and started stripping off his wrinkled, once-white dress shirt, she told herself to look away, but all those lean muscles snagged her attention and wouldn't let go.

Powerful pecs, amazing biceps and six-pack abs that laddered down a rock-hard stomach. The man clearly stayed in shape. When he pulled the long-sleeved camouflage T-shirt over his head, covering his magnificent chest, she managed to bring her lust under control and start getting dressed herself.

As she fastened the bra she had unhooked for sleeping last night, a memory arose of Derek's big hand cupping her breast, his finger sliding over her nipple, making it ache and tighten. Desire slipped through her. Considering they were in the middle of a Honduran jungle, it was insane, yet there it was, making her ache for him all over again.

With a sigh, she took off her dirty pink-flowered blouse and pulled on the V-necked camo T-shirt that must have belonged to Pilar, a woman close to Bree's same size.

"How are the boots?" she asked Derek as she turned her back to take off her jeans and pull on the cargo pants.

"Pilar seems to have a good eye for sizes. The clothes and the boots are a pretty good fit."

Bree wasn't so lucky. Pilar was thinner. The borrowed T-shirt stretched uncomfortably across her breasts, and the cargo pants were a little too long and a little too snug over her hips. She remembered the feel of Derek's hand sliding over her curves last night and bit back a moan.

Forcing her thoughts back to the task at hand, she slipped on the boots, which were slightly too narrow, but the socks would keep them from rubbing. She prayed that by the end of the day, her feet wouldn't hurt too badly.

"Once they get wet, they'll stretch a little," Derek said, looking down at the leather boots. It had already started to rain, a light patter that could rapidly turn into a downpour.

Bree stepped off the platform into the foliage to take care of her needs while Derek kept watch for the snake and any uninvited men who might wander in her direction.

Pilar arrived with more *baleadas*, these more heavily spiced and stuffed with some of the leftover meat. "You must eat quickly," the woman said. "We will be leaving soon."

As Bree ate her makeshift breakfast, she gazed at the jungle-covered mountains stretching into the distance around them. There was no sign of civilization as far as she could see.

She looked back at Derek. "Another day of traveling out here and no one will ever be able to find us."

He followed her gaze into the forbidding wall of green. "That's the idea. Let's just hope your dad comes through with the money."

Bree shivered. She didn't doubt it. The question was, would the hijackers let them go after the ransom was paid?

THE LONG, MISERABLE day seemed to go on forever. The rain had been manageable for a while, then the sky opened up and poured down in earnest. Rivulets of water cut the trail, turning it muddy and making it even more difficult to hike. The wind came up, blowing leaves and sticks with enough force to dig into their skin. They hadn't had enough water and had only eaten a handful of nuts since breakfast.

Bree was exhausted to the point of collapse, and Derek was worried about her. He'd offered to carry her, but she had indignantly refused.

"Don't be ridiculous. I'm tired, but I'm okay. Besides, it's going to be dark soon. Hopefully, they won't make us go much farther."

Mercifully, her wish was granted an hour later. By then

the rain had stopped and the sun had come out, a bright spot in an otherwise wretched day.

Derek spotted the camp ahead, a large open space dotted with canvas tents set up in a circle. Campfires burned in the middle, where what appeared to be Indigenous women worked to cook meals for the men who lived in the camp—somewhere around forty of them, Derek guessed.

Some of Batista's soldiers came to greet their esteemed leader and his group of weary travelers, but the women continued their tasks, working to finish the meal before darkness swept over the camp.

"We made it," Derek said, sliding an arm around Bree's waist, keeping her close beside him.

"Thank God," she said.

Pilar brought bottles of water, and this time they drank their fill. Derek could smell the juice of roasting meat dripping into the fire, and his stomach growled.

"Sounds like you're as hungry as I am," Bree said.

"Yeah, and the good news is, it looks like they're actually going to feed us."

Cisco showed up just then and prodded Derek with his rifle toward a row of tents off to one side of the clearing.

"You will stay in here," he said, lifting the canvas flap and motioning Derek inside. Derek urged Bree into the tent first, and the cooking smells disappeared as they entered, replaced by the odor of wet socks and jungle rot.

"Tonight the women roast *un cerdo* to celebrate the arrival of El Defensor," Cisco said, using the Spanish word for pig. "You will wait in here." Cisco turned and walked away, the tent flap falling closed behind him.

Derek made a brief survey of their temporary quarters—at least he hoped they were temporary. He glanced over at Bree, who was doing the same thing.

"How do you like the new digs?" he asked. There were two narrow cots with a striped wool blanket folded on each and a small wooden table with a kerosene lamp on top and two wooden chairs.

Bree sank down wearily in one of the chairs. Both of them were wet, tired and hungry. "I guess it's better than sleeping out in the jungle."

"Yeah." Derek made a cursory inspection of the interior but found nothing useful. He sat down across from Bree.

"How are your feet?" he asked.

"Not too bad. How about yours?"

"Not much worse than they were last night. But walking out of here could be a bitch."

Bree gave him a worried nod, then looked up at a sound overhead, the *whop, whop, whop* of helicopter blades. Derek had noticed an open space through the trees off to one side as they had entered the camp. Now he knew what it was used for.

"Sounds like El Defensor is arriving in style," Bree said, but Derek's thoughts had already jumped ahead to how he could get his hands on the chopper and get them the hell out of there.

"Wait a minute." Bree eyed him warily. "I can almost see your mind spinning. What are you thinking, Derek?"

"I'm a pilot, remember? I was just thinking we might not need to wait for your dad's money."

"You can fly a helicopter?"

He shrugged. "I took a few lessons. I never got my license, but I could manage to get us in the air."

Bree's eyebrows shot up. "You could manage to get us in the air?" she repeated, incredulous. "No way. We need to wait. Dad will pay and they'll let us go."

Derek didn't press the issue. No need for her to worry unless they had no choice. "I hope you're right," he said.

A few minutes later, Pilar arrived with dry clothes, a long, gathered red skirt and off-the-shoulder white blouse for Bree and a clean pair of cargo pants and dry camo T-shirt for Derek.

"You will put these on and Cisco will take you to El Defensor," Pilar said and left the tent.

Bree cast Derek a look, then turned around and started stripping off her clothes. Derek did the same, managing not to imagine Bree standing behind him naked, but it was a near thing.

They had just finished getting dressed, sliding their feet into woven leather, open-toed, huarache-like sandals, when Cisco opened the tent flap.

"You will both come with me."

CHAPTER EIGHT

BREE HELD DEREK's hand as they crossed the clearing in the wake of Cisco's stout, thick-shouldered frame. Night had fallen, the darkness lit by the orange-red glow of burning campfires.

A large tent had been set up a short distance from the rest of the camp. Cisco motioned them inside. Derek led the way, ducking his head, stepping onto a thick wool carpet that covered the floor in a bright-colored native design.

Bree let go of Derek's hand as Rafael Castillo rose from an ornately carved wooden chair at a round, leather-topped table. A second man rose from the opposite side—blond, blue-eyed Julio Montez. His gaze ran over Bree, and a shiver of foreboding crawled up her spine.

Only Castillo approached, but it was Montez whose presence chilled her. She focused on the man with the scarred eyebrow, El Defensor, the leader of the group.

"Ms. Wingate." Castillo took her hand and brought it to his lips as if he were a courtier instead of a terrorist. "A pleasure to see you again."

Bree made no reply.

"I spoke to your father," Castillo continued. "As you know, tomorrow is the last day for him to gather the necessary funds for your release. He assures me he will have them ready by the end of the day. Should that occur, the following morning, you will be transported by helicopter to the rendezvous site, where the money will be transferred by computer, deposited into an offshore account. After the transaction is complete, you will be released."

She squared her shoulders. "Along with my fiancé, correct?"

He shrugged. "If that is your wish."

"I won't leave without him. You may tell my father that."

Castillo flicked a nearly imperceptible glance at Montez before he answered. "As I said, that is your decision." His lips tipped into a smile. "Enough talk of business. Tomorrow our goal will be met, our task here completed. Tonight we celebrate. You will enjoy a meal of roast pig served with *machuca* and boiled mashed plantains. Also *pupusas*, thick tortillas served with frijoles. You will drink our special *horchata* mixed with *guaro*, a liquor made of sugarcane. It is quite delicious."

Montez said nothing, but his smug, predatory gaze made his intentions clear. No way was she drinking alcohol tonight.

"You are both dressed for the evening," Castillo said. "Shall we join the festivities?" He offered her his arm, and though it was the last thing she wanted to do, she accepted, lacing her arm through his. She didn't miss the dark look on Derek's face as Montez held open the tent flap and she and Castillo walked past him into the night.

They paused next to the largest campfire in the circle, where a makeshift table and chairs had been set up and draped with a bright-colored, striped woven cloth. Castillo pulled out a chair and seated her, waited for Derek to sit down, then seated himself. An empty chair beside him waited for Montez.

Then one of Castillo's men came forward, bent and whispered something that Bree couldn't hear.

"I'm afraid you will have to excuse me," Castillo said, rising. "Enjoy the meal, and perhaps we shall speak more later."

Bree sincerely hoped not. The only thing worse than being with Castillo was the thought of being with Montez. She caught the glint of his blond head as he bent to speak to one of the young women who worked in the camp. They were prostitutes, Derek had told her, probably brought in for the occasion. Bree prayed Montez's lascivious attentions would fix on the other women and he would leave Bree alone.

Derek must have sensed her worry. As soon as Castillo walked away, he leaned toward her. "Stay close. I don't trust that bastard. Hell, I don't trust either one of them, but it's Montez who's set his sights on you."

"There's something scary about him. He gives me the creeps."

A muscle tightened in Derek's cheek as Pilar and another young woman walked up to serve them. They set two steaming plates of food on the table in front of Bree and Derek, along with two glasses of a milky-white liquid that smelled like cinnamon.

"Eat," Pilar said. "You will want to be in your quarters before the men get drunk and go after the women." She looked at Bree. "They will not care whose daughter you are."

A chill swept through her. "What about you?"

With her onyx-black hair and high cheekbones, she was exotically beautiful. Her slender figure caught the eye of every man she passed.

"I am Cisco's woman. They will not bother me." Pilar turned and walked away.

Thinking of what could happen, Bree looked down at her steaming plate of food, but she was no longer hungry.

Derek reached over and took her hand. "I'm here. I won't let any of them near you."

But it wasn't a promise he could keep. If the men or Montez decided they wanted her, there was no way one man could stop them.

Derek squeezed her fingers. "Eat, baby. We don't know what's going to happen tomorrow. You need to keep up your strength."

He was right. As she watched him dig in with the gusto of a starving man, Bree forced herself to shovel a forkful of the roasted meat into her mouth. After the first two bites, her hunger returned, and she cleaned the rest of her plate.

She had just finished when she felt a presence and looked up to see Julio Montez standing next to her chair. Her stomach contracted, and she swallowed to keep down the food she had just consumed.

"Did you try the *horchata*?" Julio asked with one of his lascivious smiles.

She'd tasted the drink just to see what was in it, a combination of milk, sugar, cinnamon, vanilla and strong sugarcane liquor.

"I tried it," she said.

"Perhaps you would join me for another glass. We could discuss your upcoming departure."

From the corner of her eye, she saw the muscles across Derek's shoulders tighten.

"I'm afraid I'm not feeling very well. The day was long and tiring. Perhaps another time." She smiled, hoping to placate him at least for tonight.

He gave her a nod of understanding. "Of course. Tomorrow then. I'll enjoy talking to someone from the United States. My mother is American. I went to college there for a while." His English was perfect, she'd noticed, and he oozed enough charm to impress any number of women. But there was something in those ice-blue eyes that put her on alert.

Bree followed his gaze to the edge of the clearing, where a young prostitute stood waiting.

"Good night." Montez gave her a final smile and strode off in the woman's direction.

Bree's stomach settled as relief filtered through her. She turned back to Derek, whose hard body still vibrated with tension. She rested her hand on his cheek and felt the roughness of his unshaven jaw. "It's okay. He's gone."

The muscles across those broad shoulders relaxed. "He won't bother you tonight. He's got another woman to take care of his needs."

The minute the words were out, a flash of heat darkened the gold in his eyes. It reminded her that Derek had needs as well. So did she. She wished they were somewhere else, a place where they could explore their attraction.

"Come on," Derek said, rising. Taking her hand, he urged her up from the chair and led her back to the false safety of the tent.

"No lamp," he said. "The less attention we draw, the better." Fortunately, the moon shining through the canvas brightened the interior enough to see.

Bree eyed the narrow cots. "I wish we could sleep next to each other the way we did before."

"Maybe this will help." Derek rearranged the cots, pulling them together. "Best I can do." She couldn't get as close to him as she wanted, but she was really glad to have him there.

"When this is over—"

He caught her face between his hands and kissed her, long and deep. "When this is over, princess, I'm going to make up for all the hours I've wanted you and couldn't have you."

Bree nodded. "Yes, please," she said.

WHILE BREANNA SLEPT, Derek lay awake considering his options. If there'd been any way he could have taken control of the helicopter and flown them out of the jungle that night, he might have tried it. But it would be dangerous enough in the daytime.

He'd never soloed in a chopper. Hell, he'd only flown one a couple of times. Aside from that, he needed to use landmarks to get his bearings. He only had a vague idea where they were, or which way would lead them to civilization.

Resigned to playing whatever hand they were dealt, he finally managed to fall asleep. He was the kind of guy who woke at the least disturbance, so he figured he'd be awake before danger could reach them. Since he'd barely napped on the plane or in the jungle, he needed the rest, needed to be at the top of his game for whatever they faced tomorrow.

There was no way to know what the terrorists would do when Wingate paid the ransom—assuming he managed to get it done. What happened tomorrow could mean life or death for one or both of them.

It was late when a noise near the tent penetrated his slumber—the grunting sounds of a man and a woman having sex. He felt Bree stir beside him. They weren't touching, but they were as close as the cots would allow. The mating sounds grew louder, panting, harsh breathing, the woman's moans of pleasure.

"They're having sex," Bree whispered. "Right outside the tent."

"Yeah." His voice sounded thick as he tried not think of

Bree's pretty breasts, of kissing a path down her tempting curves, of burying himself inside her.

She rolled onto her side and slid her arms around his neck. "Touch me, Derek. Please…"

"Jesus, baby." But he couldn't resist leaning over to kiss those soft pink lips. She tasted as good as she had before, something sweet and as wild as the jungle. Every nerve ending in his body ignited with desire for her.

"I need you, Derek." She pressed her mouth against the side of his neck, trailed kisses down to his collarbone. It took every ounce of his will to ignore the plea in her voice and the blood burning through his veins.

"If they hear us, they might come into the tent. I'm not willing to share you with half a dozen men."

She made a little sound in her throat, shuddered and eased away. "I know you're right. I just… Tomorrow anything could happen. We could both die, Derek."

"We could. Or we could get the hell out of here and spend the next week in bed somewhere safe. I could make love to you until neither of us could move."

He caught the hint of a smile on her face. "I bet you're great in bed."

Derek grinned. "I'm pretty sure I won't disappoint you."

Bree turned to smother a laugh in his shoulder. Thank God, the grunting had stopped and whoever was out there had drifted off into the night.

"Get some sleep, darlin.' We need to be ready for whatever happens tomorrow."

She nodded and moved away from him. A few minutes later, he heard the sound of her deep breathing. He must have fallen asleep after that.

Light streaming through the canvas finally woke him.

Bree was already up and dressed, sitting on the cot next to his.

"Good morning," she said.

He smiled. "Well, look at you, princess. Already up and ready for the day. You been keeping watch so I could sleep?"

"You needed the rest, and it was my turn."

Derek swung his legs over the edge of the cot and stood up. With the drunken men and women in the camp last night, both of them had slept in their clothes, or at least he had only stripped off his long-sleeved camo T-shirt. He plucked it off the end of the cot and dragged it on over his head, ignored the sandals and pulled on the heavy leather boots he'd worn in the jungle.

"Maybe we can find some coffee," he said.

"I sure hope so."

The morning air was humid but not yet hot. A layer of clouds circled the top of the mountain, but it was sunny this far down the hill. After making a stop at the camp latrine, they found Pilar, who rustled up tin mugs of the boiled coffee the women made in big blue porcelain pots.

Though the helicopter still sat in the flat spot Derek could see through the trees, there was no sign of El Defensor or Julio Montez, which suited Derek just fine. It wasn't until the middle of the afternoon that trouble arrived in the form of Montez.

CHAPTER NINE

BREE WAS WORKING with the women to prepare the evening meal while Derek worked with the men, digging a trench for a new latrine on a rise at the edge of the jungle. Cisco had insisted both of them work, saying they must contribute to the efforts necessary to keep the camp running.

Bree didn't mind. Doing something helped her pass the hours while they waited for word from her father. Derek worried it was just an effort to separate the two of them. Bree prayed he was wrong.

Shoving back a loose strand of blond hair that had escaped her ponytail, she tightened her grip on the bare tree branch she was using to stir the men's dirty clothes in a big iron pot of boiling water. It was a hot, cloudless afternoon, worse working over the flames of the fire. She was careful to keep her ankle-length, gathered red skirt safely out of the way.

"Well, Ms. Wingate, I see they've put you to work." The sound of Julio Montez's voice sent a trickle of fear down her spine. She didn't know what it was about him that put her on edge, but she trusted her instincts, particularly where this man was concerned.

He smiled, all Mr. Charm. "It pains me to see you treated no better than a servant. It's much cooler in my tent. Why don't you join me? We'll have something cold to drink, and it'll give us a chance to talk."

She glanced around for Derek and spotted him through the trees, shovel in hand, digging at the top of the rise. "I don't think so. I wouldn't want Señor Castillo to get the wrong idea."

"Señor Castillo is busy making plans. He has given me use of the tent for the afternoon. Shall we go? Or do I need my friends to escort you?"

She glanced around and saw two soldiers standing by, obviously there to do his bidding. The message was clear. She could go willingly, or they would drag her there by force.

She started walking toward Castillo's big tent, off in the trees at the edge of the lush jungle. The soldiers followed. A knot formed in her stomach and began to squeeze tighter with every step closer to the tent. One of Montez's men opened the flap, and she walked inside. Montez followed, and the flap closed behind him.

"Some refreshments?" he asked as if they were friends, but she didn't miss the icy determination in his blue eyes.

Her survival instincts grew stronger, and her heart began to speed erratically. "All right." Anything to draw out the moment and give her some time. Perhaps Castillo would return. General Batista was somewhere in the camp, but she hadn't seen him since Castillo's arrival. And general or not, Montez was one of El Defensor's soldiers. No help there.

Montez poured her a glass of white liquid, the *horchata* with *guaro* the men had been drinking last night. He handed it over, poured himself a glass and drank down a good portion of it.

"Now you," he challenged.

She took a sip and set the glass on a nearby table.

"Finish it," he commanded.

"I'm not in the mood to get drunk."

His mouth hardened even as he smiled. "It might make things more pleasant for you."

Her heart was beating hard now, pounding in her temples. "What things?"

He set his empty glass down on the table next to hers. "We both know why I brought you here. I intend to have you, Ms. Wingate. The beautiful daughter of one of the world's wealthiest men? It will be a memory I treasure."

Her mouth dried up. She forced a calm note into her voice. "Are you sure you want to take that kind of risk at this crucial stage of your operation? Aren't you worried about my father? If you hurt me, he won't pay you."

"Your father wants you back alive. He'll pay whatever we ask."

It was true.

"You're not a virgin," Montez continued, moving closer. "Keep your mouth shut and you and I will be the only people who ever know."

She was standing next to the table. As Montez came up behind her, she picked up his empty glass and gripped it in her hand as tightly as she could. When Julio pressed his lips against the back of her neck, she whirled, smashed the glass into the side of his head and ran.

She had almost reached the tent opening when Montez caught up with her. His head was bleeding, his jaw clenched into a line of fury. Gripping her wrist, he spun her around and slapped her hard across the face.

"You shouldn't have done that." Dragging her deeper into the tent, he slapped her again, and Bree cried out.

The glass of *horchata* she had been drinking crashed to the floor as Montez pushed her down over the table and came up behind her.

Bree screamed and started fighting.

DEREK WAS ALREADY moving as Bree and Montez entered the big canvas tent. Shovel in hand, Derek disappeared off the rise into the rain forest. Whatever Montez had in mind, it wasn't good.

The sound of Bree's scream sent him running. One of the men guarding him shouted for him to stop, but he just increased his speed. The guards, a brawny man with greasy black hair and a shorter man with rotten teeth, took off at an angle, cutting a path between him and the tent.

As the men drew near, Derek whirled and used the shovel as a weapon, holding it like a bat, cracking the metal spade against the brawny man's head, jamming the handle into the shorter man's chest, then knocking him in the head. Both men went down, and Derek kept running.

Montez had two guards posted outside the tent. Derek wielded the shovel again, taking one of the men down with a blow to the shoulder, then shoving the blade into his stomach. The guy's eyes rolled back as he hit the ground.

The other guard moved in. With no room to maneuver, Derek dropped the shovel and swung a punch that sent the second guard crashing into a tree. Derek yanked him up and hit him again. A spray of blood flew into the air. The man groaned when he hit the ground, clearly unconscious.

Derek jerked open the tent flap to see Bree bent over a table, her skirt up around her waist as she fought Montez with every ounce of her strength, kicking and screaming while Montez held her down and tried to work the zipper on his pants.

Derek's teeth clenched. Blind rage burned through him, and an urge to kill Montez with his bare hands.

Grabbing the man by the back of the neck, Derek dragged him away from Bree, whirled him around and smashed a fist into his pretty-boy face. Montez cursed and swung a counterpunch that Derek dodged. Derek threw a series of punches that had Montez bleeding from his nose and mouth, but Montez got in a solid blow that cut into Derek's cheek.

Keeping his weight on the balls of his feet, he threw a hard right that sent Montez flying across the table, landing in a heap on the patterned carpet. Derek jolted to a halt as a big semiauto appeared in Montez's hand, retrieved from a leather satchel on the floor next to where he'd landed.

Derek cursed. Montez's smile looked demonic. He regained his feet, his finger tight on the trigger.

"You shouldn't have interfered," he said. "Now I'm forced to call my men in here to hold you down while I enjoy your woman."

Derek's jaw tightened. "Touch her, and I'll kill you."

Montez just laughed.

Derek considered his options, which were slim and none. Then, from the corner of his eye, he spotted Bree, gripping the handle of the shovel like a baseball bat.

"I won't let you hurt her," Derek said, holding Montez's attention as Bree silently approached.

Montez smiled cruelly. "On second thought, I think I'll just shoot you. Gives me more time with your woman."

Bree swung the shovel with all her strength, hitting Montez squarely in the side of the head. Bone cracked, blood spurted and Montez's eyes rolled back in his head. He hit the floor with a soft thud and lay unmoving, staring into nothing.

Bree started shaking. "Oh God, I think I killed him."

Derek knew a dead guy when he saw one. Montez would never hurt another woman.

He grabbed hold of Bree's hand. "We have to get out of here. No choice now but to leave." The tent was far enough away from the main part of the camp that Castillo's soldiers hadn't come running. Derek figured Montez must have ordered them to ignore Bree's screams and let him do whatever he wanted.

Fresh fury hit him as he pried the gun from Montez's dead fingers and stuck it into the waistband of his cargo pants. He quickly searched the satchel and said a silent thanks when he came up with a four-inch folding knife.

Flipping it open, he hurried to the rear of the tent and sliced a hole large enough for them to climb through, slipped outside and urged Bree to join him. He made a quick check of the area, but the soldiers still seemed unaware of the happenings in Castillo's big tent.

Bree's eyes moved toward the flat spot she could see through the foliage. "The helicopter, right?"

"No choice, baby. Let's go."

They hurried toward the open area, Bree hampered by her loose-fitting sandals. Derek helped her over roots and fallen logs as they made their way through the dense jungle undergrowth. There was no trail here, nothing but plants, tall grass and tree branches blocking their way.

He managed to find a game trail, which made things a little easier. Bree's sandals and long gathered skirt worked against her, making the climb more difficult, but she kept pressing forward. Derek led her up a thickly vegetated hill and came out at the edge of the flat spot where the chopper sat waiting for Castillo's return.

"What about the clouds?" Bree asked, looking up at the dense white fog circling the mountain a few hundred feet over the ground. Spotty sunlight shone through here and there, but the heavy white mist was too dense to see the hilly, tree-covered terrain surrounding the clearing.

"We'll have to get above the clouds." It wasn't good

news. The rain forest was mountainous. If he chose the wrong direction, he could fly straight into the side of a hill.

The good news was that from the moment Derek had seen the chopper land, he had worked to memorize their surroundings as far as he could see in case they found a chance to escape. The knowledge was going to be crucial. He prayed he remembered everything correctly.

Bree started into the clearing, heading for the chopper, but Derek pulled her back.

"No way would they'd leave the helo unguarded." He eased her back into the cover of the leafy foliage. "Stay here while I take a look."

He started moving, stopped when he felt her hand on his back. Wordlessly, Bree pointed to a man with a pock-marked face sitting on a stump not far from the chopper. Derek had seen him around the camp—not the pilot, just one of Castillo's *soldados*.

He nodded to let Bree know he had spotted the threat. "Be ready to move," he whispered and slipped off into the jungle.

CHAPTER TEN

BREE WATCHED DEREK circle around the helicopter to the right, planning to come up on the guard from behind. It was a risky move. There was twenty feet of open space between the dense jungle foliage and the stump where the man sat smoking a hand-rolled cigarette.

His relaxed posture said he wasn't expecting trouble, but a semiautomatic pistol rode in a holster at his waist, and an assault rifle spanned the width of his chest.

Bree held her breath as Derek appeared out of a thicket choked with dense green leaves. He moved silently across the open space toward his target, the knife gripped in his hand. In his waistband at his back, Montez's pistol glinted in a thin ray of sunlight, but firing a shot would be a death sentence, alerting the entire camp of their escape.

As she watched Derek close in on his target, she wondered if he had ever killed a man. He'd been a pilot, not a regular soldier, but he would have been trained in enemy combat, and he was using that training now.

The knife flashed as Derek grabbed the man by the hair, pulled his head back, and sliced the blade across the *soldado's* throat. Blood gushed from the wound, and a wave of nausea hit her.

She thought of Julio Montez, the man she had killed. It hadn't been her intention, but she and Derek were fighting for their lives. She had ducked out of the tent in search of a weapon and spotted the shovel. She'd used it in self-defense and would do it again if she had to, but she didn't feel good about it.

Careful not to look at the man on the ground, Bree swallowed the bile in her throat and rushed into the clearing toward the chopper. Derek was already aboard when Bree opened the Plexiglas door and climbed into the copilot's seat.

"Strap yourself in good and tight." Derek was busy flipping switches as if he actually knew what he was doing. Bree prayed that he did.

The engine began to whine, and the rotors slowly began to spin. Derek continued checking gauges and dials, going through some sort of pilot checklist.

"Put your headset on."

She found it and was lifting it over her head when she heard the first gunshot. Fear jolted through her. Whirling toward the sound, she saw a dozen armed men cresting the hill, surging onto the open patch of ground.

"Hang on, darlin'. Time to get out of Dodge."

Bullets pinged on the metal struts, and her heart seemed to stop as the chopper lifted away. The nose tipped forward, skimming along the ground, eating up the distance between them and the men. Her stomach swirled for an instant before the helicopter swept them into the air.

Even with the headset over her ears and the roar of the engine noise, she could hear the echo of gunshots. Derek worked the controls, trying to get the chopper out of range, his features set in a hard, determined line.

He was in his element, she realized. She trusted him to do what he was trained for, trusted him as she had from the moment she had met him. The last thing she saw was a thin man who looked like Castillo charging up the hill, leading a group of men coming in from another direction.

Then whiteness engulfed them, and she started praying again. The helicopter kept climbing through the cloud layer, but she had no idea whether they would get high enough to see where they were before running into the side of a hill.

Please, God...please, God...

Seconds that seemed like hours passed before the helicopter popped into sunshine so bright it hurt her eyes. Derek swooped left to avoid a mountainside that appeared right in front of them, and they were away.

"Looks like we're in the clear," he said through the headset.

Her heart was still pounding. "I can't believe we made it."

"Yeah, now all we have to do is figure out where we are and where to find civilization." But she could hear the smile in his voice. Typical cocky pilot.

"What are we going to do?"

He explained how he had been mentally keeping track of their location since the hijackers took over the passenger jet and forced the airplane off its course, veering east to the abandoned airfield. He'd added the two-day trek up into the mountains and figured he knew approximately which way to fly to get them to safety.

"This is an old R22 Raven," he said. "It's got a piston engine, fairly easy to fly. This one has Garmin avionics, so we can see what's out there."

"So we're headed back to the airstrip?"

"It would be a good place to land, but we could still be miles from a village, and it's the first place Castillo will look for us."

"So where are we going?"

"Our best course is to head for San Salvador. I figure the closer we get to a city, the more population. The more people, the better the chance of finding a place to set down and a phone we can use."

Unfortunately, as the chopper continued west, Derek's voice over the headset sounded a lot less cocky.

"We got a problem," he said, and a fresh rush of adrenaline jolted through her.

"What kind of problem?"

"One of those bullets must have nicked the gas tank. The fuel level is dropping way faster than it should be."

Bree glanced down, seeing nothing but green. At least it was flatter here, the mountains mostly behind them. But dense vegetation and trees covered the ground.

"Look for an open spot," he said. "Someplace we can land."

While Derek checked the GPS, Bree scanned the ground through the Plexiglas bubble, but flat jungle was jungle nonetheless, and she couldn't see any end to it.

"Just jungle and more jungle." *How long before the fuel runs out?* she thought. *How long till we crash?*

"Keep looking," Derek said.

"I think I see a road down there, but it's pretty overgrown."

"I see it."

"Can you make it work?"

"Don't have much choice." He swooped down to the road, which followed a stream, looking for a wide spot that wasn't too overgrown. She heard the engine begin to sputter, and her heart jerked.

"Hang on," he said. The chopper continued to sputter and jerk uncontrollably. Her pulse was hammering, her sweaty hands gripping the seat. Then she saw where Derek was headed—a spot on the river wide enough to handle the blades—and felt a fresh shot of hope.

The helicopter rapidly descended, and her fingers dug into the seat. For an instant she closed her eyes and said a silent prayer. Her eyes flew open as the struts settled neatly on the ground and Derek shut down the engines.

Bree looked over at him and grinned. "We made it!"

Derek smiled. "Yeah, baby, we did. Now we just have to follow the road till it leads us to a village."

"Might be a long walk, but at least we don't have to hack our way through the jungle."

"Or fight our way through Castillo's men."

But as they climbed out of the helicopter and Bree went around to join Derek, ten rough-looking men stepped out of the heavy foliage onto the road, two of them with pistols drawn and pointed squarely in their direction.

Derek swore softly. He and Bree both raised their hands.

CHAPTER ELEVEN

IT WAS AMAZING how circumstances could change. What to Derek had looked like another group of hostiles was actually a bunch of villagers working together against a local band of thieves.

The thieves had been raiding nearby settlements, and the men had set out to catch them. They'd been searching when they'd spotted the chopper and heard the engine misfire. The guns were only a precaution.

The men spoke Spanish, making it easy for him to communicate. Since he wasn't sure where the villagers' sympathies lay, he told them he and his wife were on vacation when they had been kidnapped by hostiles. Although they managed to escape in a stolen chopper, they needed to report the bandits to the authorities and call Bree's father, who would be worried about his daughter.

The story seemed to satisfy the men, who led them into the tiny village of Santa Margarita. It was little more than a scattering of wood-framed houses painted an array of once-bright colors, clustered around a block-long dirt street.

The leader of the group, Paco Arnolde, a sinewy man with darkly tanned skin and a heavily weathered face, was the local *alcaldía*—mayor of the town. There were no police, Paco said, but there was a cantina.

"In the cantina, you will find food," the mayor announced, "and there are rooms upstairs. Also there is a telephone. You will need money, though, for the room and the food." He grinned proudly, exposing a missing tooth. "Or you can pay with Visa."

Derek grinned back. "We can do that." His card was in the wallet the hijackers had taken, but he knew the number. Hopefully that would work.

Paco led them down the dirt street while children in ragged clothes darted around them, surveying them with smiles and curiosity as they played some kind of stick-and-ball game.

El Gato Azul cantina, the Blue Cat, looked like a two-story shed, with a roof that sloped away from the street and doors off a second-floor balcony.

There were glass-paned windows in the rooms upstairs, but the ones downstairs were covered by wooden shutters that had been propped open. Paco led them into the cantina and introduced them to the owner, Bernardo Garcia. Bernardo was short and fat, and his black eyes seemed to gleam with dollar signs when he looked at Derek and Bree.

"You and your wife wish to rent a room, Señor?"

"*Si*, and we need to use your telephone."

"*Si, si.* I will take very good care of you."

Derek turned back to the mayor. "We appreciate everything you've done, Señor Arnolde. I'd appreciate if you'd let us know if any strangers show up in town. I don't think the hostiles will come after us, but there's no way to know for sure."

"*Si*, I will let my men know to keep watch."

"*Gracias.*" Derek stuck out a hand. The men shook, and Paco departed.

"First, I show you the telephone." Bernardo waddled ahead of them to an old-fashioned pay phone mounted on the wall.

"*Gracias,*" Derek said. He waited till Bernardo returned to work behind the cantina bar and turned to Bree.

"We need to call your dad first. Let him know we're safe before he pays the ransom."

She nodded. "I'll make the call. Dad will send someone to pick us up, but it might take a while for them to get here."

Lifting the receiver off the hook, she pressed it against her ear, called for an operator and gave them a credit card number.

"It worked," she said, smiling.

"So far, so good."

He could only hear Bree's half of the conversation, but from what he could tell, Jonathan Wingate was nearly in tears.

"It's okay, Dad, really. I'm okay. Both of us are safe." Her eyes filled, and she swallowed. "I love you, Dad. Tell Mom I love her and I'll see you both soon."

Her dad said something else, and Bree took a moment to compose herself. She wiped away a tear, glanced at Derek and smiled as she continued the conversation. "I can't wait for you to meet Derek," she said. "He saved my life, Dad. He saved both our lives."

Derek felt a sudden chill. The rest of the conversation was lost as he thought about what Jonathan Wingate would say when they met. By now, the man would know everything about him, including his ugly past. No father, a drunken, drug addict mother. His years in one foster home after another. He was Texas trailer trash, and Bree was Seattle royalty.

Didn't matter that he was a corporate executive now. Nothing could change the past.

Bree hung up the phone. "I told him what happened, how we got away and where we are now. He flew into El

Salvador after he got the ransom call. He's working on getting us out of here, but it may take a while."

Derek just nodded. As soon as they got back to San Salvador, he'd call the office. He didn't have any family, aside
from a few distant cousins he refused to claim. But his staff
and the close friends he had made in the company would
be worried about him.

Bernardo waddled up beside them. "You must be tired.
I will take you up to your room." He handed Bree a paper
bag. "My wife sends you some *baleadas*." Bree's gaze
flashed to Derek's as she accepted the bag. No way were
either of them hungry enough to eat more *baleadas*, they
silently agreed.

"Thank you," Bree said.

"Dinner will be ready at six," Bernardo added. "It will
be served downstairs, and it comes with the room."

"That sounds great," Bree said, her Spanish as good or
better than Derek's. They followed Bernardo up a set of
stairs that opened onto the balcony, then followed him to
the last door at the end. He opened the door and waited for
them to walk inside.

Linoleum floors, two double beds with worn fringed
bedspreads, a battered nightstand with a lamp covered by
a faded red-fringed silk shade.

"There is a bathroom behind that door." He pointed in that
direction. "If there is anything you need, just let me know."

Bree smiled. "Thank you, Señor Garcia."

The room wasn't much, but the bathroom was a bonus,
and the place was clean. And there were actual mattresses
on the beds.

Garcia waddled back the way he had come, closing the
door behind him, and Bree headed for the bathroom. Derek
watched the gathered skirt sway as she crossed the room,

her hips moving enticingly. He remembered the feel of her breasts in his palm, and his groin tightened. The shower went on, and he clenched his jaw against the need to join her.

Bree came out a few minutes later dressed once more in the skirt and off-the-shoulder white blouse—the only clothes she had. Derek walked past her into the bathroom, just a toilet, sink and rusted stall shower.

When he came out a few minutes later in the camo pants he'd been given last night, he felt a hundred pounds lighter. Barefoot and shirtless, he walked over to where Bree sat on the bed and sank down beside her.

"It's almost over," she said, combing her fingers through her thick, damp blond hair.

Derek tried not to think how pretty she looked with her big blue eyes and her face freshly washed, her cheeks pink in the sunlight streaming in through the window. She was naturally beautiful. There wasn't a thing about her he would change.

He tried not to think about what it had felt like to kiss her, to touch her. He tried not to want her again. It wouldn't be fair. Not when he knew there was no way they could be together.

Bree reached up and cupped his cheek. "I don't know how long it will take my dad to get us out of here."

"We'll make the best of it, same as we did before."

"Before there was an army of men with weapons ready to kill us. Now there's just you and me." She waited for him to kiss her. When he fisted his hands to keep from touching her, she leaned over and settled her mouth over his. Her lips were plump and warm, and it took every ounce of will to capture her wrists and ease her away.

"There are things about me you don't know, Bree. My past…it isn't exactly sterling."

"I don't care about your past. That has nothing to do with the man you are now."

He shook his head. "I'm not like you, Bree. I never had a father. My mother was a drug addict. I was raised in foster care, shifted from one place to another. Your parents... they'd never accept me. I'm not the guy for you, Bree."

She looked up at him, her pretty blue eyes filled with tears. "I don't care about your parents or what happened to you in the past. I care about the man who stepped up beside me on that plane. The man who risked his life to protect me."

His chest ached. He just shook his head.

"Tell me you don't want me."

Everything inside him tightened. His fist clenched so hard, his hand shook where it rested on his knee. "I've never wanted a woman the way I want you."

"I want this moment, Derek. I want you. The future will determine itself. If you want me—"

There was no way he could refuse. Not now. His mouth crushed down over hers, stopping the words. He wanted her. So much he ached with it. And Bree wanted him. Whatever happened, he wanted this memory, these precious hours with a woman who meant more to him than any woman he had ever known.

He wanted to kiss her. He wanted to touch her beautiful body. He wanted to be inside her.

There would be no stopping now. Not this time.

He kissed her with all the feelings he knew he shouldn't have. He showed her how he felt by the way his hands slid reverently over her body, showed her with another deep kiss how much she had come to mean to him.

In seconds her blouse was gone, his mouth fastened on

a pale, perfect breast. Bree made a soft sound in her throat and arched her back, giving him better access.

Derek eased her down on the bed and unbuttoned her skirt, drew it over her hips, down her shapely legs. Her calves were nicely muscled, her ankles trim. He pressed his mouth there and felt the rapid beat of her heart against his tongue.

Neither of them wore anything under their clothes. They had long ago abandoned the wet garments to the jungle. He kissed his way up over her knee, along her bare thigh. He wanted her to remember this, remember him. When she belonged to another, more suitable man, he wanted a faint memory of their time together to whisper through her heart.

She cried out as he pleasured her, her hands combing through his damp hair, then fisting in the sheets. Her climax hit hard, drawing a moan from her throat.

Derek felt a surge of male satisfaction. He couldn't have her, but she wouldn't forget him, he vowed as he drove her up again.

Bree whimpered as he moved above her. Claiming her mouth, he kissed her deeply, took his time and felt her respond again, pleased that he could arouse her so easily, proof she had wanted him as much as he wanted her. He kissed her softly, then fiercely, kissed her until she was saying his name over and over, her nails digging into his shoulders. She was begging him to take her as he slid himself deeply inside.

He didn't have a condom. He would have to pull out, have to be careful, but his own pleasure didn't matter. He wanted this, wanted just to be with her, to claim her in some way. As the pleasure increased, he realized part of him would like nothing more than for Bree to end up with his child. She would have to marry him then.

The knowledge hit him like a brick. He was in love with her. After what they had endured and the strength she had shown, how could he not be?

He took her hard, took her deep, did his best to claim her mind as well as her body. Her release struck and she tightened around him, driving him to the brink. He pulled out before he reached release and rolled away from her, protecting her as he'd done from the moment he had met her.

"Derek…" The soft sigh of his name made his chest ache. He wanted to turn back to her, take her again. Instead, he got up and used the bathroom, returned and pulled her close beside him. For a time, he just held her, memorizing the way she felt in his arms. They dozed for a while, feeling safe for the first time in days.

At the touch of her fingertip running lightly over the muscles on his chest, he opened his eyes.

"I was right," she said. "I knew you'd be good in bed."

He smiled, caught her hand and kissed the back. "I'm glad you were pleased."

"I knew we didn't have a condom."

His body pulsed with unspent desire. "I figured you'd trust me to take care of it."

"I trust you, Derek. I haven't had the best luck with men, but the luckiest day of my life was the day you sat down in the seat next to me on that plane."

Derek said nothing. Nothing he could say would change the way things were.

"Kiss me, Derek. Make love to me again."

"We took a big risk the first time."

She leaned over him and smiled. "All right, then I'll make love to you."

And she did.

CHAPTER TWELVE

IT WAS ALMOST time for supper. They showered together this time, being careful and passionately creative as they made love once more. Neither of them had had unsafe sex before they'd met, so they knew they could enjoy each other freely.

Bree held onto Derek's hand as they headed downstairs to the cantina and sat down at a rough wooden table, the aromas of roasting meat and beer floating in the air. Señora Garcia served them a meal of *chile colorado, frijoles* and freshly made tortillas. The food was delicious.

Bree leaned back in an old wooden chair that rocked on uneven legs. For a while after their afternoon of lovemaking, she'd been relaxed. Now Derek's words were rolling around in her head.

Your parents...they'd never accept me. I'm not the guy for you, Bree.

Derek was the best man she'd ever known. Besides his amazing body, fantastic lovemaking and being the sexiest man on the planet, he was smart and loyal and protective. She hadn't been looking for a man when she'd met him, but Derek had won her heart completely. He was everything she'd ever wanted, and she wasn't letting him go.

Not without a fight.

On the other hand, he had never mentioned his feelings for her. The idea nagged her...maybe Derek didn't feel the way she did.

There was no doubt he wanted her. Under different circumstances, she was certain they would still be in bed making up for lost time. But sexual desire wasn't enough. Not when her heart was already fully committed. She needed to know Derek's feelings ran as deep as her own.

She took a drink of Salva Vida, Honduran beer, hoping to calm her emotions. Derek had already finished eating. He was leaning back in his chair, his golden eyes watching her as if he touched her, but there was no way to tell what he was thinking.

Her head swiveled toward a commotion in the cantina.

"Señor Stiles! Señor Stiles!" A small brown-skinned boy rushed through the door and raced toward them. "Men come! Men come!"

Bree and Derek both shot up from their chairs, and Derek's whole body tensed as Rafael Castillo and half a dozen men pushed through the cantina doors, General Batista among them.

Derek moved toward Bree and eased her behind him. Bree fought not to tremble. *Dear God, Castillo found us!* She steeled herself. No way was she letting a man like him see her fear.

"So, we meet again," Castillo said with a look of dark satisfaction. Bree had never seen such fury in his cold brown eyes before. Next to him, General Batista's smooth, dark features were marked with silent rage. He'd been made to look like a fool in front of his commander. Payback was etched into every line of his face.

"You're too late," Derek said to the men. "Wingate knows we escaped. He won't pay your ransom now."

Castillo's hard mouth flattened out. "Oh, he will pay. But only for his daughter. You, my friend, will be rotting in your grave."

Bree stepped out from behind Derek. "If you hurt him in any way, I'll make sure you never get your money."

"Perhaps not. But one way or another, you will both pay for the death of my friend."

The general motioned to his soldiers, and two of them moved into position behind them, guns drawn.

"*Vamanos!*" Castillo raised his hand and started leading them toward the door. The soldier behind Derek shoved him forward. Bree hurried to catch up with him, her heart beating hard, her skin icy cold as they pushed through the door into the narrow dirt street.

An eerie quiet settled over her, the town strangely empty. Something shifted in the air around them, and her heart beat even harder.

"Put your hands in the air! All of you! Do it now!"

Bree clutched Derek's arm. At least thirty armed, uniformed soldiers stepped out of their hiding places on each side of the cantina, rifles and pistols pointed at Castillo, the general and his ragged band of men.

Derek and Bree raised their hands but eased a little away from Castillo and the others, who stood frozen, hands held high, in the middle of the street.

"That's my daughter! Breanna Wingate!" Bree recognized her father's voice an instant before she saw him, just an average man with short brown hair and square-rimmed glasses. But there was nothing average about Jonathan Wingate. Her father's authority crackled in the very air around them.

A soldier who stood opposite them walked toward her. He had epaulettes on his shoulders and a billed cap on his head. Brass buttons gleamed on the front of his khaki uniform.

Gripping Derek's arm, she drew him along beside her,

making sure he stayed close. Bree's eyes stung. She let go of Derek, ran into her father's open arms, and held on tight. "Dad. I can't believe you're here."

He kissed her forehead. "You didn't think I would come? My darling daughter, I told you on the phone I flew down as soon as I got the ransom call."

"Yes, but I thought you'd wait for us in San Salvador. I didn't think you'd bring an army to rescue us."

"Colonel Zepeda got word Castillo and his men were looking for you. He was worried about your safety. Fortunately, we got here in time."

She went up on her toes and kissed his cheek. Around them, Colonel Zepeda's men were rounding up the terrorists and disarming them. General Batista stood at the head of his men, his usually graceful posture stiff and jerky as he was marched off down the street. At the rear of the column, Castillo walked in the middle of a group of soldiers, his hands cuffed behind his back.

At the least, Castillo would be facing years in prison for his terrorist activities as well as kidnapping. A sentence he more than deserved.

Bree returned her attention to her father. "Dad, I want you to meet Derek." She looked over to where he stood tall and straight, talking to Colonel Zepeda.

Her father nodded. "Of course. I look forward to meeting the man who helped my daughter." She had told him on the phone Derek wasn't really her fiancé, just a passenger on the plane who had come to her aid.

Holding on to her father's hand, Bree led him toward the man who had risked his life to save her.

"Dad, this is Derek Stiles. I'd probably be dead if it weren't for him." Or brutally raped or forced into a life of prostitution, never to be seen again.

Her dad extended his hand. "It's a pleasure to meet you, Derek. I'll never be able to thank you enough for what you did for my daughter."

Derek's expression never changed. "Bree's an amazing woman. I'm glad I was able to help."

"He did more than help, Dad." She began to tell her father all the things Derek had done to protect her, but her dad cut her off.

"You can tell me all about it back at the hotel. I took the top floor of the Sheraton El Presidente to use as a command post. You both have rooms there. You can rest and refresh yourselves."

"How do we get to the city?" Bree asked, glancing at the activity around them.

"The colonel has a helicopter waiting to take us back. I've got the jet on standby at the airport whenever we're ready to leave." He smiled. "Your mother sent several changes of clothes. She figured you would need them."

Her mother was a rock, the matriarch of the family, the person who held everyone together.

She glanced at Derek, whose expression hadn't changed. Bree just nodded. "Okay."

"All right, let's go." Her dad set his hand on her shoulder and ushered her around the building toward a military Jeep parked out of sight behind a faded yellow, wood-frame house. Derek walked a few paces behind them. She could already feel him distancing himself, preparing to leave.

Her throat tightened. She loved him. There was no way to pretend it wasn't so.

They all climbed into the Jeep, and the driver turned onto the road, heading in the opposite direction the soldiers had escorted Castillo, General Batista and his men. They followed the dirt track to where a big jet helicopter sat in an open field, nothing at all like the much smaller Raven that Derek had flown.

The blades were slowly revolving, waiting for orders. They all climbed in and belted into their seats, Bree making a point of sitting next to Derek. He flicked her a sideways glance but said nothing.

Just as they were ready to lift off, Colonel Zepeda climbed aboard. Then the engine revved, and the chopper lifted away. She still hadn't had a chance to talk to her dad, but as the helicopter roared back to the city, she looked at Derek's stony face and swallowed back the tears collecting in her throat. Nothing she said was going to matter.

Derek's mind was made up. Whatever they had shared was over.

Bree's heart ached as if a knife had been stabbed into her chest.

CHAPTER THIRTEEN

DEREK OPTED NOT to stay at El Presidente. He'd borrowed a phone and called the Garrett Resources office in Houston as soon he'd returned to San Salvador to let them know he was well and safe. As soon as word of the hijacking had reached Bogotá, his meetings had been canceled indefinitely.

He hadn't expected the phone call a few minutes later from his employer, Reese Garrett, CEO of the company, though the email he had sent from the plane had gone to Reese.

"Thank God you're safe," Reese said. "As soon as I got your email, I called Bran, and he insisted on flying down."

Brandon Garrett was Reese's younger brother, a former special ops solider. During his years in the army, Bran had been deployed many times to South America, though he never talked about it.

"Bran managed to make contact with a colonel named Zepeda," Reese said. "Zepeda was familiar with El Defensor, and once he understood the situation, the colonel was eager to help. Bran wasn't allowed to go in with the colonel's men, but that's never stopped my brother. Apparently, he was in Santa Margarita when the operation went down. Soon as he saw you and Ms. Wingate were safe, he disappeared."

That sounded like Bran. They were friends of a sort. Clearly Bran Garrett was a good friend to have.

"Tell him I owe him a beer."

Reese laughed. "Tell him yourself. Bran's still in San Salvador. Company jet's waiting to bring you both home. Where are you staying?"

"Intercontinental. Room 515."

"I'll let him know."

Since Derek's phone was somewhere in the Honduran jungle, he'd picked up a disposable, but it didn't have his contact list. "That'd be great."

"Anything you need?"

He thought of Bree and how much he missed her. *A new heart*, he wanted to say but didn't. "I bought myself some clothes, so I'm good to go."

"Take a week off when you get back," Reese said. "Two if you need them. Rest up and relax. I'll be in touch." The call ended, and Derek lay back on the bed in his hotel room. Shoving his hands behind his head, he stared up at the ceiling.

Tired and depressed, he must have fallen asleep. A knock on the door awoke him an hour later. When he looked at the clock, it was a quarter to five in the afternoon. With a sigh, he stumbled out of the bed and answered the door, stepped back to let Bran Garrett into the room.

"Reese told me you were in the city," Derek said to him. "I really appreciate what you did."

"No problem." Bran looked him up and down, taking in his rumpled clothes, uncombed hair and unshaven face. "Man, that jungle must have been even harder on you than I thought."

Derek scratched his days' growth of beard. All he could think of was Bree, but Bree and her father had already left for Seattle. She had wanted to see her mother, reassure her mom that she was okay.

With her father eager to leave for home, they hadn't had time to talk, which was good. Derek had nothing to say.

Bran held up a brown paper bag. "I figured you might need a little lift. I got something here that'll cure whatever ails you." Carrying the bag over to the small round table in front of the window, he took out a bottle of Ron de El Salvador Cihuatan Grand Reserve rum. Bran cracked it open and poured two fingers each into a pair of water glasses, then carried one over and handed it to Derek.

"*Salud.*" He waited for Derek to lift his glass.

"*Salud.*" Derek tossed his drink back, and so did Bran. "All right, now tell me what's going on."

They sat down at the table. The room was nicely furnished, done in shades of pale sea green. The queen-size bed was a hell of an improvement over a cot in a tent. On the other hand, he'd rather be sleeping in the jungle with Bree than sleeping by himself in a wide comfy bed.

"I guess this is all just catching up with me."

Bran cocked a dark brown eyebrow. He was a good-looking guy, tall, with light blue eyes, and amazingly fit. "Is that so? I don't suppose it could have anything to do with that luscious little honey you rescued in the jungle."

Derek's head came up.

"Breanna Wingate?" Bran continued mercilessly. "She's been all over the news. Couldn't sing your praises enough. Said she'd be dead if it weren't for you."

Derek glanced away. "She needed help. I helped her."

"That's it? You got off a hijacked plane to protect her when you could have stayed aboard. You two didn't get close while you were fighting for survival out there? Because I've been where you are, bro. I married the woman I rescued. Or maybe she rescued me."

Derek sighed. "Okay, fine. I'm crazy in love with her.

Breanna's beautiful and strong and sexy as hell. What guy wouldn't fall for her?"

Bran took a drink of rum. "So why aren't you in Seattle? That's where she is, right? Up there with her parents?" He went to the table and poured a little more rum into his glass, brought the bottle over and poured more for Derek.

"She's just visiting her family in Seattle," Derek said. "She lives in Dallas, runs a nonprofit there called Shelter the Children, among others, I guess."

"Dallas. That's even better. You two only live a few hours apart."

Derek drained half the rum in his glass. "Don't you get it, man? She's Breanna Wingate. Her dad's one of the richest men in the world. I'm not in her league. My mother was a druggie, and I don't even know my father's name. I'm not good enough for her. Her parents would probably have me shot if they knew I'd even touched her."

"Bullshit. You're one of the top executives at Garrett Resources. You had to have a college degree, right?"

He nodded. "I studied hard and worked my way through school. So what?"

"You were a jet fighter pilot, Derek. That didn't come easy, either. Far as I'm concerned, Breanna Wingate would be lucky to have you."

Derek looked at his friend. He and Brandon had only talked a few times, yet Bran had flown all the way to South America to help him.

"Look, Bran, I appreciate your advice, but—"

"You think she loves you? Because she sure sounded like it on TV."

Derek glanced away. "Everyone would say I married her for her money."

"So who cares? There are assholes everywhere, Derek.

Nothing you can do about that. She said you didn't even know who she was when they took her off that plane."

Derek downed the rest of the rum in his glass. "Like I said, she needed help, and there was no one but me."

"Yeah, well, maybe this time you should help yourself." Bran rose and set his empty glass on the table. "You can think about it while we're on our way home. You ready to get the hell out of here?"

Derek pushed up from his chair. "Damn straight. More than ready." While Bran slid the bottle of rum back into the paper bag and tucked it under his arm, Derek grabbed the few items he'd purchased at the local Sanborns department store, and they headed out the door.

An hour later, he was leaning back in a butter-soft leather seat in the Garrett Resources jet on his way back to Houston.

All the way there, Derek thought about Bree.

CHAPTER FOURTEEN

"I WISH I could stay longer, Mom, but I've got so much work to catch up on back home."

"I know, honey. Maybe we can plan a vacation together this year. We haven't done that in a while."

Bree smiled. They were sitting at the big oak table in the breakfast area of her parent's gigantic kitchen. Huge plate-glass windows looked out at a turbulent sea. "I'd like that."

Allison Wingate was an older version of Bree, only a little shorter, with the same blond hair and blue eyes. "Anywhere but South America, right?"

An image of Derek popped into her head, and her throat tightened. She remembered the way he had looked at her the last time she had seen him: not the least sign of emotion in his face, nothing that could give her the slightest indication of his feelings. It was as if they had been strangers. Bree turned to stare out the window, afraid her mother would see the tears that sprang in her eyes.

"I can tell what you're thinking," her mom said softly. "You're thinking of Derek again."

She turned away from the window. "You should have seen him, Mom. Derek was amazing. He took incredible risks to protect me."

"I know how much he means to you, sweetheart. You need to talk to him, tell him the way you feel."

"If he loved me, Mom, he wouldn't have let me go."

Her mother toyed with the handle on her coffee cup. "Maybe you should consider it from his point of view. No matter whom you marry, people will say he married you for your money. He'd have to put up with that for the rest of his life."

It was true, but still... "Derek's strong, Mom. You can't imagine how strong he is. I think he could handle whatever anyone said. The thing is, Derek comes from a broken home. His childhood was dark and ugly. He doesn't think you and Dad would ever accept him."

Her mother sat up a little straighter. "I wasn't going to tell you, but your father and I talked about this. He knows all about Derek's past. He had him checked out thoroughly when he found out the name of the man you were with."

"If he doesn't think Derek is good enough for me, he's wrong! I would be lucky to have him."

Her mother smiled. "Your father admires Derek for the things he's accomplished. The man dragged himself up by his bootstraps and made himself a success. He's exactly the kind of man your father and I hoped you would find."

Bree sighed. "If I told him that, he wouldn't believe me. Even if he did, the fact is he just might not love me. At least not the same way I love him."

"Talk to him, sweetheart. Tell him how you feel and ask him how he feels about you."

Her throat ached. She wanted to believe her mother was right, but deep down she couldn't convince herself.

"I'll call him when I get back to Texas." But she didn't think it would matter; she didn't want a man who didn't love her.

"Don't just call him," her mom said. "Talk to him in person."

She swallowed and nodded. The sad truth was, even if

she stood right in front of him, there was no way she could read Derek's thoughts if he didn't want her to.

Her father walked into the kitchen just then. She had told her dad about Derek on the jet as they were flying home. He knew she was in love with him. She had asked him not to interfere in any way.

"What is it?" her mother asked, far better at reading a man than Bree was.

"Apparently, there's some kind of disturbance at the front gate." The brown eyes behind the glasses fixed on Bree. "The man's name wasn't on the visitors list. The guard asked him to leave, but he refused. Turns out his name is Derek Stiles and he's here to see you."

Bree's heart jerked.

Her dad looked at her and smiled. "Shall I let him in?"

Her heart was pounding. She had no idea why Derek was there, but she prayed with everything inside her he had missed her as much as she had missed him.

"Maybe he just came to say goodbye," she said. "We didn't get to talk before we left. Maybe he just feels like he needs to clear the air." Or officially put an end to their brief relationship.

"You won't know until you talk to him," her mother said, reaching over to squeeze her hand. "Whatever happens, I'd really like to meet him."

Bree nodded.

Her dad gave her an encouraging glance. "I'll tell the guard to let him in. Why don't you talk to him in the library? It's nice and quiet in there."

Bree would rather talk to him in a little coffee shop in town—anyplace but her family's palatial home. But maybe it was better this way. Better if he saw the world she had been born into, the world she still sometimes lived in.

She waited nervously in the library, a two-story, wood-paneled room lined with acres of books. She had always liked it there, had spent hours sitting on the dark green velvet sofas, curled up with a favorite novel.

She stood up when Derek appeared in the doorway, his wide shoulders nearly filling the opening. He was dressed in a navy blue blazer, tan slacks and a white dress shirt with no tie. His dark brown hair had been neatly trimmed. He looked amazing.

"Hi," she said dumbly, wishing she could have come up with something clever.

"I needed to see you," Derek said, looking every bit as nervous as she was. "I wanted to talk to you. I probably should have waited until you got back to Texas, but I've already waited too long."

She just stared, thinking how wonderful he looked, wishing he was holding her the way he had in the jungle. She thought of the way she had felt when he kissed her and wished he would do it again.

"I missed you," she said, the words just popping out.

"I missed you, too, Bree. So much."

And then somehow he had moved and so had she, and she was crushed against his chest, his arms wrapped tight around her. He looked into her eyes, tipped her chin up and very gently kissed her.

He ran a finger down her cheek. "I know I'm not the guy your dad would have chosen, but I love you. If you love me, too, I promise to do everything in my power to make you happy."

Her throat closed up. Before she could speak, her father's voice rang from the doorway.

"You're exactly the man I would have chosen for my daughter, Derek. You risked your life more than once to protect her, and you never let her down. And I know all about you, son. From the moment the kidnappers mentioned your name, I started digging. I know about your past—which you managed to spectacularly overcome—but also about the things you've accomplished. You represent everything I believe a man should be. Now I'll leave you two alone so you can finish the conversation I so rudely interrupted." Her dad closed the door.

Still wrapped in Derek's arms, Bree looked up at him, her eyes filled with tears. "I love you, Derek. So much."

"Will you marry me? I know it's too soon to ask, but whenever you're ready—"

"I'd love to marry you." She smiled, her eyes glistening. "Anytime. Anyplace. Whenever you want."

The sweetest, sexiest grin spread over his face. "I should have come sooner." And then he kissed her. A deep, time-less, endless kiss that promised everything she had ever dreamed. Both of them were breathing hard when he finally let her go.

"I've got a week off, two if I want. I know you probably have a lot of work to catch up on, but we deserve to spend some time together. So what do you think?"

Bree smiled. "You owe me a week in bed. I'm holding you to it."

Derek laughed, and she could hear the relief in his voice. For once, she knew what he was thinking.

He kissed her very softly. "I almost didn't come. It took me a while to work up my courage."

Bree cocked an eyebrow. "So asking me to marry you was harder than fighting a jungle full of terrorists?"

His mouth edged up. "When you put it that way—yeah."

Bree laughed. She went up on her toes and lightly kissed him. "My mom wants to meet you."

"Good. She can help us plan the wedding."

Her eyes stung, but they were tears of joy. "I didn't think you loved me."

Derek wiped a tear from her cheek. "I think I fell in love with you on the plane when you held a stranger's baby in your arms."

Her heart squeezed. "I was coming to Houston. I was thinking I wasn't going to let you go so easily."

"Yeah? Well, now that you're mine, baby, I'm never letting you go." Then he kissed her, and Bree had never loved him more.

Except maybe in the jungle when he had saved her from that python.

* * * * *

PHKMBPA0221MAX